This is the novel of a glittering time...when the kings of Hollywood held omnipotent sway over millions...when fortunes were smashed and re-created at the edge of a marble swimming-pool — between the satin sheets of a starlet's bed.

It is the story of men with gargantuan appetites—for women—for money—for power.

It is the brilliant, epic-sized saga of Hollywood's Fallen Angel—the story of

CZAR

CZAR

THOMAS WISEMAN

AN AVON BOOK

All major characters, incidents and events in this story are fictitious although sometimes placed in a historical setting, and any similarity to actual people and events is purely coincidental and unintended.

T.W.

AVON BOOKS
A division of
The Hearst Corporation
959 Eighth Avenue
New York, New York 10019

Copyright © 1965 by Thomas Wiseman.
Published by arrangement with Simon and Schuster, Inc.
Library of Congress Catalog Card Number: 66-16154.

First Avon Printing, September, 1967

Cover illustration by Robert Foster

AVON TRADEMARK REG. U.S. PAT. OFF. AND
FOREIGN COUNTRIES, REGISTERED TRADEMARK—
MARCA REGISTRADA, HECHO EN CHICAGO, U.S.A.

Printed in the U.S.A.

For Malou

BOOK ONE

PART ONE

CHAPTER ONE

As a child he was alone a great deal, and he spent much of his time looking out of the windows of the apartment, or building high towers with the playing blocks that his father had bought him. Looking out of the windows was what he liked to do best because he had already made the towers as high as they could be made with the available blocks, and as he couldn't make them any higher he had become bored with this form of play. But looking out of the windows was always rewarding: there was so much going on in the streets below, so much to see and wonder about. The house in which Alexi lived was on the corner of Allen Street and Delancey Street, and he liked to do his watching from the triangular-shaped kitchen from which he could look down on the two converging streets. One window looked out on the huge tenement building opposite, the other was on the same level as the Elevated, whose channel was Allen Street, and that side of the room was always dark, and the whole house underwent a spasm of shivers and shakings every few minutes when a train roared by, making the windows rattle as in a storm, and abruptly extinguishing what little light normally percolated down to that level. To Alexi, who had never been outside the city in his seven years, these things were as natural as thunder or the clouding of the sky.

In the corner of the room there was a large iron stove on which, in the winter, there was nearly always a great pot of soup on the boil, filling the whole apartment with the good smell of his mother's cooking, making his nose tingle with pleasant anticipation, the soup spilling over every so often to hiss against the stove, the lid of the pot dancing on a jet of steam, and the condensing steam running down the window-panes and making a curtain against the cold world outside. From this triangular-shaped room, whose walls had in time become impregnated with the smells of his mother's cooking, Alexi could watch what was going on in the turbulent street market beneath the El, and from the other window he could see into some of the rooms of the tene-ment building opposite, and without ever speaking to any of the neighbors, something his father had forbidden him to do, he had learned a good deal about them. He knew, for instance, that the man who lived on the second floor op-posite, with his wife and five children, did not think much of his wife's cooking because sometimes, when he got angry, he emptied it, like slops, into the street. And Alexi knew that the woman on the third floor, with the unkempt white hair, was mad; sometimes she came to the window and tried to force her head and shoulder between the bars, and emitted a shrieking laugh that was unlike any human sound Alexi had ever heard and was as much of a scream as a laugh. It always had the effect of draining the blood from the boy's face, and when he thought she had seen him his heart pounded and he shrank to the floor, not daring to expose his head in the window again until she had disappeared. Also, he had come to be familiar with a good many of the family quarrels that flared up from time to time: voices rising suddenly to a high, terrifying pitch, made unnatural and ugly by anger. The frenzied way in which they poured words at each other, in languages he did not understand and in rhythms that seemed to be working up to some terrible climax, frightened him almost as much as the sight of the madwoman. Sometimes—and this was the most frightening thing of all, more frightening than the mad-woman—his mother and father shouted at each other in this way, and what made it worse, somehow, was that they did their shouting in hoarse, strangled whispers.

On the other side, in the permanent twilight beneath the El, there was the market, whose noise and smells and unceasing activity and good-humored bargaining comforted him and fascinated him and, for some reason, made him feel safe. All along the curb, as far as he could see, there were the pushcarts, and also some horsecarts harnessed to

10

big, heavy dray horses, piled with the most extraordinary assortment of wares: samovars and hand-wrought vessels of brass, secondhand clothing, pots and pans, kettles and garbage bins, kerosene lamps and potbellied stoves, chamber pots, wash basins, hip baths, old bedsteads, mattresses, secondhand books, carpet beaters, the sheet music of songs popular several seasons ago and now rather moldy looking, *tallithum* and *tvillim.* . . . The street was rich in sounds— of bargaining, of street traders calling their wares as they led their plodding horses along, looking up to the windows of the houses in search of buyers; of women shouting down to friends or relatives or tradesmen in the street and sometimes conducting long harangues in a variety of languages, at the tops of their voices—even trying to shout through the din of the El which, every three or four minutes, blotted out all lesser noises.

In the summer fruit appeared on the pushcarts and all the windows were open and the streets were full of small children eating watermelon, their faces virtually obscured as they burrowed deep into huge, messy slices of the succulent fruit, the green rinds like masks over their faces, only re-emerging to spit out the seeds. Flies and other insects buzzed and swarmed around the discarded rinds and the overflowing garbage cans that stood all along the street, outside the entrances of the houses, like squalid sentinels. Around them the dogs and the cats of the neighborhood sniffed and searched and fought, and sometimes rats joined fleetingly in the scrimmage, and when they were not fast enough in escaping with their plunder the dogs and cats pounced on them and made a meal of them. For all that, the summer was a good time, and it was when Alexi was happiest. The drab tenement was bedecked, as if for some festivity, with eiderdowns and bedsheets placed out to air at open windows. And in the very hot weather, tiny children pranced naked in the spray from the water wagons that came from time to time.

The house in which Alexi lived was a brownstone with iron-railed front steps rising to a first-floor entrance, and an iron fire escape making a zigzag scar down the front. From the first floor up it was given over to private apartments; the ground floor, by the side of the steps, was a pharmacy. With the choice of two windows to look out of, there was always something for the boy to see, and sometimes by running

11

from one window to the other he could see things on both sides of the corner—for instance, two massive, overloaded horsecarts converging with no possibility of being able to pass each other. Being able to look down on both sides of the corner gave Alexi a feeling of being in the know about things nobody else knew about. (Sometimes a woman left her husband on the tenement side and joined another man waiting for her under the El.) There was a lot that Alexi learned about, just by watching.

The apartment itself was small but scrupulously clean and tidy, consisting of a bedroom and a kitchen, which was also the living room and contained a folding bed on which Alexi slept when he was not allowed to sleep in the big bed with his mother. This happened whenever his father came home, which was not all that often. There was a framed photograph of his father on the washstand, but it was of a man who bore little resemblance to the father Alexi knew. It was of a very handsome man, with a very grand air, who looked like an ambassador or other such important personage. The necessity of keeping still while the photographer made his exposure had perhaps added to the pomposity of the stance, and given his eyes the unseeing look that very important people always seemed to have, but which, in his father's case, may have been caused by the effort not to blink. He was wearing a closely buttoned frock coat with high lapels, a flower in the buttonhole, a tall silk hat, spats and patent leather shoes, holding chamois gloves in his left hand and a gold-topped cane in the other. He was posed in a rather contrived position, against a fiacre. Alexi knew from the date on the back of the photograph, 1896, that it had been taken in Vienna, before the misfortune, which his parents hardly ever talked about but which he knew was the cause of their having come to America. The misfortune was also the reason why they now lived in this poor neighborhood. It was only for the time being, his father always pointed out, until they were on their feet again. Meanwhile, Alexi had to remember, always, that he was a Sondorpf, that he came from a good family of professional people, and while they were temporarily obliged to live here, on the lower East Side, he must watch out not to mix with the kids of the street.

In the big bed he felt safe, knowing that, later, his mother would get in next to him and that he would be able to curl up against her big, warm, comforting body and be cushioned by her breasts as he slept. Knowing this, he could allow himself to fall asleep lightly; the deeper sleep came afterward—was sometimes just a transition from one to the other—when his mother gave him the final good-night hug that made everything all right, for the rest of the night at least. He was at the falling stage, the pleasant thoughts of his mother had become blurred and whooshy but were not yet dreams, when he heard something that made him immediately wide awake: his father's cough on the stairs—he always coughed, in this distinctive way, just before taking out his keys and unlocking the door. Alexi's heart was thumping. The sound of the door being closed noisily; his father's voice calling "Leushka? Leushka!" and, a moment or so later, mother gently shushing him, "You want to wake the child? You know what time it is?" A door closing, very softly this time, the voices fading away into a continuous drone. In this new, fraught silence, so different from the silence of a few moments ago, Alexi moved restlessly in the bed. For a long time he struggled to go to sleep again, but the light under the kitchen door was a constant reminder of something going on in the other room that concerned him. It probably meant that he would be bundled out of the big bed—just because his father had chosen to come home—and be made to sleep on the folding bed, deprived of the comforting presence of his mother to guard him against the dangers of the night. He had to find out what was going on in the other room. Creeping on hands and knees, he made his way to the door, which his mother had kept slightly ajar so she would hear him immediately if he called her. Through the narrow aperture he could see into the kitchen where his mother and father sat at the round table covered with the tasseled and embroidered tablecloth. The kerosene lamp was turned down low and gave out only just enough light to illuminate the area in which they were sitting. "You are going to make a sissy of him," his father was saying, filing and cleaning his fingernails with the nail file he always carried with him. He looked gray and tired; the flesh of his face, so tight and firm and polished-looking in the photograph, was loose and drooping, and the skin had many folds and creases in it, as if it had been kept for a long time in a trunk. The little hair on his head had

13

been brushed straight back very flat, and was shiny from the lotion that he used. The structure of his face was such that from certain angles he looked hollow-cheeked; his face curved inward from the high cheekbones and came to a sharp point at the chin. As he talked, he had a habit of lightly feeling the texture of his skin, the way men do after they have shaved. "He can't sleep by himself?"

"He's frightened, he's only a child," Leushka said. Though Oskar had been in the room only a short while she had already discovered that a button on the cuff of his jacket was loose and she was sewing it on with quick, deft stitches while he, rather imperiously, held out his arm to enable her to do this.

"Frightened?" said Oskar. "Frightened—of what?"

"It's not enough there's the *meshuganeh* across the street, always at the window, with her laughing and her mad screams?" Leushka said in a whisper, glancing toward the bedroom door as she spoke. She had spoken very softly, very reasonably, but Oskar seemed to react to her words as if they were an accusation. He pulled his arm away roughly, and Leushka had to get up and go around to his side of the table and bend over him in order to break the thread with her teeth.

"You think I like it here so much?" He hurled the words at her. "You think I like this high-class neighborhood we live in? A man like me who always had only the best? In Vienna—I need to remind you?—we lived on the first floor, in the best district. . . ."

"Shhhh, Oshkerle, you want to wake up the child?" she implored. "I'm not accusing you," she added in a low whisper. "I said the child's frightened, that's all I said."

"What you want me to do?" he demanded violently, forgetting about lowering his voice and incurring another remonstrating look, on this score, from Leushka. "You think overnight you get to be Rockefeller? It's not so easy I can tell you. I can tell you it's not so easy."

"I know," she said soothingly, "I know. I'm not accusing you."

"For me, you know quite well, it's automatic the child comes first. The first consideration, Leushka, is the child."

"I know, I know, Oskar. Don't upset yourself."

Oskar's anger subsided with a suddenness characteristic of him. He smiled and leaned across and stroked Leushka's

14

face. "Sometimes I forget you're still only a girl almost. I'm getting old, Leushka, I'm going to be fifty this fall."

She had very black, straight hair, combed back very plainly over her ears, dark, large, warm eyes, a full mouth, a prominent nose—all her features were bold and generously proportioned: heavy breasts, fleshy hips, a curving belly. She was not yet fat, only well-fleshed; but she was the type who would not be able to avoid becoming fat eventually. Nobody would have called her pretty—she wasn't made with sufficient delicacy for that—but sometimes she was almost beautiful. "Madonna," Oskar called her, ironically, at times. "Is the madonna ready? Has the madonna finished beautifying herself? Is the madonna going to remember one day where she put her keys a little earlier than the last minute before we're going out? Has the madonna finished spoiling the child for one night?" Though he used the term ironically, you could see why he should have chosen it: Leushka was the sort of woman who looked incomplete without a child in her arms.

"You did good business?" she asked.

"Leushka," he said, "you know suddenly I'm dog-tired." He felt the texture of his skin. "I need to shave," he said, "I need to shave twice a day. Leushka, I didn't make any money, I lost money. I lost money. I lost a lot of money, Leushka." Her dark eyes were soft and unamazed; she had heard this before. Oskar could no longer tell her anything that would truly shock her, after what had happened in Vienna.

"How much was it you lost?"

"A lot of money, Leushka. Plenty. Almost a thousand dollars. I know, I know, you don't have to tell me, you don't have to put those accusing eyes on me, with a thousand dollars we could get a nice apartment in Tompkins Square, we wouldn't have to live here. What do you want I should do? Lie down in front of a train? It looked like a certainty, we could have got on our feet from that one deal."

"What deal, Oskar?"

"I'd rather not talk about it right now." He sighed deeply. "I don't seem to have any luck these days, Leushka." She looked at him silently, pained by his pain, unable to remonstrate with him at a time when he was so obviously full of remorse and regrets. That was the trouble, he was always so self-recriminating after he had done something of this sort, and it was pointless then—and cruel, as well—to

15

rub it in that she had warned him in advance. But when she did warn him before the event, he would dismiss her misgivings contemptuously. What did she know about business? Why didn't she keep quiet about things she didn't understand? A man had to take risks to get somewhere. He'd made a lot of money once, in Vienna. Hadn't they lived on the first floor in the best district? Didn't they sit at the opera in a private box? And drive in a fiacre! He'd made money once, he'd make it again.

"What we going to do now, Okshkerle?" she asked tenderly.

"We'll have to write to the family," he said. "We'll have to write to the family to send more money."

"What reason do we give this time?"

"I don't know, Leushka, I don't know. I'm beat. We have to write to the family and say . . ."—he was making an effort to think of something—"and say the child is sick, he needs an operation. No, I know—he's got sick with consumption, he needs sanatorium treatment. That's expensive. They know that's expensive. The child's dying, *he's got to have sanatorium treatment*. They should send fifteen hundred dollars at once, or it'll be too late." Oskar had brightened a little on thinking of this idea.

"You shouldn't say such things," Leushka said, rebukingly. "You shouldn't bring such thoughts to your lips."

"You know something, Leushka, with fifteen hundred dollars behind me I could get on my feet again. I tell you something, I suddenly have got a very good feeling. I can still make a fortune. This is America, there's opportunities all the time. This is a country where anything is possible. Leushka, I've got a good feeling all of a sudden. . . . Maybe you make up the bed for the child so I can get a good night's sleep, I've had a strenuous time and I'm dog-tired."

This was what Alexi knew would happen; it always happened—his father came home and immediately Alexi lost all his rights, his right to sleep in the big bed in his mother's arms, his right to be fussed over and looked after, to have his needs immediately satisfied. He crept back into the bed and pretended to be asleep. His father, he knew, would be very angry if he discovered that Alexi had been listening at the door. When, some two or three minutes later, Leushka tiptoed into the room, he was simulating the steady breathing of deep sleep. Carefully, she removed the bedclothes

16

and took him into her arms, holding him very soothingly and very gently so as not to awaken him, and he, still pretending to be asleep, snuggled up close against her breasts as she carried him into the kitchen, lowered him gently into the little bed she had prepared for him, tucked the bedclothes around him, and gave him the good-night kiss that he had been waiting for earlier. Then, taking the kerosene lamp with her, she joined Oskar who had already gone into the bedroom and was now sprawled out on the big bed.

"I'm really dog-tired, Leushka," he said, without opening his eyes, the effort being too much for him. "You think you could take off my shoes, Leushka?" Lovingly, with the same tenderness she had shown the child, she unbuttoned his shoes and pulled them off. "You won't forget to put in the shoetrees," he said, "because otherwise the shoes get ruined. You're an angel, Leushka. And the trousers, Leushka. Suddenly I don't seem to have a drop of energy left. That's good." She was unbuttoning the trousers at his waist and easing them carefully down his legs. "An angel I've married. You won't forget to take the things out of the pockets otherwise it ruins the pockets." She smiled. He was nearly always dog-tired before he went to bed, and she nearly always took off his clothes and hung them up, and took the things out of the pockets. Now, as in the past, she emptied the contents of his pockets and, together with his other accessories, laid them out on the washstand: nail scissors and nail file; cigarette case; cigarette holder; pocketbook; watch and watch fob; cuff links; silver collar studs; tie pin. She carefully folded his trousers so they would keep their creases and hung them up. Noticing that she had left the door open, she sighed at her own carelessness and went over to close it.

As the darkness became enclosing, Alexi felt the familiar panic surge up inside him. The room, with his mother so far away on the other side of the door, was cold and desolate, like the grim landscape in a nightmare, full of menacing shapes. A sob was forming in his chest and swelling and swelling until it filled him. He tried to hold it back. His father had warned him of what happened to little boys who were always crying like little girls, they turned into little girls, that was what happened to them. The dark was tangible, oppressive, smothering. The madwoman's disembodied face was in the room; she had a strange, knowing,

17

laughing expression: there was something that she knew, something terrible and unspeakable that she had found out in the dark regions to which she alone had access. The madwoman's face was his mother's face, emptied of kindness and tenderness, grimly knowing, a fixed expression of tragic suffering in her eyes, as if she knew something that he didn't know. His mother, the mother who loved him and cared for him, was a long way away, in the other room, and unreachable. Her face was receding from him at terrifying speed, drowning in the darkness. He was being torn from her, wrenched bleeding from her body by the waves of darkness. He pulled the bedclothes over himself and tried to shut out these images by closing his eyes tight. But under his eyelids the darkness grew denser, became almost solid and had no end, it stretched as far as the moon and further, and his mother's face kept receding further and further into this immensity of space. The panic rose in him like vomit, it could not be held down any longer, it began to force its way up into his throat, and he began to scream and sob with all his force: "Mama, Mama, Mama. . . ." If only she would come, if only she would come to him. For a long time he cried and nobody came. He could hear low murmurs from the next room, movements, creakings. She had heard him, but she did not come. He was completely alone. The panic got worse, he was drowning in it; he was dissolving like a snowman in the sun, becoming nothing. The door opened, and in the light from the other room he saw his father coming toward him, an angry expression on his face.

"What for is all the crying?"

"I want Mama," the child demanded.

"You had a bad dream?"

"Mama! Where's Mama?" he sobbed.

"Your Mama is a hard-working woman, Alexander. She's also entitled to sleep sometimes."

"I got frightened."

His father came over slowly and sat on the edge of the bed, and looked at the child tenderly. "Frightened—hm? What's to be frightened about? When you grow up you'll find plenty to be frightened of, that's for sure. But what's to be frightened of in the dark? The dark can't hurt you. Your mother spoils you, that's the trouble. Pampering you all the time. Tell me, Alexander, how are you going to be a man —and one day look after your Mama—if you can't be

18

alone in the dark five minutes? You get to be a man and you got to be alone in the dark all the time. Or you want to grow up to be a sissy, always crying for Mama? You got to be a bit tough. You got to have a bit of toughness in you to get anywhere in this world. Here." Oskar picked the boy out of the bed and sat him on his lap and carefully dried his tears away with a corner of the bedsheet. "You know, Alexander, your Papa and Mama love you very much. Everything we do, it's for you. So you should have a nice life. But your Mama can't be with you all the time. You're a smart boy, you understand that. Hmm? Better now? Go to sleep now." The child seemed to have become calmer, and Oskar kissed him and put him back in the bed. "I bring you the lamp," he said, "so you won't be frightened." Oskar went out of the room and returned after a few moments—during which Alexi could hear him and Mama talking in whispers—bringing the kerosene lamp with him. "There, you be a good boy now. No more crying."

When his father had left again, Alexi felt better for a while; the terrible, overwhelming panic had gone, but there was a raw, hurting emptiness inside him that could be healed only by his mother, and she hadn't come to him, she hadn't come when he needed her so badly. He lay awake, listening intently. Presently he began to hear movements and sounds from the next room which suggested that his parents were not asleep—and, later on, he heard his mother cry out as if in pain. He knew that something unimaginable was going on in the next room, it must be something awful to make his mother cry out like that: perhaps the madwoman knew what it was, perhaps that was why she had gone mad and had that strange, knowing look on her face—it must be something so terrible that if you found out about it, it made you mad. When he fell asleep eventually he had one of his recurring nightmares. In this version, he was part of a garrison that was going to be attacked. The enemy was approaching and arms were being handed out to the defenders. Alexi wore the uniform of an officer, but he had no pistol. He went to the arsenal and said he was an officer and that he wanted a pistol. All the other officers had pistols. But at the arsenal they said, smirking, that they didn't have one to give him. The enemy was very close. He went to a superior officer and complained that he had not been given a pistol though, being an officer, he was clearly entitled to one. The superior officer, who had a strange, knowing expression on his face, which was the face of the madwoman, agreed that Alexi ought to have a pistol, and then gave a derisive laugh. Alexi was out in the streets which were full of the enemy, marching in formation and bayoneting everyone who crossed their path. The sidewalks were littered with the dead and the bleeding. Alexi hid in a ditch, and observed the slaughter on all sides. Fires were burning in the distance, and the streets were full of screaming, panicky women. He saw some of them being ripped open by violent bayonet thrusts. Alexi was very agitated because he did not know where his mother was and if she was safe. A woman lay on the ground, her belly cut open, and out of her bloody entrails a baby crawled, screaming. Alexi started to run, pushing and shoving his way through the densely packed streets. He could see his mother in the distance, standing on some high ground, wringing her hands in great anxiety, and searching for him. He called out to her, but she didn't hear him, and though he struggled to get nearer to her the tide of panicky, stampeding women swept him further and further away. The enemy was in among the crowd, bayoneting everyone. He kept thinking, "If only I had a pistol. If only I had a pistol." One of the enemy was on top of him, and others were all around him, he was hemmed in, trapped. The bayonet was leveled, it was thrusting toward him, it was piercing him, he felt it going through his body and knew he must be dead, and yet as he was aware of being dead he knew he was alive, and that he was dreaming and that he could save himself by waking up or changing the dream. He was in a dark place and a train was rumbling overhead. He was trying to get back to the apartment where he knew it would be safe, but the streets were full of people and one of these people was after him and he didn't know which one. He started to walk toward the house, all the time terrifyingly aware of being followed by someone. This someone was out to kill him, or to do something even more terrible to him, but Alexi could not hide from him because he did not know from whom he had to hide. Alexi had got as far as the house and he was inside the door. He was waiting, fearfully, in the dark by the stairs. The door was opening and a man was approaching very slowly; it was someone Alexi had never seen before but he knew, with a sudden feeling of profound dread, that it was *him*. Though

20

he had never seen him before, he recognized him instantly as his pursuer, as the one who was always after him in all his dreams. "It's *him*," he thought. "Yes, it's *him*." This man knew something, some terrible secret that the brain cannot encompass, and that was why he had that strange, knowing look on his face. This incommunicable knowledge gave his face its distinctive mocking expression. It seemed to be saying: "You don't know, do you? You don't know. But I know, I know." As he came closer, Alexi took out his pistol and pointed it at the approaching man, but he did not seem in the least perturbed and continued to come closer, and the expression on his face did not change. Alexi pulled the trigger, but nothing happened, he kept pulling the trigger again and again but no bullets came out. He knew now that there was no way of evading the ultimate confrontation with *him*, but it could be postponed, it could be postponed by waking up, for the time being that was a way out. This was a dream that he had had before, in various forms, but always Alexi was being pursued and hounded and then there came this horrendous moment of confrontation with *him*, who was always different and unknown to the boy, but was none the less unmistakably *him*.

In the morning Alexi had a temperature and whatever his mother gave him to eat he brought up. The constant vomiting made him very weak. Whenever he had to be sick, his mother held him over the pot, pressing the sides of his forehead with her hands as if in this way she could squeeze the badness out of him. Afterwards, she made him sip plain, unsweetened tea. To reduce the fever she boiled some sheets in water, wrung them dry and wrapped the child from head to toe in the steaming linen and covered him up to the chin with the bedclothes. To revive him after a bout of vomiting she bathed his face and chest with vinegar and held a cloth soaked in vinegar under his nostrils. All the time she watched him with her large, anguished eyes, sitting up all night at his side, sleeping only intermittently, waking up immediately if the fever got worse and made him toss and turn. The doctor came, took his temperature and pulse, listened to his chest, looked in his throat, frowned, smiled, tested his reflexes, scratched the soles of his feet with something sharp, frowned again to himself, smiled again at Leushka, murmured something reassuring and said he would come again the following

21

day. What Alexi remembered always of this illness was his mother's tired, tragic face from which, even when she was pretending for his benefit to look cheerful, she could not exclude the fears she was feeling. On the third night his temperature went up to 105, and through the delirium of his fever he could see his mother standing over him for what seemed like hours, wringing her hands, nodding her head tragically, biting her lower lip, looking up to the ceiling and imploring God's help in German phrases that she kept repeating endlessly in a sort of rhythmic chant, sighing deeply every so often, crying sometimes, and in such a pitiful way that Alexi, seeing this, became more agitated and so gave the impression that he was getting worse, which made her cry even more.

Oskar came in from time to time, and then there were ominous whisperings. He was better able to conceal his feelings than Leushka, but he also looked desperately worried. Sometimes Leushka would look at him meaningfully and say, "It's God's punishment, it's God's punishment. God hears, God hears," and then Oskar would stand by the bed rhythmically beating his chest with a clenched fist, as Jews do on the Day of Atonement, intoning that Hebrew prayer of contrition. On the third night, when his temperature was 105, Alexi's breathing was just a series of rapid gasps alternating with sudden, desperate, choking gulps for air. He was falling, at a controlled speed, as if held by elastic that gave and gave; it was stretching and stretching, not arresting the fall, but slowing it slightly, stretching further and further—now it must break, now, now, now, now it can stretch no more. . . . In the middle of this long, slow terrifying fall, Alexi felt a sudden calmness, as if he were standing outside his own body and watching himself fall, and really it was not such an awful thing this fall, if you could look at it with the eyes of a spectator; there came a point when sensation ceased and what remained was detached awareness, as if it were all happening to somebody else. Alexi was unconscious for no more than a few seconds; he came to with the smell of vinegar in his nose and his mother's white, terrified face before his eyes. She looks so pale, he thought, I must look after her. He gave her a reassuring smile and murmured, "Don't worry, Mama, don't worry, please." Then he fell into a deep peaceful sleep. When he woke twelve hours later, he was better.

Though the fever had gone, he was still very weak and now Leushka devoted herself to making him well again. To begin with, she decided, he must eat only light, easily digested food. At first she limited his diet to soups. Sitting him up in the big bed, three enormous pillows supporting him, she fed him the strengthening soup, a spoonful at a time. "A drop more soup? Yes, you'll have a drop more. Gives you strength." And she smiled happily as his appetite returned. "A piece of chicken? Plain, boiled chicken can't do you harm. I give you the white of the meat, tender like butter, can't do you any harm. That's right, eat. Eat and get well." Alexi responded to his mother's loving care and got stronger. She was insistent that the child could not sleep alone; he might need something during the night, he might be hungry or thirsty, and so it was necessary that she should be close by him. For about a week Oskar slept in the kitchen, and then Leushka returned from shopping one day to find a note from him saying he had had to go off on business and would be away for a little while. He had had to borrow her wedding ring and her engagement ring, he explained, because there was nothing else in the apartment that could be pawned. Just as soon as the family sent some money, the very first thing he would do would be to redeem the rings.

Slowly Alexi was becoming stronger. At night, in his mother's arms, he usually slept well; if he did have a bad dream or had a sudden fright his mother was there to soothe away his fears and make him feel better again. During the day, Leushka began taking him out in the open air on short walks. "That's better," she was able to say after a few days, "now you got some color in your cheeks." When Oskar had been away for three weeks, Alexi asked his mother one evening, "Where is Papa? Why is he away always?"

"Your Papa has got a living to make, that's why he's away," she answered. The child considered this for a while, then he asked, "Do I have to go away to make a living?" She smiled at this. "One day," she said, "maybe. But you got time."

"I don't want to make a living," he said, "if I have to go away from you."

23

She pressed his head to her breast. "You got time," she said. "First you got to grow up into a big, strong boy, a clever boy you got to be so your Mama will be proud of you."

"What does Papa do when he goes away?"

"Business," she said. "Your Papa is a highly intelligent man. When I was a girl in Vienna, you should have seen your Papa then. The way people looked up to him! He was a businessman, but he never handled goods. It was done all on paper. Can you imagine? Buying, selling—all on paper. To handle goods, with his own hands, that was not for your father. He could sell anything, your father. Always he could find a buyer, because everywhere he was known, he had connections everywhere. One time, I remember, he sold five thousand ashtrays that none of the stores could sell, steel ashtrays. Who would want to buy five thousand steel ashtrays? Your father figured out; who could need such a lot of ashtrays, who?—a shipping line! It's logical. On ships there's rough weather, always things get broken, five thousand steel ashtrays at a low price, to them it's a bargain. Your father always got such good ideas. What a highly intelligent man! Everybody admired him. That a man like that should be interested in me was something remarkable. In a fiacre he took me to the opera . . ."

"Why did you leave Vienna, Mama?"

It was a question Alexi had asked before, and never had he got a proper answer. "That's another story," said Leushka. She sighed. "Your Papa had a piece of bad luck . . ." For a moment it seemed as though she might go on and explain, but she stopped herself. "It was a misfortune," she said.

All the time Oskar was away there was always enough food in the kitchen so that if he should return unexpectedly she would be able to give him a meal immediately. Often, while she was sewing, she would stop momentarily and listen to identify footsteps on the stairs. When she was sure they were not Oskar's she gave a deep sigh and went on with her work. From time to time, during each day, she would go to the window and look down into the street, searchingly. Sometimes the fear rose in her that Oskar would never come back, that he had had an accident and was dying, that he had found another woman whom he pre-

24

ferred—she knew he had other women, could sometimes smell their smell on him when he came home. But she quickly put such thoughts out of her head. No point in having bad thoughts. Anyway, she had to get on with her work, otherwise how would she be able to feed the child.

Once Alexi was completely well again she often took him with her when she went to collect or deliver the sewing work—mostly small repairs and invisible mending—that she did for various men's-wear shops who hadn't the staff to do such work on their premises. While his mother was transacting her business in the stores, Alexi was allowed to remain outside, on the understanding that he must not wander too far away and get himself lost. There was one shop that Alexi was always glad for his mother to call at because there was a place next to it that fascinated him, a converted store that showed moving pictures. His father considered this a very low form of amusement, catering to illiterates and ignoramuses who couldn't speak the language of the country they were living in and so could only follow stories if they were told in pictures. Alexi was not allowed to go inside one of these places, but there was no way of stopping the child from looking at the posters and the placards and the pictures outside and in the vestibule. Above the colonnaded plaster-work entrance, the arches of which were studded with colored electric light bulbs, the name of the theater was spelled out in giant letters, two stories high. During the daytime, when the sign was not illuminated, you could see the windows between the letters, and sometimes people leaning out, looking very small and insignificant in relation to the enormous sign. The name Bijou formed the base of the display; out of the "i" rose a fountainlike eruption of colored light bulbs that spread upward over the façade of the building to a height of several stories, and there, at the top, like balls supported on a column of water, was a cluster of stars, each containing a different message: Admission 5c; World in Motion; Show Going on All the Time; The Family Show; No Pictures Shown Here That Are Not Perfectly Moral and Clean—Bring the Kids; Continuous Performance—8 A.M. Till Midnight. At night these stars were illuminated in sequence, starting with "Admission 5c" and ending up climactically, with "Bring the Kids," by which time the

25

entire façade of the building was ablaze with many colored lights. Inside, beyond the colonnaded entrance, in the center of the vestibule, there was a box-like structure with a cupola-shaped roof where you bought your ticket for the show. The vestibule was always full of people, either waiting in line to buy their tickets or looking at the posters and pictures. They were in their working clothes mostly, some of the men were in need of a shave and wash, and Alexi could understand why his father disapproved of this kind of show: its clientele could certainly not have been described as high class. "You don't know what diseases you can pick up in a place like that," Oskar would say when Leushka requested permission to take the child to one of these shows. "And you think it's good for a child's mind to see such rubbish? You're forgetting, Leushka, I'm used to the best of the best, and I want the child he should get used to that too." He did not explain how this was to be achieved on their small and irregular income, but meanwhile, at any rate, he would not tolerate the child's mind being corrupted by such lurid rubbish. Lurid it certainly was. The Bijou, which prided itself on being "the home of showmanship," was always bedecked with crudely colored posters and placards advertising the current attraction. What Alexi was not allowed to see, he created in his imagination as he walked home with his mother or when he was alone in the apartment, using the placards and the posters and the display pictures, the boldly printed hints and the promises of the streamers as a starting-point for his own opulent imaginings. In this way, he made up dozens of stories for himself, visualizing in rich detail the situations that were alluded to on the hoardings, but which he was not allowed to see. SHE-PANTHER, screamed one of these streamers. The Queen of the Underworld. Why Were the Cutthroats of Paris Afraid of Her? What Was Her Terrible Power? Talk About Excitement, This Is the Limit. Thrills, Thrills and More Thrills. Her Look Spelled Death. The artist's representation of the She-Panther showed a rather solidly built and bejeweled young woman, with a great deal of thick black make-up around her eyes, staring hypnotically (the artist conveyed this by showing rays coming from her eyes) at an agonized cutthroat who, arms akimbo, mouth hanging open in terror, was in the act of dropping his pistol. Alexi spent days

26

working out that one. In the version that he finally settled for, she was a mesmerist (in an earlier version, which he had not been satisfied with, she had been a witch) who, during the day, was a leading figure in Paris society and at night became the leader of a gang of criminals and rogues whom she got to commit dreadful crimes, the victims being her society friends. Alexi decided that the reason she did these terrible things was because she was not really an aristocrat at all, but a working-class girl abandoned by her husband, who needed money to feed her small child.

CHAPTER TWO

On a Saturday, soon after his tenth birthday, Alexi was taken on an outing to Fifth Avenue. It was by way of being a birthday treat, and one of the rare occasions when he went out with both his parents. It was a fine summer's day and they all wore their best clothes: Leushka wore a pale blue muslin dress with short sleeves, high waist and a flounced skirt, the hemline of which she had raised slightly to conform with the new fashion, so that you could just see her ankles. With it she wore the white straw hat, with the low crown and very wide brim and the luxuriant outcrop of feathers curling over the brim, that Oskar had brought her a couple of years earlier and which she had kept, ever since, in a box under the bed, not having had an occasion to wear it previously. Oskar, in high, white collar almost obscuring the narrow knot of his tie, gray cutaway coat, stiff white cuffs, pearl-gray spats and pointed shoes, and a gray, rather low, top hat with curled brim, looked decidedly distinguished. And Alexi was allowed to wear, for the first time, the Panama, the Norfolk jacket and the knickerbockers that his father had bought him for his birthday. When Oskar had made some money his homecoming was always an exciting and joyful occasion —then there were parcels to unwrap, trips to be planned, treats for the child to be organized, and discussions about the furnishing of the new apartment they would take in Tompkins Square.

There was a great to-do as they got ready, almost as if they were setting off on a long journey and must not miss the train. Oskar kept shouting to Leushka to hurry up, to stop dawdling and dreaming, to bring him his hot water so he could shave, to find his nail clippers, to make sure the child had cleaned under his finger nails, to hurry up and get ready herself; and Leushka lost her temper several times and said how could she get dressed herself if she also had to dress Oskar and the child. Once or twice, in fact, Oskar threatened to call off the whole outing as it seemed beyond their capabilities to get ready in time. But eventually they were all ready—though the apartment was in a shambles, littered with items of clothing that had been considered, debated and then discarded: the breakfast things hadn't been washed, the shoe brushes had somehow got on the kitchen shelf, the clothesbrush was lost, and now Alexi had to go to the bathroom. When he returned, Oskar subjected him and Leushka to a rigorous, final scrutiny. If they were going to be seen in his company along Fifth Avenue he had to make sure that they were properly turned out. He was liable to run into important business friends, he pointed out, and it was imperative that his wife and son should make a good impression.

After making the first part of the journey by El and streetcar, on which the boy had often traveled before, Oskar hired a hansom to take them the rest of the way. This was a completely new experience for Alexi. As the traffic moved at a sociable six miles an hour along Fifth Avenue, he had a lordly view of the elegant parade of carriages and automobiles and promenading swells. Oskar had insisted that the top of the cab should be lowered so that they might enjoy the sunshine, and this enabled them not only to see better, but to be better seen. Alexi felt very proud to be traveling in this luxurious, high-class way along this fine street, and he looked avidly about him, his eyes plundering wildly, as if by just looking the things that he desired might become his. Sunlight falling on brass coach lamps and door handles and automobile headlamps and wheel hubs and the buttons of liveried coachmen made the whole length of the Avenue shimmer and sparkle. There was so much to see, he became quite dizzy from twisting and turning and craning his neck. . . . A nifty little yellow and black barouche insinuating its way through the heavier traffic, its owner-driver, reins in one hand, doffing his boater with the other to a . . . palely pretty girl in an

28

open landau, rigid as if sitting for a family portrait, around her a haze of frilly white women, all busy gossiping and fanning and recognizing and cutting. . . . A magnificent coach, liveried coachman and footman on the box, a heavily mustached man and a bosomy woman inside, holding on to velvet, tasseled straps that were like the bell-pulls in a great house. . . . A sporty-looking young man, affecting aviator's goggles—though they were now on his forehead—and duster, in a Bugatti. . . . Fashionable ladies under enormous, flowery hats, lolling against very high, buttoned-leather tonneaus, that seemed almost a part of them, of their extravagant outfits. . . . A big, heavy, long-bodied roadster, its surfeit of nickel and brass blazing in the sun: a colored sun-umbrella contained in a wicker holder mounted on the running board, next to it a strapped-on picnic basket, and then the tool box and the spare wheel. . . . "Look over there, Alexander," his father instructed. "Not too obvious. Just casual—it's not good manners to stare. Those two men, see them? Getting out of the hansom. Know who those men are . . . ? Rob Collier and Sam McClure. Great figures in the magazine publishing business. And over there, walking all alone, can't you tell from that distinguished way he walks . . . you know who that is? You don't know? Leushka, the boy doesn't know anything. What do they teach him?" He shook his head with incredulity, pained by the shortcomings of the educational system. "That," he declared, "is Charles M. Schwab, iron and steel. Very big man. That's who that is, and remember it, Alexander, remember his face. To know important people is always useful." Dutifully Alexi absorbed this advice. A tally-ho and six belonging—Oskar informed them—to Mr. Vanderbilt was making its way to its stand at the Waldorf. All along the sidewalks people were watching this great parade of which Alexi, by virtue of being in the hansom, considered himself to be a part. There were vulgar gapers, from out of town clearly, looking and pointing in such an ill-bred way, and fathers lifting up their children to give them a better view. There were young swells, standing about idly chatting, rather as if they were at the races, and eyeing the girls in the passing carriages. There was a woman in a hobble skirt and a high straw bonnet trailing ribbons, descending from her carriage, assisted by her footman. . . . There were small, neat children, the boys dressed not unlike Alexi, the girls in knee-length dresses and short socks, being taken out by their governesses. . . . Alexi felt very superior to them, being in a carriage when they were only walking.

As they got out at Holland House, Oskar nodded to a tall striking looking man who was just coming out of the hotel; the effect was dramatic. With an exaggerated flourish, he doffed his topper and gave a deep, theatrical bow. And he repeated this elaborate gesture three times, once for Oskar, once for Leushka and once for Alexi, and then went off, weaving slightly. "That," said Oskar, highly pleased, "was James K. Hackett, the famous actor. Leushka, that is an actor to compare with the finest—even in Vienna. That is not an exaggeration. And what a character —I've met him personally, several times, bought him a drink. Alexander, are you listening? There is an actor for you—" (Oskar kissed the tips of his fingers to express his unqualified admiration) "—tiptop, with culture, with education. You see, Alexander, your mother and I are used to the finest of the finest in theater, in opera, in music. To see a great performer—a Bernhardt, a Duse, I've seen them both—is not just a matter of looking. Any jerk can look. To see great artists you got to be *part* of an audience, and that means you got to be dressed elegant, you got to smell good, you got to appreciate what you are seeing, you got to be a connoisseur, that's what theater is. Not just a lot of flickering pictures in a dirty room full of unshaven bums who don't know to speak the language of the country they live in." Oskar had become so carried away that he was unaware of the fact that he was blocking the entrance to the hotel, and Leushka had to tug his sleeve to draw his attention to this. Inside, they were shown straight away to their table by a headwaiter who had a knack of rolling names off his tongue as if they were all as familiar to him as Rockefeller or Stuyvesant and, what's more, as important. "This way, Mr. Sondorpf, please, follow me, sir. Very nice to see you again, Mr. Sondorpf. And Madam,"—and giving a slight bow to Alexi—"and sir." Bills of fare were produced with a flourish, a waiter arrived with a jug of iced water, and they settled themselves comfortably in the red plush seats against the wall, from which they had a perfect view of the rest of the restaurant. "Best eating place in New York," Oskar pronounced. "Some people, they say they prefer Sherry's or Delmonico's. Fine places, both of them, I have nothing against them, but for my own personal preference I take Holland House. They say the Americans don't know how to prepare good food, which is true of a lot of places, but not Holland House. Now, Alexander, if you like some soft-shell crab, I can recommend it. Or a lovely canvasback, roasted, served in its own gravy, with a dish of milk-white fried hominy. Take my word for it, delicious. You want to share a bird with me, Alexander? Leushka? I can assure you it's good. You don't believe me, look at the price. Four dollars—the most expensive thing on the bill of fare, more expensive than imported English pheasant. Or maybe you like some terrapin —Leushka, you prefer terrapin? You know what terrapin is? It's not kosher, that I can tell you, but it's delicious. It's . . . well, it's . . . tortoise."

"Tortoise?" Leushka said. "Tortoise is to be eaten? I never heard of such a thing."

"Don't be so prejudiced," Oskar retorted. "Don't turn your nose up just because you don't know. There exist other things in the world to be eaten than always boiled chicken and boiled beef. Be a bit adventurous. I take you out to Holland House to lunch so it should be a new experience for you. And for the child, he should see a bit of life, the kind of life I want him to have."

"All right," Leushka said, capitulating. "I'll be adventurous. I'll take a canvas—what?"

"Canvasback. It's duck, it's the most delicious duck." At this, Leushka's face brightened. "Duck," she said, "duck I like, it's almost the same like chicken." When they had given their order and were waiting for the food to be served, they sat back, sipped their iced water, and savored the dynamo-hum of the many conversations that made the room vibrate with a special sort of excitement. Oskar, sitting back very much at his ease, pointed out the important people to them. The big, fat man, eating alone, napkin tucked in his collar, was a famous impresario. At the next table was a well-known journalist and author, Stephen Raille, who had recently written an article in Pearson's magazine exposing the corruption in Minneapolis city council where, he had revealed, a crooked mayor and council had granted water, gas and street-railway franchises for fifty years to private corporations, with the legal right to charge exorbitant fees. "It happens everywhere," said Oskar, "New York, Chicago, St. Louis, San Francisco, Los Angeles, everywhere corruption, makes you sick in the stomach." He hardly paused for breath as he continued his celebrity-spotting tour of the restaurant. "Over there, by the window, the man with the pince-nez, that's Daniel Cranston, a big noise in the banking house of Kuhn, Loeb & Co. . . ."

"Papa, how come you know so many famous people?" Alexi wanted to know.

"Well," said Oskar, "I have to know them in my line of business. It's necessary I should know such people."

"What business are you in, Papa?"

"Well, Alexander," Oskar said, "there are some businesses you can put a name to just like that, like saying Mr. Smith is in the hardware business or Mr. Jackson is a haberdasher. But then there are other businesses you can't put a name to so easy. It's like asking what business is J. P. Morgan in. The business of making money, that's the business he's in . . ." and Oskar emitted a thin laugh. "Well, that's the business I'm in too. You could say that I'm an entrepreneur . . . yes, an entrepreneur."

"Is that a good thing to be, an entr . . . entre . . . ?"

"Entrepreneur. Well, Alexander, it's like with everything else, depends on whether or not you're successful at it. . . ."

"Are you successful at it, Papa?"

"I'm building up, I'm in the process of establishing myself. That isn't always easy, and it takes time. But I'm building up, things are beginning to move, I'd say I was doing all right. If I weren't doing all right you think I could afford to take you and your mother to an expensive restaurant like this? The people you see here, Alexander, are successful people. Have to be to be able to pay the bill."

"If we're doing all right, Papa," Alexander persisted, "why do we live in a slum?"

"We don't live in a slum," Oskar corrected him. "We live in an inexpensive neighborhood, and I'll tell you the reason for that. The reason we don't live in a more expensive neighborhood, the way your mother and I did in Vienna, where we lived on the first floor in the best district, the reason we don't live in such a good neighborhood here is because in my line of business you got to have liquid capital, you see. No good having it tied up in houses and furnitures. Liquid capital, that's what you need. Because you never know when the opportunity you been waiting for is going to come along, and when it does you need liquid capital. Always remember this, Alexander, America is a country where a man can multiply his riches, if he just has the nerve to seize his opportunities and the patience to bide his time. Nerve and patience, those are the two qualities, Alexander, that make for success. But first of all, you got to have capital, without capital you never get anywhere. The banks, they're the ones who run this country. Not the President. The President has to go to Pierpont Morgan."

"Isn't that a bad thing, Papa?"

"I tell you something, Alexander, there is a lot that's wrong with this country, but I'm glad you were born in America, although in Vienna we lived better. Because, I tell you something, in America nothing is impossible. America is a country that's unformed, like a big, gawky youngster with spots on his face still—for whom everything is possible, the best and also the worst. There's a lot of dishonesty, sure, but that also is a sign there are opportunities, even for crooks there are more opportunities here."

This dissertation was interrupted by the arrival of the waiter with the canvasbacks, the birds nestling against each other tenderly in the big silver dish. The waiter displayed them to Oskar, to Leushka and to Alexi, inviting their approval, and having received it, placed the silver dish on a side table and proceeded to carve. With quick, deft movements, he inserted a long, two-pronged fork astride the breastbone and then with the minimum number of carefully calculated strokes of the carving knife, laid half of the bird on either side, leaving the carcass on the fork between. "The only way to carve a canvasback," Oskar pronounced. "Unheard of to slice it. Divide, but do not slice. Bear that in mind, Alexander. It's all useful for you to know. Knowledge is what counts: to know more than somebody else—even to know how to carve canvasbacks—it gives you an advantage."

Soon after this excursion Oskar had to go away again, and for Alexi life returned to the normal routine he had become accustomed to. School. Looking out of the window.

Visits to various men's-wear stores. Helping Mama carry the groceries home, helping her with the dishes after they'd eaten, listening all the time for the sound of father's footsteps on the stairs, which might mean anything—riches such as he talked about, or calamity and disaster. The opportunities that Oskar had spoken about, and the things and the people that the child had seen in Fifth Avenue and Holland House, even the long-lingering taste of the canvasback, made Alexi restless, impatient to be out doing something to advance himself. And yet, while his mind was inflamed by such images, he was prohibited from even venturing outside the house on his own, he was not allowed to visit the picture houses but had to fall back on his own imaginings which grew more and more extravagant and sometimes made him quite dizzy with vague indefinable longings. He was a special person, his father had frequently told him, a Sondorpf, different from the other kids who ran around the streets. When he tried to express some of these longings to his mother, and asked her when they were going to be rich, she smiled and said it was nice to have dreams, but meanwhile you just had to live like the whole rest of the world, and be grateful for what you'd got, health and enough to eat and a roof over your head.

He had to get out. Running down the stone steps, Alexi felt very adventurous. He had never gone out before without telling his mother where he was going—and usually he went for a specific purpose, to get something from a store, to fetch something, and on those occasions he would come straight home without dawdling in the streets. Now he was going out for the express purpose of going out. There were several kids sitting on the steps outside the house, but they took no notice of Alexi as he came out: they knew the snooty Sondorpf kid never played with anyone. "Hi!" Alexi called to them uncertainly as he ran down the steps. They didn't even hear him. Well, he didn't want to play with them anyway. Slouching, in the way that his father had always forbidden, his hands stuck in his pockets, making bored blowing noises with his mouth, he ambled on down the street. It was a warm spring afternoon. Alexi turned the corner and continued along under the El where it was cool and dark: the overhead steel structure made intricate and sharply defined patterns of light and shade on the ground, and as a train went past the whole ground shuddered and trembled. Alexi emerged into the daylight again, and the sun got into his eyes and made him blink. Dogs and cats, lean, scrawny, dusty-gray creatures of the streets, were everywhere, sniffing around the garbage cans, searching the refuse for scraps of food, but finding nothing more edible, most of the time, than potato peel and fruit rinds. They growled and snarled at each other, and then catching a glimpse of a choicer catch, a large rat almost the size of a rabbit, which had flashed out from under the Elevated, they immediately set after it, yelping and barking—a zigzagging hunt that took them back and forth across the street and the sidewalks, under the El and out again, and back under again. . . . Alexi did not stop to see the outcome of this chase: it was something he had observed many times from the window of the apartment, and it always sickened him.

A few blocks further on, Alexi turned right, for no particular reason, into a street that was unfamiliar to him: neither his father nor his mother had ever taken him in this direction. The houses along here were mostly of the same type as the one he lived in: three- or four-story brownstones with iron-railed steps leading up to the front entrance. The lower floors of most of them had been turned into stores and business premises while the remaining floors continued to be used as living accommodations. A profusion of drab and enticing signs, some in Hebrew lettering, others in English and in languages that were unfamiliar to Alexi, contributed to the defacement of these houses. The iron pillars supporting the doorway of one such house had been repainted as a barber's pole. The window of a semibasement had the word Delicatessen painted on it. Another window, on the first-floor level, bore the words: trusses and abdominal belts. There were many signs saying: Rooms $1.50 or $2. A horsecart full of large wooden barrels was being unloaded by two men, who were rolling the barrels down some steps to a semibasement restaurant called Tregano's. The bill of fare was scrawled in chalk on a blackboard outside the entrance: lamb stew, 25 cents; beef stew, 25 cents; potted chicken, 35 cents; roast chicken, 40 cents; roast beef, 40 cents. The smell which wafted up to street level was not particularly appetizing, and Alexi walked on more rapidly. Further along, there were several tailoring establishments and through the windows Alexi could see

35

women at sewing machines and men in shirtsleeves and braces wielding pressing irons, which, on being applied to the dampened materials, produced great enveloping clouds of steam.

Some of the kids in the street called out to Alexi as he mooched along, but he knew that any contact with them was forbidden and whenever such overtures were made, whether friendly or abusive, he ignored them, and walked faster. Coming to an intersection, the boy hesitated about which way to go. Never before had he had such freedom of choice. Whenever his mother had sent him out it was on the firm understanding that he would take the route she had previously shown him, and that he wouldn't stray from it. Now here he was—and it made him feel tremendously wicked and adventurous—on his own in these prohibited streets, defying his mother, pondering which way to go next. For a moment he felt apprehensive: if his mother knew he had disobeyed her she would worry—but why should she know? She was not due back until the early evening and it was such a fine, bright day and there was so much to see and he felt so good, so excitingly alive. Every step he took increased the dimensions of the world as he knew it, made him keenly aware of all the possibilities for adventure that existed. There was so much going on—people coming and going, streetcar bells ringing, children like himself playing games, hopping and skipping and running after each other. At every intersection he came to, new and surprising vistas opened up. Now, standing at a corner, and hesitating about which way to go next, he could see on all sides a rich variety of happenings. Further along the street that was the continuation of the one he was on, a house was being pulled down. In a street to the left furniture was being carried out of a tall building and piled on a cart; a man on a high ladder was panting a sign; a woman, leaning out of a fourth floor window, was having a heated argument with somebody on the ground; another women was spreading her wash on the iron fire escape. Looking the other way, the boy could see in the distance a main thoroughfare along which a continuous line of traffic was moving. He decided to turn left, partly because he had heard the sound of music coming from that direction: on investigation he found that it came from a basement restaurant where the proprietor, not having any customers just then, was teaching his small

36

boy how to play the zither. For a while Alexi stood there, happily watching, but when the man beckoned him to come down and join them, Alexi shook his head and quickly ran off. He continued to run, he felt so full of energy. Pretending that someone was after him, he turned into a back street and from there into an intricate network of even smaller and narrower streets. As he ran he made up stories about why he was being chased. Suddenly a sadness came over him. He had been out for over an hour and he hadn't talked to anyone. The other kids weren't forced to sit in their room and look out of the window. It was true they looked dirty and rough, but they seemed to be enjoying themselves. He picked up a stone and threw it with all his strength along the street; then he picked up another one and tried to throw it further. For a while he became absorbed in this game, picking up stones and trying to exceed the length of each successive throw. He kept this up for some time, and following in the direction of his throws came eventually to a dilapidated house. Several of its windows were broken; after a few attempts, he succeeded in lobbing a stone through one of them and heard it landing inside, making a clattering echo. The front steps must have been fouled by all the dogs of the neighborhood and, in addition, were littered with bits and pieces of refuse which must have been accumulating there for months. The door was defaced by words, the meaning of which he did not understand, scrawled in paint and chalk or scratched into the wood. Climbing up the steps he could see into the semi-basement area, which was apparently used as a sort of communal garbage dump: the smell which rose from this filth was very unpleasant and made him pull a face and hold his nose. Coming up to the door, he hesitated, undecided about whether to explore further. The windows on this level were boarded up, preventing him from seeing inside, but he could now hear the sound of voices and movements. Kicking at the door, he found that it swung open. He went inside.

After the brightness of the street it seemed very dark in here; particles of dust swarmed like insects in the beams of sunlight which penetrated several gaps in the boarded-up window. At first Alexi saw only the crumbling plaster-work; then, as his eyes adjusted to the dimness of the interior, he saw shapes moving in the shadowy parts of the

37

room. Several kids, not much older than himself, were engaged in some kind of game. They were rolling about on the floor, laughing, panting, wrestling; there were cries of "Get off," and "Stop it," and "Hey, you're hurting me," and "Lemme go," and "Cut that out." Alexi had observed enough scraps to know that this was not a serious struggle because clearly the object of this game was not to inflict injuries—there were no blows, only the pulling of arms and legs and hair and clothing and the constant jockeying for position. He could see now that of the five kids involved in this game, two were girls, and they were the ones the others were fighting with. One of the girls was being held down by a dark-haired boy who sat on her chest and was trying to keep her flaying arms pinned to the floor; another boy was struggling to keep hold of her legs which she kept kicking and twisting to free herself. At the same time she was heaving upward to try and unseat the boy on her chest. The other girl was trying to help her friend on the ground by pulling at the arms and legs of the two boys, but she also had to contend with the third boy who, though smaller and weaker than her, was none the less succeeding in holding her off. In any case, Alexi could see that the girls were not making any very determined attempt to fight off their attackers, and the struggle was punctuated with giggles and playful screams. While Alexi watched, the respective positions of the participants in this scrimmage changed several times: once the girl on the ground actually succeeded in freeing herself and even managed to get to her feet, but she was soon recaptured and back in the former position. Now, apparently tired out, her struggling diminished and though she still put up a show of unwillingness she made no strenuous attempts to stop the boy sitting on her chest from feeling inside the top of her dress. Nor did she offer much resistance when the boy who had been grappling with her legs began to push up her skirt. The other girl who had just a little earlier fought so hard to help her friend had also apparently tired of struggling and was just standing there, looking on, while the boy with whom she had been fighting fumbled, unhindered, under her dress. Alexi found these sights very exciting and strange: his face was flushed and his heart thumped because he knew that of all the things that were forbidden him this, which was happening now, was the most forbidden and secret of all. The girl on the floor now had

38

her skirt bunched up around her waist and the boy was pulling at her drawers, pulling them down over her hips as far as her knees, and now he was prising her knees apart; the boy on her chest was watching this over his shoulder and moving rhythmically, as if on a rocking horse. The other two were also on the floor, rolling and struggling and heaving in the dark places of the room where Alexi lost sight of them. It was the most thrilling game Alexi had ever seen: he was trembling from excitement and fear, and his mouth was very dry and he knew that he wanted terribly to be a part of this game. It had become quiet in the room; the shouts and exclamations and cries had stopped quite abruptly, and now all that could be heard was the sound of quick, shallow breathing, as if they had all been running very hard, and the rustling of clothing. There was a sharp intake of breath from the girl on the floor; in this new quiet every sound seemed exaggeratedly loud—strident; from the far corner of the room came the rasping sound of boots scraping against the wooden floorboards, a steady, continuous scraping sound that did not seem related to any human activity that Alexi knew of. The girl who had been on the floor at the start was now just part of a melee of threshing arms and legs. It was a curiously inhuman heap, a many-limbed monster. Alexi felt both repelled and, in a deeply shameful way, excited by this sight, and by the sounds which accompanied it. The girl was uttering a series of short, shallow gasps, and then she made a curious gurgling, choking sound, followed by a long drawn-out Ahhhhhhhhhh, a protracted exhalation that seemed to go on and on, frighteningly, and did not seem to be the product of a human voice. In the other part of the room, the girl was murmuring throatily, "Bastard! Bastard! Get off, I said get off. Oh, Jesus! Oh Jeeezus—not that. Get off, you bastard: Get away, *get away*. Oh, Christ. You filthy little bastard, it's all over my dress. . . ." Presently the room became still and quiet, except for the irregular sounds of breathing. There was no movement. Uncertainly, wide-eyed, heart pounding, almost in a state of shock, Alexi dropped on his knees and crawled closer to where the first girl sprawled, unmoving, her clothing a rumpled mess around the upper part of her body, her drawers awkwardly entangling her knees. The two boys were now clear of her, on the floor. Alexi reached out to touch her, he touched her feet, experimentally, and she did not stir, his hand moved hesitantly along her leg. Abruptly she sat up and looked straight at him. Seeing this strange face, and realizing what he was doing, her eyes flashed angrily, and her mouth curled into a childish expression of disgust. She kicked out at him viciously and Alexi drew back, terrified.

"Hey!" she called out, "look what's crawled in—look what's crawled in out of the garbage."

Awkwardly, Alexi got to his feet and started to retreat. They were all sitting up now, looking at him. For the first time Alexi saw the girl clearly. She was older than himself, about twelve or thirteen, with dark hard little eyes, a surly petulant mouth, brownish hair. She was quite pretty in a chubby, coarse sort of way.

"Who said you could come in here?" one of the boys demanded.

"You been spyin' on us?" the one in the far corner called out accusingly, coming forward, buttoning his trousers.

"The little rat," said the first girl. "You see what he was up to, feeling up my legs, the filthy little pig!"

"We oughter teach 'im a lesson, bash his head in," the biggest of the boys said.

"Yeah, let's teach the brat a lesson."

Terrified, Alexi started to move away toward the door, his accusers converging on him menacingly; he stumbled backward feeling for the way out. One of the boys gave him a brutal push which sent him reeling against the door. The girl who had discovered him stuck her face very close to his, a contemptuous, cruel look in her eyes; she was hollowing her cheeks as if she were sucking candy, her mouth was moving in a peculiar way, and suddenly Alexi realized what she was doing; she was filling her mouth with saliva and now, very deliberately, she opened her mouth and spat full in his face. Somebody was kicking his shins, somebody else was jabbing an elbow into his stomach. Alexi struggled to open the door, but all the others were pressing against it to keep it shut. He managed to get it open a little and insert his foot in the gap; they were all hitting him and kicking him, and now both the girls were spitting at him in rapid succession. With a great effort, he squeezed most of himself through the opening, while still being held from inside by his arm. For a while it became a tug of war, with those inside trying to pull him back, and Alexi pulling

40

desperately to free himself. At last, with a supreme effort that made him think his arm was going to be torn from its socket, he managed to wrench himself clear, falling onto his knees at the top of the steps. The two girls were the first to come through the door after him. As he picked himself up they kicked at him and continued to spit in his face, frenziedly hollowing their cheeks and spitting, hollowing their cheeks and spitting . . . his face was running with their spittle. He was swaying at the top of the steps, his hands in front of his face to protect himself against this humiliating attack; moving backward, away from them, his foot missed a step, he lost his balance, and fell over sideways, hitting his knees hard against the concrete; his hands tried to clutch at something to arrest his fall, but not finding anything to hold on to he tumbled all the way down the stone steps, coming to a stop only when his shoulder hit the iron railing at the bottom. The pain of the impact was such that for a moment he blacked out, but his fear was stronger than his pain, and he scrambled to his feet and started to run as fast as he could. After he had gone about a hundred yards, he looked back and saw he was not being pursued, but he continued to run, and now the pain in his shoulder, together with the humiliation and horror of this experience, forced dry, breathless sobs out of his chest. Every part of him ached and hurt, but his shoulder hurt most, and he had to try and keep his left arm rigid, because the slightest movement caused such a violent pain in his shoulder that it made him feel he was going to faint, it was so unbearable. He was bleeding in several places—his shoulder, his knees, his forehead, and he couldn't seem to get enough air into his lungs.

It was beginning to get dark, and suddenly a new terror seized him: he had no idea of where he was, the streets were completely unfamiliar to him. With mounting panic, he ran on to the next intersection, where he looked around desperately for some familiar sight, but everything was strange and menacing. He tried another direction; the further he ran the more lost did he feel. He was sobbing continuously, and the physical pain was the least of his hurts. Even in this state, to ask help of any of the people in the street was something he could not bring himself to do. A few passers-by did stop and call out to ask what was the matter; as he took no notice of them and just ran on they

41

shrugged and did not bother to go after him. The idea of asking somebody's help terrified him even more than the thought of being lost. These strange streets and houses had a harsh and cold and cruel look, but to Alexi the people seemed even harsher and crueler, and, also, he felt much too ashamed to ask their help. All the time it was getting darker, and he was sure that with nightfall any chance he might still have of finding his way back home would be gone. He became more and more frantic as he ran around —often in circles—looking for some familiar outline. In the dusk, and in his state of pain, confusion and dizziness, many buildings—from a distance—seemed familiar and caused hope to surge up in him, and made him run faster, but on approaching closer he saw with bitter dismay that he had made a mistake. He ran around in this way for almost two hours and then he began to feel so bad he thought he was going to die, his head was going round, his legs had the consistency of Plasticine, he saw the houses toppling toward him as if the whole earth had shifted on its axis. When he recovered consciousness, there was a small group of people around him and a big man in a uniform was bending over him asking him where did it hurt. Hearing the words hospital and ambulance made him very agitated, and he started to cry: "Mama, my Mama, what will my Mama say? Mama! Mama! I want to go to my Mama, I want to go to my Mama!"

"Where does your Mama live?" the big cop asked him. "Tell us where your Mama lives and we'll see you get there. Just you tell us where you live."

Alexi just managed to mumble his address before fainting again. In the police wagon which took him home he kept coming to and then fainting again; but he was conscious when it passed under the El and stopped outside his house. As he was being lifted out he saw his mother in a small group on the sidewalk, her face pale and anguished, and he could sense the hysteria in the air, and as she saw him being carried toward her in the arms of a policeman she let out a terrible cry which, in a way, was more painful to Alexi than anything else that had happened to him that terrible day.

"I'm all right, Mama, I'm all right," he called out to her, fearing she might think he was dead. As she took him in her arms, and he felt safely enfolded by her and her tears

42

washed his face, he said, as if it were the most important thing he had to tell her, "Mama, I didn't do anything bad."

At school he made no friends, hardly ever talked to any of the other kids, and did badly at his lessons. He couldn't seem to concentrate. Conquest of Peru by Pizarro, 1532–34. Or was it 1632? or 1562? That special school smell: dust and chalk and new books and freshly sharpened pencils and urine and disinfectant. The heavy lethargy, coming as the light went outside and it grew darker and darker, and the teacher rambling on, through a fog of stifled yawns . . . what about? Must concentrate. What is he saying? What is he saying? If *a* equals *b* and *b* equals *c*, then *a* equals *c*. Why? Why? The streets outside, with that desolate look of sameness: nothing would ever happen here: it would all go on for the next hundred years just like this—wars of the Huguenots, 1562–98; desk lids slamming, bells ringing, the hot asphalt underfoot. Oh, that heart-sinking, early-morning, empty-stomach feeling of dread. Sometimes the lamps on in the morning when it was very dark, and the sleep still in his eyes—pencil box, ruler, compass, exercise books, crayons, forgotten anything? The smell of the gym. Leather and sweat and new wood and thick matting—cold flesh, shivering in the morning. Come on, Sondorpf, try harder. Make some effort, lad. The bleeding Jesus on the cross—excused from kneeling, against my religion. Again, the smell: the stale smell of celibacy, of ingrown passions curdling. Everything in unison: getting up, sitting down, kneeling, picking up hymn books, putting them down, singing, praying. He was glad that his religion permitted him to stand outside all that, so that when all the others were behaving in this curious, trancelike way, he was always doing something different: sitting when they were kneeling, silent when they were singing, detachedly examining the church when they were rapt, or pretending to be rapt, in prayer. Feet scraping against the stone floor—the *scraping sound*. Ahhhhhhhhhh! Why did she cry out like that? Did it hurt? It was like a wound, a bleeding wound. He did not practice his own religion either, he resented the fact that it was all predetermined, that it had all been settled before he came along, without anyone consulting him. In the can, standing on the seat and looking over, you could get a good look . . . they didn't mind you looking. Hannah bathing him when he

43

was little, such a funny-nice feeling, like wanting to pee and not being able to, drying him on her lap—oh such a lark, such games, rocking backward and forward, backward and forward, drying him on her lap till he hurt wanting to pee-pee, then putting his hand there, where it was all wet, all sticky and wet. Hannah's a bad girl, Hannah's wee-weed in her bloomers. Anything I *think*, can happen. Anything. They're all frogs—all the teachers are frogs. Quack, quack, quack. Q.E.D. Algebra is a lot of rubbish. "For his brilliant work in demonstrating the fallaciousness of algebraic and geometric theories, going back to Euclid and Pythagoras, something that nobody else has dared to do, or indeed has possessed the intuitive genius to be capable of doing, we award to Alexander Sondorpf the highest honor we are able to bestow: the first doctorate in Sondorpfian mathematics, a system which will henceforth replace all previously known systems." On your knees, dogs. All teachers of the now discredited algebraic and geometric systems will be executed at dawn.

"Sondorpf! Sondorpf!" The disagreeable spray of saliva on his face, caused by the exaggerated enunciation of the pf in his name, was what made him conscious of the teacher standing over him. "On your feet, Sondorpf, hold up your exercise book. Let everybody see it." Alexander's exercise book contained all the evidence needed to prove that he had not been paying attention. The page on which he should have been solving the algebra problem they had all been set was covered in strange scrawls and patterns and ink blots. Triumphantly holding up the shameful page, so that the rest of the class could see it, the teacher declared: *"This* is Sondorpf's solution of the problem." The derisive laughter of the class was unanimous. Turning to Alexander, he said with heavy sarcasm: "As some of us are not as advanced as you are, perhaps you'd like to tell us what all this means, Sondor*pf?*" The teacher's exaggerated articulation of the pf made the name sound highly comical, and was rewarded with the expected titters from the rest of the class.

"I'm waiting for an answer, Sondorpf."

"It doesn't mean anything, sir."

"Then why do I find this filthy mess in your exercise book?"

"I couldn't understand the problem."

"You couldn't understand it. Too hard for you? Too

advanced for your miniscule brain? Well, now, let's see if we can find a problem more suited to your limited intelligence. Could you multiply seven by six for us?" Alexander went very red; the figure forty-two flashed into his mind, but he distrusted it—it came out of his memory, it was not arrived at by any logical process of reasoning. He tried to do the calculation by means of the mind pictures he normally employed, but somehow in his embarrassment and confusion he couldn't find the right images to represent six and seven.

"Too hard for you?"

"I'm a bit confused . . ." stammered Alexander.

"That is almost certainly the only accurate statement you have made all day, Sondor*pf*. Come now, boy, try and concentrate your mental faculties, such as they are. Seven multiplied by six. A child of seven would know that."

"Is it fifty-six?"

"It is not." The teacher's voice changed in tone, and he assumed an air of mock surprise. "I'm really very surprised, Sondorpf, that you can't tell us the answer to a simple arithmetical problem. I had always thought that members of your tribe were very good at figures. Never ran across one before who was quite so slow in multiplying seven by six, if it was his profit he was calculating. Perhaps if I put the problem to you in a different way. Say you were lending seven Christian boys three dollars each, at one hundred per cent interest. When you came to collect, how much would you get? *Well?* Now don't tell me a Hebrew doesn't know the answer to that! How much would you get, boy?" The class was tittering expectantly, in anticipation of some new foolishness that would come from Alexander's lips.

"I expect I should get about three months in jail, sir," said Alexander with every sign of outward calm, but with his heart thumping violently at his own audacity. There was a sudden, puzzled hush in the classroom.

"Three months in jail, boy?"

"For usury, sir. One hundred per cent interest is usury, sir, and punishable by imprisonment." This time the titters were on Alexander's side, and the teacher frowned.

"You're not only a fool, Sondorpf, you're also impertinent." Alexander could see that the teacher was angry, and this reassured him and calmed him; if it was so easy to make a man lose his temper he could not be a very formidable opponent. Alexander suddenly felt an ecstatic upsurge of confidence, his paralyzing shyness disappeared, he found that he relished standing up with all eyes on him, the center of attention—his heart was beating very, very fast now, but no longer with fear. It was excitement that made his heart race, the thrilling taste of victory. He suddenly felt as sure of himself as in his fantasies: sure of his superiority to this man who, until now, had loomed so large and menacing in his mind. Now he saw him quite clearly as a trivial and insignificant little man, and he was no longer afraid of him, or impressed by him, or intimidated by him.

"I said something, Sondorpf."

"Did you, sir?" Again the class tittered, trying to suppress this inclination—for this was punishable laughter now—but unable to.

"I said you were a fool, Sondorpf, and impertinent as well. What do you say to that, Sondorpf?"

"Do I have a choice, sir?"

"Don't you cheek me, you grimy little Hebrew."

Alexander looked at him icily. "It is perfectly true, sir," he said, "that I am small and that I was born of the Jewish faith, but as for being grimy, I am quite sure, sir, that I wash as often as you do, sir."

This time there was a horrified gasp from the class; nobody had ever dared to go this far in answering back a teacher, beatings had been earned by far less. The teacher's lower lip was twitching in a curious way; Alexander observed this with complete detachment, almost with pity, as he calmly awaited the expected blow across the face or the savage rap across the knuckles with the ruler. The teacher's face seemed to be out of control; from the corner of his mouth right down to where his thin, scrawny neck disappeared inside his high, tight, winged collar, he seemed to be suffering some kind of muscular spasm, the effect of which was to wrench his face out of proportion and distort his features. Spittle oozed out of the corners of his mouth and ran down his chin. His hot, moist breath smelt very unpleasant to Alexander, who was getting it full in the face. The teacher's frog's eyes seemed on the verge of popping out of his head. But the expected blow for which Alexander was waiting did not materialize.

"I don't intend to waste any more of the class's time on a useless idiot," he said. "If you want to remain a fool,

Sondorpf, then I shall not do anything to dissuade you from your chosen course." Alexander noted that his name was no longer being comically mispronounced, and the disagreeable spray of saliva that usually accompanied the exaggerated enunciation of the pf had consequently not occurred.

He started going to the movies, without telling his mother. At first he was disappointed: they were not nearly as lurid and as fantastic as his own imaginings. What, eventually, he found so appealing in the films he saw was their revelation of the way in which people lived in other strata of society. This interested Alexi tremendously. He loved the High Society dramas with Francis X. Bushman and Beverly Bayne. He was thrilled by adventure stories like *The Count of Monte Cristo*. He saw Robert Z. Leonard and Hobart Bosworth in *The Code of Honor*. He saw Florence Lawrence—"The Biograph Girl"—in innumerable films. If a film was showing within walking distance—or a short streetcar ride—from Allen Street, and if he could think of some pretext for going out for an hour, he was off. And always, at the approach to the theater, his heart beat faster, and as he went inside he felt very daring to be defying his father in this way. As soon as he was in the dark, and the compelling images started to move and live on the screen, he forgot about everything else and became completely immersed in the story he was watching. He was not conscious of being in a shabby room, of sitting on a bench or a rickety chair, of the other people near him, of the woman (to be encountered at pretty well every show) who had to read the titles aloud to herself. As soon as the story started he went into a kind of trance, from which he did not emerge until "The End" had appeared. Then, conscious of being in a forbidden place, he slunk out. Going to the movies became an obsession for him; once, when his mother said she would be away for most of the day, Alexi saw four different programs, going from one theater to the other.

At the beginning of his secret movie-going he saw and enjoyed everything; then, when the initial novelty and the thrill of doing something forbidden had begun to wear off, though he still saw every movie he possibly could, he became more critical and selective. But even if the stories

47

themselves were silly, as they often were in his opinion, the settings, especially if they were High Society, always appealed to him. He loved to peer into these fine houses, full of faithful servants who were invariably so devoted to the interests of their masters. He loved to watch the elegant men and women using the bewildering array of cutlery laid out for a big banquet. He watched attentively to see how a gentleman opens a door for a lady, how he assists her out of a carriage, how he escorts her in to dinner, and how he seduces her. These were all things that he felt he should know.

One day, coming out of a Dick de Lopez thriller called *Deathly Pale at Breakfast,* the proprietor of the theater called to him. For a moment Alexi felt guilty; perhaps his father had somehow found out where he was and he was now going to suffer the consequences of his misbehavior. But the proprietor did not look at all severe; on the contrary, he was smiling ingratiatingly. His name—as everyone knew who went to the Bijou—was Willi Seiermann. He was a plumpish man in his early thirties, with a head that was rather too large for his short, squat, powerful body; he seemed to have virtually no neck. He was standing in the foyer, hands stuck deep in his trouser pockets, jacket open, several loose cigars in his vest pocket, and a heavy watch chain with fob ornamenting his paunch. He wore a rather snazzy bow tie and he peered at the boy through pince-nez. As Alexander came up to him, he withdrew his hands from his pockets and rested them on his belly with the self-satisfied air of a man who has just eaten a good meal.

"Enjoy the show, sonny?"

"It was all right," Alexander replied.

"You must have enjoyed it," Seiermann insisted. "You been in three times this week."

"It wasn't bad, Mr. Seiermann," Alexander agreed, grudgingly.

"Well, I tell you what I'm gonner do, sonny." Alexander nodded suspiciously. "I like to encourage a good customer. I seen you here before, haven't I? Lot of times I seen you here. A good customer we gotter look after. So what I'm gonner do is I'm gonner give you a special pass, reserved for very special clients. Every time you come here with two friends, one of 'em can get in free. Three tickets for the price of two. How about that?"

"I don't know," said Alexander doubtfully, not wishing to admit that he didn't have two pals.

"What don't you know, sonny? I'm putting money in your pocket. All you gotter do is persuade a few of your pals. . . ."

"I don't know," said Alexander. "I don't know that you have such good movies here."

"If you don't like the movies, why d'you come?" A note of exasperation was creeping into Seiermann's voice. "Three times to see a lousy movie, that makes sense?"

"I like to work out why it's lousy," Alexander said. "It interests me."

"You pay three times to figure out why you don't like the movie? What kind of a nutty thing is that? Listen, sonny, you trying to kid me or something?"

"No," said Alexander, "it's like I say, it interests me. Now this movie you've got on now. I could tell you why you got an empty house."

"Summer business is never so good."

"It's got nothing to do with the weather," Alexander said. "The picture is put together wrong. It's supposed to be a thriller and it's got no suspense." Seiermann laughed uproariously, holding his stomach.

"You're a boy maybe twelve, thirteen years old, and you're tryin' to tell me you know better how to put together a picture than people that make their living making pictures?"

"They won't make a living for long if they make pictures like that," Alexander retorted, not in the least abashed. "I know, I see a lot of movies."

"All right. We got a rule in this business. The public is never wrong. So you're the public. So you tell me what's wrong with this picture? Okay, I'm listening. You tell me."

Alexander took a deep breath. "I'll tell you," he said. "I'll do more, I'll tell you how you can make that picture a success. All you got to do is cut it different. It's easy. You've got a story here about a woman who thinks somebody is trying to kill her, but she doesn't know who. That's a pretty scary situation. At the beginning of the picture she tells her husband this, and he says she must be crazy. Then, in the next scene, we see he's the one who's trying

49

to kill her. That scene when he starts buying weed-killer. The moment we see that, the picture is over. It's got no more suspense. Instead of her being in danger *all the time,* she's only in danger when her husband is around. You take that one scene out of the beginning, and put it in at the end, and nobody knows *who* is trying to kill her. It could be the husband, or it could be one of half a dozen other guys, and so she's in danger all the time. In a thriller the heroine has got to be in danger all of the time."

"Well," said Seiermann good-naturedly. "I'll pass on your criticisms to the makers of the picture. I'm sure they'll be very interested. But isn't there one thing you've forgotten, young feller? If they don't show that the husband is the killer from the start, then you cut out all of Dick le Lopez's best scenes, and he's the star of the picture, he's the one they're paying to see."

"I thought about that," said Alexander. "It's a problem, sure. They made a mistake in casting Dick de Lopez in that part, because it's actually the girl's picture, and the husband should have been played by an unknown. That's the mistake they made. That's why they've got a flop."

Seiermann chuckled benevolently. "With ideas like you got," he said, "you oughter be in the picture business."

CHAPTER THREE

Alexander was fifteen. He felt his youth to be a terrible handicap, something that had to be overcome, surmounted by some supreme effort, before he could go on. To do so seemed impossibly difficult to him. Merely to speak to somebody strange was for him a dreadfully painful experience that made his heart thump, his palms sweat, his mouth go dry and his cheeks go white with apprehension or burn with embarrassment. He could not envisage how he could ever establish a sufficient degree of intimacy with anyone —other than his mother—to be able to kiss that person. And yet, beyond that kiss, was the grown-up world he longed to enter.

It was very hot. The kids who usually ran around barefoot had tied the soles of old discarded shoes, salvaged from the rubbish heaps, to their feet to avoid getting them scorched. Everything smelled about ten times worse than usual. There didn't seem to be enough air to breathe. Everywhere windows and doors were wide open, and at night some people slept on mattresses put out on the iron landings of the fire escapes. In the height of the summer nothing was private. The nights were often turbulent with quarrels that resounded throughout the neighborhood, and for Alexander, lying awake by the open window, it was very disturbing to see the night-faces of people, the secret faces of anger and hatred that seemed to belong to other people than those he saw during the daytime, going about their daytime business. The shrill laughter of the mad-woman provided an ominous—and completely unnerving—finale to most of these rows that Alexander overheard, and observed in glimpses. At such times he would long for the purifying daylight, the first tinge of light in the sky that dispersed the shadows of the night and enabled him, at long last, to fall asleep.

And now there were also disturbing sights of another sort. A woman going through the stages of undressing, tantalizingly and maddeningly and heartbreakingly disappearing at a crucial moment to re-emerge within his field of vision some time later, perhaps wearing a robe now, or else in her underclothes. He saw segments of people's lives, passions divorced from their context, movements, gestures, acts unrelated to emotions: he saw truncated bodies making love, and the ecstasy of limbs. For long hours he sat by the open window, his entire mind burningly concentrated, like the rays of the sun by a magnifying glass, on one tiny point of distant activity—blurred movements, fragments of passion from which he could attempt to reconstruct the original. In a kind of permanent semifaint, which made the real world seem distorted as if seen through a heat haze, he would teeter for long periods on the very edge of that sharp pleasure which, when it came, was both a relief and a letdown. That what he was doing was wrong and shameful, he knew: long ago, his father had told him what happened to boys who did such things, and Alexander had heard—from other sources—that it could give you terrible diseases; it could make the brain dissolve, the spine disintegrate, the hair fall out, the loins rot away: it could make you mad. And yet he could not stop himself. He willingly accepted the possibility of his early death, the shame of possible discovery, the inevitable feelings of disgust and lassitude that followed the brief, searing, mind-emptying, body-emptying moment. The possibility of doing such a thing with another person, with a girl, seemed very remote, all of growing-up away. In this state so much was meaningful. Once he sat in a streetcar opposite a girl of such delicate, dark prettiness that just looking at her made his heart beat with exquisite pain: the agony of seeing and not having, of wanting and being unable to ask. She was so cool and crisp and shiny and brand new, like something very fine and very expensive wrapped in the softest tissue paper. To think of her in terms of the coarse, crude acts that filled his mind, against his will, like bad thoughts on a beautiful day, was a kind of vandalism. Yet her eyes were bold, fastening on him so boldly, so meaningfully—for an instant; they seemed to overflow, against her will, with a gush of feeling that originated in some deep spring inside her. The bold, sparkling, daring eyes, so incongruous in that sedately molded face—long skirt, shirtwaist blouse, all very proper and concealing, no hint of the body's secret places, no suggestion in the way she held herself, so properly, that her limbs could ever take those forbidden attitudes. Thinking of her in this way had the inevitable effect, and it being a warm day, and Alexander wearing only shirt and trousers, concealment was impossible. She saw; but what changed the situation from one of acute embarrassment into a thrilling adventure was that, instead of huffily looking away, she gave Alexander a tiny smile of complicity. It was almost as if, without being able to admit to this openly, she was enjoying this evidence of the effect she was having on him. Never before had he achieved such instantaneous intimacy with anyone. Dispensing with all the polite preliminaries, the endless social rituals, the elaborate pretenses, she was looking at him quite directly and smiling slightly in recognition of what he was feeling, and the smile made what he was feeling all right, took away the shamefulness of it. Encouraged in this way, he allowed himself to look at her without disguising his thoughts, and the directness and sharpness of his hunger seemed to kindle a kind of dispassionate tenderness in her eyes, closer to charity than passion, but warm, so warm. It was almost as if she could read everything in his mind, and yet did not disapprove, did not rebuke or censure or

52

scold or frown. He saw that her knees were slightly parted; in other circumstances it would have been of absolutely no significance, but in this situation the fact that she had not primly closed them on becoming aware of his look created in him such a strong sensation that he felt himself beginning to topple, beginning to topple over that sweet-painful edge, and he bit his lips hard to stop himself, and her eyes were still unhorrified and understanding, and indeed seemed flattered by this nice, strong masculine thing that was happening to him as a result of her. At the next stop she got up and left the car. Everything had happened and nothing had happened. Not a word had been uttered between them, they had not touched even fleetingly, and yet this was the deepest and most intimate relationship he had ever had with anyone outside his own family. Perhaps, he often thought afterwards, it had all been in his imagination; perhaps he had misinterpreted the look he had seen in her eyes—perhaps she had been absorbed in thoughts of her own that had no bearing on what he had been thinking. Perhaps she had been totally unaware of him; perhaps the look that he had taken to signify complicity was only one of preoccupation. It was such an insubstantial incident, and yet her face would not leave him. And in the ensuing months she became the principal figure in his fantasies, and with her he experienced all the permutations of love that he was capable of imagining.

It was that moment of the evening when darkness seems to come on with a sudden rush. Alexander was by the window, near him a discarded book: in a room on the first floor of the tenement a woman was undressing—impossible to tell at this distance if she was attractive or not. But certainly she was not young, and certainly she was rather too fleshy . . . and she was taking her dress off because of the heat, which made her gasp and try to cool herself by sprinkling water over herself. But Alexander did not see her; he saw the girl from the streetcar, so cool and delicate in her movements, and she was undressing not because of the heat but solely for his benefit, because she had seen him watching her and because it excited her to display herself before him. She had already removed her dress and was exhibiting herself, half boldly, half shyly, in her long lingerie garment that had straps coming over the shoulders and very fine

53

embroidery—like his mother's best pillowcases—at the hem and the neckline. She was sliding the skirt of this garment upward, very sensuously, and he could hear the silk against her skin, and her eyes were half closed as she savored the pleasure of what she was doing. The girl in the streetcar was not the only girl in his life; in his mind he created dozens of imaginary paramours; he dressed them, and determined how they walked and how they sat down, how they gestured, what words they spoke and when. These imaginary creatures were immediately responsive to his every whim and wish. They were infinitely preferable to real girls. Real girls could not be relied upon to respond and react exactly as he wished, they might snub him or mock him or laugh at him, turn him down flat, humiliate him. Sometimes he tried to picture the worst that might happen if he overcame his fears and made some sort of approach to a girl, but the images of what she might do were so terrifying as to put such a possibility out of his mind. In any case, how would he ever get the opportunity of making such an approach: he never met anyone: and just the effort of talking to somebody strange—not even a girl—reduced him to a state of paralysis so that, try as he might, the words simply refused to come out of his mouth. Much better—safer—to daydream. In his mind he could create such exquisite obedient creatures. Inside him there was a deep conviction that he could, by some superhuman effort, by some tremendous assertion of himself, by some knack the secret of which he had still to learn, eventually manipulate reality in just this way. It had to be possible. To live on other people's terms was too painful; they would have to be made to live on his terms. At the moment the world was still brutally indifferent to his needs: life was uncompliant and refused to be shaped. But one day . . . one day he was sure. . . . What conceit, he thought immediately; what horrible conceit. And yet I have no choice, this is what I must do, the alternative is too terrible.

Once he had a real experience. On a bright afternoon in the artificial dark of a cinema. A girl took the seat next to his when many others were unoccupied. The sudden heart-pounding awareness of her next to him, a fleshy shadow. For a long time there was nothing between them but silence, with both listening intently for a sign: their unnatural breathing—that was the only sign: the meaning of it slowly spreading, from one to the other, like mounting panic. Their hungers intertwined in the dark: leg against leg, the dizzying pressure was maintained for several seconds. No words, no looks, just touch: material, cloth, coarse, and so alive with what it covered; searching, fumbling, inexperienced fingers —and then the jolting contact: a stockinged knee, a new texture, the excitement tasting so strongly of fear in the back of his throat; intimate material, sweating palms, but—her thighs were parted; a confusion of materials; his hand lost in this slippery silkiness. Drawers: layer after layer of frilly flounces, from knee to thigh. Where? Where? Her hand guiding his through all these materials, toward the secret apex. Now no more cool, crisp, freshly-laundered freshness: now the body's hot breath coming through, through the material, the contours slightly disguised—his fingers, all his awareness at their tips, moving slowly, searching, not knowing the way. How soft can flesh be? How moistly can lips breathe? Wet palms against wet thighs; becoming one, mingled, wetness. Satisfied, she daintily removed his hand, as daintily as if she were taking a lump of sugar from a sugar bowl. She continued to watch the movie as if nothing had happened. Slowly consciousness returned from his fingertips to his mind. He looked at her, struggling to formulate words that could bridge the gaping silence between them. But he could think of nothing to say. All the words that suggested themselves to him sounded too silly, too inadequate, too nervous and inappropriate. He would only make a fool of himself. Once or twice she glanced at him wonderingly, surprised by his silence. When the lights came on, she got up to leave. She was a woman in her thirties. She glanced at him as she was passing and the realization of how young he was brought an involuntary look of horror to her face, as if she had discovered a nasty insect crawling over her. That look almost spoiled the whole experience for him.

Outside, in the lobby of the theater, the proprietor, Willi Seiermann, recognizing Alexander as one of his regular customers, called out to him. "Hello, youngster. I see you see a lot of movies. We could do with more like you."

"Business not good?"

"Can't complain—no, can't complain. Considering there's all these regulations now—ventilation regulations, and fire regulations. And a war in Europe, and all this talk now that we're gonner be in it any day now, ourselves. Still, last year was a good year, a very good year I don't mind saying, and this year, so far, touch wood, it looks like it's going to be even better. But what happens we get into a war, who knows? I guess you're too young to be drafted?"

"I'm fifteen," said Alexander.

"I thought you was older."

"I look older, I know."

"You still at school?"

"Yes, but I'm going to leave soon."

"You're the kid who was going to be in the picture business—am I right? Well, I could use a bright young feller like you. I'm expanding, negotiating for a couple of theaters right now. If you're interested, come and see me."

"I'll think about it," said Alexander.

Out in the street, walking home, he felt good. He'd had an adventure, a real adventure. And he'd been offered a job. All in one day. He felt a sudden exhilarating surge of self-confidence. The girls he passed in the street were no longer totally inaccessible; he knew their secret. Walking along the street he watched the people he passed for some sign that they had noticed this new assurance in him, and, indeed, it did seem to him, now, that girls noticed him, whereas before they had passed him as if he didn't exist. He stopped by a shop window and examined his reflection in the glass: deep, dark, intense eyes; thick, fine, dark hair; a taut, hungry smile; his face—like his father's—coming to a point, the skin stretched tightly over high cheekbones, concave cheeks; full, girlish lips. A worried frown making such interesting identations on his forehead, which could be erased so quickly, so completely. What girl could refuse to unruffle that fine brow? To feel like this was worth anything. If only he could feel like this all the time.

The war was something they didn't talk about. It was going on a long way away, and even though Austria was involved, it wasn't their Austria any longer. Still, their relatives were there, and that was hard. They could no longer, in an emergency, rely on the family helping them out financially. And it was hard to think of the family as being on the other side, hard to realize that victory for the Allies, which might soon include America, was defeat for them. It was all too complicated, the conflicting emotions

56

were irreconcilable. Better not think about such things—at least, one good thing, Alexander was too young for the draft.

When Alexander told his parents that he wanted to leave school and go to work for Willi Seiermann, Oskar gave a weary sign and said he would think about it. His health had not been good lately, and he was no longer as vehement about things as he used to be. Alexander, like so much else in his life, had turned out to be a disappointment. With the kind of marks the boy was getting, there wasn't much point in keeping him at school. He had turned out to be a dullard and a lazybones, loafing about the apartment, spending most of his spare time at picture houses, filling his head with cheap rubbish! The boy had no drive, no initiative. A couple of days after Alexander had raised the question of being allowed to leave school, Oskar took him aside and gave him a talk.

"You know something, Alexander," he said kindly, "sometimes it's necessary a father should say some hard things to his son, things that it hurts him to say, but that he has to say, because it's necessary they should be said. Alexander, I got to be frank with you: I don't like what you're turning into. Now let me tell you something, so you understand that what I'm telling you I mean it for the best. Alexander, I'm getting older and my health is not so good any more, and I don't kid myself any longer I'm going to make a fortune. There comes a time a man has to face certain things. All my life, Alexander, I lived for what was going to be tomorrow. Tomorrow everything was going to be all right, we were going to be rich, it was just round the corner. I never had much enjoyment, because I always wanted what I hadn't got but was sure I would have—any day now. Well, 'any day now' stretched into five years, ten years, thirty years. And now what have I got to look forward to? Dying? That's the only thing round the corner for me that I can count on for sure. I'm telling you this, Alexander, because I don't want you to make the same mistakes. I never had any trade and I never had any profession, that's why I never got anywhere. I was always doing deals. I was always betting on some new miracle that was going to change our whole life. I had a lot of hopes for you, Alexander, and now I see you're going to make the same mistakes I did. You want to work in a picture house? Is that a profes-

sion for a young man? Is that a career? Picture-houses, cir-
cuses, fairgrounds—that's for Bohemians, for drifters. What
future is there in that? One day, maybe I won't be here .You
know I'm not going to be here forever. You may have to
look after your mother. Your mother is still a young woman,
you know. She's almost twenty years younger than me. How
you going to look after your mother if you have got no profession, no trade? Alexander, I had hopes for you, you
would be an architect, an engineer, a lawyer, a doctor—
there's security in having a profession. Or you want to be
like your father, at the age of fifty-seven I got to hang
around cafés and bars to arrange deals—deals! You know
what my business is—you asked me once. I'm a salesman
for junk. A manufacturer has some goods that he can't get
rid of, because they're faulty or they're the wrong article or
he's over-estimated the demand, I get rid of them for him, at
a cut-rate price. I find a buyer who can shift these goods,
who can make them look good when they're faulty, and can
kid his customers they're the latest when they're out of
date. I know all the people on all the fringes of all the businesses, so when anybody has some goods they can't shift
they call in Oskar Sondorpf. And, sometimes, if I've had a
good month I get the idea I'm going to clean up, and I play
a little bit the stock market, and I put a few dollars into this
crazy idea and a few dollars into that, and soon I've lost all
the money that I made in the good month, and I'm out
sniffing around for another deal. I tell you Alexander, it's
not a nice life for a man of fifty-seven, and I'm beginning
to get tired. Which is why I'm telling you this—you
should reconsider, work harder at school, go to univer-
sity and have a profession. It is something that would please
me, Alexander. At least if I could feel I sent you to uni-
versity I would feel I had done something useful with my
life."

His father's words had pained him so much, Alexander
could hardly answer. Never had he loved his father as at
this moment. The words had torn into his heart. How gray
his father looked, how tired. He wished he could say to
him: "Don't worry, Papa, I will look after you. You've had a
hard time, but now it's all right. You've fought hard, and
you've brought the gift of optimism and hope to your fight,
and those are noble qualities even though you were fighting
in an area where you had no chance of winning. But I'm

not going to be like you. Things are crystallizing in me that you have no idea of. So don't worry about me. I will find my way." This was what Alexander wanted to say, but he couldn't because, though this was what he felt, how could he trust his feelings? If he talked like that—a boy of fifteen who couldn't get even average marks at school—everybody would think him mad. Only to his most private self could he say such things. He could not say them to his father. So, instead, he just said, feebly: "I know you mean it for the best, Papa, but I think I'm wasting my time at school. They don't teach me anything I'm interested in. I think I can teach myself all the things I need to know—and I want to get out and do something that interests me, and the picture business interests me."

Oskar sighed. "Pictures," he said, "moving pictures— another miracle just round the corner."

PART TWO

CHAPTER FOUR

The first place that Willi Seiermann talked himself into was an orphanage. Having found out that the German-Catholic orphanage of All Souls provided more and better food than any other in New York, he was not going to allow himself to be deterred by the fact that both his parents were still alive and, moreover, Jewish. The mouth-watering stories of the lamb stew and the black bread baked by the nuns, and of the potato soups, were quite enough to convert him to Catholicism. At home, with two brothers and three sisters to be fed, Willi felt that his own needs in the way of food and attention could not be satisfactorily met. The idea of going to an orphanage came to him in a flash of inspiration, when he noticed that of the kids in the street those whose parents were dead looked better fed than those whose parents were alive. Having made up his mind, he acted quickly. Two days later, having taken no food for twenty-four hours to make himself convincingly weak, he arrived at the orphanage, rang the bell of the heavy wooden door, which was studded with rosettes of blackened iron, and as soon as it was opened by one of the nuns, stammered a few words and then fainted. His story, when he was called upon to tell it, was heartbreaking. For weeks now he had been walking the streets of New York, begging for dimes and scraps of food, sleeping on park benches, under bridges and in doorways. But all this was nothing, really. What really weighed on him was the terrible fate of his mother, who was surely burning in hell this very moment. Three weeks ago, before his own eyes, she had thrown herself from the sixth story of the tenement building where they lived—she had died, without receiving the sacraments, without repentance, in mortal sin. But surely, the nun said, he was a little Jewish boy. Ah yes, he replied, that was the trouble. His father was a Jew, a wicked man, a sensualist, a corruptor of devout Christian girls—and he hadn't seen him for two years—but his mother had been a good Roman Catholic, until his father had seduced her and forced her to become a Jewess. As a result he, Willie, had never been baptized, and now his great fear was that if he should die before being received into the holy church of Jesus he might burn in hell like his mother; he had come to the orphanage, he explained, not knowing what sort of place it was, but drawn mysteriously by the cross which he had seen as a blazing light in the darkness of his delirium. He felt that God had guided him to this place, and now that he was here he felt more peaceful than ever before in his life, and if they sent him away he would no doubt be admitted to a Jewish orphanage and then his soul would be eternally dammed. The nun who conducted this interview was so impressed by Willi that she took him to the Mother Superior, who was equally impressed: perhaps, strictly speaking, it was a breach of the rules to admit him to All Souls, but what mattered rules when there was a soul to be saved, and one that had already undergone such torment.

Willi liked it at the orphanage. Once inside its high and rather somber walls it was actually quite a cheerful place. The dormitories, church and schoolrooms were grouped around more than an acre of untidy gardens and overgrown lawns; an arched quadrangle surrounded this open space and connected the various buildings. In the summer you could find narcissi and jonquils and fleurs-de-lis sprouting up haphazardly along the sides of the paths and in the thick grass. There was even a small orchard of perhaps a dozen trees, which produced quite a reasonable crop of apples and pears, and there was a good vegetable garden producing potatoes and lettuces and cabbages and carrots. As a special case, a reluctant infidel now being triumphantly brought back to the true faith, Willi received the kind of personal attention from the nuns that pleased him enormously and made him feel very important. The price he had to pay, attendance in church and endless religious instruction, did not seem to him excessive in return for a comfortable bed and

61

at least one substantial and satisfying meal a day. Not altogether surprisingly, some of the others at the orphanage resented this special treatment he received. One day four of them were waiting for him.

They were engaged in kicking a heavy stone about the street and pretended not to notice Willi as he approached. He called to them cheerfully, and they made out they hadn't heard him. As he came closer, he found his path blocked; whichever way he turned his way was barred by one or other of the kids. "Come on," he said. "Come on, quit foolin'. Come on, cut it out." One of the kids stuck out his foot and succeeded in tripping Willi. "Hey! Whadya wanner do that for?" he demanded plaintively, sitting up on the ground and rubbing his grazed knees. "I never done nothing to any of you. Come on, fellers, quit foolin'."

"The Jew-boy wants us to quit foolin'," said the boy called Freddy. "How about that! He thinks we're foolin'." And he aimed a savage kick at Willi's backside, which sent him sprawling on his face, just as he was attempting to get up.

"Where you going, Jew-boy?" the boy called Walter demanded tauntingly. Willi looked up at him and found the sole of a shoe descending toward his face; he tried to avoid it, but when he tried to get up somebody pushed him down again, and however much he moved his head about, in the end he could not evade the slowly descending sole. It was pressing on his face, on his nose and mouth, making his lips bleed; somebody else was standing on his arms, preventing him from using them to defend himself. While he was held down in this way, the boys took it in turn to wipe their shoes on him, on his face and clothes, until he was covered in the filth and grime of the streets. When all of them had had their turn, the first one, who had taken the opportunity meanwhile to dirty his shoes some more in a heap of horse dung, returned to wipe his feet a second time on the prostrate Willi. One after the other, they dirtied their shoes in the horse dung—and in dog excrement as well—and then returned to wipe their feet on Willi. Though he struggled desperately, they were too strong for him and held him down.

"Ugly little sheenie," said the boy Walter.

"Yeah, ugly little Jew-runt," said Freddy.

"This'll learn yer what we think of Jew-boys," said a third boy.

"God, don't he stink?" said Walter, holding his nose.

"That's the Jew smell," said Freddy. "They all smell like that."

"Come on, let's get out of here."

When they had all run off, Willi sat up painfully. About ten yards away stood a very neatly dressed little girl, aged about eight, holding her nose. "You sure smell bad," she said and giggled.

"You seen what they done?"

She nodded vigorously and giggled again. "Whatcha goin' to do about it?"

"I'm gonner fix 'em."

"You goin' tell on 'em?"

"No. I'm gonner fix 'em."

"There's four of *them.*"

"I know."

"How you goin' fix them?"

"You wait and see." He could hear them in the next street, kicking the stone along, shouting, horsing around. Without moving, Willi wiped as much of the muck off himself as possible. For over an hour he sat in the street, waiting for them to come back, and the girl waited too.

"You better clear off," she said. "I can hear them comin' back."

The boy Walter was running down the street, kicking the stone ahead of him, followed by the others. The final kick sent the stone toward Willi, who stopped it with his feet. Standing there, panting, the four boys examined their recent victim. "Jew-boy's come back for some more," said Freddy.

"That's right," said Willi.

"Give back the stone," said Freddy.

"Come and get it," Willi replied.

"You asked for it, kid." Freddy came forward, still breathing hard; the other three were propped against the wall, getting their breath back after their recent exertions. As Freddy got within range, Willi made as if to punch at his head, and the boy's arms shot up to protect his face; at the same time Willi jabbed his other fist, hard, into the now completely unprotected stomach. The blow made Freddy gasp and double up, the little breath he had left in him was forced out; seizing his opportunity, Willie followed

63

up by ramming his knee into the other boy's crotch, which brought forth a bellow of pain. The three other members of the gang were converging on Willi, still breathing hard; they tried to grab hold of him, but were squeamish of touching him because of the filthy condition of his clothing. All their movements were heavy and slow; Willi had no difficulty in shrugging off their attempts to grapple with him and in dodging the clumsy, tired blows they aimed at his head. He danced around, just beyond their reach, tiring them more. Then, carefully choosing his moment, he went in to the attack. Walter was the first boy to receive the full impact of Willi's flaying fists; blow after blow landed on his face, on his nose, mouth and eyes; the two other boys attempted, feebly, to intercede, but they had no strength left in them, and even their combined efforts were ineffectual. Having finished off Walter, Willi now turned on the remaining two. One just turned and ran, the other was too slow, and Willi had him by the neck and arm and was twisting his arm behind his back until the boy screamed. Contemptuously he pushed him aside, and turned back again to Freddy, who was still rolling on the ground in great agony. Bending over him, Willi pushed his knee against the other boy's throat, and began to strip his clothes from him. When he had got all Freddy's things off, Willi began to undress and to change into the other boy's clothes. His own filthy and befouled clothes he left on the ground; Freddy would have to choose between wearing them or going through the streets in his underwear. The girl, who had watched all this, now turned admiring—and incredulous— eyes on Willi, who was swaggering away from the scene of his triumph. "You could've gotten a beating then," she said.

"What yer talking about?"

"You could've got your head beat in."

"I knew I could lick 'em."

"You knew?"

"Sure."

"There was four of *them*."

"Yeah, but I knew I could lick 'em."

"You must be tougher'n you look."

"No. Just smarter. They was all tired and I was fresh. They're dumb in the head so they're gonner think I licked 'em 'cause I'm so tough. . . ." He began to roar with laughter. "That's what theyre gonner think, and so they're gonner leave me alone from now, I bet, because they're gonner be scared to meddle with me after today."

Willi stayed at the orphanage from the age of nine until the age of thirteen. During this time he often visited his family and sometimes brought them food which he had succeeded in smuggling out. He got on well with the nuns because he was always ready to undertake tasks on their behalf—or rather to organize others to undertake these tasks. Until Willi's arrival the orphanage had relied on one elderly and ineffectual handyman to keep the garden in order and attend to the innumerable repairs that were necessary every day in those old and badly maintained buildings. As a result, a leaking roof might go on leaking for months before anything was done about it; the garden was overgrown with weeds; the iron entrance gate was rusting for need of a fresh coat of paint; ancient wooden window frames were rotting away; a broken windowpane would be temporarily repaired with a piece of cardboard, and thereafter the chance of a more permanent repair ever being effected was very slight. For the nuns it was all too much; they did not know where to start in the matter of putting things right and so they did not start anywhere; they put their trust in God and prayed that He would do something about the leaking roof and the broken windowpanes and the fact that the priest's wardrobe in the sacristy could not be made to remain shut. Willi found the remedy to these problems. There were forty-three children at the orphanage, of whom at least thirty were capable of being trained to carry out simple repairs. Willi had no idea of how to repair a leaking roof or a broken windowpane, but he was ready to find out how it was done by means of trial and error. With the whole orphanage to draw on for his labor force, he began to get things done. He realized that success depended largely on organization; on deploying the available forces and talents to the best possible advantage; no point in getting one boy to de-rust and paint the iron gates—he might start enthusiastically, but soon the apparent enormity of the task before him would drain his energy, he would become bored and restless and, as a result, slapdash. What Willi did was to assign eight boys to the gate, divide them into teams of two, and give each team one section of the gate to work on. The team that finished first would be excused lavatory duty—cleaning the lavatories was the least agreeable of the tasks to be shared out—for a month. The children for the most part were willing to accept the duties that Willi allocated to them because he was always willing to do the worst tasks himself—at any rate he would start on such tasks and put so much enthusiasm and energy into the work that, soon, disgruntled onlookers were transformed into more or less willing helpers. Once the job was reasonably under way, Willi would slip away to attend to something else.

It was during his stay at the orphanage that he embarked on his first business venture. He had come to hear of a store that was closing down—the owner had died, and the widow was too sick to run the business herself. The stock, consisting mostly of cheap leather goods, handbags, pocketbooks, school satchels, traveling cases, was being sold off at well below cost price. Willi was not interested in any of these leather goods. But he was interested in a stock of over fifty umbrellas which, apparently, nobody else wanted. He went to the executors and made them a proposal. He said he was sure he could find a buyer for the umbrellas but he had no money to lay out. Would they, for a start, let him have ten umbrellas on credit? They said no, they would not. How could they trust a kid of ten or eleven to meet his financial obligations? Undeterred, Willi found the address of the widow and went round to see her, bearing a bouquet of flowers he had picked in the orphanage garden. By the time he left she had agreed that he should be allowed to have the umbrellas, ten at a time, on a sale or return basis. Willi's plan for selling the umbrellas was very simple. He had figured out that the desire to buy an umbrella was at its lowest on a dry, sunny day, and at its highest in the pouring rain. Therefore the time to sell umbrellas was when it was actually raining. Once he had collected his first consignment of ten umbrellas, Willi waited impatiently for a suitable day. It occurred a week later. It had been warm and sunny from morning until early evening, and then, at around eight, it had begun to rain heavily. Together with five previously selected salesmen, recruited from the orphanage, Willi set off for Broadway. As people, wearing light, summery clothes, came out of the theaters and restaurants, and saw the drenching that was in store for them, Willi and his salesmen popped up with their umbrellas. It was not the sort of moment to quibble about prices. If any of the buyers expressed disapproval of the fact that the umbrellas were being sold at four times their normal price, the young salesmen had been instructed by Willi to say that they came from the All Souls Orphanage and that the proceeds from the sales would go toward repairing the church roof, which was at present leaking so badly that the Virgin Mary was being drenched every time it rained. Within half an hour they had sold all their umbrellas. The remainder of the stock was sold in the course of the next two weeks. Willi came to the conclusion that if only one could rely on a really bad summer there was a fortune to be made in selling umbrellas on Broadway in this way.

Willi's stay at the orphanage came to an end in this way. Though his parents were not excessively religious, they did insist that Willi, on attaining the age of thirteen, must be *bar mitzvah,* like any other Jewish boy. The fact that he was living in a Catholic orphanage did complicate matters. His dual religious status would obviously have to be kept both from the rabbi, who was to prepare him for the *bar mitzvah* ceremony, and also from the nuns and the priest who were instructing him in the Catholic faith. Willi's attitude was that if God did exist the chances of getting into His good books must be higher if you subscribed to two religious beliefs than if you confined yourself to one, which might possibly be the wrong one. God could not possibly object to such an excess of zeal. The nuns, however, proved to be very narrow-minded about the whole business when they found out how Willi had been deceiving them. They found out because of an unfortunate accident. With so much religious information to absorb, and rather overwrought by his impending *bar mitzvah,* Willi made the stupid mistake on being asked to say his catechism of reciting a portion of the Haftorah he had recently been committing to memory. After that it all came out, and soon afterward Willie was expelled from the orphanage.

CHAPTER FIVE

Willi's lack of physical attractiveness was something of which he was being made more and more aware as he grew older. He did not feel ugly; he had the shoulders of a pugilist, he told himself; no doubt about it, he was a powerfully built fellow, a bit of a rough diamond maybe, not what you would call a pretty-boy but, so it seemed to Willi, a fine-looking figure of a man. It pained him that to others he often seemed ridiculous. At first, he was perplexed to discover how often he aroused people's mirth. He could not understand it. What was so funny? All the time he was encountering people who were in the act of suppressing a grin. He was always catching complete strangers, people he passed in the street, for instance, in the process of erasing a smirk from their faces. Sometimes they didn't bother to conceal their mirth and just laughed in his face. On one occasion he had demanded outright: "What's so funny?" and received the forthright answer: "You should see yourself, fella, you wouldn't need to ask." Willi examined himself very carefully in the mirror but could find nothing to explain the widespread hilarity his presence aroused. Despite his heavy build he was extraordinarily light on his feet, almost dainty. His legs were very short and as he was always in a hurry he gave an impression, when walking, that was extraordinarily funny. But it was not only his gait that aroused people's mirth, it was his whole manner, which suggested someone compelling you to like him at the point of a gun. His desire to get on, his naked eagerness, his way of looking at things that he wanted without being able to conceal or even politely disguise his desires, the obvious way in which his innermost feelings registered on his face, his ability to alternate between obsequiousness and aggressiveness, dependent on which attitude was the more profitable—all this made him seem something of a buffoon.

At first it distressed Willi that people should laugh at him, but slowly he came to accept it, and indeed to encourage it. To make people laugh was better than being laughed at, so he made people laugh. He took note of those of his mannerisms that seemed to cause mirth, and deliberately exaggerated them. From a very early age he had the reputation of being a character and a funny fellow. "You should go into vaudeville," people would say to him, not intending it as flattery.

Willi often watched the young men who were considered handsome, who radiated attractiveness and made everyone, not just girls, wish to be in their company. How easy it was for them! What an asset it was to have personal charm!

What a mystical thing was a smile—that could make people come running. How pleasant to have an appealing personality and a well-proportioned physique! What was more to the point, what a lot of bother it saved. To get a girl, if you were not good-looking, was a lot of work, Willi had discovered. Some people had it easy—because their nose was a different shape and they had a bit less flesh on them. What did such trivialities matter? Willi was sure that when it came to it he was a better lover than any of those fancy fellows. He had such appetites within him! Such insatiable hungers—for food, for love, for women, for pleasure, for fame and wealth and power and possessions. What could these slender youths, sipping life through a straw, feel in the way of real passion? Willi was sure they did not feel a tenth of the things he felt. Did the blood roar like an ocean in their veins? He doubted it. But they were considered attractive and he was considered ugly. It was all wrong.

The wholesale tailoring firm of Hermann Glantz & Sons was housed in a three-story building: the workroom was on the third story; the bales of cloth were kept in the stock room in the basement; when they were required upstairs it was Willi's job, in his early days with the firm, to get them upstairs. There was a hatchway through which the goods were hauled up by means of a system of pulleys. A sort of halter, with a strong loop on one side, was fixed round the bales of cloth; the iron hook at the end of the pulley was inserted in this loop; and then Willi ran upstairs, up three flights, to the hatchway opening, and began to haul up the goods. As the hatchway was rather narrow, and the cloth heavy, this operation might have to be repeated several times in the course of one morning, until a sufficient supply of material had been transported to the workroom. Once the stuff had been brought up, it had to be carried to the huge cutting tables, and this too was Willi's job at the beginning. It was a back-breaking job, but he quite enjoyed handling the materials, getting to know the different textures of gingham and seersucker and linen and duck and muslin and taffeta and crepe and satin and tarlatan and velvet and batiste and organdie and crinoline. The first thing the cutters did on receiving the material was to measure it, using a rule attached to the cutting table for this purpose. Then the material was spread out, and paper patterns attached to it by means of pins, and arranged in such a way as to reduce wastage to the minimum—it was the sign of a bad cutter if his remnants were too large. Carrying the bales of cloth to all the cutters, Willi got to know which of the cutters were habitually wasteful and which were excessively careful. He saw that a balance had to be struck between wasting time and wasting material; the cutter who endlessly rearranged his patterns because he was nervous of wasting a little more material than was absolutely necessary was almost as bad as the one who was so careless that he was always left with the largest remnants.

At six-thirty in the evening, when the employees went home, there was always a bunch of young men hanging around in the street, waiting for the girls who worked at Hermann Glantz & Sons to come out. More than twenty girls and women worked in the firm—as seamstresses, as clerks, as salesladies, as machinists and in various other capacities—and some of them were decidedly pretty. Coming into the street to run the gauntlet of avid male eyes, they became transformed from the self-effacing creatures who plied needles, or wrote letters and bills all day long, into mysteriously alluring coquettes, whose eyes sparkled with secret invitations. In the dusk they seemed to glow and glisten with the magic of their warm blood, whose exciting flow recommenced so punctually at six-thirty.

For the young men this was the moment of triumph or defeat, when they found out if the fleeting looks or casual exchange of words, all that was possible during the day, meant anything or not, and the air was charged with expectation. Among these young men there were some with the confidence of their acknowledged charm and looks, who lolled and lounged full of the conceit of previous successes, while others, less sure of themselves, were as tense and fidgety as runners waiting for the starter's gun. The successful young men talked in a coarse and boastful way of past conquests, and the unsuccessful ones either tried to bluff it out and pretend to experiences they hadn't had or else remained glumly silent, hoping that their silence would be taken for gentlemanly reticence.

Every day Willi stood with the young bloods, offering himself as the victim of their often cruel humor, grinningly accepting their taunts and jibes. They liked to have him

70

around, because when the approach to a girl was made Willi fulfilled the function of a stooge, at whose expense these young men who considered they had a chance could be amusing, and thereby make an impression. One approach was to pretend to find a girl for Willi, and this was the kind of fun that appealed to the girls because it gave them an excuse to hang around and so expose themselves to more interesting offers. A good-looking boy called Ed Sayler was the principal exponent of this technique. He was tall and well-built and had a savage grin, and all his gestures and looks were sexual overtones.

"Willi," he said one evening, "that pent-up expression of yours bothers me. What d'you say, fellers? We gotter help Willi make out. We gotter find him a real juicy number. How you like that un, Willi?" While the rest of the group guffawed, Ed indicated one of a group of five girls coming out of the building. "The blonde, Willi." The others were now bellowing with uncontrollable mirth. Willi's eyes were feasting gluttonously on the girl, and he smacked his lips with relish, which produced a further outburst of laughter. "Hey, Trina!" Ed called out. "Come on over a minute, honey. Want yer to meet a friend of mine who's just dying to meet you." Trina looked up and gave him a secret smile, and being familiar with this game motioned the other girls with her to come along too. In an affectedly unhurried way, they strolled toward the boys. "Trina, honey," he said when the girls had approached, "my friend, Willi Seiermann, is just pining away for lack of female companionship. See how thin he is, at this rate there soon won't be nothing left of him. I hear tell that under that spotty skin, he ain't as bad as he looks. Well, stands to reason. It ain't hardly possible for *anyone* to be as bad as Willi looks. . . ." Some of the girls laughed, and Willi, who was used to this jocular abuse, joined in wholeheartedly. "Seriously, kiddin' aside, there must be one of you girls bighearted enough to take pity on this poor, love-starved feller. It ain't his fault he's repulsive. Now is it?"

After all this badinage, the first words uttered by Willi were singularly inappropriate. "I sure would appreciate it," he said to Trina, "if I could walk you home." This got the biggest laugh so far; they were all convulsed with laughter, they were holding their sides and gasping for breath and unable to bring words from their lips because of the

71

cataclysms of mirth which shook them. "Willi wants to walk her home," one of the boys eventually managed to bring out and, having done so, was immediately rocked by a further spasm. Trina didn't deign to reply even; she pretended the invitation had never been made.

When they had all quieted down a little, one of the girls whom nobody had really noticed, because she was easily the plainest of the group, said in a small but firm voice: "I think you're all very nasty and cruel. I would be very glad if Mr. Seiermann wished to walk me home." This elicited a chorus of derisive remarks. "There you are, Willi. Your big chance, boy. This is your big day, Willi-boy. Go on, what are you waiting for? Won't get an offer like that again." Willi was reluctant to accept this offer. He had seen the girl every day for more than a year, and she was among the few about whom he had never entertained any ideas. It was not that she was totally unappealing, but she had a severe expression and a dignified carriage, which suggested that there was not likely to be any hanky-panky where she was concerned. Moreover, she was thin, almost frail, and the way she dressed there was scarcely a suggestion of any bosom. Mostly she wore, as now, a very high dress with ruffles or lace trimmings at the bodice, and her hair was done very plainly in what Willi regarded as the schoolmarm style, with a flat knot at the top. She was one girl about whom none of the boys made any lewd boasts, and it seemed very unlikely to Willi that he would succeed where nobody else had. He fancied his chances with Trina far more, simply because of the stories he had heard about her. But now he was being playfully-savagely pushed toward the plain girl, whose name was Sarah, and it was hardly possible for him to avoid taking her home. "I'll be glad to see you home," he said feebly, and, when she was not looking, gave a miserable, despairing shrug at Ed.

"Never mind," Ed whispered. "You won't get laid, that's for sure, but you'll get fed. Her old man has a delicatessen store."

The girl's name was Sarah Essberger, and she was about eighteen or nineteen; her job at Hermann Glantz & Sons was to write bills and letters—Willi could notice the ink-stains on her fingers. After they had walked in silence for a couple of blocks, and were out of sight of the others, she said: "You don't have to see me home, Mr. Seiermann. I

72

just said it because I thought they were getting nasty and . . ."

"Oh, they're only kidding," Willi said. "They don't mean nothing by it. I can take a joke."

"I hate cruelty," she said.

"They were just having a bit of fun."

"At your expense."

"Oh sure. So what?"

"You're a very good-natured man, Mr. Seiermann. Not many people would put up with that sort of thing."

"It don't hurt me any," said Willi, beginning to feel extremely noble. "If they wanter horse around and be mean— I guess they're entitled."

"You really don't mind? Or you just covering up?"

"I guess I mind a bit, Miss Essberger. It wouldn't be human not to mind a bit. But the way I look at it, it's them that's gonner suffer in the long run. Now don't get me wrong. I don't mean I'm gonner get back at 'em, or anything like that. I don't bear grudges, it ain't in my character. What I mean is that doin' cruel things hurts the doer more'n it does the one that it's done to. That happens t'be my philosophy in life, you see."

"It's a very fine philosophy."

"It's nice of you to say so, Miss Essberger."

For a while they walked on in silence, and then Sarah Essberger gave Willi a shy, sidelong appraising look. "You know, Mr. Seiermann," she said, "apart from being pretty mean, the things they said about you, I'd say they were dead wrong. I don't think you're . . . bad-looking like they say."

Willi chuckled. "I don't claim to be any Adonis."

"No, you're not that," she said, looking him over carefully. "But your face has got—character. And, if you don't mind my saying so . . ." She hesitated, feeling that perhaps she had already been more forward than she should have been.

"Go on, Miss Essberger. You can say anything to me."

"Yes, I think I can. What I was going to say, Mr. Seiermann, is that you could dress to . . . to better advantage."

Willi was pleased that anyone should take this amount of interest in him. "Well," he said, "I guess you're right about that. The thing is I don't spend a lotter money on myself, because I got plans. I aim to get on, and to do that you gotter have money in the bank, capital. There's all sorts of opportunities for a man that's been thrifty and has got some capital behind him. Some time, when you're not too busy, I'd sure like to tell you about my plans, because I've seen you around the firm, and I always thought—that Miss Essberger is a smart young lady, with a head on her, and your point of view is one point of view that I sure would respect."

"I'd be glad to listen to you any time, Mr. Seiermann, and thank you for saying such a nice thing about me."

"You really would? That's great."

As they continued to walk, they kept looking at each other from time to time in a shy way, and it seemed to him that she was flushed. Willi was thinking that perhaps she wasn't the prettiest girl in the firm, and she probably didn't have all that many passes made at her because of her rather off-putting manner; maybe with her he had a chance.

"This is where I live, Mr. Seiermann."

He looked around. They were in a good-class neighborhood, the houses were well kept up, there were some trees in the street and, most significantly, there were no barefoot, snotty-nosed kids running around. The area exuded respectability, just as Miss Essberger did herself. A little further along the street, the residential district gave way, very discreetly, to a small avenue of shops with living accommodations above.

"My father runs a little grocery business," said Miss Essberger. "Perhaps you would like to come in a minute."

Inside, tantalizingly displayed, Willi saw barons of cooked meat, and big bowls of chopped liver, and bottles of schmaltz herring, and plates of potato salad; there were wicker baskets full of freshly baked chalehs and black bread and seed rolls; on one counter there was tier after tier of cold, fried fish; and there was a huge carp embedded in jelly, and there were little pancakes of gefilte fish; and long chains of frankfurters and knackwurst, and jars of borscht, and long trays of cheesecakes and strudels. Willi had never seen so many good things to eat; the smell of all this food made his nostrils quiver.

"Papa," said Miss Essberger, "I want you to meet a friend of mine, Mr. Seiermann, who is one of the cutters at Hermann Glantz."

"I am very pleased to make your acquaintance, Mr.

74

Seiermann. You have come to try my strudel? Please. You help yourself. Take a piece."

"Thanks a lot," said Willi, carefully selecting the largest piece, and biting off more than half of it in his first mouthful. A sort of ecstasy came over his face.

"It's beautiful," said Willi, "tastes beautiful . . ." His mouth was so full, and he was so busy masticating, he couldn't speak.

"Take another. Please. It gives me pleasure to see you enjoying it."

"Thank you, Mr. Essberger, I will—you got such lovely things here, somebody like me, who enjoys to eat good, appreciates such things."

"I can see, my dear," said Mr. Essberger, his eyes sparkling with approval, "that your young friend is a man who appreciates good food—that I like to see."

"Sometimes," said Willi, slapping his stomach disapprovingly, "I wish I didn't have such an appetite."

"What is this!" said Mr. Essberger. "A bit of a stomach! A man shouldn't have a stomach! What for did God give men stomachs—they should keep them empty, they should hide them? Eat some more, Mr. Seiermann, and don't let me hear you talk this nonsense—let me give you a nice piece fried fish. Or a little carp?"

Willi's relationship with Miss Essberger progressed very satisfactorily; other boys who had taken her out, for a while, had lost interest when it became clear, as it rapidly did, that there was nothing doing, but Willi was quite happy to walk her home and spend an evening gorging himself on the delicacies in her father's delicatessen. It became an established routine that, four or five times a week, he would eat with the Essbergers, and when Passover came along he spent the Seder nights with them and accompanied them to the synagogue, and it became accepted that Willi and Sarah Essberger were going together. Once or twice he made a tentative, fumbling attempt to kiss her, but when she pulled away he behaved in a gentlemanly way and did not press his attentions. When Willi was not eating, he talked about his plans, and this was the time that Sarah liked best, because she loved to hear him talk of all the money he was going to make, and somehow it was assumed that these dreams of the future included her. When they had been going together for about two months, Papa Essberger took the opportunity one evening, when his daughter had been sent out of the house on some pretext, to have a man-to-man talk with Willi.

"My boy," he said expansively, "you know that I got the best opinion of you, and that as a father I naturally have got the interests of my daughter at heart. The point which I am coming to, and I think you must know what I am about to say to you, my boy, is that it would make me very happy to think that my daughter's future was settled. I have only one child, and my late wife, God rest her soul, always used to say the future is with the child. . . ."

"Mr. Essberger," said Willi, getting up from the table which was piled with the remains of the colossal meal they had just eaten, and beginning to pace the room in a solemn way. "Mr. Essberger, I don't have to tell you my feelings for Sarah—I think you know what they are, and so does she. And nothing would make me happier than if I was in a position to say to you now—what you, I think, would like to hear. But it so happens I can't, for a very good reason . . ." and he stopped dramatically to let the weight of his utterance have its full effect. "For one thing," Willi continued, "I am not at all sure that Sarah . . . returns my feelings."

"But that's nonsense, my boy . . ."

"Mr. Essberger, you are a man of the world, and you know that between two people who love each other there are certain feelings, cretain expressions of feeeling, and I can only say that Sarah don't give any indication of having those feelings . . ."

"Sarah is a shy girl, and she's a good girl and perhaps she listened a bit too much to what her mother taught her, but she is a girl with feeling—that I can guarantee you. A man could be happy with her, I give you my word."

"Mr. Essberger, you forgive me, but on such a matter *your* word, for which I got the greatest respect, isn't enough. In fact, *words* isn't enough; love, Mr. Essberger, is not only to be said with words."

"Willi, I will have a talk with Sarah, I promise you. I will straighten out this whole question."

"Unfortunately," said Willi, "there is also another problem, which is even a bigger problem. I got a good job at Hermann Glantz and I take home twenty dollars a week, which is a good wage for somebody my age, and you

76

could start a family on such a wage. Except I don't want always to be a twenty-dollar-a-week cutter, or even a thirty-dollar-a-week cutter, and so every week from that twenty dollars I save eight, which goes straight into the savings bank, and I already got a tidy little bit put aside. But on twelve dollars a week to get married, to start a family . . ."

"So maybe for a little while you won't save so much, till you get on your feet."

"No, Mr. Essberger, I got my eye on a little business, a little tailoring business of my own, and with another four hundred dollars I could get started."

Mr. Essberger was silent while he stroked the one day's stubble on his face in a thoughtful way. At last he said, "Tell me something, Willi, for my information, this question of the four hundred dollars you need to start this business— that is the only thing that stands in the way of you and Sarah getting married?"

"That, and the other matter."

"The other can be taken care of."

"Then it's just a matter of four hundred dollars," said Willi.

"And you also got to have some place to live, that also costs money. That's another two to three hundred dollars at least."

"I thought of that," said Willi. "If we have a big wedding we're sure to get a lotter presents, right? So we say to everybody—instead of giving presents we don't need or don't like they should all give money, and with this money we buy a little place. How much furniture do we need? A bed, a table, a few chairs."

"Willi," said Mr. Essberger, "I'm a man who don't like to mess around too much so I tell you what I do. The day you and Sarah are married I give you as a wedding present four hundred dollars to start the business."

"Mr. Essberger," said Willi, smiling broadly, "it's a deal."

The immediate effect of this conversation was that when next Willi tried to kiss Sarah she did not pull away. She wasn't what you would call passionate, but she was a little more permissive. She permitted him, in a resigned sort of way, to fondle her breasts and to press close against her and to feel the outline of her body through the many layers of clothing that she wore. It did not give him any very accurate indication of her true shape, but it was intimacy of a sort, and it excited him sufficiently to make him overcome his scruples about spending money on whores, and he paid several visits, with Ed Sayler, to Fat Annie's place.

CHAPTER SIX

Willi had no intention of starting a garment business, but this was not something he proposed to tell his prospective father-in-law at this stage. From their first encounter he had made a fairly shrewd assessment of Mr. Essberger: that he was a man who doted on his daughter, that he must have a tidy bit of money put aside—for it was easy to see that the delicatessen store was successful—that he was fairly stingy, that he would not cough up any money for what he considered a speculative venture, and that he was in poor health and would probably not last very long. Only in this last respect was Willi's judgment wrong. Having come to these conclusions at the beginning, and having had them more or less confirmed in the course of subsequent encounters, Willi had settled on a course of action. From the time of his successful enterprise with the umbrellas, he had been on the lookout for other business opportunities. He knew that the tailoring business could, in due course, provide him with a reasonable living, and he might even build up a prosperous concern eventually. But Willi had long ago come to the conclusion that this was no way to get rich, not for him. He knew from his observations at Hermann Glantz & Sons that the margin of profit, though reasonable, was not enormous; a lot of people were involved in the manufacture of every single article of clothing, and they all had to earn enough to exist, and furthermore there was a limit to the number of dresses and skirts that a woman would buy in the course of a year. It did not seem to him the sort of business in which there could be a sudden and dramatic increase in the demand—it was a matter of competing with established firms for the existing demand. What Willi was on the lookout for was some venture that might yield a quick profit of several hundred per cent, as in the case of the umbrellas. He was sure that the big money was to be made out of some of these new inventions that one was hearing about all the time—the telephone, the electric light bulb, the automobile, the airplane, the Kinetoscope, wireless telegraphy. People sneered at this notion—indeed it was rather poetic and fanciful to express it, and much of his courtship of Sarah Essberger had consisted of such high-flown talk about the way in which life would become transformed in the next few decades. Quite ordinary people, he had said in these moments of poetic speculation, would talk to each other across vast distances by means of the telephone. Great airships would be built to fly people across the continent of America. It was all very well to talk in this way to a girl one was courting, but it was quite another matter to persuade hardheaded businessmen, or even Mr. Essberger, that one of the junior cutters at Hermann Glantz & Sons might have some kind of stake in this scientific Utopia. For this reason Willi, though he talked in a grandiose way about the things he planned to do one day, did not let on that he had more immediate and practical plans. If Mr. Essberger knew the purpose for which Willi needed four hundred dollars he would never have agreed to the loan, and he might, in fact, have changed his mind about the young man's suitability as a son-in-law.

There was a place on Fourteenth Street at this time called the penny arcade, and before he started going with Sarah Essberger, Willi had been in the habit of dropping in there quite regularly, whenever he had some spare time and nothing better to do with himself. It was one of the many amusement arcades that had been springing up in New York. It contained all the contraptions normally to be found in such an establishment: punching bags that purported to show, on a dial, the strength of your punch; phonographs; weighing machines; chewing gum machines; Kinetoscopes; and various other devices for relieving passers-by of their loose change. It was a place that fascinated Willi, not so much because he wanted to have the strength of his punching measured, nor because he wished to know his exact weight, but because he loved to watch what went on in the basement of the penny arcade. To him it was one of the most beautiful and impressive sights in the world. There, under the machines, was a miniature railway track, and on this track ran an open car; at each stop that it made, nickels from the machines on the floor above cascaded into it, and it went round and round the track until it was quite full, whereupon it shunted on to another track, made the journey to the far end of the basement and emptied its cargo of nickels into a funnel. This was not just business being done, but business being seen to be done, and the sight of all those nickels pouring into the funnel—and thence, in imagination, into the pockets of the proprietor—moved Willi profoundly. Unlike in the tailoring business, there was no sweat, no labor, no worry about canceled orders, no large staff to employ and supervise—it was all done by machines. The customers came in, they dropped their coins in the slots, the little railway cars collected them, and the owner pocketed them. Only one person was required to look after the machines, and as the basement could be locked, and as there was no need for the attendant ever to venture into it, the opportunities for an employee to be dishonest were minimal. There was no need for the owner of such an establishment to look in more than a couple of times a week—just to collect the pile of nickels and take them to the bank. To Willi this was making money scientifically. It was being truly modern.

When Willi visited the penny arcade very few of his nickels found their way into the machines, most of his time he spent closely observing the other patrons and talking to them, and he came to certain conclusions. These people had nothing to do with themselves after they had finished their day's work, he found. The workingman did not earn enough to enable him to go to vaudeville shows, even had he wished to do so. He could have a few beers in the saloons, but he had to be a pretty heavy drinker to make this form of entertainment last the evening. Moreover, if he was a married man his wife probably disapproved of this form of recreation, particularly if, as was usually the case, she was excluded from it. From his own experience Willi knew what a desperate business it was to fill the empty hours, the dawdling end of a day, and he knew all about the heavy lassitude that came with dusk and the vain yearning for excitement and adventure. Some young men, like Ed Sayler, had special ways of occupying themselves, but the majority were like Willi—permanently at a loose end. It came to Willi, in a moment of tingling discovery, that he was like the majority of men, and that what he wanted they would want. The main difference between himself and all the others lay, he told himself, in that he possessed the energy and the determination—and daring—to exploit this discovery. These thoughts had been occupying him for several years. All this time he had been saving up for the moment when he could translate his thoughts into actions. During these waiting years he had carefully watched, and noted, the ebb and flow of business at the existing places of entertainment—how a rainy day filled the burlesque shows more effectively than a star attraction, how a new craze (like the Salomé dance) would suddenly flare up, earn brief notoriety for its performers and fat profits for its promoters, incur the wrath of self-appointed civic reformers and smut hunters, thrive on this for a while, and then abruptly die out to the accompaniment of the hoots and jeers of outraged, morally offended audiences. As a bachelor, starved of actual sexual contact, he enjoyed these sort of shows, and regretted that moral crusaders were always trying to clean them up; but as an aspiring businessman it seemed to him common sense that a show to which a man could bring his wife and children was going to yield more profit, in the long run, than one to which he had to sneak in on his own.

These considerations persuaded Willi that his first big business venture would be to acquire one of these penny arcades, and he had made all the preliminary inquiries about hiring the machines and leasing a suitable store which could be used for this purpose. He had spent weeks juggling with the figures, cutting costs to the absolute minimum, but however he worked it out it was clear that he would need at the very least $1,000 to get started. He had $600, which meant that somehow he would have to find another $400.

Shortly after his man-to-man talk with Mr. Essberger, Willi became officially engaged to Sarah, and the wedding date was set for three months hence. The following day, during the half hour that he had off for lunch, he paid one of his periodic visits to Mr. Brailey, of the local real-estate firm of Brailey and Bergenson.

"It's a fortunate thing you came in to see me today," said Mr. Brailey, "because I just happen to have got a property that I think is what you're looking for. And at the price they're asking, they're giving it away."

"How much they're asking, may I ask?"

"I don't want to mislead you, it needs fixing up. But for the purpose you are thinking of, it's perfect. The minute I

81

seen it I said that is the place for Mr. Seiermann. Knock down a couple of walls, a bit of paint, fix it up a bit and you got yourself an amusements *palace*."

"Where is it located exactly, this place?"

"Just round the corner from here. A few blocks—Rayburn Street."

"Rayburn Street is a pretty slummy street."

"What you want—Longacre Square?"

"How much they asking?"

"I tell you something, Mr. Seiermann, this property is owned by a man, he owns a lot of real estate, and this is a property he don't want to be bothered with. So he's prepared to let it go to a go-ahead young fellow for next to nothing."

While he was talking Mr. Brailey was studying Willi carefully, assessing his financial resources the way a pawn-broker assesses the value of an article brought in for hock. "Eight hundred dollars will buy you a twelve-year lease," he said.

"Eight hundred dollars—that's a lot for this locality."

"A lot? That price includes one year's rent in advance. Listen, a place like that will rent for five, six hundred, easy. You're getting a lease for nothing. For a couple of hundred. Have a look at it. I walk you there."

"I take a look at it," said Willi.

The property at number 14 Rayburn Street had until recently been occupied by a barber and tattooist named Charlie Goff. The main display window had been smashed and was now boarded up; a sign hanging over the entrance announced: Shave 5 cents; Haircuts 10 cents. Beneath this was a small sign, which said: Tattooing downstairs. And on each of the glass panels of the double entrance door there was a crude painting of a human eye and beneath it the words: "Black eyes made natural." Further down, painted in fading and irregular lettering, were the words: "Charlie Goff, Master Tattooer. All Kinds of Work. 20 cents. Walk in."

It was a pretty dingy street. Next to Charlie Goff's there was a junk shop, its wares piled and stacked up to the ceiling, leaving only a narrow corridor of free space inside; the contents of the shop overflowed on to the sidewalk where there was a clutter of objects which included picture frames, a brass bedstead, a stuffed moose head, several basins and jugs, three carved oak chairs (on which stood an oil lamp, a large circular brass tray containing a vast assortment of tiny objects, and a rather fine samovar); slabs of discolored and chipped marble, salvaged from washstands and butchers' shops, leaned against the wall. On the other side of Charlie Goff's there was a rooming house that offered a night's accommodation for thirty cents, and further along there was a shop selling buttons and babies' ware, and after that a restaurant that announced, somewhat starkly: "Bean soup—5 cents."

Willi knew the street; there was a saloon on the corner where prostitutes hung out, and a bit further along, past the intersection, Fat Annie had her place. It wasn't a very salubrious street, but Willi knew that good business was done there, and he calculated that all the people who spent a night at the rooming house or at Fat Annie's, and all those who had to wait while a prescription was being made up at the pharmacy on the corner, and of course the men on their way to and from the saloon, were potential customers of his. He wasn't so sure about the people who patronized the babies' ware place, nor about the junk shop customers. But certainly it was a lively area, close to main roads, and within easy walking distance of some of the big tenements.

"Look at that frontage," said Mr. Brailey. "Thirty foot at least. For you, it's perfect. Don't need to put in a new window because you're going to have an open front anyway. You know what you save yourself just on the window—plate glass comes expensive."

Willi's features formed into an ambiguous expression; he was keeping what he was thinking to himself. "Let's go on inside and take a look round," he said.

Mr. Brailey unlocked the padlock on the door and led the way into the interior of the premises. The hairdressing and tattooing accouterments had been removed and the place was depressingly bare. There was one large room that had served as the barber shop; behind that there was a back room where Charlie Goff used to fix himself a meal or have a snooze when business was slack. From there a spiral iron staircase led down into the basement, where the tattooing was formerly done. The basement was spacious, dry and not too dark, and Willi realized with a sudden feeling of excitement that it would be perfectly adequate as living

83

accommodations; in the back room upstairs there was a big iron stove, and, having been a barber shop up till now, a water supply was available. If he took this place, he would not need to also pay rent for living accommodations. "It's in a bad state all right," said Willi when they came out into the street again. "Cost a packet to fix up. Still, it's got possibilities."

"With a smart go-ahead young fellow running it I'd say it could be a gold mine."

"I tell you what," said Willi, "I don't want to haggle. The lease practically ain't worth anything 'cause of the amount I got to spend on fixing the place. Let's say six hundred dollars a year rent, and I put down one year's rent in advance."

"Mr. Seiermann, I'll be honest with you: I think my client can get a better offer and I would not be acting in his best interest if I advised him to accept your offer. The only thing that would persuade me to persuade my client to accept your offer would be if we could settle the whole deal in twenty-four hours. For him that would be an attraction because he don't want to be bothered with a lot of negotiations."

Willi was thinking rapidly. "Twenty-four hours is impossible," he declared firmly. "But I can have the money for you and the whole deal can be settled in forty-eight hours, if you give me your promise not to sell before."

"Forty-eight hours—that's Wednesday at twelve-thirty—you come to my office with six hundred dollars, I'll have the papers ready and the place is yours."

That evening Willi walked Sarah Essberger home in silence, responding to her tittle-tattle with vague murmurs and grunts.

"Moody," said Sarah eventually. "My Will's very moody tonight. What's making my Will moody?"

"Sarah," said Willi, allowing himself to be coaxed into speech, "it isn't nothing I could tell you about."

"We're engaged now and we're going to get married and we're not supposed to have secrets," she said.

"Well," said Willi, "it's kind of hard for me to say." Then, in a sudden rush, he blurted it out none the less: "It's all this waiting, Sarah, waiting till we're married. You don't know how tough that is. What do you think, I'm made of stone? Seeing you every day, thinking about you. Sarah, I wish we was married already." In the street, he stopped

84

suddenly, and to her amazement—because he had never done this before so publicly—put his arms around her and kissed her passionately.

"Willi!" she remonstrated breathlessly, when he let her go.

"That's the way I feel," he replied defiantly. "A man can't help his feelings, Sarah. Its my fault I happen to have a highly passionate nature? Its a sin that I should love the woman I'm going to marry? Sarah, my darling, you know I wouldn't ask you to do anything that's against your beliefs because I respect your beliefs and I respect you, but you must know a man in love is an impatient feller, and it's not easy to wait three months."

She gave him a half-reproachful, half-coquettish look. "You must learn to be patient, Willi," she said.

"In that case," said Willi, "maybe we better not see each other till we're married because for me, like this, is torture. Soon it'll affect my health. Already I have trouble sleeping."

"Oh, Willi, Willi," she sighed.

Mr. Essberger was understanding about Willi's impatience to get married, but he pointed out that it wouldn't look good if they did it in too much of a hurry. It would look as if Sarah *had* to get married. On the other hand, perhaps it was not necessary to wait three months. It was then that Willi told of his other reason for being impatient. That day, he said, he had been offered a place that was not only ideal as premises for a garment business but also could provide them with a home. It was a great opportunity, one which might not occur again so soon. The thing was that to clinch the deal he had to make the down payment within forty-eight hours. He needed $900 and he only had $600. Mr. Essberger said he would like to see the place, and the next day Willi, having obtained a key, took him there and showed him around.

"It's not exactly what I call a good neighborhood," declared Mr. Essberger, "but you got to start somewhere and I can see you could do business here. The price is reasonable, and, like you say, you also got somewhere to live. I tell you what I do. I let you have the four hundred dollars now so you can settle the deal, and then you get married. Considering everything, it's possible to move forward the marriage for a month from now." At that moment Willi believed passionately in God and that He was on Willi's side.

There was a great deal to do in the four weeks before the wedding. For Willi had had the idea of combining the wedding reception with the grand opening of his Amusements Arcade. Papa Essberger was a respected member of the local Jewish community; his friends and customers included aldermen and civic dignitaries, prominent members of the chamber of commerce, lawyers, teachers, doctors, other shopkeepers and businessmen, religious leaders, and the editor of the local newspaper. In the twenty-three years that Papa Essberger had been running his delicatessen store he had made a great many friends, and the marriage of his daughter was a big occasion for the neighborhood. It was seriously being discussed whether the Police Commissioner and the Mayor of New York should be asked. For Willi this was an opportunity not to be missed. What better way to acquaint the local notables with the fact that he was in business? How else could he get so many distinguished people to his Amusements Arcade?

On the Wednesday Willi arrived at the office of Brailey and Bergenson with the check for $600. Half an hour later, the deeds of his newly acquired property stuffed in his pocket, he tendered his resignation to Hermann Glantz, and he walked out of the building savoring the delicious flavor of no longer being an employee, of being instead a businessman, a man of property. On an impulse, he stopped at a hatter's and bought himself a brown derby. The brand-new hat looked out of place on him, considering that the rest of his clothes were so shabby, but it made him feel very jaunty, almost dashing. As he walked along the street, he practiced smiling like a proprietor—it had to be warm, polite, friendly, but not subservient; polite, welcoming, but definitely not subservient. He was a proprietor now. He practiced smiling in a nonsubservient way, indifferent to the curious glances of passers-by, trying to inject just the right degree of aloofness into his expression. It wasn't going to be all that easy to eradicate the obsequious habits of years. He must stop agreeing with people quite so readily: a proprietor didn't have to agree with everything other people said. He must assert himself more, be less accommodating.

CHAPTER SEVEN

Despite the cold there were a few curious spectators outside the synagogue to gape at the guests as they arrived in their carriages and coaches. A dark blue, rather worn, strip of carpet stretched from the end of the sidewalk to the entrance, where men who had arrived without hats were provided with skull caps; this occasioned some jocularity among non-Jewish guests, unaccustomed to this type of headgear. There was a great deal of smiling and bowing and handclasping and emotional embracing, and Papa Essberger's bows became lower and lower, and more profuse, as it got closer to the time of the ceremony, and the most distinguished guests, who were the last to arrive, made their appearance. When the Police Commissioner and his wife stepped out of their coach, Papa Essberger was so overcome by the honor of their attendance that his forehead practically scraped the ground.

Willi, accompanied by his father, mother and eldest brother, arrived in a hackney. (The rest of the family had to make their way to the synagogue on foot as he considered it extravagant, in view of all his other expenses, to hire more than one carriage for the occasion.) He looked exceedingly uncomfortable in his tall silk hat, black frock coat, light-gray striped trousers, pearl-gray vest and high winged collar, which cut into the flesh of his neck and made his double chin more pronounced than ever. Everything he wore was brand new, from the collar down to the buttoned shoes. He wore his newly acquired finery as if afraid that any uncalculated movement might cause it to come apart and expose him naked to the assembled congregation. His face was very red, partly from the cold and partly from the excitement, and he kept looking nervously at his pocket watch (a present from his father) as the moment for the start of the marriage ceremony approached. He had so much on his mind just now that he was afraid he might forget, or mix up, the Hebrew words he was required to say, and he kept mumbling them to himself under his breath while his eyes kept going over the guests, trying to pick out the important ones, estimating the size of the congregation and coming to the conclusion that it was, despite a few notable absences, a most creditable turnout.

His bride he hardly looked at. After all, he knew well enough what she looked like, and there was no point in reminding himself of that unnecessarily and thereby marring a beautiful and important occasion in his life. As they stood together under the *chupah*, a silk awning supported by four posts under which the bride and bridegroom, their immediate family and the officiating rabbi had gathered for the ceremony, he did give her a sidelong glance. She looked very pale and was swaying a little and for a moment he had the horrible feeling she was going to faint. He could imagine the ribald jokes that would result from such a catastrophe. He gave her a loving—and he hoped reviving —look. She gave him a slight smile in return, and he prayed that God, who had been pretty good to him so far, was not going to let him down now. If Sarah was already feeling faint now, how was she going to stay on her feet throughout the lengthy ceremony and the rabbi's address: the latter might last for half an hour or more, as the rabbi would certainly want to take the opportunity of impressing such a distinguished congregation. Willi wasn't surprised that she was feeling faint with all the things she was wearing. He had never seen a wedding dress—or any other sort of dress —that managed to use quite so much material to cover what was, after all, a fairly limited area. There were layers upon layers of the elaborate dress. He could only guess at what she might be wearing underneath, but knowing Sarah he was sure there would be a lot of it: undressing her was going to be like dismantling an elaborate piece of machinery. These thoughts flashed through his mind as the rabbi chanted the (to Willi) incomprehensible Hebrew words of the marriage ceremony. As he waited for his cue to assent to taking Sarah Essberger as his wife, he was, in his mind, worriedly comparing the size of the synagogue with the size of his Amusements Arcade and wondering whether he was going to be able to get in all the guests. So preoccupied was he with this thought that he missed the cue words, and the rabbi had to repeat them twice before Willi responded correctly. He had forgotten exactly what the vows, which he was now being asked to make, amounted to, but he made them in a voice that was strong and firm and full of sincerity. His bride, who understood Hebrew, spoke in a much more hesitant voice. Then the flow of Hebrew words came to an end, the rabbi smiled broadly, everybody relaxed and there was the shuffling, scraping sound of people sitting down, and Willi realized he was a married man. The address, as he had feared, was a long one, and though the congregation was able to hear it sitting down, the bride and bridegroom had to hear it standing up, only a few feet from the rabbi. Willi was shifting his weight from one foot to the other; at one stage one of his feet started to tingle with pins and needles and he had to try stamping it, very discreetly, to disperse the numbness creeping up his left leg. It was a very tricky business. How does one stamp one's foot discreetly in full view of the congregation? The rabbi gave him a sharp glance and Willi smiled back feebly, frantically seeking to awaken the sleeping limb by wriggling his toes inside his shoes, without actually moving his foot. A frown was creeping over the rabbi's benign features as he became increasingly aware of Willi's fidgeting movements, but he went on and on, ignoring, or failing to understand, the difficulty in which the bridegroom found himself. To make matters worse, Willi's eyes were beginning to water, which the rabbi interpreted as emotional reaction to his words and took as encouragement to go on in the same vein. Sarah, too, was under the same misapprehension, and the looks she kept shooting at her husband became more and more tender as the tears trickled down his cheeks. At long last it was over. The relief of being able to stamp his foot openly! He embraced his mother, he embraced his father, he embraced Papa Essberger, he embraced both his brothers and his three sisters, and he remembered to embrace his wife. For a moment, as he held her rigid form, he thought about the pleasures of the night, to which he was now legally entitled, but quickly he dismissed these thoughts: there was much still to be done. Extricating himself from the embraces and the handclasps, rapidly dispensing kisses to proffered cheeks, or manly shoulder clasps to men who slapped him on the back, he struggled out of the synagogue, his bride in tow, got into the waiting carriage, and urged the driver to proceed with all possible speed to Rayburn Street. It was essential that he should arrive ahead of the guests.

As they were approaching the Amusements Arcade he told Sarah to close her eyes because he wanted to give her a surprise. Giggling, her eyes clenched shut, she allowed

89

herself to be helped out of the carriage. He had gone to elaborate precautions to prevent Papa Essberger and Sarah from finding out in advance the kind of business he was setting up in. The machines had been installed only two days before; the sign had been put up only that morning, and it had been arranged that the food and drink, which Papa Essberger was providing, should be conveyed to Rayburn Street while the wedding was actually going on. Willi was himself seeing the result of his labors of the past weeks for the first time in its final glory; the last time he had been there, the day before, tarpaulin had still covered the frontage from view. Now, his heart swelling with pride, he made the prearranged signal, and from inside the arcade one of the phonographs started to blare out "Here Comes the Bride." Some of the guests who had arrived early, mostly unimportant ones, his former co-workers at Hermann Glantz, joined in, singing loudly, if not exactly in unison with each other or with the phonograph. At this point Willi told the giggling Sarah that she could open her eyes. Her reaction was not exactly what he had anticipated. She was surprised, certainly; but the surprise was such that it made her go weak at the knees, and he had to hold her to prevent her falling. The look on her face was one that might have been occasioned had she, a well-brought-up girl, just been forced to witness an act of public indecency. "Willi," she stammered at last, "this isn't a garment business."

"No," he replied, quite unruffled by her reaction, beaming with pride. "It's Willi Seiermann's Amusements Palace. One of the finest of its kind."

Other carriages were approaching as Willi, for the benefit of a photographer from the local press, lifted his bride in his arms and held her, in the traditional pose, on the threshold of the Arcade. Realizing that the expression on her face was still one of shocked horror, and that this might not seem appropriate to the occasion, he contrived to obscure her face with his own as the flash exploded.

The other guests were now arriving. Some seemed amused to discover the kind of business that Willi, unbeknown to Papa Essberger, had set up in; others were barely able to conceal their shocked dismay. The ones who were amused by it all were feeling in their pockets for small coins to operate the machines. An alderman was measuring the strength of his punch while his portly wife, who had obvi-

ously had a few snifters before the wedding ceremony, was
being induced to step on to the machine that spoke your
weight, and when it spoke hers—and it was a considerable
weight—this was the signal for an outburst of hilarity that
spread around the Arcade. Several of the phonographs
were playing simultaneously now: Sousa marches competing with "The Hottentot Love song," "I'm Afraid To Go
Home in the Dark," "You Splash Me and I'll Splash You,"
and other such current hits. On the walls, amid innumerable signs and notices with instructions on how to operate
the machines, were posters drawing attention to the pictures to be seen in the Kinetoscopes. One of these announced boldly:

    The Wonderful Kinetoscope
    Moving Pictures Photographed from Life
    Drop nickel in slot—keep turning crank to the
        right and you will see
    HOW THE PUERTO RICAN GIRLS ENTERTAIN
        UNCLE SAM'S SOLDIERS

Beneath this there was a picture of three coquettishly
smiling girls, wearing large feathery hats and dresses that
were presumably meant to pass for their native costume.
One of Uncle Sam's soldiers, in a peak cap, had his arm
around the waist of the girl in the middle and was staring
intently at the nape of her neck, while the other two girls
peered at him over their spread-out fans.

One of the young men from Hermann Glantz had already dropped his nickel in the slot and was discovering—
to the accompaniment of a good deal of bawdy badinage
from his co-workers grouped around—how Uncle Sam's
soldiers *were* entertained. "How about that," he kept murmuring as he cranked the handle. "How about that!
Wowee! I don't believe it!" When it was finished he mopped
his brow, pretending to be overcome by the torrid nature of
what he had just seen, and declared in a loud voice: "Just
as well Willi got himself married. With inflammatory stuff
like that in his hands no girl'd be safe . . ." Above another
machine was a poster declaring—"WARNING: This moving
picture should not be seen by young people under 18 or by
members of the fair sex liable to shock easy. It has been condemned by the clergy as 'a lyric of the stockyard' on account of the long kiss between the principals. The Manage-
ment of this Establishment don't agree. So we're giving the

Public the opportunity of making up their own minds, which is their entitlement in a democracy. Thank you! (signed) Willi Seiermann, proprietor."

This notice had been discovered by Ed Sayler, who was reading it out loud to the merriment of several girls around him, one of whom was actually bent double with laughter. (Waiters had been serving generous amounts of a potent punch from the start of the reception, and also bringing round the delicacies prepared by Papa Essberger.) The bride was standing with her best friend, an even plainer girl than Sarah, given to abrupt, embarrassed peals of laughter, which came out as shrieks of the kind uttered by nervous women in ghost trains or on roller coasters. In this situation, being embarrassed pretty well the whole time, she was shrieking fairly continuously, which soon became accepted as part of the general hubbub. Sarah, a sagging smile on her face, kept looking around for her father, and asking people who came to congratulate her if they had seen him. One of the guests told her that he was arriving together with the Police Commissioner. Willie was moving among the guests, asking them if they were having a good time and if they needed anything, and handing out business cards. To their boisterous inquiries about where the honeymoon was going to be, he replied: "Right here. I got a big bed fixed up downstairs."

"Well," declared Ed Sayler, "that's somethin' somebody oughter make a moving picture of, that'd be somethin' to see—Willi's honeymoon night."

The raw talk, the punch, the arrival of more guests, which forced those already there closer together, the train of thoughts started by Willi's wedding—and Willi's posters, and Willi's moving pictures—were having their effect. Some of the young men, finding themselves squashed up against some of the girls, felt inclined to seize the opportunity: kisses were being snatched, breasts fleetingly fondled, hands pressed against thighs until they were playfully slapped away, legs insinuated between legs and subtle secret pressures exerted under cover of what was rapidly becoming a scrimmage. Ed Sayler was enmeshed with one girl, against an electric shock machine, and they were moving against each other in a way that made several guests, who happened to see what was going on, decide to leave immediately.

It was over an hour before Papa Essberger finally arrived,

without the Police Commissioner and his wife. Their carriage had driven up to the Amusements Arcade about twenty minutes after the start of the reception, but Papa Essberger was sure that it was the wrong place. He was very confused. Was it Rayburn Street? It couldn't possibly be. Some vulgar celebration going on at one of those new amusements arcades, but no sign of a garment business or a wedding reception. Maybe it was Romund Street. He told the driver to take them there, muttering apologies to the Police Commissioner and his wife; in the confusion and excitement he must have got the address mixed up—well, it wasn't every day that an only daughter got married, and he had to admit he'd had a small glass of wine, before the ceremony, for his nerves. At Romund Street—more embarrassment, dire perplexity. No sign of a garment business, or a wedding reception. To lose one's daughter, quite so literally, on her wedding day, and moreover to commit this act of carelessness in the company of the Police Commissioner, was a singular blunder. Perhaps the best thing, in the circumstances, was to go back to the synagogue. Somebody there was bound to know where the reception was being held. But at the synagogue they were told that the only people who knew where the reception was were already at it. Papa Essberger said, in desperation, that at his delicatessen there was bound to be written down somewhere the address of the reception, because all day long people from his store had been taking food there. But, by this time, the Police Commissioner had to beg to be excused; unfortunately, he was already late for another engagement. Before taking his leave he told Papa Essberger—and somehow this just made matters worse—that if he hadn't found his daughter by the evening to be sure to inform the police. Personally, the Police Commissioner did not think it was a case of kidnapping: he had never heard of a bride and groom *and* all of the wedding guests being kidnapped. . . .

When Papa Essberger turned up at the reception, having decided to explore Rayburn Street for a second time, he was not in a very congenial frame of mind. And when he saw the scenes of—what seemed to him—bacchanalia going on at his daughter's wedding reception, in an amusement arcade decorated with indecent posters, he, a nonviolent man normally, could not control the anger that welled up in him. He pushed his way through the crowd, found Willi,

93

struck him across the face, and then fainted. Sarah screamed; there was a great commotion as Papa Essberger was carried out into the fresh air, where he came round. This was the signal for the guests to start leaving; some, who had not been informed of what had happened to Papa Essberger, came to the conclusion, seeing him sitting on the sidewalk, his collar loosened, his daughter pressing a water-soaked handkerchief to his brow, that the old man had had a few too many, and sniggered as they passed him, much to his irritation.

When all the other guests had left, Ed Sayler and some of the other boys and girls from Hermann Glantz were still there. Willi and Sarah were gloomily waiting for them to go. But all hints, requests and outright demands that they should leave had absolutely no effect. "Don't worry about us, Willi," Ed Sayler replied. "Just you get on with whatever it is you gotter get on with, feller, don't need ter worry about entertainin' us, we're real happy. . . ." Eventually, as the only alternative was to call the cops and have them thrown out, Willi and Sarah crept downstairs to their wedding bed, while the party continued, noisily, above them.

"I guess we better go to bed then," said Willi when they were alone.

Sarah didn't answer; her breast was heaving and she looked as if she was about to faint. She wanted him to turn round and not look while she undressed, but Willi insisted that it was his right, as her husband, to undress her himself. What with all the drink he had downed, and the exhausting nature of the day, and Sarah's far from erotic manner, he felt singularly unpassionate, and he feared that unless he could get himself worked up a bit he might not be able to fulfill his marital obligations. Clumsily, roughly, he made a grab for her, pulled her close and forced an animalistic kiss on her mouth: he felt far from animalistic, but he thought it behooved him to make the effort. At first Sarah simply looked disgusted, and then, an expression of martyrdom on her face, she resigned herself to woman's inevitable lot. As Willie feared, there was a great deal of clothing to remove, and his fumbling fingers were quite unfamiliar with the intricate way in which women's undergarments were fastened. After the wedding dress, he had to remove starched white petticoats, very elaborate, delicate things edged with pleated ruffles. Then there was the bust improver to be removed—

without it, Sarah was virtually flat-chested, he now realized —and also the *figure improver,* a kind of small bustle, worn over the rump, to be unfastened. Then came the corset, laced front and back. He tried to derive some excitement from the unlacing, which he had always thought of as being highly erotic, but his hands, roaming over her body, encountered only the hard texture of her whalebone stays—and her bones. Her drawers were a very elaborate affair, with lace flounces as wide as a petticoat. He got them down with difficulty. She was shivering—and not with passion— shoulders hunched, thighs clenched together, as he removed the white shoes and silk hose. She was naked, and he felt nothing, only a sense of amazement that such a miserly distribution of flesh over a fairly common-place arrangement of bones should be considered capable of arousing any feeling in anyone. At his failure to react to the sight of her naked body, he began to panic. He began to undress quickly, keeping on his long shirt to conceal his unaroused condition from his bride—which she took as being done, out of regard for her modesty, to conceal the very opposite state. Crudely—to try and arouse himself—he forced her back on the bed and tore her thighs apart; crudity was an excusable male failing on such occasions, but nonconsummation was an everlasting disgrace. He searched for the place between her thighs, but she did not help his inexperienced fingers to find their way. He had never felt so unaroused in his life. He closed his eyes and tried to picture Ed Sayler with Trina: the girl bending over a chair—it was a method Ed had described in detail—holding up her dress, her drawers around her ankles, her well-fleshed buttocks, her juicy lips, exhorting Ed to greater fervor. . . . Thinking about this had a slight effect, and Willi felt it was now or never, the effort must be made; girding himself for the task, he made the lunge, and missed. Feeling in the dark, he guided himself for the second attempt, all the time aware that he must achieve his objective quickly, otherwise the effect of his imaginings would have worn off. He applied pressure—nothing: no give at all, just solid flesh. Was that the place? How the hell could one know? Drat it, now he'd have to stop and think some more about Ed and Trina. Once again he conjured up the provocative images, again they had the desired effect, again he tried, again no success. He didn't dare ask Sarah for help. She hadn't volunteered it, evidently assuming he knew what he was about. For almost an hour Willi made attempt after attempt to deflower his bride, but, eventually, exhausted, tired, incapable of being aroused for a further attempt by even the most extravagant imaginings, he had to admit defeat. Sarah kissed him tolerently, relieved that he had had his beastly male pleasure and was through for the time being: and she went to sleep. Upstairs, the party was still going on. Willi couldn't sleep. After nearly an hour of tossing and turning, he got up, put on his trousers and shirt and went upstairs, in order to tell Ed Sayler and the gang how could a man sleep on his honeymoon night with all that racket going on, and couldn't they please show a little more consideration. But when he got up there, before he could say a thing, he was immediately subjected to all sorts of lewd inquiries. How had it gone? So, finally, Willi had got himself laid. Well, well, well! Who'd have believed it possible? And how had Sarah been? Some of these quiet mousy creatures were dark horses. The disheveled clothing of the boys and girls indicated to Willi that however disastrous his experience had been, they had been having a good time of it. Well, thought Willi, looking around his Amusements Arcade, now littered with the debris of the wedding party, I got myself launched in a good business.

BOOK
TWO

PART ONE

CHAPTER ONE

After the last show, Willi Seiermann always came down into the foyer and saw the customers out. He liked to talk to as many of them as possible, to find out what they thought of the film they had just seen; he liked to find out if they had enjoyed themselves, and if not, why not. "Enjoy the picture, sir? Glad to hear it. Very glad to hear it. A satisfied customer is music in my ears. Hope to have the pleasure to see you again real soon. Your little boy? Lovely boy. What's your name, sonny? Enjoy the picture? He's a lovely boy. I'm a married man myself, haven't had the blessing of a son so far, but we're hopeful. Glad to see you, sir, madam. . . ." To an unsatisfied customer he went out of his way to be equally agreeable. "A shame you didn't enjoy the picture. It hurts me, because if I find a customer didn't enjoy herself I take it personally. But I tell you what I'm gonner do so you won't think bad of me. I'm gonner give you my card, signed by me personal, which entitles you next time you come—and I hope we may have the pleasure of that real soon—to three tickets for the price of two. Is that a fair offer? You excuse me for one second. . . ." Going to where a huge bowl of flowers was standing on a display pedestal, in a recess, he extracted a slightly drooping, long-stemmed tulip and returned with it to the dissatisfied customer. "You allow me?" he inquired with exaggerated courtliness, gave a little bow, and handed the solitary flower to the somewhat startled woman. "It should bring a little sweetness to your life. With my compliments."

When the last customer had left, Seiermann went into the

auditorium and watched as the girls shone their flashlights between the rows of seats to see if anyone had left anything behind. As he surveyed his domain, he took a cigar from his vest pocket, removed the cellophane wrapping, bit off the end and spat it out so forcefully that it plonked against the wall, making an additional stain on the already bespattered paintwork. Shifting the cigar from one side of his mouth to the other, he rapidly enveloped himself in the comforting aroma. "All right, girls," he said when they had completed the search. "You can go home." He locked up himself, and then climbed the stone stairs to his first-floor office, where Alexander was checking the day's taking, which the cashiers of Seiermann's four theaters had brought up in the black tin boxes.

"Not so good, not so good," said Seiermann, able to estimate the takings at a glance. "But business has been bad everywhere, there isn't the money around. The war will be over this year, God willing, and business will pick up again. I got a lot of ideas. Trouble is they keep turning out war pictures and the public don't want them. They got sons and husbands in the war, they come to the pictures to *forget*, not to be reminded. Comedies, sure. *Shoulder Arms,* a lovely picture. They want they should be able to laugh. *Birth of a Nation,* beautiful, it's an old war—they don't have sons fighting in *that* war, it's entertainment. But *Beast of Berlin?* They haven't got enough with horror?"

"What you want me to do about this letter from Essanay, Mr. Seiermann?" asked Alexander. "It's nearly three weeks and they said they wanted a check by return. . . ."

"Money, money, money," broke in Seiermann. "All they can think about is money. Imagination, artistry, pictures the public are going to enjoy—that they're not in such a hurry about. But money. . . . All right, they don't want to do business with Willi Seiermann, it's their funeral. I go to my friends at Vitagraph, at Lubin, at Pathé, at Biograph, at I.M.P. There are plenty picturemakers, and they make better pictures. . . ."

"I.M.P. and Pathé are also insisting on payment before they supply any more film," Alexander pointed out.

"They got it made," sighed Seiermann indignantly. "They make lousy pictures which don't take a cent, they keep people at home with their lousy pictures, and they want money. Alexander, you know what we're gonner do, we're gonner

100

write them a letter. All of them. I tell you what to write and you make it sound good. I find out I'm writing ungrammatical, you're fired. Understand? You say to them I got plans for opening up ten more picture houses, so it's understandable my capital is a bit tied up right now, and if they want to lose a good customer with fourteen theaters because of a stinking few dollars then good luck to them and I'll take my business elsewhere. If they wanner be cut out of the Willie Seiermann chain of theaters, that's their funeral. I got big plans, tell 'em; if they don't wanner give me their pictures, I make my own, you tell 'em that. Up their lousy ass holes they can stick their lousy films, and good luck to them. Tell 'em that, but *grammatical.*" Seiermann puffed violently at his cigar and paced the room, which was really too small and too filled with a clutter of objects to be entirely conducive to satisfactory pacing. But, insinuating himself between wooden filing cabinets and rickety office chairs and stacks of film cans and piles of papers and trade journals, Seiermann somehow or other managed to pace, a look of intense concentration on his face.

"You know something," he said at last, lowering himself into a leather swivel chair. "It isn't such a bad idea."

"What isn't, Mr. Seiermann?"

"I make my own pictures. Why not?"

Working for Willi Seiermann was hard work. Alexander wrote business letters for him, and typed them as well; he took cans of film from one theater to the other; he helped to plan and arrange advertising displays in the foyers; sometimes he did a spell in the ticket booth; he learned how to project films, and when a projectionist was ill or left because he had got a better job somewhere else Alexander stood in for him until a replacement was found. Sometimes the film broke, and Alexander learned how to join it together again. Discovering that to join film together was a comparatively simple matter, once you knew how to do it, he experimented secretly, joining film together in different ways, slightly, but significantly, altering the rhythms and structure of a story. He discovered that a film, which bored audiences when shown in the form in which it came in, could sometimes be made to hold them if some of the sequences were rearranged. With comedies it was possible, often, to get more laughs out of a particular situation by

101

leading up to it differently; sometimes it was a matter of leading up to it more slowly, and sometimes of leading up to it faster. You had to play it by ear in the first place, and then by trial and error you could rearrange the sequence until the maximum number of laughs had been got out of it. Alexander experimented with various devices: for instance withholding, by means of cutting, some information that the makers had felt the audience ought to have from the start. The withholding of such information could create a suspense otherwise lacking. In other cases, the converse was true: a bored audience could be interested if it was told something that the makers, originally, had not revealed until much later.

Once, Alexander came into the office and found his employer sitting behind his desk, his big, heavy head propped in his hands, weeping without restraint or shame.

"What is it, Mr. Seiermann?"

Seiermann focused his eyes on Alexander; he made no effort to dry his wet cheeks. "For ten weeks I been waiting, I wait and I wait and I wait. You know I'm not an impatient man. I been promised ten thousand dollars for my place in Rayburn Street, promised for sure—I need the money. Still they keep me waiting." Seiermann got up, stuck his hands into his trouser pockets, and his neck sank even deeper into his shirt collar. "Alexander," he said in his most tragi-philosophical manner, "you know the difference between a nobody and a somebody? I tell you. When you're a nobody, you got to wait; when you're a somebody, you keep others waiting. Ten weeks I been waiting, and still they stall me. I hate that man's guts, but can I tell him? How can I tell him—then I got *no* chance. I got to wait and keep smiling and say 'Thank you, sir,' and 'I look forward to your early decision, sir,' and 'I hope we can bring our negotiations to a rapid and satisfactory conclusion.' That's what I got to say. Meanwhile how do I find the money? My creditors, they don't wait for me. 'If payment is not made within seven days we shall be obliged, etcetera etcetra.' *They* know when they got you in a corner, that's when they kick you in the guts."

His current troubles had made Seiermann reflective. "Alexander," he continued, after pacing for a while more, "I'm not a happily married man. I married a woman that

102

don't attract me. I married a plain girl, what's worse I married a skinny girl. I brought it on myself, Alexander, because I didn't marry for love. I married her for her dowry, for her lousy few hundred bucks. I thought I get myself started in business, it'll make up for it. Never do a thing like that, Alexander. You pay for it. Now I pay for it. A man has a hard time in business, at least he comes home to a woman he loves, who can give him some pleasure, some satisfaction, that's something at least. But with me—it's like going home to a grave. Sarah, understand me, is not a bad woman, a good mother, a good, sweet nature, but skinny—you know? Skinny to look at and skinny in her heart." He banged his own heart for emphasis. "How she can be so skinny, I don't know. The daughter of a man who had a delicatessen store. And with such things—to make your mouth water. Cold meats and gefilte fish and seed rolls and those long chains of frankfurters and bottles of borscht and freshly baked chalehs and carp deeply embedded in jelly and knackwurst and cold fried fish and strudels. But she's skinny. Don't every marry a skinny woman, Alexander. They open their legs for you like they're performing a tragedy."

While he had been talking Miss Tolby, the cashier, had come in with the black metal box containing the evening's takings. In silence, Seiermann watched her movements as she crossed the room, put down the box, said a perfunctory "Good night," and left again.

"Now that's what I call a woman," Seiermann declared with lewd enthusiasm. Alexander gave a smile of agreement. "She don't look at me," said Seiermann, "I know that. Why should she? I don't blame her. I give her a little slap on the ass—an innocent little slap, no harm meant—and she says 'Please, Mr. Seiermann, don't do that, Mr. Seiermann, or I'll have to give in my notice, Mr. Seiermann.' One day it'll be different, Alexander. They'll be grateful. I know I got a funny appearance, *I know*. I tell you something, Alexander, one day they won't notice."

"I don't think you're so funny looking, Mr. Seiermann."

"Thank you, Alexander. You're a good kid. I wish I had a son like you."

Seiermann went to the window and watched Miss Tolby moving down the street, her every movement an incitement to him, and he remembered how it had always been. When

103

he had been a junior cutter at Hermann Glantz & Sons. At six-thirty in the evening—the girls coming out of the building, running the gauntlet of avid male eyes. There were no eyes more avid than Willi's, even then. How those girls changed! During the day, at work, so drab and proper looking. But at six-thirty! In the dusk they seemed to glow and glisten from the heat in their blood. Like fireflies!

"You're not eating," said Leushka.

"I don't have much appetite," Alexander replied.

"Come, eat a little. A person has got to eat."

"I'm not hungry."

"At least eat the white of the meat, it's so light, an invalid can eat it."

"Leave me alone, Mama, don't keep at me."

"What for I cook, you don't eat?"

"I've got a lot on my mind, I'm just not hungry. Now can we change the subject?"

"You're thin like I wouldn't give you enough to eat."

"For God's sake, will you stop going on about it!"

"A mother has got a duty."

"You irritate me sometimes, Mama."

"I don't mean it for your good?"

"I know you mean it good, but you irritate me, always wanting to push food into me when I'm not hungry. Let me decide when I want to eat and when I don't."

"I make you a little mashed potato with milk."

"No. I don't want to eat *anything*." He pushed the plate away violently.

"I never heard of such a thing."

"Well, you've heard of it now."

"You're not well, Alexi?"

"I'm fine, and I've asked you a million times not to call me Alexi or Alexile. My name is Alexander."

"What's the matter?"

"I tell you what's the matter with me," he said with mounting violence, "you're what's the matter with me. A person could go mad the way you keep on all the time. . . ."

"That's a fine thing to say to a mother. I could drive him mad, such things he can bring from his lips. . . ."

"Can't you see, the more you go on the worse you make it. Leave me in peace, please."

"It's sticking at home all the time," she said knowingly.

"I said plenty times to your father it's not good for the boy to be home so much. Never sees anyone. That's a life? You think too much, that's why you got trouble with your nerves. You shouldn't be shy with girls, you're a nice-looking boy . . ."

"For God's sake, Mama," he said, jumping to his feet and banging the cutlery on the table, "will you shut up! Will you stop all your conniving. It makes me sick to hear you go on and on and on. I can't stand it any more, don't make me lose my temper. All the time, all the time, it's like nails going into my head!" Her face became tragic and grim and assumed the contorted expression which he knew presaged tears.

"That's how you talk to a mother," she said. "I deserve that? With pain I brought him into the world—with pain! And this is what I get? That is my reward?"

"Oh stop it, stop it!" He could feel the anger rising uncontrollably inside him, he could feel the coming explosion in himself; soon he would be screaming at the top of his voice like the other neighbors. At such times his carefully cultivated American manner of cool, self-possessed calm seemed to desert him, and he felt himself reverting to a type he hated and despised. Waving his hands about, talking emotionally in a loud voice . . . it was like some other person inside himself breaking out.

"Don't cry!" he shouted threateningly, hoarse and tense with emotion. "Don't use that weapon against me." His mother was crying now, an expression of martyrdom on her face, a hand pressed to her heart, as if to quell the pain he was causing her. He felt a sort of frenzy. She was using the tears to silence him, to make him acquiesce, to make him come to her—as he used to do—so that she could hold him in her arms and shower him with kisses and tell him how much she loved him, that she lived only for him, that she only wanted what was best for him. But he could not bring himself to go to her in this way any more. He could not bring himself to kiss her in this way. There was a great barrier that prevented him from doing any of this. He knew that, later, he would feel terrible remorse at having treated her in this way, but he couldn't help it. He would have to make it up to her in other ways, to show his love indirectly. Angrily, he stormed out of the kitchen, slamming the door after him, and threw himself down on the big bed. These scenes were so exhausting. After he had calmed down a little, he returned to the kitchen. He had to make it up with her or he would be unhappy all evening. "Mama," he said with calm, cool self-possession, "I don't like having these quarrels with you, but you must try and understand. Whatever other people may consider the right way of behaving doesn't interest me. I can't help that. I'm not like other people." And then he added with a slightly sheepish smile—alluding to his father's oft repeated words: "After all, I'm a Sondorpf, aren't I?"

By 1919 Willi Seiermann had eight picture theaters, good houses doing good business in predominantly working-class neighborhoods. In addition to owning theaters, he had gone into distribution in a small way. The fact that the distributor, who neither made the pictures nor showed them—but merely *distributed* them—always took a nice slice of the takings had at first annoyed Seiermann and then prompted him to go into this business himself. If there was this easy profit to be made, Seiermann didn't see why *he* shouldn't make it. His firm—the Fine Pictures Exchange—was a pretty small concern; most of the leading production outfits were already tied up with the established distribution organizations. He dealt mostly with foreign films and one-reel comedies and travelogues that bigger concerns didn't want to be bothered with. He regarded the exchange as a sideline: his main interest was the theaters, which brought in the real money. For this reason he entrusted a good deal of the running of the Fine Pictures Exchange to Alexander. On the whole, it was a fairly routine operation. The distributor put down an agreed sum for the franchise to distribute a particular picture—or series of pictures—in his own area. This initial outlay was against a remittance to the makers of between 35 per cent and 50 per cent of the eventual gross takings. The makers had the right to inspect the books to make sure that they were not being cheated, but the bookkeeping practiced by the smaller exchanges was often erratic and unreliable. As Seiermann also owned theaters it was a comparatively simple matter—he regarded it as normal business practice and didn't think of it as being dishonest—to substantially reduce the takings on paper, thereby remitting the absolute minimum to the makers.

106

Knowing that the small exchanges were run in this way, and that they could count on getting for their movies little more than the initial down payment, it was only the low-grade producers who came to Seiermann, and then only after they had tried, and been turned down by, the more reputable companies. In these circumstances, it was unlikely that the Fine Pictures Exchange would ever grow into anything very much. Alexander's suggestion that he should see some of the movies before the Fine Pictures Exchange agreed to distribute them did not evoke much enthusiasm from Seiermann. He thought it was a waste of time. A travelogue about Africa was a travelogue about Africa, and a Stanley Lupino one-reeler was a Stanley Lupino one-reeler. Why waste time seeing a lot of cheap pictures? There was a generally accepted scale of payment for such stuff, and if he paid a little less than the current market price Seiermann was well pleased. But if Alexander wanted to waste his time—his *own* time it would have to be, Seiermann made it clear—he had no objection to his going to trade shows. Alexander liked to do this because in this way he got to know some of the picturemakers, and in his talks with them he learned about the cost of picturemaking, and found out how much the producer could count on getting back from different markets. Soon—though he had been no good at arithmetic in school—he was able to do complicated calculations in his head while talking casually about something quite different. In his dealing with the producers he was not shy or embarrassed—as a buyer (or the representative of a buyer) he was treated with courtesy and respect. His opinions were valued. If he liked a movie, the producers were naturally delighted. If he was disappointed in it, they were disappointed that he was disappointed. It was true that he was dealing with people in the lowest echelon of the business, but none the less it was flattering to be courted by them, even if only in the most perfunctory and automatic way.

At these showings he had on several occasions met a young man, Lewis Sholt, who was on the sales side of an outfit that specialized in making travelogues designed to show America to the Americans. They mostly dealt with out-of-the-way communities and were of the Would-You-Believe-It? variety. Alexander had not seen Lewis Sholt at any of these showings for some months—which he discovered later was because the firm he had been working for had gone bust—when he turned up one day at the office above the Bijou. It seemed he now had a new job, and he had a proposition to put to Alexander. He had come to Alexander because he had a high regard for his acumen, and he wanted to let him in on something big. Alexander, who did not think much of Lewis Sholt—he thought him shifty and flashy and distrusted him—was immediately suspicious. But he had learned to curb such reactions, and expressed interest with just the right degree of casualness.

"I've got a Walter Staupitz picture for you," Lewis Sholt declared. It was not necessary, he knew, to dress up this information: for Alexander, Staupitz was a god, ranking with Griffith and Stroheim and Chaplin and De Mille as one of the great figures of the American motion-picture industry.

"What do you mean you've got a Staupitz picture for me? He releases through I.M.P. They finance him."

"I know. But he has a deal whereby, under certain circumstances, he can take his picture away from them, go to someone else."

"Any of the big outfits would be glad to take a Staupitz picture," Alexander said, "why are you bringing it to us?"

"It's like this," said Lewis Sholt confidentially. "There are some tricky angles to this picture and I think a small outfit like Seiermann's is the best one to handle it. Anyway, I'm the sales director, and I'm offering it to you—if you want it."

"What are the tricky angles?"

"I'll tell you about that after. In principle, are you interested?"

"I'd have to talk to Mr. Seiermann, but in principle I'm sure he'd be interested."

"I thought maybe you should see it first, and then you could sort of sell Seiermann on it. If the deal goes through there'd be something in it for you, naturally."

"That's not necessary. But why d'you think I'd need to sell Mr. Seiermann on a Staupitz picture? His last two cleaned up. You *are* talking about *Arlesia?*"

"Yuh, that's right. You know it? Lousy title, but that can be changed. What d'you know about the picture exactly?"

"I know he's been making it for four months—I kept reading about it in *Variety*. The story was being kept secret, they said."

"That's right," said Lewis Sholt, "that's the picture."

"What's the deal exactly?"

Lewis Sholt considered his words carefully, then with a becoming show of frankness he opened up. "I'll be honest with you, Alexander, there are problems with this picture. That's why I'm prepared to offer you a very advantageous deal, fifty thousand dollars against twenty per cent of the net."

"What are the problems?"

"I'd rather you saw the picture for yourself, it's sort of difficult for me to explain, not being an artist myself. It's a problem of theme. It's a tricky theme. It's a great picture, maybe his greatest, but it's tricky."

"All right," said Alexander, "when can I see it?"

"Tomorrow. Afternoon? I'll provide a theater."

"All right," said Alexander, "let me know where."

"See you tomorrow, then," said Lewis Sholt, "and don't make any early dates. The picture runs four hours twenty."

The following day, in a small, private projection theater off Broadway, Alexander saw *Arlesia*. Lewis Sholt kept watching him to see how he was reacting, and Alexander had to make an effort to conceal his feelings, which wasn't easy. It was the most remarkable film he had ever seen. It made all the other pictures he had seen up till then seem crude and clumsy by comparison. It was stamped with the extraordinary personality of its director, Walter Staupitz. Instead of being the standardized product of a factory, this picture was as personal as a man's fingerprints. But Lewis Sholt had been putting it mildly when he had said the theme was tricky. The story was about two attractive sisters who destroy the man who becomes involved with each of them in turn. It gave a mordant twist to the cliché situation, very popular just then, of two sisters fighting for the same man. In *Arlesia*, though this was what they appeared to be doing, at first, the man was only a pawn; a device for revealing the sisters' "unnatural" feelings for each other. The first shock scene of the picture was when Arlesia spied on her sister, Lotte, and the man, an Austrian cavalry officer played by Staupitz himself, making love. At first it seems as though she is conventionally jealous, because she is in love with the cavalry officer herself; but when she goes in to break up their love-making it becomes clear that it is the sister she is in love with. The man, a typical Staupitz creation, was a victim of sensuality: the callous seducer who unwittingly stirs up passions that destroy him in the end, in two women he had regarded as fairly conventional prey. The theme apart, there were many individual scenes that audiences would clearly regard as obscene or hilariously funny, or both. There was one scene in which Arlesia touches and feels her sister's silken underwear and shows every sign of being aroused by what she is doing. In the scene in which Arlesia breaks up the love-making between her sister and the officer, there appeared to be a suggestion, from the man, that he would gladly oblige both sisters simultaneously. There were other scenes of this sort. Alexander's first reaction was that the film could never be shown.

On his way home he thought about it a great deal, and he had an idea which he thought would be worth trying on Seiermann. Accordingly, the next day, he broached the subject with him. As soon as the title was mentioned, Seiermann said he knew all about *Arlesia*. Every distributor in the country had turned it down. The company that had made it had already decided to write it off. It would be madness to put down one cent for the film because no theater in the country would show it. Even if they wanted to play it, they would be prevented from doing so by public morality groups who would undoubtedly instigate police action and have any theater that played the film closed down. Alexander listened to all this and agreed.

"But I've been thinking," he said. "The picture runs four hours twenty. You could cut that picture so that it was a story of two sisters in love with the same man—it would still have a hint, for those who wanted to see it, of the other thing. But, on the surface, it would be a perfectly reasonable story, if you cut out all the sex scenes, or most of them. It would still be daring, but it would be daring in a permissible way. *I* could cut that film so it'd stand up. You'd get the public in because it has the reputation of being a controversial picture. We could build up that angle. We could sell it on the line—the picture nobody else dared to show. And they're offering a very advantageous deal, financially."

110

The financial aspect of the deal had certainly attracted Seiermann. He had never before put down such a large sum of money as $50,000, but this was against 20 per cent of the net—the normal arrangement was between 35 per cent and 50 per cent of the *gross*. Obviously the company didn't expect to get more than $50,000 out of the area. This was quite a large sum if the picture got only very limited showings here and there. But if it were given a normal release, a picture of this sort could take very much more. He hardly dared to think how much more. But it was impossible. He was just going by some kid's fancy notions. If there had been any way of making the picture showable, the company that had financed Staupitz would have done it.

"There must be a snag," said Seiermann.

"I'll tell you what the snag is," said Alexander. "Staupitz has got a contract that his pictures are not to be cut without his permission, and he refuses permission to cut one foot."

"Then how do we cut the picture?"

Alexander smiled. "We don't tell him."

"You think he's not going to find out?"

"By then it'll be too late," said Alexander. "We make a hundred prints, and we open simultaneously in a hundred spots. He'd have to get an injunction to stop the picture being shown. And I'll make a gamble he wouldn't go to court. He knows he can't justify those scenes to a jury. He's using his contract as a threat to intimidate I.M.P. into releasing the picture as it is. But I guarantee that if they just went ahead and broke the contract he wouldn't sue. Mr. Seiermann, I'm so sure of what I'm saying I'm willing, personally, to put five hundred dollars into the picture."

Seiermann laughed. "So now I only need to raise another forty-nine thousand, five hundred dollars."

CHAPTER TWO

Those evenings when he was not required at the theaters Alexander made his way along Fifth Avenue to the corner of Forty-second Street, up the gently rising steps, past those superior-looking lions who guarded the entrance, and into the marble splendor of the Public Library. In the main reading room with its Italian Renaissance ceiling, its supply of free paper, pencils and ink, its perpetually changing population (students, researchers, priests, writers, biologists, chemists and other information seekers), varying in appearance from smartly-dressed matrons to rather scruffy-looking youths—here Alexander spent much of his spare time. He preferred the Public Library to the smaller branch libraries because of its cosmopolitan air (you could usually tell a newly arrived foreigner from the fact that his leather heels clicked on the marble floors whereas native Americans, or acclimatized immigrants, wore rubber soles). He enjoyed the opulence of the place, and always when he came into its reverential silence he was conscious of being in the presence of knowledge, the way a devout believer is conscious of being in the presence of God. Here, among the two million or more books, he felt sure there was to be found the key he was looking for, which would open the world to him and make its treasures his. It was to be found, this magic key, this open sesame, in those endless cliffs of books; if only he chose the right volume and opened it at the right page it would tell him something—he could not even guess what it might be—which would make everything comprehensible to him. Instinctively, he felt that there was something he had to find out—perhaps the meaning of that knowing look on the face of his perennial pursuer in those recurring nightmares. At first he had read haphazardly, selecting a book because its title contained some promise of a revelation; and then, his interest having been aroused by a particular topic, a philosophical argument, a scientific phenomenon, some aspect of nature or the mind, he chose other books on the same subject, searching for the elusive answer in the jungle of irrelevancies. The more he read, the more complicated things seemed to become; ideas which had clicked satisfyingly into place in one book, giving him a temporary feeling of contentment and of having mastered something, were often questioned and disparaged in the next book he happened to choose. He learned to read very quickly, to dredge the closely-packed pages for the core of significant meaning contained in them, reading faster and faster with mounting excitement as if he were racing everyone else to the end of the story, when surely everything would be clear. But the end of the story was always receding

112

before him, a perpetually postponed climax that seemed to get further and further away as he raced faster and faster toward it. At such times a feeling of despair welled up in him: he would never be able to catch up.

Eventually, dizzied and confused by all the contradictory information he was absorbing, he made a practical decision: henceforth he would read only encyclopedias, starting at the letter A and working through—skipping those things that didn't interest him—to Z. Then, at least, he would know everything there was to be known that people were reasonably sure about.

Ten months after he had put this plan in operation, he had got as far as Aristotle—and was beginning to think that, with all the distractions of his job, he had perhaps set himself an impossible task. So often a pretty girl would take a seat near him, and then his concentration would go: instead of reading the thirty thousand words he had allocated himself for the evening, he would endlessly reread the same sentence while his mind took fanciful leaps in directions that were not the least bit self-improving, elevating or ennobling. Imaginary parted thighs, rich in mysteries more compelling than those the encyclopedia was capable of illuminating, stood between him and the enlightenment he sought. He felt himself helplessly carried away in the strong current of his daydreams. Now, for instance, there was a plumply attractive brunette leafing through a book on costume design, while her eyes flitted restlessly about the room, almost pleading for somebody to interrupt her in what she evidently found a far from absorbing study. Alexander was not the only person who had noticed her and the coded plea in her eyes. At a near-by table sat a young man he had seen before at the library: he had rather long, straw-colored hair, wide nostrils and permanently smiling blue-gray eyes. Alexander could not place his country of origin; he looked foreign, vaguely Slavonic. He was giving the girl a cool, appraising look that was searching without being the least bit unsure; it did not remotely resemble a leer, though the thought behind it was the same; it was imbued with an easy, relaxed confidence that Alexander found very enviable. Their eyes met, acknowledging their mutual interest, and the Slavonic-looking young man raised his eyebrow in a polite, sporting inquiry. It was rather like being offered the only remaining seat in a full streetcar. Alexander declined with a tiny shake of his head, whereupon the young man got up and went over to the girl.

"Are you going to be reading that book long?" he asked.

"As a matter of fact . . . no. You can have it. I was just glancing, sort of."

He picked up the book and looked at the title. *"Costume Through the Ages,"* he read out. "Why on earth are you reading that?"

"I was interested. Why do you want it?"

"I don't."

"But you said . . ."

"No, I didn't. I said were you going to be reading it long."

"Oh, I see," she said with sudden coolness.

"Well, what other reason could I give, on the spur of the moment, for coming to talk to you? Do you mind?" She shrugged as if it was a matter of supreme indifference to her.

"The thing is," he said, lowering his voice to a mock-confidential whisper, "I'm almost as bored with my *Schönsten Heiligenlegenden in Wort und Bild* as you are by your *Costume Through the Ages.* . . ."

"Your what . . .?" she said, laughing.

"It's a book by a nineteenth-century German priest called Expeditus P. Schmidt. I was reading it to find out if I would hear the call of God. As I haven't yet, and I've spent nearly twenty minutes listening for it, I'm at a loose end for the rest of the evening, and I suspect you are too."

"Actually, I'd arranged to meet somebody here."

"Well, as he's kept you waiting for over half an hour at least, you are entitled to let him wait until the library closes. What's your name?"

"Joanna Pringle."

"Are you argumentative . . . because I must warn you I hate argumentative women . . . I ask very little of women, other than total obedience and total compliance. Apart from that I'm very undemanding. What's more, I sometimes go so far as to buy them supper when I'm not too broke." His mock-aggressive manner was softened by the delicate smile that played all the time on his lips and the disarmingly boyish laughter in his eyes. "Now stop clutching *Costume Through the Ages* as if it were a life belt, pick up your

114

gloves, stop thinking so hard—it ruins the complexion—and come along. All the best and most momentous decisions are made on the spur of the moment. If you decline my invitation, you may regret it for the rest of your life—you will never know what it was you declined. Your curiosity will torture you forever after. On the other hand, if you accept, you will be able to live to a ripe old age, secure in the knowledge that what you declined (if you do decline it, that is) wasn't worth having. You see the logic of that, don't you? Well then, Joanna Pringle, give me your hand . . . *give me your hand . . .*" Obediently, a questioning, puzzled look in her eyes, she did so. He took it, examined it, clasped it firmly in his, the way an older person does with a child he is going to lead across a busy street, and led her out. As he left, he looked over his shoulder at Alexander and gave him a wink.

Alexander had watched the entire operation in admiration. He had seen American boys making up to girls, and invariably they had seemed to him clumsy, undignified, embarrassingly banal in their choice of lines and dreadfully self-conscious. But the way this young man had done it had been so relaxed, so improvised and natural and light, not the least bit subservient. Alexander had always thought that approaching a girl entailed a certain degree of subservience—it was after all asking for something—but this young man had somehow managed not to put himself in this situation. He had simply taken charge. It wasn't that he was especially good looking; it was simply that he was so authoritative.

Some days later he was again in the Public Library, and seeing Alexander, came over to talk to him. He did not allude to the girl. "My God," he said, sitting down next to him, "you work hard. Hard at it every time I'm in here. If I'm interrupting at some vital moment, just say and I'll clear off." (But he continued without giving Alexander a chance to say anything.) "People interrupting you when you're trying to work is hell. Isn't it? That's why I come here, for some peace and quiet and a chance to think. My place is always full of people. Trouble is I like people, love to have them around, but how do you get rid of them when you no longer want them around? I can see you don't have that problem, working away, iron discipline—my

115

God, I envy you. You're fantastic. What is it you're studying?"

"I'm just reading."

"My name's Paul Krasnor," he said, looking to see what Alexander was reading.

"Mine's Alexander Sondorpf."

"German?"

"Austrian, by origin."

"Forgive me for saying this, but why are you reading up Aristotle in an encyclopedia?"

"I'm not reading up Aristotle. Not *especially* Aristotle, that is. It's just that he comes under the A's."

"You mean you're *reading* the encyclopedia?"

"Yes."

Paul Krasnor burst into a rich, unrestrained peal of laughter. "I know of course that Americans are hell-bent on self-improvement and all that, but reading the encyclopedia from A to Z! It's fantastic. It's so absurd it's almost heroic. In fact it *is* rather touching—this Promethean struggle with culture."

Alexander had gone very red. "I don't see what's so funny about it," he said defensively, looking away to try to conceal the hot flush of shame that colored his cheeks.

"I'm sorry," said Paul Krasnor, "I do apologize. I always forget that one shouldn't be offensive to people until one knows them really well. Every time I've been in here I've seen you sitting there, concentrating so intensely. I like to think I can tell what somebody does—I'm a writer, myself —from just looking at them. Well, I've watched you and I'd decided that you were Jewish—right?—born in America but of foreign origin: German, Rumanian, Austrian. And I had the idea that what you were doing here was cramming—for some exam—chemistry, law, history. I couldn't quite decide what it was you were going in for, but it was something like that. I didn't think that anyone worked that conscientiously just to, just to . . . well, what exactly *is* the purpose of reading an encyclopedia?"

"I just wanted to be well read," said Alexander, feeling very silly as he said it, his face going an even deeper shade of red. Paul Krasnor looked at him uncertainly, restraining the initial impulse to laugh out loud. The seriousness behind the naïveté was curiously impressive.

"How old are you?"

116

"Seventeen."

"Only seventeen. You look older."

"I know."

"What work do you do?"

"I'm in the picture business."

"In the picture business? You mean making pictures?"

"No. Showing them, at the moment. I work for a man called Willi Seiermann, who owns theaters."

"What do you do for him?"

"Well, I buy pictures—I see them, at special shows, and if I like them I buy them. I just bought a Walter Staupitz picture that nobody else wants to show."

"You've bought *Arlesia?*"

"Yes. You know it?"

"You're going to *show Arlesia?*"

"It's a masterpiece," said Alexander defensively.

"All my theories about people have gone to pot today," said Paul Krasnor. "I know it's a masterpiece. But how do *you* know? How can a person so naïve as to start reading the encyclopedia from the letter A in order to cram some culture into himself also have the perception to recognize as a masterpiece a movie that is at least fifteen years ahead of its time, *and* is the nearest anyone working in America has got to making a specifically *sexual* tragedy? Strindberg has done it and there are other Europeans who understand this, but Americans don't. The American writers who are any good—Mark Twain, Melville, Crane, even Henry James—they're asexual basically. They don't even reach the rather superficial sophisticated realism of a Schnitzler. In American writing, sex is what people do *after* and *in between* solving the main problems of their lives, which have to do with making money, becoming somebody, proving their heroism etc. Here sex is always incidental to the main theme, which is why Staupitz is such a giant, and quite alone. They will hate *Arlesia*. They must. Every image in it shatters their cosy, complacent attitudes, it puts the pain into sex whereas they like to think it's all candy floss. Look, I'm sorry, I'm interrupting you in the middle of Aristotle . . . and it's a long way to Z. But if you feel like calling it a day and continuing this discussion, why don't you come round to the apartment and I'll put on a pot of coffee. I have a feeling I must do something about you. Somebody who can appreciate *Arlesia*—and, moreover,

117

can actually manage to get it shown—shouldn't be allowed to waste his time reading encyclopedias."

Alexander was glad to accept the invitation, and he accompanied Paul Krasnor back to his apartment which was in a run-down old mansion on West Eleventh Street, on the western fringe of Greenwich Village, not far from the Hudson River. Like most of the once elegant houses in this street, it had been turned into an apartment building and allowed to deteriorate to such an extent that it was now virtually a slum. Paul Krasnor had what was called a studio, on the top floor. It was called a studio because it consisted of one vast room (the walls having been knocked down as part of some reconstruction project that was later abandoned) which had once had a skylight. But most of the glass panes had been broken and replaced by wooden boards. The first impression, on entering, was of a warehouse full of objects that had no relation to each other. Certainly there was no conventional order about the way in which things were arranged. Bang in the center of the enormous room stood a four-poster bed, hung with heavy drapes. To the far right, under what remained of the skylight, stood a long table of raw, unvarnished wood. On it there was a typewriter, almost totally obscured by the mass of papers, magazines, books and other objects which surrounded it and almost buried it. Behind it, its back to the window, was an adjustable barber's chair. The floor, which consisted of bare, unvarnished floorboards—with a couple of batik mats here and there—was in this part of the room stacked with books that either just lay one on top of the other or filled orange crates to overflowing. These piles and stacks of books, and crates, had been put down in such a way as to leave an erratically twisting network of alleys through which it was possible to crawl or squeeze in order to get from one point to the other. Against another wall stood an enormous wardrobe of intricately carved wood, near it a marble washstand, then a very fine but threadbare French sofa. The room was lit by gas jets. The walls and ceilings were almost black from grime; one section had been washed down (which emphasized the dirtiness of the rest), and somebody had started to paint a huge, life-size mural of a nude, but for some reason the artist had had to stop before he got around to giving the girl's face any features, and he had allowed his colors to run with the result that

118

the featureless nude seemed to be dripping red, green, mauve and yellow blood. An attempt had been made to brighten up another part of the wall (and conceal the dirt) by creating a huge *collage* on it—a kind of expressionist visitor's book, which all guests were asked to sign in their own way. One had left the glassless frames of a pair of lorgnettes dangling from a picture hook; another had nailed a pair of drawers to the wall; somebody else had decorated these with silver tinsel of the kind used on Christmas trees; a wooden steering wheel was suspended as a sort of mobile from the rafters; newspaper headlines, dust jackets, pages of manuscript, sheet music, rolls of toilet paper used as bunting, a great morass of ticker tape—these were some of the other ingredients of the *collage*. It was, apparently, still growing. At present it covered only about one-third of one wall. In other parts of the room, placed more or less at random, could be seen a phonograph with a huge trumpet loudspeaker, a couple of couches made up as beds, the sheets of which could not have been changed for months, a big round stove with the flue going straight up to the ceiling and through it.

"This," said Paul Krasnor with evident pleasure, "is where I live. It's a hell of a place. Impossible to heat in the winter—we all sit around in overcoats, fur caps and gloves looking like Russian refugees. Three flights down to get to the toilet and the water. Gaslights. Spiders. No possibility of privacy—people are in and out all the time, looks like a cross between Grand Central Station, a New Orleans bordello and *The Cabinet of Dr. Caligari*. But I love it. And the rent is only four dollars a week. First, let us find out if there's anyone home. Anyone home?" he shouted, looking around as if expecting people to creep out from under the books or step down from the *collage*. When he had repeated this question three times, a sleepy girl's voice did respond: it seemed to come from the direction of the draped four-poster. "The books, incidentally, can be borrowed, but as I've had to steal most of them I insist on them being returned to me. There is no point in going to the trouble and risk of stealing books from public libraries and bookstores if your friends just steal them from you. If there are any you want to keep you'll have to steal them yourself, but not from me." Another shout from Paul Krasnor, "Lala! . . . Lala?," resulted, some moments later, in a

119

disheveled and sleepy girl's head being protruded from the drapes. "What time is it?" she demanded.

"Almost ten."

"Oh," she said. Then: "Any coffee?"

"Just going to make some."

"Time to get up, I suppose," she declared sleepily. "Where is everyone?"

"They must have left," said Paul Krasnor. "I've been out."

"Oh," she said. She pulled at the drapes, using them as a sort of climbing rope, and heaved herself up out of the bed, looking like a half-drowned water nymph reluctantly surfacing. She looked uncuriously at Alexander. "What are we doing?" she demanded.

"I don't know about you," said Paul Krasnor, "but I propose to sleep tonight. Tomorrow—work."

"Well, if you're going to be like that," she said grumpily, and disappeared again behind the drapes.

Paul Krasnor smiled at Alexander. "Lala," he said. "She's fantastic." He offered no further information or explanation. "Come on," he said, "I promised you some coffee—and advice. The only things of which you will find a plentiful supply in this establishment. Apart from odd women, that is. Are you interested in women? Well, of course you are. Like the books, they can be borrowed but not stolen. How d'you like your coffee? Black?" As he prepared the coffee, first grinding the beans in a coffee mill, he went into a long, autobiographical monologue.

He had come to New York in 1909, at the age of seventeen, in order to write. His people were middle-class, boring and in the button business in Prague. They had a small factory, were quite well off, with a typical bourgeois hatred of the artist and nonconformity. The prospect of going into the button business had so depressed him that he had seriously considered suicide as one of several possible alternatives. In the end, he had decided to come to America. It was further than Paris, and moreover he was fluent in English—having been brought up bilingual because the family did a lot of business with England, and it had been planned that one day he would take charge of the London branch. Besides, reading Conrad had given him a great love of the English language. It was the only language in which he wanted to write. Unfortunately, it was not until he had got to America that he had found out Americans

120

didn't speak English, that they were what he called "sexual cripples," and that they were seeking to perpetuate a culture based on Buffalo Bill, Jesse James and Mom. As a result, he now felt enormous nostalgia for Europe, and as soon as he had got together enough money for the fare he was going to Paris. He was writing a novel, for which he was hopeful of getting a sufficiently large advance to finance this trip, the current rate of exchange being extremely favorable to the dollar. Besides, in Paris, you could always make some money, if you were broke, by writing pornographic books, which was an agreeable and easy thing to do and not so corrupting—as one was merely required to be more rather than less honest—of one's talent at turning out commercial trash for the big-circulation American magazines. Meanwhile, he was trying to finish his novel, which was damn hard, the demands of the flesh being what they were, and women being what *they* were.

Alexander was very taken by Paul Krasnor; never before had he heard anyone talking in such a free and open way. Here was somebody, not all that much older than himself, living exactly as he chose, evidently not giving a damn about what anyone thought of him, having no money, but not unduly worried about this, having achieved nothing solid by the age of twenty-seven, but not feeling bitter or a failure as a result. Paul Krasnor's attitude was one of casual, humorous acceptance. But, above all else, what impressed Alexander was that Paul Krasnor had such enormous assurance, which must come from within himself, because there was really nothing in his external life, unless it was his success with women, to justify it. It was true, as Alexander was now learning, that Paul sold articles or stories, from time to time, to obscure reviews and periodicals, but they paid very little and sometimes not at all. Paul's principal source of income was writing "True Confession" stories and, when times were really hard, taking tourists on conducted walks in Greenwich Village—"to see the artists and Bohemians at work and at play."

Alexander got into the habit of dropping in quite regularly at Paul Krasnor's studio. When there were other people there he did not stay long, for he was still shy of strangers and nervous of expressing his thoughts in public. But with Paul he did not feel this way. He did not mind saying foolish things to him, and having his foolishness pointed

121

out. He did not mind revealing the extent of his ignorance to Paul. And because Paul was always absolutely blunt, and never hesitated to point out to Alexander the fallaciousness, the superficiality, the triteness, the speciousness, the stupidity, the tastelessness, the philistinism, the conventionality, the absurdity, or whatever, of something he had said, or something he was proposing to do, or some attitude he was taking; because of this extreme honesty on Paul's part, such praise as he gave Alexander was valuable. One day Paul said to him: "You know when you say something that you haven't picked up from somebody else, from some second-rate book or something your father said, you're usually sound. Even if previously you knew nothing about the subject, you have the capacity to understand certain things in a flash. You cut out all the tortuous processes of reasoning, calculating, weighing up, assessing—and arrive at the solution, without having to go through all the preliminary stages that other people have to go through. Your mind seems to have the knack of making very quick connections. It's very curious. You seem to be able to test propositions by the sound of them. They sound right to you or they don't sound right, isn't that só? And when you trust this sound that they make inside you, you usually come to the right conclusion, whereas when you reason things out you nearly always come to the wrong conclusion, because you don't have enough knowledge to work things out intellectually. It's a great gift, Alexander. Of course it's very infuriating for people like me that you come along, uninformed, ignorant of some of the most elementary things, and see in a flash something we have ploddingly arrived at after months of reading and discussing and analyzing. We are trying to ride a bicycle by working out the exact angle at which the handlebar has to be turned to prevent us falling off. You just get on the damn thing and ride it." Paul's other friends did not share his belief that Alexander was somehow remarkable, because with them he did not dare to express himself freely. He could not yet assess the quality of his own ideas, could not differentiate between those that were very naïve or stupid and those that were original; therefore he did not like to expose himself before strangers who might be derisive at his expense. At Paul's, nobody felt bound by rules of politeness. Alexander made himself as inconspicuous as possible, never joined in any of the long and often intensely emotional arguments about Freudian psychology, Marxism, the Russian revolution, expressionism, diabolism, capitalism in America, the rights of women, Chaplin, Walter Staupitz, D. W. Griffith, Negro prejudice, Gertrude Stein, Nietzsche, J. Pierpont Morgan, Stephen Raille, and other related and unrelated subjects. While these arguments raged, the proponents often coming to the verge of blows, Alexander sat listening intently but saying nothing. In his absence he was always being talked about disparagingly, because in that circle to be that noncommunicative was considered very perverse—and also rather affected. Nobody accepted his shyness as an excuse. Shyness, they all agreed, was just an extreme form of arrogance.

Apart from Paul's studio, the other place frequented by this group was a saloon known as the Rat Hole, where you could get a mug of beer or a whisky for five cents and have a free lunch thrown in. (Most of the saloons were at that time still providing free lunches with drinks.) The Rat Hole got its name from the dank, gaslit cellar where the artists tended to gather, leaving the upstairs to the Irish, the retired prize fighters, the poker players and the racing types. The cellar smelled of damp, of spilled beer and of sawdust; there was a dumb-waiter in which food was sent down and which also served as a speaking tube up which orders could be shouted. The plates of free lunches were on display upstairs, on the mirrored shelves that lined one wall of the saloon. Alexander was finding out how people could live, sometimes for weeks, on literally no money. Paul, and others like him, could always be relied upon to supply a bed for the night or for several nights; at the Rat Hole they could always get free lunches, even without buying any drinks, provided they were in a group of drinkers. And it was not too difficult to get an extra lunch, which could be wrapped up and kept for the evening.

It was an indication that he had been accepted in the circle that, about a month after first going to the studio, Alexander was allowed to read the manuscript of Paul's unfinished novel, *The Innocent and the Guilty*. Up till then he had wondered about Paul's seriousness as a writer. But now he felt sure of his talent, and ashamed of ever having entertained doubts about his new friend.

CHAPTER THREE

In the late autumn Oskar returned home unexpectedly from one of his trips. Alexander was alone in the apartment—Leushka had gone out to deliver some sewing. His father's cough on the stairs sounded very strident: a hard, convulsive bark in the course of which his vocal chords seemed to give out and the spasm continued with increased violence but without any sound, as if all the sound-making energy had been used up. Alexander opened the door quickly: "Papa, what is it?" Oskar was standing by the door, bent almost double by the cough, a strange, straining expression on his face as he tried to draw air into his lungs. He was sweating coldly, and the features on his face were all disarranged, like a dining table on a storm-tossed ship. "I haven't been feeling so good," said Oskar. "Where's your Mama?"

"She's out," said Alexander.

"Well, I think I lie down a bit."

Alexander helped him to the bed. "You want to take off your things, Papa?"

"No, Alexander." He put a cold, damp hand to the boy's face and felt it lovingly, almost in the way that a blind man might do. "I wish my Leushka was here," he said, and his eyes were moist.

"Papa, are you all right? Perhaps I should call the doctor."

"No," said Oskar, "not necessary. I'm dog-tired, that's what it is. Tires me to talk, isn't that a funny thing. I take a little sleep, in half an hour I'll be a bit rested. You go, Alexander."

Alexander went out of the room, a terrible fear around his heart and in his bowels. He did not know what he should do. Should he go for Dr. Fryerhof? That meant leaving his father alone. Should he ask one of the neighbors to go for the doctor? He had never spoken to the neighbors and it embarrassed him to do so now, in these circumstances. Perhaps he should wait until Mama came home, and then go for the doctor. That was the best thing. He put his knuckle in his mouth and bit on it hard to try and quell the rising panic. "Please, God, don't let anything happen to my Papa," he pleaded. "Please, God. Please. He hasn't had a very nice life and I want to make it up to him. Lately, he always looked so disappointed when he looked at me, sad and disappointed. Please, God, give me a chance to take away that disappointed look from his eyes." There were tears in Alexander's eyes and the bad taste of fear in his mouth. He went out of the kitchen and stood by the closed bedroom door and listened. Nothing. Not a sound. He continued to listen, feeling the fear diminish slightly—his father was sleeping quietly, as soon as he'd had a rest he'd be better. He was run-down after the bad cold he'd had; with his tendency to bronchitis, it had exhausted him; he needed a holiday, sunshine, a little relaxation without worries. At that moment Alexander felt he would gladly rob a bank, if necessary, to give his father these things. "He's entitled," he said out loud, with a sob in his voice, "my God he's entitled." And then he heard it. It was a long hissing sound, like the sound of air coming out of a punctured tire. Though he knew immediately, by the ice around his heart and the grinding pain in his bowels, what this sound meant, his first reaction was to look around—desperately—for some other explanation. He opened the door and went in. "Oh my God!" he said as he saw. "Oh my God! Oh my God! Oh God! Oh God! Oh God! Oh God! Oh God!" He did not know what to do. His father's body and legs were on the bed, but his head and arms were dangling over the edge. His face was a dreadful mauve color, and the air was hissing out of him in sudden spurts, as if out of a pair of bellows. Alexander ran to him and tried to lift him back on to the bed, but he handled him clumsily and the result was that he slid off the bed and on to the floor. His teeth were rattling, and there was a gurgling noise in his throat.

"Papa," Alexander cried, desperately. "Papa!"

He was conscious; he peered at Alexander through an immense distance and his eyes seemed to be saying, in that characteristic Jewish way he had always tried to avoid, "Well, you see, Alexander, that's life." He was moving his lips but no words came.

"Papa, Papa, listen to me, I'm just going out a second. To ask the neighbors to get a doctor." His father's expression appeared to be one of disapproval; he was shaking his

125

head and making a desperate effort to speak through the chattering of his teeth. "Not necessary," he managed to say. Then with a supreme effort: "Your Mama, tell her gentle. . . ." His face seemed to become terribly ugly; it had become an even deeper shade of purple, and Alexander could see all the tiny little veins just under the skin, as if the skin had become transparent. The lips were colorless, and the mouth hung open; his chest heaved several times, with long intervals in between, the gurgling sound in his throat became softer. Alexander felt for the pulse but could not find any; he put his head to his father's chest, but could hear nothing. He ran out of the apartment and banged on the door opposite. There was no answer, presumably no one was in. He tried the one upstairs. A woman in a housecoat came to the door. "My father has been taken very ill," he gasped. "Please get a doctor. Please. Quickly." She took in the boy's white face and panic-stricken eyes.

"I get a doctor," she said and, turning to her husband just behind her: "Elmer, give the boy a sip of something. And go down with him. Don't let him go down alone."

She left immediately, and her husband searched in a cupboard and found a half-full bottle of cherry brandy. He poured Alexander a drink in a tiny liqueur glass, and the boy swallowed it down in a gulp, the sweet, thick, burning liquid sliding down his fear-lined gullet. "Have some more," the man said, handing him the bottle. Alexander put the bottle to his mouth and swallowed avidly—it made him feel sick, but it also slightly dulled the fear and the pain. "We go down," the man said kindly. "We take with us the bottle."

The man came down with Alexander and he looked at Oskar on the floor and felt his pulse and his heart, and then he took the boy's arm and led him into the kitchen. There were several neighbors standing outside now, on the landing, and throughout the building doors were opening and people were coming out on to the landing and leaning over the rails and calling to the people on the landing below to find out what was going on.

When the doctor came—he was a young man and a stranger to Alexander—he listened to Oskar's heart with a stethoscope, felt his pulse, took out a long hypodermic, which he filled from a glass phial, and injected it into the chest. When he had done this he waited for a few moments, holding the limp wrist, his fingers on the pulse. Half a dozen of the neighbors were in the room now, watching silently, their heads shaking sorrowfully. Eventually the doctor released the limp hand and placed it gently on the floor. He turned to Alexander. "Your father? Poor man. I'm afraid he's gone." At this, as if it were some kind of signal, the women gave sympathetic sobs—though none of them had ever had more than a "Good day" out of Oskar. The doctor looked sharply at Alexander. "Help me get him on the bed," he said firmly. He took the legs himself and Alexander took the arms and they lifted his father on to the big bed and covered his face with a towel, which was the only thing Alexander could find on the spur of the moment. While the doctor was washing his hands in the kitchen, he asked: "Your mother is out? So she doesn't know anything?"

With the realization that he would have to tell his mother, Alexander began to sob uncontrollably. The doctor finished drying his hands. "That's it," he said approvingly as he watched Alexander sobbing, "get rid of it before your mother comes back. You'll need to be calm then. To be able to look after her. I'm going to give you something for your mother, something to calm her and make her sleep. It's for her. I don't think you need anything, do you? You're all right now." And he wrapped a single pill in a piece of paper and gave it to Alexander. "There are some formalities," he said, "but we'll take care of all that tomorrow."

"How am I going to tell her?" Alexander gasped.

"D'you want me to do it?" the doctor asked. "There is no way of doing it that won't cause her suffering. You just have to accept that. But it might be less of an ordeal for *you*, now, if I told her. You tell me what you want."

"No," Alexander said after a while. "I'll tell her. Thank you, doctor."

The doctor left, but the neighbors remained on the landing and on the stairs, and the woman on whose door he had knocked, and her husband, remained with Alexander in the kitchen. It was getting dark outside and here and there lights were coming on in near-by buildings. Alexander looked out of the window and saw that outside everything was the same, unchanged. In the market some of the stall-holders were packing away their goods and calling good-humoredly to each other; horses were being given their feed; a woman was taking in her washing from the fire escape where it had been hung out to dry; two women, leaning out of windows on different stories, were having a loud gossip— and in the bedroom his father's face covered with the towel.

It was almost an hour after the doctor had left that Alexander saw his mother coming down the street, walking very unhurriedly, a shopping bag in each hand, her eyes going up to the window because she knew that Alexander often looked out for her. He hid his face as he watched her getting nearer; about ten yards from the entrance she became conscious of the group of neighbors silently watching her approaching, and a look of fear came into her face. She started to walk faster and then to run; Alexander saw her run inside and then he heard her coming up the stone stairs. As she came up she was looking at the faces of the neighbors she passed, not daring to ask, trying to decipher the meaning of their tragic looks, their hand-wringing, their headshaking. Outside the apartment she saw Alexander coming to her, and for a moment she felt a surge of relief: the child was all right. Then, taking in his terrible pallor, his anguished eyes, the headshaking neighbors, her face screwed up into an expression of unbearable pain. "Oshkerle!" she screamed. Alexander helped her into the kitchen and made her sit down on a chair: she was still holding the shopping bags. She looked at Alexander's face, and at the faces of the strangers.

She insisted on seeing him; the towel was removed and she stood for a long, long time at the foot of the bed, crying silently, taking a deep gulp of air every so often, and then going on with her silent crying that seemed to alter the whole shape and structure of her face. She was swaying on her feet, Alexander tried to make her take the pill the doctor had left for her, but she refused it. "What for?" she said. "So I shouldn't feel? A pain like this is meant it should be felt." It took a lot of coaxing and urging and persuading to get her out of the bedroom; once in the kitchen, the torrent of pain poured out and her weeping and wailing could be heard throughout the entire building, and it carried across to the other buildings, and in a dozen different apartments people turned questioningly to each other and closed their windows, and the madwoman came to her window and laughed.

That night Alexander and his mother slept, when they

could manage to drop off for a few moments, on the folding bed in the kitchen, fully clothed, and pressed close together.

Alexander held together, like a cracked plate, until after the funeral. He was all the time on the brink of something, he could feel that. In his nightmares he relived his father's death in innumerable variations. He felt stretched so taut that the slightest touch would break him; he felt dehydrated of all energy, the reservoir was empty, there was nothing left in him that he could call on.

The violent palpitations started about ten days after his father's death. His heart beat so hard he thought it would burst, he could not calm its frantic thudding; he lay on the bed, choking and gasping for breath while his mother put ice from the icebox around his heart and made him smell a handkerchief soaked in vinegar. He felt his pulse and it was so fast the individual beats were indistinguishable; there was a terrible tightness in his chest and a dull pressure all around his heart, as if it were slowly being crushed in a vise. His mother sent for the doctor and the one who came was the same young man who had come to his father at the end.

"Well, now, what's the matter?" he asked, reaching for Alexander's pulse.

"I can't breathe," Alexander gasped, "and my heart hurts. . . ."

The doctor listened to his chest with the stethoscope, made him sit up in bed and touch his toes several times, then he made him get up and touch his toes, then he made him run while standing still; after each of these exercises he listened to his heart.

"Did he have rheumatic fever as a child?" he asked Leushka. She shook her head: "Measles. And some trouble with his tonsils and his adenoids. He had to have them out."

"Well," he said, "there's nothing wrong with his heart."

"Then what is it, doctor? He had such a terrible attack."

"Nerves."

"He always suffered with his nerves," she agreed. "So it's only nerves?"

"I'd like to talk to him alone," the doctor said.

When Leushka had left, the doctor, whose name was

129

Dirrer, said thoughtfully: "Your father's death hit you hard? Of course it was a big shock for you, seeing him die."

"I felt so ill today," Alexander said, "I felt I was dying."

"Well, you're not," the doctor said firmly. "There's nothing organically the matter with you. I'm sure of that, though if you like we can arrange for a more thorough examination in a hospital."

"Then what's the matter with me? I feel so ill. I can hardly walk. I have no energy. And I feel these pains around my heart all the time."

"It's nerves," said Dr. Dirrer. "What we call neurasthenia, one of the symptoms is the patient's conviction that he is physically ill. Believe me, there's absolutely nothing the matter with you organically. Your heart is sound."

"But what do I do, I feel so awful?"

"What's your sex life like?" he said in a matter-of-fact way.

"Oh, all right," said Alexander.

"You practice *coitus interruptus?*"

"I don't understand."

"Withdrawal. As a form of contraception."

"No."

"Good. Don't, if you possibly can help it." Dr. Dirrer was putting away his stethoscope in his bag. "Stimulation without release plays havoc with the nervous system. That's why I'm glad you don't practice *coitus interruptus.* Much better to do what you do—use a condom, a simple French letter. Well, I'm sure you're going to be fine. Neurasthenia is largely something one has to cure oneself of. If you feel you'd like to, come and have a talk with me at my office, if ever you have a problem on your mind. I'm going to give you a prescription. Something for the palpitations. But the thing is just don't worry about your heart beating fast, does it no harm. Think how fast an athlete's heart has to beat."

For a time after Dr. Dirrer had left Alexander felt much better, and during the next few days it seemed as if a great weight had been taken away and he was able to breathe again and taste the sweetness of the air. And then he became ill again. Going up the stairs to the apartment he fainted; neighbors had to carry him up; as they were about to put him down on the big bed he came to, and the most terrifying panic surged up inside him. "No," he screamed,

130

"not there!" After that he hardly dared to venture outside; he had only to walk half a dozen yards down the street and he would suddenly become dizzy, everything would go round and round, his breathing would become labored and he would have to stagger back to the apartment and lie down on his narrow bed. The fear was like some dead thing inside him.

He was examined by several doctors, and they all said more or less what Dr. Dirrer had said, that there was nothing organically the matter with him, and he was suffering from nerves, partly due to the shock of his father's death, partly due to the normal emotional disturbances of adolescence. But Alexander did not believe the doctors with their pat, reassuring phrases, their glib little labels. He believed what he felt: the drowning fear that hardly ever left him now, the heaviness in his limbs, the lack of blood in his head, the horrors of the night. He did not go to work. He felt he might have an attack any time, and the thought of being far from home when it happened, among strangers, multiplied the fear. He behaved like an invalid. Any exertion exhausted him. He spent much of his time in bed, and if he moved as far as the window, or remade his own bed, he felt tired out and had to rest. He had decided that he could not go out because coming up the stairs would be too much for him, it would kill him. He ate very little, and he became even thinner, and his face began to look very drawn and there were great dark rings under his eyes. Looking at himself in the mirror, which he did constantly, he was sure he was dying: he had the appearance of a dying man. The doctors were lying to him; they didn't want to tell him the truth, which was that he was incurable: that was why they were giving him no treatment. Why else would they do nothing for him when he felt so bad all the time? Obviously there was nothing they could do. Several times he thought the moment had come, felt himself slipping away, and when the doctor came he always felt a little better, and actually believed for a while that maybe he was not dying. But what was the use? If he felt this bad all the time, and he was getting worse rather than better, he might just as well be dead. Before him stretched an endless vista of sickness and decline.

When he had been away from work for four weeks, a letter came from Mr. Seiermann. It said, "My dear Alexander,

It grieves me greatly to hear of your sad loss and I would like to send you my condolences. To lose a father at your young age is a terrible thing to happen to anyone, and my heart is full of sorrow for you. Still, it is now over four weeks since he passed away and though I am fully understanding your grief, and it does you credit, I got to point out to you that usually nobody gets off this long from work, even if they have lost a father. In view of this, I have got to tell you, Alexander, that as your mother has written to me to say that you are not yet well enough to return to work, I got unfortunately to replace you in the organization. I am sure you understand that in a business matter I cannot allow my personal sentiments to interfere. Incidentally, I am returning to you your $500 investment in *Arlesia* as I have now heard from my other partners in this venture that they do not feel it is right for a former employee, who is not a regular investor and has not invested in any of the other ventures, to have a piece of this picture. Hoping you will soon be better. With best wishes of health and prosperity and condolences on your sad loss. William Seiermann, President, Fine Pictures Exchange."

There was a check for $500 in the envelope. No payment had been made for the period since Alexander had stopped coming to work. It seemed yet another sign of the inevitable downward slide he was taking. He had been fired. He had no job. In his precarious state of health, how could he start a new job—with all that entailed in the way of asserting himself—or even find one? Everything seemed to be collapsing all around him and he could foresee nothing but disaster. If his mother should become ill there would be no money coming in at all. How would they live? He was sinking deeper and deeper into this mood of despondency and he was in the grip of a terrible, dull inertia: he sat for hours looking straight ahead of him, not even out of the window, but at the blank wall, and Leushka seeing him like this feared that he must be losing his mind.

Five weeks after his father's death, Leushka came into the bedroom—nowadays he had the big bed to himself all the time—to tell Alexander that somebody had come to see him. It was midday, but the room was dark, Alexander having insisted that the heavy curtains, which he had made his mother put up, should be kept drawn, as the daylight hurt his eyes. The windows had not been opened for perhaps two weeks and the room had a musty, damp and airless smell. Paul Krasnor stood in the doorway, staring into this murk, his eyes trying to find Alexander among all these shadows, his nostrils twitching with distaste.

"Alexander? Where the hell are you? It's Paul Krasnor. D'you mind if I draw the curtains, can't see a damn thing."

"No. Please don't." A pause. "The daylight hurts my eyes."

Paul started to feel his way across the room, toward the sound of Alexander's voice, swearing as he bumped into things; eventually he took some matches out of his pocket and struck one. In the flickering flame he could see Alexander, very pale and with the look of someone slowly wasting away, sitting up in the bed, propped up by three large pillows.

"I'll light a candle," Alexander offered belatedly.

Paul sat himself next to the bed and gave Alexander a sharp, assessing look: he took in the dullness of his eyes, the pallor, the lack of reaction to his arrival.

"I heard you've been sick," Paul said.

"As you can see," said Alexander, "I still am."

"What is it?"

"The doctors don't seem to know. Or they won't tell me."

"You took sick soon after your father's death?"

"Yes." There was a silence and then Paul asked what Alexander considered a very strange question, in the circumstances.

"What sort of a man was he?"

"What?"

"Your father. What sort of man? Did you get on with him?"

"I was a great disappointment to him. He wanted me to study and have a profession. You know, I saw him die." He gave a little sob.

"Yes," said Paul thoughtfully. "Yes. Well, the thing is, what do we do about you? First of all we have to get you out of here. If you continue to breathe in this foul air much longer you really will be sick."

"You're like all the others," said Alexander bitterly. "You think I'm a hypochondriac—do I have to die to prove I'm sick?"

"Would you let me do one thing? Would you let me draw the curtains and open the windows?" In the candlelight, Paul could see the consternation on Alexander's face at this suggestion.

"If you want to," said Alexander at length. "All right."

Moving quickly and purposefully, Paul pulled open the heavy curtains and opened the windows wide: early winter sunlight came into the room, stirring up the dust; and a moment later the sharp, fresh-tasting air was sucked in through the open window, as if into a vacuum. Alexander was covering his eyes, almost as if he wanted to tear them out, against the sudden blinding brightness.

"Where are your things?" Paul demanded. "Ah yes, here, trousers, shirt . . . where are the other things?"

"What for?" stammered Alexander.

"I thought we might go for a walk," said Paul. "It's such a nice day."

"You don't seem to realize," said Alexander, "that I'm sick. I get faint just walking along the street, and I'm too weak to climb up the stairs."

"That's all right," said Paul in a matter-of-fact way. "We'll hire a cab to accompany us as we walk, and if you should feel faint we just put you in the cab. If you should have an attack . . . well, with a cab standing by, you are a lot nearer to medical help than in this room. We just drive straight to the nearest hospital. As for getting you up these stairs, should you be too weak to make the climb, I will happily carry you up. You're so thin it is not going to be any great burden. Have you any other objections to going out?"

Every day, for the next eight days, Paul came to fetch Alexander to take him for a walk; the length of the walk increased each day, and by the seventh day Alexander was prepared to take the risk of dismissing the cab. He still carried a hip flask of brandy, and took the occasional swig when he felt the faintness coming on, but now that he was beginning to eat properly again he was no longer so weak.

"You're getting better," Paul told him. "You really are."

"I still get these terrible fears at night," Alexander said, "and I can't sleep because I'm afraid I shall have an attack in my sleep and I keep seeing my father's face, all purple and ugly. I think it's the ugliness of it—of death—that horrifies me most of all."

134

Paul laughed. "Fortunately you can't see yourself when you're dead."

"Aren't you afraid of death, Paul?"

"No. Not in the least. As a matter of fact, I don't think *you're* afraid of death. I think you're afraid of not being, which is something else entirely. But if you still think you're going to die, I have a suggestion. First reassure yourself that you're not dying—put your mind at rest. Then, having done so, start going seriously into this whole question of dying—from the philosophical, the artistic, the metaphysical points of view. I think once you are able to accept the idea of your own death—once you are able to be unhorrified by it—you won't worry about it any more. First, however, you must reassure yourself you are not actually dying. This kind of intellectual exploration ought not to be undertaken in a state of fear. The trouble is you don't believe the doctors who have examined you and said that there's nothing the matter with you. Even if you believe them at the time, when you have one of your panic attacks you think maybe they lied to you, maybe you *are* desperately ill. Have I summed it up accurately? Yes? Good. I have a simple solution for you. How much money have you got?"

"About four hundred dollars."

"All right then. Go to an insurance company and take out the biggest life insurance you can get for four hundred dollars. Before they insure you, they'll send you to a doctor, who will give you a thorough examination. If they accept you, if they insure your life for whatever it is—ten thousand dollars say—even you will have to be convinced that you're all right. The insurance doctor is not going to lose the company $10,000 as part of a conspiracy to keep you from finding out the truth about your state of health. This is a good, sound, rational argument which you can make to yourself when you have a panic attack. It ought to convince you you're not dying."

Alexander did exactly what Paul had suggested; he was examined by the insurance doctor; he was given a clean bill of health, he was accepted as a first-class life by the insurance company; and now, slowly, he began to feel better.

In the dream he was in a place near the ocean, in a sort of tunnel where there were many other people, some of them sleeping huddled together, like refugees, their meager belongings piled around them. Others were dancing, their movements curiously slowed down, to the music of a hurdy-gurdy. One of the sleeping people was his mother. He reached up to where the empty socket of an electric light fixture hung from the ceiling, at the end of a length of cord, and he inserted a light bulb into the socket. As he switched on the light, water started to trickle out of the bulb, which was perforated with holes like a shower head. Alexander said, "Oh my God, oh my God." The water was pouring down, drenching the dancers and the sleepers; the dancers went on dancing in their unnaturally slow way, but those who had been asleep were scrambling to their feet in a state of panic, gathering up their belongings and their children, and looking for a way out of the tunnel—they were running, packed close together, toward a distant point of light. His mother was being swept forward in this mass of stampeding humanity, desperately looking around for Alexander, whom she could not see. The water was around their ankles, and it was rising fast: now it was up to their thighs, now their waists, now their necks. Now there was only space for a head between the water and the ceiling of the tunnel. Alexander was outside in the open, running along a twisting mountain road; from far below him came the screams and cries of the drowning. They were a long way away in the valley of the earth. He was safe; he knew he was safe up here, and he continued to climb higher, and presently he saw that the world was a great flat lake from which only the peaks of the mountains protruded, like many icebergs. He was on one of these peaks, and he was safe. Then he saw it: in the far distance the sky was black, and this blackness was moving slowly but inexorably toward him; as it came closer it moved faster, and he saw that it was an enormous wave—as if a dam a thousand feet high had crumbled and all the water it had been holding back was now sweeping toward him. This wave was as high as the sky, and there was no peak he could climb to escape it. As this mountain of water came closer, and he looked up to see its great height, the man who had been standing nearby turned to face him. It was his father, whom he recognized from the knowing look in his eyes as the perennial pursuer of his dreams, though in appearance he resembled Moses receiving the Commandments. He was shaking his head sadly—and knowingly—as they waited for the great wave, which was coming nearer all the time, and there was such a disappointed look in his father's eyes, and Alexander thought: it's my fault for switching on the light. There was only one way out and that was to wake up.

Alexander had not worked for five months. He spent much of his time at Paul's studio. When his mother brought up the question of finding a job, he said he did not yet feel well enough to go to work. His father had had life insurance, and under the terms of his will about a thousand dollars went to Leushka. They had never had as much money as this when Oskar was alive. Moreover, now that Leushka had to provide food only for herself and Alexander, and did not have to count on some of her housekeeping money being "borrowed" by Oskar to finance one of his trips, her earnings from sewing and private dressmaking were quite adequate to maintain their modest standard of living. She was worried that Alexander did not seem to have any desire to work, but there was no hardship, and she thought that perhaps it was best that he should not embark on a career until he was really fit again. The terrible time he'd had all winter must have exhausted him, and she was happy that he seemed to be getting better now, recovering his strength. Her main concern was that, though he was certainly looking better and eating regularly, he did not seem to have any drive, any desire to get on, and was content to loaf around with his Bohemian friends. She had to admit that Paul had done a great deal for him, in the way of taking him out of himself, and that he had helped Alexander in a way that none of the doctors had been able to, but still she could not really approve of these new friends of his, layabouts living from hand to mouth, without jobs or regular incomes. Still, she didn't want to interfere; many boys were married and had a family by his age, and a business as well, but Alexander was different from them, more sensitive and nervous—probably due to having been alone so much as a child—and it might take him longer to find his way.

CHAPTER FOUR

The item in *Variety* read: "Exchange man William (Willi) Seiermann, who did the lifesaving surgery on *Arlesia*—by cutting out the dirt—says he's going into production for himself. Cleaned up, *Arlesia* has been doing socko business everywhere, and because of unique deal most of the coin is going to Seiermann. It's estimated (but uncorroborated) he'll make close to a million dollars out of the picture everybody else considered a write off. Sign of the former smalltime theater operator's rise: this week he moved headquarters of his Fine Pictures Exchange into swank new premises on top of the 3,500-seater Broadway Dome." Alexander read the item several times before showing it to Paul.

"Yes," Paul said, "I saw the new *Arlesia*. It's ruined—butchered. They've cut out one and a half hours and they've turned it into a conventional story about two sisters in love with the same man. It's still ten times better made, and better acted, than the equivalent thing made by somebody else, but it's meaningless. It's not the same film."

"To think," said Alexander, "that I persuaded him to take *Arlesia*—and now they say he's made a million dollars out of it."

"That's the sort of man who makes money," said Paul. "You need to have his brand of philistinism and insensitivity and ignorance to be able to butcher a masterpiece. You and I couldn't do it. We'd put out the uncut film, go bankrupt in the cause of culture, probably land in jail for obscenity. It's the Seiermanns who take over everywhere—in films, in magazine publishing, in newspapers, in the theater. And now it's going to happen with radio. They'll control everything. And it's because we—those who think like us—don't want to dirty our hands getting involved in commerce. We sit here theorizing, but we don't do anything. It's the Seiermanns who do things. They have an instinct; they are of the herd and with the herd—they know what they can get away with. We're always going to be defeated because we have no power, and we're squeamish about the process of acquiring power. So the most we can ever be are court favorites, licensed jesters, the recipients of patronage. Here you have a towering genius like Walter Staupitz, you'd think nobody would dare to meddle with his work, and along comes some illiterate with nothing inside his head except a sort of animal instinct for smelling where the money is, and he not only makes a fortune out of ruining Staupitz's picture but, in the process, puts himself in a position where he can *employ* Staupitz—and others—and decide what sort of work they will do. Did you read Stephen Raille in *New Republic?*" He picked up the paper and read from it: " 'There is no artist alive,' " he read, " 'who can, by virtue of his artistry alone, keep open the increasingly complex channels of communication on which he is dependent in order to be able to continue to practice his art. The irony of the situation is that the businessmen, who control these channels, are even more dependent on the artist than he is on them. Without the businessman, the artist can reach only a very limited public. But without the artist, this type of businessman ceases to exist: he has nothing to sell. The solution would seem to be for the artist to overcome his natural reluctance to become involved in commerce and seek to gain control of the channels of communication on which he depends.' " Paul put down the paper, and said: "This is something Raille understands, because he's worked on newspapers and he understands the machinery of commerce. His books sell, he makes a lot of money, the machinery of commerce is working in his favor, he is in a position to say all this without laying himself open to accusations of personal bitterness. I admire that man almost more than anyone else writing in America today. He has courage and he has never written a dishonest word. I think *The Manipulators* is the best American novel of our generation, and the most uncompromisingly honest one, and I think he understands better than anyone else writing today the way in which, in a puritan country like America, the unrealized sex drives, the desires for sexual conquest and triumph, are expressed—are to some extent replaced by—the money-making and the getting-on and the making-something-of-myself urges."

"I'm glad you like Raille," said Alexander, "I've hero-worshiped him since I was a child. I remember once my father pointed him out to me in a restaurant. Raille had written one of those exposés of corruption in . . . New

Jersey, or somewhere like that. I remember that seemed very noble to me: standing up against great big powerful concerns—the Mayor, the City, the police force—just with words, and winning. I read all his stuff after that day, and it gave me a great respect for words, for their power."

A dozen times Alexander had approached the entrance of the Dome, peered—with a forced air of casualness—into its opulent interior, where there seemed to be a permanent guard of some half a dozen uniformed ushers, their beige tunics ablaze with gold epaulettes, gold braid and scarlet piping. One, who had more gold than any of the others and carried a short swagger stick with a mother-of-pearl tip, looked particularly intimidating as he paced up and down, scrutinizing the incoming crowd, with the air of a general just waiting for the right moment to give the order to attack. Each time Alexander approached the entrance, and caught a glimpse of the wide, white marble staircase, the heavy crystal chandeliers, the paneled lobby, the green marble columns supporting the dome, he felt his heart begin to thump and his mouth go dry at the audaciousness—the impertinence—of his plan. To march into Mr. Seiermann's office and demand his rightful share of the million dollar profit of *Arlesia*. He had invested $500 in the venture, and surely an investment once accepted could not be returned, Alexander felt this must be so. And yet, it seemed he couldn't muster enough courage to walk past that over-dressed doorman (who would be sure to stop him and ask what he wanted); then how would he ever be able to confront Mr. Seiermann and make his demand sound convincing? He was angry with his own body, that it should let him down in this way, making it so difficult, virtually impossible, to do what in his mind he had already decided to do. As he made the umpteenth approach to the entrance— by now he felt he was being watched by all the ushers—his heart was pounding so hard that he was as out of breath as if he had just run a mile. What the hell! he thought. If I collapse, they'll just have to pick me up and send me home by ambulance. What the hell! I can't allow myself to be blackmailed by my own body! Determinedly, he walked into the theater—it seemed an immense distance to the marble staircase. The thick carpeting was like quagmire under his feet—he was staring straight ahead, mesmerized by the huge monogrammed BD, wreathed by twisting loops of film, in the center of the rug. He marched straight ahead. An usher appeared from behind one of the pillars. "Yes, sir? Can I help you?"

"It's all right. I know my way," barked Alexander, his nervousness making him sound gruffer than he would normally have dared to be. He kept straight on, ran up the marble stairs two at a time, strode across the mezzanine, his eyes probing into niches and under arches for the door of the private elevator that he had been told would take him straight up to Mr. Seiermann's office. There it was, glittering bronze. He gave a forceful wrench of the handle: no movement—it was locked. What to do now? He was conscious of an usher watching him. Alexander turned and called to him: "Come and open this elevator, please."

"This is Mr. Seiermann's private elevator, sir," said the usher. "The main entrance to all the offices is from Fifty-first Street."

"I know, I know," snapped Alexander irritably. "Just do what you're told. Open this elevator."

"Is Mr. Seiermann expecting you, sir?"

"What's your name?" Alexander demanded. "Are you new?" He spoke in a clipped, authoritative manner, dictated more by his lack of breath than by self-assurance. "Don't you know my face?"

"I'm very sorry, sir," said the usher and unlocked the elevator door.

As he sped upward he wiped the soaking wet palms of his hands on a handkerchief and tried to slow his breathing to a more normal rate. On the seventh floor the elevator opened on to a large empty hall. By coming up this way he had avoided the secretaries he knew would be sitting in the outer office. He was faced by a semicircle of three doors. He knocked on the first—no answer. He listened. He thought he could hear the sound of a voice from the middle door. He knocked and turned the knob simultaneously, at the same time fixing an innocent-surprised expression on his face.

"Oh, Mr. Seiermann, I'm sorry—did I come in the wrong way?"

Hearing the door open, Seiermann had swiveled round in his chair to face his unexpected visitor. He was in the process of giving dictation to a secretary.

"Alexander!" said Seiermann, momentarily startled. For a moment he looked angry. "You came up in my private elevator?"

"I guess so," said Alexander, grinning sheepishly. Now that he was in the office his nervousness had diminished. "I didn't know it was your *private* elevator, Mr. Seiermann."

"Well how about that! How about that!" said Seiermann. "With the rent I pay, and any Tom, Dick and Harry—I'm sorry, Alexander, I don't mean it personally—can just march into my office. What for do I have a secretary and a receptionist? Well, well! Not your fault," he added magnanimously. "It's those lion-trainers in the lobby. So busy polishing their buttons they got no time to do their job. Well, Alexander. You feeling better?"

"Much better, thank you, Mr. Seiermann. I was wanting to have a word with you."

"Sure, any time, any time. But you should make an appointment. Right now I'm very busy."

"You don't have a few minutes now?"

Seiermann gave his secretary a weary, martyred look. Then he said: "Of course, Alexander, for you I always have got a few minutes' time. Miss Troe, leave us a few minutes."

When she had left, Seiermann got up and waved his hand around the office. "Bit better than the old Bijou—hmm?"

Alexander took a quick look round: oak paneling, black leather armchairs and settees, an entire wall consisting of a vast window, the Venetian blinds of which were three-quarters closed at the moment, shutting out the view of surrounding buildings.

"It's impressive," said Alexander. "Very impressive."

"Sit down, Alexander. Tell me, your health is better now? It worried me a lot you were sick. I thought a lot about you, Alexander. You know I always took a personal interest in you, not like employer and employee. You were just a kid you started with me, and now you're grown and you're getting to be a good-looking young man. What was it you wanted to talk to me about, Alexander?"

"Well," said Alexander, taking a deep breath. "I feel I've got some money due to me. Not I feel—I know."

"I didn't pay you all your salary?" Seiermann asked, innocently. "If that is the case you can be sure I put it right immediately."

142

"It's not my salary. It's the investment I made in *Arlesia*. You remember I put up five hundred dollars?"

"Yes, I got some vague recollection. Now what happened about that? Didn't I send you back the money? If I remember correctly I sent you back the money, explaining I couldn't accept the investment on account of . . ."

"That's not the point, Mr. Seiermann."

"If you didn't get your five hundred dollars back, of course, I see to it straight away."

"Mr. Seiermann, the point is I made an investment. That five hundred dollars, the way I understood it, gave me a one per cent share in the profits—your profits—on *Arlesia*. I read in *Variety* you made a profit of close to a million dollars. That means my share is ten thousand dollars."

A stunned, pained expression came over Seiermann's face. "I'm afraid I got to correct you there, Alexander. It's quite true you offered to put up five hundred dollars, and it's true I was considering accepting your investment. But, as you remember, after consultation with my other investors, I was obliged to return your money, which canceled your investment."

"Mr. Seiermann, you returned the money *after* the picture had opened, when it was already possible to see it would be a big money-maker. I don't think any court of law would accept the validity of an investment being returned in those circumstances. If the whole fifty thousand dollars had been lost for some reason, my five hundred dollars would have gone down the drain with it—isn't that so? If that's so, then I'm entitled to a share in the profits."

"Alexander, are you suggesting that I want to trick you or something? Is that a nice thing to say, when I always regarded you more like a relative, a son almost, than an employee? When I let you walk into my office like a close friend, when I let you come up in my private elevator—anybody else would have had you kicked out on your neck. Now is that a nice thing to even think about me?"

"I'm not saying you're trying to trick me, Mr. Seiermann. I'm just saying I'm entitled to ten thousand dollars, and I haven't got it."

"Entitled, entitled," sighed Seiermann. "All of a sudden every Tom, Dick and Harry is entitled. Let me explain something to you about business, Alexander. When you came to me and asked me if I would allow you to invest five hundred dollars . . ."

"*Allow!* Mr. Seiermann, you were desperately looking around to raise the money, you even asked me if I knew anyone else who'd like to invest."

"I think your recollection is misleading you there, Alexander, but we won't argue about that. As I was saying, when you asked to invest five hundred dollars, I let my personal feelings for you, which you know have always been the warmest, to influence me. As far as I personally was concerned, it would make me happy to see you make some money, but what I wasn't considering was the business aspect. In business, like in life, Alexander, there has got to be ethics, and what sort of ethics would it be if I let all my other investors in, who had backed me up to the hilt when we didn't have such a sure winner, and they lost money? In a situation like that, Alexander, my personal feelings don't count. I have got to do right by my investors, and when they pointed out to me the unfairness, to them, of accepting your investment I saw they were right, and I returned your money to you in a right and proper—and legal way."

"Are you forgetting, Mr. Seiermann, that it was my idea you should buy *Arlesia*, that I told you how it could be cut so it would be showable, and that I practically arranged the whole deal?"

"And aren't you forgetting, Alexander, that you were working for me at the time, that I paid you a good salary, and that whatever you did was part of your job, for which you got paid? I built up the organization, I established the credit, I had the investors that made it possible to buy *Arlesia*. When Lewis Sholt came to you with the proposition, he came to an employee of the Seiermann organization. You think he would have come to you, Alexander Sondorpf, with five hundred lousy dollars in the savings bank?" Seiermann was becoming emotional. "It hurts me, Alexander, that after all I have done for you you should come in here making accusations. I ought to kick you the hell out of here. Accusations! That's what you get trying to be nice to people."

"Mr. Seiermann," said Alexander, going very red, "I'm not making accusations."

"You're practically accusing me of dishonesty," stormed

144

Seiermann. "You're practically calling me a swindler. I don't take that from nobody, and not from any snotty-nosed brat that I picked out of the streets and taught the picture business. I'm a fair-minded man, and I don't lose my temper easy, but some things I don't take. You want to make trouble and I'll show you you're up against Willi Seiermann, and I'll give you trouble, you'll be sorry you ever had the cheek, the downright *chutzpah*, to come up into my office—like a thief—in my private elevator, that nobody is allowed to use without my personal permission." He was practically screaming now. In the middle of this tirade the telephone rang. Seiermann picked up the receiver. "Yes?" he shouted into it. Then, with lightning abruptness, his manner changed. "Sarah, my dear, I'm tied up in a business conference right now. Yes? I got so much work I can't tell you when I come home. Maybe I sleep tonight at the office. Sure, I'll be comfortable. I probably be working late into the night, I rather don't disturb you and the children. I take a bite to eat round the corner. Yes, yes. Sure. Kiss the children for me." He blew kisses into the telephone and then replaced the receiver with a bang, immediately assuming again the outraged demeanor that the telephone call from his wife had momentarily displaced. "You understand what I'm saying to you?" he threw at Alexander. "I make myself clear?"

"Mr. Seiermann," Alexander said, "it wasn't my intention to offend you. I thought this was something we could discuss in a reasonable way."

"Then why d'you come in here accusing?"

"It seemed to me that I was entitled to some money out of the profits. Maybe not one per cent—but *some* money. I felt at least you would recognize that I was morally entitled to some of the profits."

"Morally entitled," said Seiermann, weighing the words. "You know what you're morally entitled? A good kick up the ass, that's what you're morally entitled." He reached into a drawer of the desk, took out a file, and leafed through some papers. "Here," he said, "this is the letter. I read it to you. 'Dear Alexander, I acknowledge the receipt of $500 from you, which you wish to invest in the acquisition of the distribution franchise of *Arlesia*.' *Wish*," thundered Seiermann, *"that you wish to invest*. Where does it say, tell me, that I *accept* the investment? Where is the

145

contract? Where does it say anything about percentages? If you think that this piece of paper entitles you to one cent you're making a big mistake." He seemed to be making a great effort to be calm and reasonable. "Alexander," he said, "you read in some newspaper I make a million dollars. It's a wicked thing they said. I don't pretend I didn't do very nicely out of *Arlesia*, but you got any idea of my expenses? You know what this office costs me in rent? Fifteen thousand dollars a year. Just rent. Some yellow press reporter jerk writes I made a million dollars, and I find I've got two brothers and three sisters, and their wives and their husbands and their children, to support. Not to mention I've got a wife and two baby girls and a father-in-law myself. Everybody's digging in my pocket, They all *want, want, want.* It's all grab and take. My two brothers, you think I ever heard a word out of them till they get to hear I make a little bit of money, and then in two seconds they're here like a pack of wolves. Relatives I didn't know I had suddenly find out I'm their long-lost cousin. Wherever I go people come up to me and say, 'You know, Mr. Seiermann, it's a funny thing, you won't believe it could be true . . .' And I say, 'Yes, I know. You're my cousin Dolly.' And they say, 'However did you guess, Willi? You must have seen the family resemblance in the face.' So many cousins I've got all of a sudden, those uncles of mine must have been sowing wild oats from here to China."

All of Alexander's artificially aroused confidence had deserted him now. He felt cheap and grasping, and he felt the absurdity of having dared to march into this office to demand $10,000 to which, clearly, he was not entitled, morally or legally. "I'm sorry, Mr. Seiermann," he said, "I'm sorry I've added to your difficulties in this way. I just thought, well I must have been wrong. . . ."

A benign, forgiving look spread over Seiermann's well-fleshed features. He now radiated good will as, a little earlier, he had radiated righteous wrath, "Alexander," he said, "I know you been sick, I understand you been suffering with your nerves, so I don't hold anything you said against you. I'm not a man to bear grudges against anyone. It's all forgotten. In fact, I'll do more—to show you how I feel about you. You want to work for me again, you can have your job back. My brother Leo is taking over the exchange side of the organization. You want to work as his assistant,

146

the job is yours. We had a good year, so I raise you your salary ten dollars, is that fair? Think it over, let me know in the next three days, because I'm going out to the West Coast to look into the studio question. Maybe you read I'm planning to go into production. I figured I seen enough what people pay to see I should be able to make successful pictures. I got a dream, Alexander, I got a dream to make beautiful pictures—pictures people *want* to see. That'll make them feel better in their lives, that will give them a little beauty and happiness. Not all this ugliness you get in pictures. Walter Staupitz—sure we did well with *Arlesia*. But I wouldn't employ that man if he came to me begging for a job. A pervert. A sick mind, full of sickness and dirt, that's Walter Staupitz. Fortunately I found a fine, decent man, Harry Rolland, he was able to dig around in all that filth and salvage something. They say Staupitz is a genius. Such geniuses we don't need. Let them be geniuses in the farmyard, which is where they belong, with the pigs, wallowing in the dirt. In my pictures, Alexander, I'm going to show people the beauty of life, I'm going to show them tenderness and love. Because in their hearts that's what they want."

All the way home there was the sour taste of defeat in Alexander's mouth and he felt the dull emptiness that comes after a great effort that has been futile. As he walked, his mind dwelt on his defeat, analyzed it, went over the various stages of the interview, trying to figure out when he had said the wrong thing that had given Seiermann the upper hand. The more he thought, the worse he felt: he had handled the whole situation clumsily. If he had given the impression of being sure of his case, he could certainly have got some money out of Seiermann. But he had allowed himself to be browbeaten and shouted down. And now he would be depressed for days, perhaps weeks. He had no resilience, no capacity for recovering quickly from some setback. Some tiny slight, real or imaginary, could upset him for days—a major rout, of the kind he had just suffered, could also affect his health: his heart was beating irregularly, occasionally missing a beat, which gave him a fright each time it happened. Why can't something good happen to me, he demanded desperately of himself. Each defeat makes it harder and harder for me. With great effort I painfully get on my feet, and immediately I'm knocked

147

down again. How many more knocks can I take and still keep getting up? Have to pull myself up by the bootstraps. Can I do it? And what is the alternative? To stay down? To die? To go on, like my father, living from day to day, without a profession or a career, trodden on by everyone? I couldn't, he thought. The depression would overwhelm me. I'd rather kill myself. Some things are worse than death. Curiously, this thought reassured him. If things were really so desperate that he was thinking about suicide, he could at least stop worrying about his health. If he died it was just too bad. It wouldn't be such a calamity. He wouldn't be giving up all that much. In that case, he might just as well stop taking his pulse all the time, stop worrying that his heart might suddenly stop, and take some risks with himself. What did he have to lose? He began to feel the headiness of extreme despair.

CHAPTER FIVE

Paul took the earplugs out of his ears and emerged from behind the screen, where he had been trying to work. "Well, children," he said, addressing Lala and Alexander, "tonight the Muse is silent. Giving me the brush. I propose to get the hell out of here."

"Goody," yelled Lala, who was lying on the bed listening to some music on the phonograph. Alexander was sprawled on the floor, in a narrow gorge between the stacks of books, reading.

"After all," said Paul, "it isn't every day that one can get the inspiration to write a *Saturday Evening Post* story."

That morning he had received a check for $800 for a story he had knocked out in one night and sent to the *Saturday Evening Post*. He had declared, cynically, that, as it was undoubtedly the worst piece of crap he had ever written, it would certainly be published. Still, he had been staggered to get the letter of acceptance and the check, and on rereading the story he had come to the conclusion that perhaps it wasn't as bad as he had first thought. Eight hundred dollars for one night's work was a fortune: it was more than he had ever made before, by writing, in a whole year.

"I propose we celebrate," he declared. "And then tomorrow it's ice bags and black coffee, and work, work, work. And as for you," he said, pointing an accusing finger at Lala, "you will remember in the future that this is now *officially* an author's establishment, and there will be no more phonograph playing or recitations of Baudelaire while I am trying to work. And you're staying in. It's going to be a stag party. As for you, Alexander, tonight melancholia, misanthropy and—above all else—misogyny are forbidden. We are going to have a gay time, and I am determined that *you* have a gay time. You will kindly be good enough to enjoy yourself. I know what we'll do, we'll start at Jack's."

Jack's was an oyster house at Sixth Avenue and Forty-Third Street, a hangout for writers and newspapermen, where, Paul declared, they served the best sea food in New York. They might see Stephen Raille there, it was a favorite place of his. Dreiser and O'Neill came there often. But that night the only writer in the place, that Paul knew, was a girl reporter from the *New York Daily News*, who complained that New York was dead just now, that absolutely nothing was going on. After they had eaten, they sat around drinking coffee and then, as there was still no sign of Dreiser, Stephen Raille, O'Neill, or anyone else who might qualify as a well-known writer, the girl—whose name was Martha Hall—said she knew a great place where they could get a drink, called the Second Half of the Night. It was in Greenwich Village, and Paul said he knew it—it was strictly for the tourists. But the girl said she had been there a few nights ago and it was very lively. Paul said all right, he was prepared to look at it. They took a cab there. At the door, the girl produced a card on which was written: "Friend Jack, this is one of my friends." The proprietor, an Italian, looked at it suspiciously, looked at them even more suspiciously, and reluctantly agreed to admit them to a small, bare and empty restaurant with checkered tablecloths. They asked for something to drink, and he brought them ginger ales which really were ginger ales. "But I was here the other night," the girl complained, "remember?" He shrugged and went away. "There's another room," she said, "that's where the action is."

"Well, it doesn't look as though we're going to get into it," Paul said.

Some minutes later the proprietor came back to their table, his manner as surly as before, and said: "Come with me." Obediently they got up, the girl reporter smiling triumphantly, and followed him through a door, along a long, unlit corridor until they came to another, heavier door, which he unlocked with a large key. Now they were in a small hall, also unlit. He locked the door behind them, and indicated that they were to go down some stairs. At the bottom there was another door on which he gave a complicated series of knocks, whereupon a spy hole opened, an eye peered through, and they were admitted. They found themselves in a medium-sized room, on the walls of which were murals of nymphs and satyrs disporting themselves in attitudes of contrived abandon, watched, from behind a tree, by a horned gentleman with a long forked tail. A wooden bench, with loose cushions on it, ran all around the circumference of the room, and close to it there were lots of tiny tables. They were shown to one of these by a waiter in shiny tails who demanded: "Whisky or red wine?" In the center of the room perhaps twenty couples were dancing to the music of a small band on a dais. Among them were several Negresses dancing with white men and one shiny-faced Negro dancing with a white woman. The girl reporter kept looking at him, as if trying to catch his eye. "He's a fabulous dancer," she told them. "It's some place, this. The other day some society dame came here, danced with some nigger boy that had took her fancy, and the next day, taking the elevator up to her Park Avenue duplex, she found she'd been having a roll in the hay with the elevator boy. Isn't that killing?"

"What about you?" Paul inquired in his slightly ironical manner. "You ever roll in the hay with one of them?"

"Now that's asking," she said coquettishly. "But I can tell you, I wouldn't mind. When it comes to *that* they've got the white race licked to a frazzle."

"I don't know what members of the white race you've been keeping company with," Paul said teasingly, "but I think you're a bit young to be that authoritative about an entire race."

"You want to prove me wrong?" she demanded provocatively.

"I never boast," said Paul, grinning.

"At least you're not American," she said. "American boys are death."

When the music stopped, the Negro bowed politely to his partner and strolled away. As he passed their table the girl reporter called out to him, "Hi there!"

"Hi!" he responded automatically. His blank face opened up into a huge grin as he remembered her. "Oh sure, *hi!*"

"Aren't you going to ask me to dance?"

"If your friends got no objection, gladly."

"Go right ahead," said Paul.

When they had gone off together to the middle of the room, and the girl had wrapped herself around the big Negro, Paul said: "I guarantee you that girl is a virgin. Thinks about nothing else, and never does it. Will do anything, except the actual act. Her thrill is talking about it, pretending, teasing; playing a bit in public, in a parked car—anywhere where it can't go all the way."

On the floor, the girl was dancing very close to the Negro, a rapt expression on her face. The music was very loud. The room was dark except for a swinging spotlight which kept moving monotonously to and fro, arbitrarily illuminating a face here, rotating buttocks there. They lost sight of the girl and the Negro. When the music stopped she returned to the table by herself. She looked very hepped-up, her expression was the kind you see on the faces of women at boxing matches when the blood has started to flow.

"What's happened to your friend?" asked Paul.

"Let's go somewhere else," she said.

"I thought you were getting on so well with him?"

"Well, he isn't *new*," she said. "I've been here before. Why don't you take me someplace new?"

"Unfortunately," he said, "I couldn't take you where we're going."

"Why not?"

"They don't allow women in there."

"But that's ridiculous," she said. She was a little drunk. "I'm press."

"Not even ladies of the press," said Paul, smiling.

"I never heard of any place like that," she said.

"We're going to a house," said Paul.

"A house . . . ?"

151

"A bordello."

"Oh," she said, and then a look of little-girlish excitement came over her face. "Take me with you," she pleaded. "I've never been to a proper bordello."

"Oh no," said Paul, "oh no. They don't play your sort of games there."

"Please," she said. "It'd be a terrific thrill."

"What would you do there?"

She considered this for a minute with a worried frown. "I could watch," she said brightly. She looked questioningly from Paul to Alexander. "I'd love to come and watch," she said. Alexander felt the fear-tinged excitement creeping through him; the girl reporter had placed her hand on his. "You'd like me to come along, wouldn't you? Make him take me."

"D'you want us to take her?" Paul asked.

"I didn't know that's where we're going," Alexander said, trying to sound casual about the whole thing.

"Why not?" said Paul. "I know a very good one, run by a fantastic Greek woman called Madame Menocoulis. She'll arrange something special for us. An *exhibition* maybe, two girls. . . . Would you like to see something like that?"

Alexander shrugged; his mouth had gone dry and he didn't dare trust his voice, over which he felt he did not have sufficient control just then.

"Are you kidding me along?" the girl asked.

"Normally," said Paul ironically, "I wouldn't suggest such a thing to a nice girl. But as you're *press* . . . I guess there isn't much you haven't seen."

"I'd like to come," she said in a small voice, from which all the bravado had suddenly gone.

"To watch?"

"Yes."

"Not to participate?"

She gave a small, frightened shake of the head; Paul was looking at her hard, with the sort of masculine toughness that Alexander had noticed in him when he was dealing with women. "Sorry," said Paul. "You come along and you open those milky-white thighs with the rest of them. . . ."

"Like a whore?" she said, tremulously. He put some money on the table to pay for the drinks and started to get up; she let her fingertips touch the notes, and for a moment the contact made her close her eyes. "You're not taking me?" she asked.

"No," said Paul, "it's not a place for little girls."

The place to which Paul took Alexander, on West Forty-third Street, had an impressive frosted glass door, ribbed with wrought iron and illuminated from inside. To gain admittance Paul placed the palm of his hand against the glass, whereupon the door was immediately opened by a courteous giant who murmured in a remarkably gentle voice, "Good evening, gents," and took their hats and coats. "Go right on in, gents," he advised mellifluously. "Madame will be right along." He drew some heavy, red velvet curtains that hung over a pair of double doors, opened the doors, and showed them into a long low room, very delicately lit. The walls were covered in quilted red satin and the ceiling was tented in the same material. In the center there was a small, sunken dance floor, where about half a dozen couples were dancing languorously and intimately to music provided by a bald, middle-aged man at a piano, who smiled welcomingly to Paul and Alexander as they came in. He was in one of the alcoves, rather like private boxes in a theater, which formed a sort of loggia all around the room, on a slightly higher level than the dance floor. Paul gave him a friendly pat on the shoulder as they went past. Some of the alcoves they passed had their curtains drawn; in others girls sat deep in conversation with their men companions, giving the impression of being involved in long and serious discussions, from which they were only momentarily distracted while they flashed quick, intimate, inviting looks at the other men strolling along the gallery, to indicate that no binding arrangements had yet been made between themselves and their present companions, and that therefore they were still open to alternative offers. In some of the alcoves groups of girls sat unaccompanied, their slightly bored expressions vanishing—to be instantly replaced by provocative, but by no means coarse looks—as the two men strolled by, Paul subjecting them all to an intense, smiling scrutiny. One or two of the girls gave Paul the special smiles that denoted pleased recognition, and then he responded with a gallant little bow and sometimes by blowing a kiss. When they had done the complete circuit of the gallery, Paul indicated to Alexander one of the empty alcoves, where they sat down. On the table there was a bottle of champagne in an ice bucket and another bottle labeled: "High & Dry Gin—Booth's. Estd. 1740. The Original Dry Gin." Another label declared: "Imported for Medicinal Purposes only." To the waiter who appeared presently, Paul said: "Take these away, Carlo. And bring us a bottle of Madame's own Grand Marnier. But the good stuff—hm?"

"Certainly, sir. I'll do that, and I'll tell Madame you're here."

"Will you? And Carlo, is there any new talent . . .?"

"Oh yes, sir." He bent down to whisper confidentially in Paul's ear, indicating various groups of girls in the alcoves opposite. He was extremely respectful, and he and Paul talked for some moments, very seriously, huddled together, mouth to ear, rather like stockbrokers at the Stock Exchange.

"It must be hellish expensive here," said Alexander, when the waiter had left.

"Don't worry about that," Paul said airily. "Madame is a good sort—makes a special price for artists. I wrote a short story about her once and she was enchanted. She's a fantastic woman. That's why I didn't want to bring that dreadful little reporter-girl here. Madame is very particular about her clientele. If she doesn't like you, it's no go. No matter how much money you've got. Now don't worry, she'll adore you. She will look after you like a Jewish mother."

Alexander, to his amazement, was feeling extraordinarily relaxed; he had drunk just enough for his normal apprehensions to be quietened, and the atmosphere in this place was so agreeable, so *elegantly* raffish, so unhurried, so discreetly exciting, that he began to enjoy the sensation of just being in this high-class bordello. He felt a blade, and allowed himself to look boldly at the girls, whose flashing eyes met his so readily, so incitingly. They looked like very nice girls. His idea of whores as tough, painted harridans, full of contempt for their clients and with permanent sneers on their faces, was delightfully disproven by these marvelous creatures. The thought that they could be had, just like that, gave him the strangest feeling in the pit of his stomach.

When Madame Menocoulis arrived, bringing the Grand Marnier herself, Paul got to his feet and kissed her hand, very correctly; she, dispensing with formality, embraced

154

him and gave him a great big smacking kiss on each cheek.

"Paul Krasnor," she said. "I'm very displeased with you. For months you haven't come to see me . . ."

"My dear madame," he said, "I'm a poor artist. I can't afford your prices."

"Nonsense!" she exclaimed. "You can come and take a little cognac with me. But—" and she turned to address Alexander "—he only comes when he wants girls, the wicked man. For my company—no."

"Ah," said Paul with great gallantry, "if I thought I had a chance with you, madame, I would be at your doorstep all the time." He introduced Alexander, and she shook hands with him, her eyes appraising him gently but searchingly. She was a short, big-bosomed woman of about fifty, with deep, dark, compassionate eyes, heavy eyelids, a rich, full, large mouth, and the unmistakable demeanor of somebody who lives well. It was a face full of energy and good humor and matriarchal toughness, and a certain melancholy as well. The initial impression she gave, of great jollity, was amended after the first few moments: it was a sort of defiant—valiant—jollity, that grew out of a great, sad, detailed knowledge of human affairs. It was easy to picture her weeping hot tears at a sad song, or a sad story beautifully told, but anyone who took these tears as an indication of feminine softness, of easy vulnerability, would be grievously mistaken. She was the sort of woman who could weep without loss of authority and command unequivocally, but without harshness.

"Madame," said Paul, "my friend here has not previously visited your excellent establishment. And as I have just sold a story . . ."

"My congratulations!" she exclaimed, clapping her hands together with genuine delight, pride in her eyes. "I always said you had talent. I am very pleased for you. And I'm flattered that you come to my place to celebrate. . . ."

"To the *Saturday Evening Post*," added Paul, a little shamefaced.

"What is wrong with the *Saturday Evening Post?*" she demanded. "I hear they pay very well. In this world you can't have always everything exactly as you wish. Is it a good story?"

"It is not exactly literature."

"You'll write better. First, you must make a little money,

then you can afford to write for yourself. First, you must establish yourself. I know writers–I know their problems. Always money problems. Always they talk about their money problems. Most of them would be very pleased to have a story accepted by the *Saturday Evening Post*. You should be proud. As it is a big occasion you will want something out of the ordinary. You've looked around?"

"Yes," said Paul, "some of them look charming."

"I don't expect you to choose here," she said. "You come up, you take a drink, and I bring you up the girls. You can look them over privately, leisurely, and decide. You and your friend. Go up, I send the waiter and the drinks. And then I bring up the girls. You would like something a little special? Special clothes? Something a little out of the ordinary?"

"Possibly an *exhibition,* two girls."

"Yes. Yes, or I have some movie film . . ."

"No, they're so badly made."

"You are right, they are very badly made."

"Perhaps two girls. But they must like each other. They must have *enthusiasm.*"

"Of course."

"I'm not sure, if we might look first?"

"Naturally, you can entrust yourself to me, you know that."

"Madame," Paul said, "I have always said it, and I mean it, you are an artist."

"From somebody who has just sold a story to the *Saturday Evening Post*, I consider that a great compliment. Now go up, I don't need to show you, you know your way. And please come and see me, *please*, we have a long talk about literature. Please? I would love to read some things you have written, it would give me great joy."

"I will, madame. You can be sure."

When she had gone, Paul ordered a drink for the pianist and raised his glass to him, they finished their own drinks and then made their way up a curving staircase to a first-floor drawing room. Paul explained that this was Madame's own drawing room, which she also used for the line-up which, nowadays, was something reserved for special customers. Most of the clients were expected to make their choice downstairs, without the benefit of first seeing the girls unrobed. Madame had had to bring in this rule most

156

reluctantly, as it went against all her ideas of how a good house should be run. But now that so many men just wanted to see a striptease, it was impracticable to provide a line-up for every customer. As no charge was made at this stage, a lot of people would come merely to see the girls undress, and this would waste a great deal of time and necessitate long periods of waiting for serious clients. But in the case of clients she knew personally, the line-up was still provided, and of course there was no obligation to take any of the girls if they did not appeal. As long as you were known to her as a serious client, she would not take it amiss if, after seeing the girls, you decided you didn't want any of them. Madame was not the sort of madam who would try and sell you on something against your inclinations.

All this Paul explained to Alexander as they waited for the girls, sipping their Grand Marniers with the air of gentlemen callers at a fine house. It was a large room, but so overfurnished it seemed almost small. In one corner there was a large ottoman heaped with many-colored cushions, and near it stood a high wrought iron lamp with a green silk shade dripping tassels. Occupying a large section of one wall was a huge painting of a swarm of alabaster-white nudes—all leaping and prancing and floating; their postures romantic and unnatural—watched by a group of dark male figures with hooves. Near the window there was a black, lacquered rolltop desk, inlaid with ornate gold patterns, and next to it a big oak-frame armchair, floral designs embroidered in petit point on back and seat. The wallpaper was black and gold with a design of Grecian urns. Potted palms and vases full of ferns stood in various parts of the room. Paul and Alexander sat down on a circular, velvet-upholstered settee in the center, the kind to be found in art galleries, and waited for the girls, As they came in, filing in rather like docile schoolchildren being taken on some outing, they took their positions against a huge gilt-framed mirror with a design of cherubs blowing trumpets at its summit. There were twelve of them. In this ornate and rather pompously furnished room they looked incongruous: neat and chic and angular and slouching. Madame brought up the rear, and having mentally counted her flock to see they were all there, came and sat herself between Paul and Alexander. Alexander noticed that

157

she had ugly hands, very thick veined, the skin mottled, something she tried to disguise by covering them with ornaments: on her left hand she wore a Cleopatra asp of beaten gold, which curled over her lower arm and wrist and extended to her middle finger.

"Delightful," said Paul, approving the girls, and she seemed pleased. For a while they merely looked while the girls stood, stoop-shouldered most ot them, inanimate, waiting to be picked in order to come alive. Their eyes went along the line and back, and along the line again, and then fastened on individuals. "The one on the right," said Paul, "four from the end."

"Yes," said Madame Menocoulis, thoughtfully, "yes—Patsy." At the sound of her name the girl showed some sign of life: her heavily made-up eyes flashed at them invitingly. She was dark and petite, with her hair worn in a bob and curl above each ear. She wore a one-piece chemise dress that gripped her just below the knees, and a cascade of black beads hung from her neck to just below her waist.

"Charming," Paul murmured politely, returning her smile. His eyes continued along the line. Next to her were a couple of girls that he obviously did not care for: then his eyes fastened on a tall blonde, rather bony and angular, with ice-blue eyes, and a band around her head, and a certain arrogance in her slouch. Paul raised his eyebrows to Madame Menocoulis. "She's new?" he inquired.

"Yes. You're interested?"

"Certainly."

She wore a blouse consisting of wide pieces crossing diagonally across the front, like a surplice, with attached ends forming a sash that was knotted at the waist. The skirt was long and sheathlike, becoming tight below the knees. "Solange, honey, would you take off your skirt for the gentlemen," Madame ordered quietly. The girl obediently fumbled at the back, undid something, and slid the skirt down her long, thin legs. She wore pointed high-heel shoes with ankle straps, champagne-colored hose, supported by fancy garter straps. "*And* the pantie, cherie," Madame added. Some of the other girls watched disinterestedly as she put her hands inside the elastic waistband and slipped off this final undergarment. She had boyish hips, a flat belly, narrow thighs and a triangle of delicate curls at the mount.

She stood there, one knee bent provocatively in the ritualistic stance, showing herself off. She did not meet any of their eyes, but stared disdainfully into the middle distance.

"A bit stuck-up," said Paul, grinning.

"A matter of taste," said Madame Menocoulis.

"What do you think?" Paul asked Alexander, leaning across Madame.

"She's very pretty," Alexander said, his eyes drawn back to the dark girl, who met his gaze with a warm, soft look that made his body tense and tighten deliciously. She was offering herself to him with her eyes. She looked inquiringly to Madame, requesting permission to undress, and on receiving it, unfastened hooks on her back, and bent down to draw the skirt over her head. Unlike the blonde, she was undressing specifically for Alexander—and watching closely for his reaction. Under the dress, she wore a pink slip with fine lacework at the bodice and hem—one hand dangled loosely at the juncture of her thighs, where the material was crumpled slightly, defining the shape of her body underneath. She did not wait for further instructions; with her eyes still on Alexander she stroked the slip up her thighs, as if relishing the feel of her own body, and held it at the waist, and showed the lower part of herself boldly— she wore nothing else—to Alexander. She, too, assumed the ritualistic bent knee stance now but, unlike the other girl, she made the movement enormously erotic. There was a slight swell to her belly, and her hips were nicely rounded with soft flesh. She waited, holding up her slip, while she was looked over, and then she dropped it and assumed again the more or less rigid posture of the other girls.

"I think Alexander has made up *his* mind," Paul said, laughing. "And I think it's a good choice."

"Patsy is a lovely girl," Madame Menocoulis agreed. "Very American, not at all exotic, of course, but very chic, very *modern*. But have a look at Tola—I think she *is* out of the ordinary." Tola was a lightbrown Jamaican girl who wore tight black breeches, laced below the knee. She had full lips, but otherwise her features—apart from being dark—were very Western. "Slip your pants down, honey," Madame commanded, "and show the gentlemen your pretty little rump." Tola did as commanded, and Paul murmured, "Exquisite . . . exquisite. You permit, Madame?" She gesticulated approval with a grandiose flourish of her

159

asp-wreathed hand, as if to say the permission he sought was granted as a matter of course. He approached the girl, drank in her heavy scent and lightly felt the outline of her buttocks; while he did this she turned her head and smiled at him encouragingly over her shoulder. Bending his head close to her neck, he took another deep, and evidently satisfying, breath of her odor, while one hand went round her front.

"Tola it shall be," he announced while she pulled up and fastened her pants. "Now what about you, Alexander? The snooty-looking blonde or Patsy? Or one of the others?" Again Alexander's eyes went along the line: there was a rather heavy-looking girl in a white dress, embroidered with white sequins. Another, older woman in a sleeveless dress with a narrow V-shaped neckline that revealed pallid skin; her eyes were sullen, seemingly seeking some desperate cure for ennui. The others made no impression on him. His eyes went back again to the ice-cool blonde, whose unchanging, haughty demeanor must have appealed to the rapist, but it was the dark girl, so hotly waiting, who attracted him.

"That one," he said, indicating Patsy. She narrowed one eye—it wasn't quite a wink—at him, in appreciation of having been chosen. Madame clapped her hands, dismissing the other girls who, like a class breaking at lunch, suddenly relaxed their postures, and started chatting noisily among themselves as they went out. Paul had drawn out his wallet and was conducting financial negotiations with Madame. The two girls waited passively, smiling.

"She'll take you to one of the other rooms," Paul told Alexander. "You'll have to give her a tip. Say—three dollars before and three after. More, if you're pleased with her. Tell her she'll get a bigger tip if she's good—but don't give the lot to her in advance. She seems sweet, but you can't blame them for trying to get the most out of a client. Say you're a poor artist if she complains it's not enough. If she tells you a hard-luck story say it's almost as tragic as your own story—and start telling her *that*. That stops them in their tracks. Oh, yes. You'll also have to buy champagne, which is a racket, but it's part of the price. Order it in half bottles. She'll drink hers very quickly—even if you order a magnum at the beginning—and want more. A couple of half bottles, especially if you hardly touch yours, will see you through the night. Anyway, here's fifteen dollars—no, no, take it, I said the evening is on me. They're absolutely trustworthy here—you can leave money loose. If any girl did steal, Madame would refund the amount, and the girl would be sacked immediately. Enjoy yourself: she's a lovely girl."

"So is yours."

"Yes, Tola is something, isn't she?"

Patsy led Alexander out of Madame's drawing room, up some stairs, along a corridor—where they passed a naked girl on her way to the bathroom—and into a small, heavily curtained bedroom, which was almost filled by a large high bed. Alexander was quite amazed, and delightfully so, at his lack of apprehension. Just being in this room with this girl was an accomplishment for him. He did not know whether it was the drink, or the expertly smooth way in which Paul had arranged the whole thing, but now he felt no fear about what was about to happen—it was like waking up at night, after a nightmare, and turning on the light to discover that there are no monsters lurking in the dark. He was filled by the elation—and the relief—of this discovery. He did not know which was the greater pleasure: the magical absence of fear or the slowly tightening knot of sensuality in himself. Inside the room, the girl lounged against the door, smiling. For a few moments he savored the thought of what was going to happen between them, postponing the actual contact for the sake of the anticipatory thrill. She was still in her slip, not having put her dress back on, and the memory of her body under the silken material was having its effect. She glanced down and then up at his face, her smile broadening. He moved up close to her, resting his hands on either side of her head, the physical distance between them narrowing, narrowing, narrowing until, with a light forward movement, she made the contact. "Mmm," she murmured appreciatively, feeling his hardness, and then added a laughing, admiring, *Wow!* He laughed too, and let his hands slide down her arms and sides, over her hips and thighs. She was moving very slowly, very purposefully, against him, exciting him as gently as if they were dancing together. It was as if a great log jam had been freed and was now beginning to drift, with ever-increasing momentum, in the desired direction, and he could feel the strong, exhilarating pull of the current. He was moving against her

161

more strongly, everything in him accelerating. He wanted to kiss her—her lips seemed almost the most private, the most sacrosanct part of her—but he knew this was something you did not do with girls like her. Her hands had gone to his trousers and she was unbuttoning deftly; he made as if to stop her, meaning he was going to undress himself, but she shook her head, asking to be allowed to do it herself; the contact of her cool fingers, the shock of feeling her soft feminine hands touching him in this unbelievably intimate way made him gasp. She stroked him unambiguously and knowledgeably, all the time watching his face for his reactions; and then, pulling up her slip and squatting slightly, she placed him against the outside of herself and continued the caresses by rhythmically rotating her lips: her curved thighs were like a hoop spinning around him, touching fleetingly, lightly, moistly. Several times he felt he had reached the point, but no . . . when she read this on his face she diminished the contacts slightly and kept him hovering on the very edge. After one such moment, she broke the contact completely, withdrew, moving backward, and threw herself on the bed, sinking so deeply into the bedding that Alexander momentarily lost sight of her. As he approached, he saw that she was tugging at a bellpull. "How about some champagne?" she said. "You'd like some champagne, wouldn't you?"

"Can't afford it," Alexander said, smiling. "I'm an artist, I'm poor."

"Oh you can afford champagne for a special occasion."

"Well," he said, "I guess. Half a bottle."

"All right. What about a little present for me?"

He felt in his pocket and took out three dollars. "Here. Have it. It's all I've got."

"And the champagne?"

"Oh, I guess I've got a few dollars in loose change."

She shrugged. "I wouldn't call you exactly a big spender, but you're nice-looking. Come on over and play with me—I like to be played with."

He lay down by her side on the bed and she spread herself luxuriantly and opened herself to his curious, playful fingers. After several minutes of this there was a light knock at the door, and before anyone could say anything a young girl in chambermaid's get-up had come in, carrying champagne in an ice bucket. "Whoops," she said unapolo-

162

getically, seeing she had come in during an intimate moment, but Patsy was unabashed and Alexander, to his surprise, found that he too was quite unperturbed by the intrusion. On the contrary, it excited him that this young girl—who was fully dressed and presumably wasn't a whore —had caught them in that form of play. There was a full bottle in the ice bucket, but Alexander calmly sat up in the bed, disengaging himself from Patsy, and said: "Honey, take that back, would you, and bring just a half bottle."

"A half bottle, sir?" she repeated with an air of calculated amazement, looking him up and down, lingeringly.

"Yes. If we want more later, I'll send for you."

When she returned with the half bottle of champagne, he opened it himself: catching a glimpse of himself in the mirror he could not help thinking how debonair he looked, how assured. Being in this place, in this situation, with this girl, was the epitome of worldliness. My God, he thought, everything *was* possible. It was an exhilarating feeling. Together they sipped the champagne.

"My," she said, "you're a good-looking boy."

"Well, thanks."

"So thin, though. Don't your Ma feed you?"

"I keep thin worrying," he said.

"You don't look like the sort who worries."

"No?"

"No. To me you look sort of cool, detached—deep. A bit aloof maybe, but that's nice. It's nice for a man to have a little mystery about him."

"You're sweet," he said, noncommittally. He put down his glass and touched her breasts.

"Come on, then," she said after a little while. Her thighs were spread, and she guided him; he felt a great strength, a great sense of masculine power, as he entered her. "Oh gee!" she said. "Oh gee!" And then, greedily: "Gimme, gimme, gimme! Come on, gimme, gimme! G-I-M-M-M-M EEEEEEE!" He moved naturally and easily and experimentally, feeling, apart from the pleasure, the deeply satisfying sense of being the instigator of her pleasure—he felt an atavistic male pride at being the planter, the seedbearer. It was a feeling that was not the same as sensual pleasure, though it was connected with it.

Later, after they had rested a little, she washed him and watched him dress and comb his hair. He had to wait for

Paul. Before they left, both paid their respects to Madame Menocoulis and expressed their unqualified admiration for her establishment.

Outside, they strolled silently through the cool darkness, which was on the verge of becoming morning, and the distant lights of Broadway, diffused by tall buildings, created a rival dawn. Alexander walked weightlessly, hardly aware of his tiredness. My God, he thought, it's possible. It's all possible.

Back at Paul's studio—it was too late to go home—he sat down and wrote a letter. "Dear Mr. Zukor," he wrote. "Although you probably do not know my name, I am writing to you as I believe I could be of great use to you in the capacity of your personal assistant. My reason for being so confident of this is that I have been for several years personal assistant to Mr. William Seiermann and was responsible for the acquisition of *Arlesia*, and for having it re-cut to make it showable. As you know, this motion picture is now expected to make for the Seiermann organization alone a profit of close to $1,000,000, which is due, in no small measure, to the highly advantageous deal I was able to arrange with the producers. I say all this to give you some idea of my background. The claims I make in this letter can of course be checked with Mr. Lewis Sholt, who conducted the negotiations on behalf of owners of *Arlesia*.

"I have a lot of ideas, backed up by years of practical experience in the picture business, which I should like to devote to your interests, as I have always regarded you as the foremost figure in motion pictures, and I would very much like to be associated with you.

"I would very much like to see you to introduce myself personally and elaborate on some of my ideas. Perhaps you would be good enough to give me an appointment, or alternatively I will telephone your secretary in the next couple of days and suggest some times that might be mutually convenient."

When he had finished this letter, Alexander wrote eleven other identical ones, each addressed to a leading figure in the picture business. The sky was already light when he went down to post the letters.

PART TWO

CHAPTER SIX

At 8 P.M. the girls were starting to arrive, singly and in pairs, silent, in a hurry, threading their way through the line of men who formed a sort of disorderly and buckled colonnade outside the entrance of the Palm Room. Calling a perfunctory "Hi" to the doorman, they made their way in, gloomy male eyes looking them up and down as they squeezed past; up a few uncarpeted stairs, past the ticket kiosk, through some swing doors, along a dim corridor, at the bottom of which they checked their handbags with a cheerful, shirt-sleeved man who stood behind an opening in the wall and gave them in exchange a piece of battered cardboard with a penciled number on it. They formed a little huddle here, a stagnant pool of femininity, making last-minute adjustments to their hair, looking at themselves in small hand mirrors, attending to their make-up, re-arranging the position of a brooch on a dress, or putting on earrings, or pinning a broken bra strap. Then, their smiles coming on like electric illuminations at dusk, they went inside, into the Palm Room.

Each time a girl came through the door Jim Kae saw her inverted image framed in his camera. He was trying to catch that sudden, pathetically seductive smile against the background of the other girls getting ready, still attending to their toilette: he was trying to get the picture that would sum up this moment: the Entrance of a Ten-Cents-a-Dance-Girl—the lights above the dance floor wrapping her momentarily in brightness, making costume jewelry and beads and tired eyes sparkle, the stance and expression

165

imitating Norma Talmadge or Gloria Swanson or Clara Bow. And he wanted to get in the same frame, in contrast, the girls outside, a blur of as yet uncomposed faces, their glamour-poses not yet decided on. That was the shot he was after. The trouble was that most of these girls were so unglamorous—they wore cheap store dresses, or else home-made ones, and once they had made their entrance, and had discovered that the huge Palm Room was almost de-serted, they quickly gave up their rather futile attempts to look gay and provocative and resumed their former dispirited expressions.

The band, its members in tuxedos that had become shiny from much wear, was tuning up, the short, harsh grunts and moans and whimpers of their instruments pro-viding an unromantic accompaniment to the entrance of the girls. Though it was already five past eight, and a ban-ner announced "Dancing Free from 8 to 8:30," there were as yet only about eight or nine men waiting to avail them-selves of this offer. They sat on badly worn leather settees arranged all around the perimeter of the dance floor, one or two neatly dressed in their going-out suits, the others in trousers and open-necked shirts, all of them seemingly dis-interested in the girls who were beginning to form them-selves into a line for the free dancing. The men and the girls seemed to constitute two separate groups who had nothing to do with each other, had just happened to find themselves in the same place at the same time. Paper lan-terns and numbers hung from the ceiling, and there were banners and bunting strung across the hall. Some of the banners contained encouraging messages like: "Winning Number Wins Ten Free Dances," and "Jazz! Jazz! Jazz!" and—"Tonight: Hoagy Brewster and His Rhythm Boys." Through the windows along one side of the wall could be seen the raised neon signs of movie houses a couple of blocks away: "Gloria Swanson and James Nelson in *Separate Beds";* "Pauline Frederick—Queen of Emotion-alism—in SALVAGE—now playing"; *"Why Be Good*—Story of Flaming Youth"; "Nazimova in—SALOMÉ."

As the band struck up the first dance tune, and the men took their positions, silently, opposite their selected part-ners in the line, a girl—a latecomer—came breathlessly through the door, and her inverted image made Jim Kae look up from his camera. As she rushed in, in too much of a hurry to adopt any artificial attitude, her expression that of a child anticipating a scolding, something strange happened. She seemed to be floating in a kind of blue haze, that hung around her like mountain mist around a peak. Jim Kae took the shot, his flash going off before she was aware of the camera. He wondered what had caused this brief optical illusion, and grinned when he saw the explanation—it was dust, thick dust rising upward from the floor; caught in the blue-filtered beam of the spotlight it became momentarily transformed into this magical mist, but just a little higher, where the blue beam ended, it was clearly dust again. He knew that he now had a picture that he could sell—for here was the shot of a pretty girl, a very pretty girl, that caught the momentary illusion of glamour that was the essence of a place such as this. For a time he concentrated on other aspects of the Palm Room: girls clutching long loops of dance tickets, their night's earnings: the plump girl, sitting by herself at a little round table, eating a doughnut: the burly man with rolled-up sleeves and the face of a long-distance truck triver, enthusiastically and sweatily doing the Charleston with a dark, heavily made-up girl affecting a vamp look. The light in the room was tricky: colored spotlights played on a spinning crystal ball suspended from the center of the ceiling. No direct light fell on any of the dancers, and the ricocheting light of the crystal ball had the effect of blurring lines and shapes, making them softer and more graceful. The girl he had photographed coming in was a blonde, her face a mask of prettiness; her looks were the looks that every girl aspired to at that moment; but, indisputably, no matter how it was achieved, by whatever conspiracy of lighting and make-up, the effect was stunning, and the evidence of this was the way in which the men clustered around her, proffering long loops of tickets. Jim Kae continued to watch her. He saw that she was quite impartial in her choice of partners, exercising no personal preference, never turning down an unprepossessing man in order to choose a more tolerable one. She danced with them all with the same degree of enthusiasm, and she put just the same amount of sex into her movements, whether the man was a small, bashful, spindly-legged clerk or a smooth-faced, smooth-haired Italian type in gangster-stripe suit and two-tone shoes. She seemed to make no distinction between any of them, and seeing the intimate way in which these men held her, Jim Kae felt a pang of something he could not exactly place. Seeing her being handled and touched in this way, so intimately and so impersonally, disturbed him. There was something about this girl. Something incongruous shining through the mask of prettiness, and it was the incongruous that made pictures. He kept taking pictures of her. His instinct for composition within the frame kept pulling him back to her, kept telling him that there were fresh angles in which she could be seen. It was this instinct that had made him successful as a photographer, it was what he had to trust. Some girls you could photograph and after a couple of shots you had used up all the potentialities; but with this girl, whatever she did, she was all the time making pictures. He kept seeing them, and each time his heart jumped, because he knew how much work and how much contrivance it took in his studio to make girls look this good; this girl kept doing things that were absolutely right, that begged to be photographed. He thought: maybe I'm wrong, maybe tonight my judgment is way out, but what the hell, I'll stick with it. Soon as I've developed the pictures I'll know if I was wrong.

He kept photographing her all evening, occasionally taking off time to take shots of some of the other girls but always returning to the original one. At around ten the place began to fill up, the smell of flesh and sweat and cheap perfume became almost intolerable, and then the girls started disappearing, after long whispered consultations with their dancing partners. Apparently there was a rule that any girl could leave after 140 dances, or after she had collected enough tickets to represent this many dances. In practice this meant that most of the men who wanted to leave with one of the girls arrived at some time between ten and midnight, and bought whatever number of tickets were needed to obtain her release. Obviously the most popular girls needed the least number of tickets to obtain their release. For this reason it was necessary to turn up early in order to leave with one of these girls. The less attractive ones still needed to have a lot of tickets bought up around ten or eleven o'clock, and consequently they were pretty readily available to anyone prepared to buy ten or fifteen dollars' worth of dance tickets. Anyone who did this was exposing himself to a risk: despite the provocative sales talk that the girls gave to their dancing partners, in order to obtain their early release, once they had left the Palm Room a whole new bout of negotiations began.

As it got later, and the more tolerable looking girls disappeared, the room, now that it was emptying, began to look depressingly drab again. For a short while a spurious glamour had been generated, as bodies and dreams coalesced in the hot, smoky darkness; but now, as the girls and the men were becoming equally bored with waiting and bargaining, it was getting to be grim. Jim Kae's camera was catching this part of it too. At around midnight, there were only half a dozen girls left, the members of the band were beginning to look at their watches, and on the leather settees one or two men had dozed off. Only Jim Kae's original girl seemed as lively as at the beginning, apparently oblivious of the deteriorating mood of the place, dancing as energetically as before. He would have to find out a bit about her—at least her name and where she came from and what her ambitions were. He bought three dollars' worth of tickets from the kiosk and, when the present dance came to an end, approached her.

"My," she said, "you're not going to have time to use all those tonight." She was smiling at the sight of all those tickets.

"They're for you," he said, handing them to her.

"This place closes in about ten minutes," she said, "You'd better keep them for another night."

"It's O. K." he said, "you keep them."

"You sure?"

"Sure."

"That's pretty generous," she said, accepting them.

"I've been taking pictures of you," he said when they had started to dance.

"Yuh, I saw." She laughed in a way that was an outpouring of all of herself.

"You photograph well."

"Yes?" She sounded pleased in a polite, disinterested way.

"Have you ever done any modeling?"

"I've been in pictures," she said.

"You *have?*"

She laughed again. "A long time ago. When I was eight.

169

I was the little girl who was kidnaped in *A Mother's Ordeal*. You ever see that?"

"No."

"I only had one scene. Say, you took a lot of pictures tonight. You must be pretty crazy about photography."

"I'm a photographer."

"You mean wedding pictures, and things like that?"

"No. I take pictures for magazines."

"You going to put my picture in a magazine?"

"I hope so. Depends how they turn out, but I should think they'll turn out all right. That's why I want to find out something about you."

"Yuh?" There was a slight edge of wariness in her voice now.

He grinned. "It isn't a line," he said. "You've probably seen my pictures in the magazines—Jim Kae is my name. What's your name?"

"Janet." She was thinking. "Jim Kae, Jim Kae—that's a funny name."

"That's why I use it. Easy to remember, and short."

"No. I don't think I ever saw your name anywhere."

"Janet?" he asked. "Janet what?"

"Janet Derringer."

"D-E-R-R-I-N-G-E-R?"

"That's right."

"Janet Derringer?"

"What sort of magazines? *Screenland* and *Movie*, magazines like that?"

"I have done pictures for them."

"Of movie stars?"

"Yes."

"You ever take pictures of James Nelson?"

"I don't like taking movie star pictures very much."

"I idolize James Nelson. You say you never took any pictures of him?"

"No. But I've taken pictures of Jack Gilbert." He felt a little ashamed of using a name like that to impress her.

"You have?" Her face had formed a tiny, disbelieving frown. "I don't get it," she said. "If you take pictures of John Gilbert why d'you want to take pictures of *me*, in a place like this?" Then an understanding, compassionate expression appeared on her face. "Maybe it isn't so easy to get to take pictures of John Gilbert?"

170

"It's not that," he said. "I get offered a lot of money to take pictures of that sort, but I don't like doing it very much." Why the hell should I want to impress her? he thought. Just get her name, her age, where she comes from, what jobs she's done, her ambitions, whether she's married or single—and that'll wrap it up. It's a picture feature, doesn't need much text. "What d'you do when you're finished here?" he asked.

She shrugged. This was a more usual approach and she understood it. "I go home," she said.

"Tell you what," he said, "I want to find out more about you. Have you eaten?"

"Oh yes," she said vaguely.

"That must have been hours ago. I'll take you for a drive and maybe we stop off some place and have a hamburger."

"No, I couldn't do that. Sorry."

"Why not?"

"I don't go with the customers," she said plainly but not unkindly. "If you like you can have your tickets back—you've only used up four. Try one of the other girls."

He sighed impatiently. "I'm not looking for a pick-up. Do I have to show you my press card? All right, I tell you what." He stopped dancing. He'd had an idea—it was a pretty cheap idea, but he couldn't think of any other way of overcoming her suspicion. "Come and sit down a minute." He led her over to one of the small tables, sat next to her and took out his wallet.

"Look," she said, laughing, "maybe you are loaded, but I told you I don't go with the customers."

"I'm not going to offer you money," he said, "I'm going to show you something to convince you that I'm a 'serious and reputable' photographer. You've heard of *Vanity Fair?*"

"Sure."

Jim Kae took a folded piece of paper out of his wallet and handed it to her. "Have a look," he said. She unfolded it, her expression, if anything, even more suspicious than before. It was a company check for $850 from *Vanity Fair,* made out to him. "Now what else d'you want? My passport?"

"Eight hundred and fifty dollars," she said, "wow! Just for taking pictures. In that case I guess I don't need to give you your tickets back."

"And I can afford to buy you a hamburger—without any strings," he said, smiling.

"O.K., serious and reputable photographer," she said, "it's a deal."

It was a heavy night. For days the sky had been girding itself for a storm that hadn't yet materialized—in this part of the world storms only came at the appointed time, and that wasn't yet. There were no stars, and the moon was just a thin smudge of silver. The lights of downtown Los Angeles pommeled the optic nerve with their various messages: C-H-E-V-R-O-L-E-T, spelled out letter by letter, and then flashed, triumphantly, in a series of short sharp jabs as a complete word; FISK TIRES; some preparation for which it was claimed that it HAS NO MEDICINAL IRRITANTS; an infinitely more ambitious sign—queening it over the sky—showing a woman caught in the rain, her raincoat momentarily blown open to reveal the label; and, behind and beyond all this, in bold red neon, the words JESUS SAVES, JESUS SAVES. Over toward Hollywood a couple of searchlights were perfunctorily sweeping the sky in search of nothing in particular. Jim Kae and the girl strolled to where he had parked his hired black Packard at Spring and Eighth. "Where d'you want to go?" he asked, enjoying the sensation of being able to offer her things—places—that would be new to her. "A night club?"

"Are you kidding? Dressed like this?"

"You look fine."

"Oh no, let's just have a hamburger like you said."

"All right. Where?"

"Let's go somewhere by the ocean."

"O.K. There are a couple of places out on Santa Monica pier. The Ship Café—or Nat Goodwin's?"

"That's where all the movie stars go, isn't it? I've read about those places in the columns. No, I wouldn't want to go to any place like that."

"Well, let's drive out there anyway. There are lots of places. We'll discover some place. We'll make it famous—shall we?"

"You're funny," she said, getting into the car ahead of him.

"Why?"

"I don't know. You're just . . . funny."

He couldn't make her out. She had been impressed—or

172

maybe surprised was a more accurate word for it—that he was a big, important photographer, she'd accepted this, but his changed status in her eyes hadn't changed her attitude toward him. She wasn't so suspicious any more, but she certainly wasn't *keen* either, the way most girls were when they found out who he was and the kind of circles he moved in. Turning off Grand Avenue, he didn't take the Santa Monica road but chose instead to go along Sunset Boulevard. The girl was quiet and contented at his side, evidently feeling no obligation to make conversation. She was quite uncurious about him, she had hardly looked at him—at any rate, she had looked at him no more than at any of the men she had danced with, who had held her body close and got whatever satisfaction they could get from this.

She was looking out of the car window. "I love driving," she said after a while. "I love the feeling of going somewhere."

At Hollywood and Vine, seeing the extras already sitting there on the stone bench under the pepper trees—so they'd be the first in line when the studios opened in the morning—a delicate sadness came over her face, and stayed there. It gave an odd, quirky kind of poignancy to her looks—a sad doll, he thought. It's crazy: that kind of look doesn't go with that kind of face. The face hasn't the bone structure to carry a look like that.

Hollywood Boulevard was not very lively: Jim Kae thought how depressingly provincial it looked sometimes, like any small-town main street. There were a few youngsters hanging about outside the Egyptian, looking at pictures of Nita Naldi and Rod La Rocque, and at the Hollywood Hotel cabs and limousines were pulling up, discharging groups in evening clothes, and their laughter and farewells carried across the cool green lawns that surrounded the low, porticoed, tree-shaded building. He drove on, fast, toward Santa Monica. The ocean was dark and still. She wasn't hungry, she said, maybe they could just walk and get some air. On the beach road, below the Pacific Palisades, he slowed down to let her see the homes of the movie stars. When they had gone a short way, he stopped the car and they got out and strolled across the sand, and then walked, parallel with the ocean, just beyond the reach of the incoming tide. Set back behind high gates, screened

173

by palm trees and cypresses, and high, shaped hedges guarded day and night by the Pacific Palisades Patrol, the movie stars' homes seemed to Janet Derringer the bastions of an impenetrable world. Occasionally, peering through the gaps in the intricate ironwork of a massive gate, it was possible to catch a glimpse of some of these fabulous people moving across a section of unscreened driveway, or appearing at an upper-story loggia to survey their private sky. Further along, not quite identifiable at this distance, a star—obviously, a star—white fox furs draped around pampered-white shoulders, a cockade of white feathers sprouting from a close-fitting black cap, was sitting in the back of a black Rolls convertible. Her chauffeur, in black leather coat and black leather gaiters, was pushing open the heavy entrance gates of her home.

A light breeze coming in off the ocean fanned the great ones in their great houses as devotedly as any slave girl. Nature was tame here, never resorting to the unexpected or the extreme. A fortuitous convulsion of the land had produced this horseshoe-shaped range of foothills opening on to the Pacific, a favored area—a windless, frostless zone. In the summer, the ocean breeze lifted the superfluous heat over the protective hills and dumped it into the surrounding desert. And in the winter the cold wind from the north passed high overhead, in any case never exceeding, in deference to this privileged community, forty miles an hour. The rains came punctually here, hardly ever exceeding the advertised sixteen inches a year, falling always between November and March, after a preliminary warning of two days of cloudy skies—sufficient rain to keep the foothills abundantly covered in wild flowers. There was snow in the mountains, for those who liked to see it, but none to inconvenience residents at inopportune moments. It was the climatic perfection of Hollywood that made Jim Kae restless whenever he came here: it provided no challenge to the body, it was a place for convalescent homes and retirement. The endless, predictable sunshine; February's warm blue skies, the soft silver beaches—this head-to-foot cosseting, part of the natural amenities of the place, made him restless. They died of pneumonia here, in this perfect climate, because the blood got lazy. He looked at the girl. He guessed she had been born around here, somewhere in Southern California: she had the look of having

174

been nurtured in conditions of perfect mildness. The two searchlights were still playing in the sky above Hollywood. Illuminations of this sort were booked for a certain number of hours and continued, irrespective of whether there was still anyone around to see them, until the expiration of that period.

"I always think those searchlights look pretty silly," said Jim Kae to the girl.

"Oh no," said Janet Derringer. "Oh, no! I love them. I like to feel that something is going on, that everybody isn't asleep. It's reassuring."

"Reassuring?"

"I like to feel that there are people awake all the time." She turned to him with full eyes. He thought of her dancing with all those men, the way they were all touching her—and her remaining curiously untouched, almost as if it was somebody else's body that was exciting them. "That's what I like about big hotels," she said. "Knowing there's always a night porter there who's awake, and always someone at the switchboard, and always someone in room service—so that at 4 A.M. you can send down for a cup of coffee or a pack of cigarettes. That's very reassuring. Think of all the terrible things that could happen to you in some little place between midnight and 7 A.M., with nobody around and everybody asleep and the whole town just dead. That's why I like all the lights—at least you know you can always go out and find some other people. You know where they are. I'd love to *live* in a hotel, not just stay in one—live there. That's my idea of real luxury. I'd like to live at the Ambassador, they've got everything there. They say you could live your whole life there, without ever going out for anything—there's a night club, and a doctor, and a bank and a pool and a post office and a movie theater and all the shops you could want."

"I know. I've stayed there."

"You have?" This seemed to impress her more than anything he had said so far. "I've never stayed in a big hotel," she said. "I just know about it from magazines, and I've heard Dad tell about it. My father's been in pictures almost from the beginning, you see."

"Really? Doing what?"

"He's a small-part player. He was the man in the front

175

row of the stalls who applauded Miss Geraldine Farrar when she played the opera singer in *A Woman's Role,* and he was the doctor who told Pola Negri, after she'd had that motor accident in *The Price of Love,* that she was going to be all right. He's been in hundreds of pictures. He's a very *distinguished* looking man. You know, silvery hair. Lots of people said he could have been a star, but he was never that ambitious."

"And you, do you want to be a star?"

She considered this seriously. "Dad says there are thousands of girls like me in Hollywood, and you only get to be a star by going with directors and people, you know—sleeping with them."

"Well, that's only partly true. How old are you?"

"Almost eighteen."

"You look older."

"Yes?" She seemed pleased. "I try to make myself look older. I always think that girls of eighteen must seem so dull, they haven't done anything yet."

"That's what some men find attractive," said Jim Kae, smiling.

She laughed knowingly. She could alternate between seeming almost incredibly innocent and then looking suddenly as if all the wickedness of the world were known to her, and in some way understood by her and excused.

"You must have found that out," Jim Kae said, "in your job."

"At the Palm Room. Oh, sure! Those men, oh, they like the feel of a young girl's body against them. Some of the things they say to you when you're dancing! Like what am I wearing underneath. What color panties? You know, things like that. But they don't get too fresh as a rule, I can control them pretty well, most of them."

"Why d'you do it?"

"The job? I like a night job. And—I guess—there isn't much else that I could do. I don't mind it that much. For every ten-cent dance I get five. If the men like you, you do quite well—though me I'm always broke. As a matter of fact, though, I'm going to give it up."

"Yes? When?"

"Tonight."

"Tonight! When did you decide that?" He laughed.

176

"Just this minute."

"Do you always make decisions this quick?"

"No, just this time. Telling you about it, I suddenly felt bad about doing it, so I'm giving it up."

"What will you do?"

"I don't know. Something will turn up."

"Have you any money saved?"

She laughed. "Not a bean."

It emerged that she was three weeks behind with the rent money— the landlady had said that unless she paid up she wouldn't be allowed in. The only way she knew of earning the money that quick was by going with one of the customers, and if she did that she might get into the habit of doing it, and so she'd decided to quit. Jim Kae offered to give her the money, which she could regard as a long-term loan if she wished, but she said no, she didn't want to go back to those lousy rooms anyway. He asked her where she was going to stay, and she said she couldn't stay with her father because he lived in a one-room apartment. She didn't know where her mother was, she hadn't seen her for fourteen years and couldn't remember what she looked like even.

CHAPTER SEVEN

When Janet Derringer woke up at one-thirty the following afternoon, her usual time for waking up, Jim Kae was in the kitchen fixing lunch. The first thing that struck her was the quietness—by comparison with the rooms she usually woke up in—and the cleanness of the sheets. For a few moments she stretched and wallowed in the luxury of freshly laundered linen. Sunshine, mellowed by soft curtains, gave the room a rich, amber glow. She felt happy. Delightedly she jumped up on the bed and started bouncing up and down, like a child, on the bedsprings. While she was doing this, she caught glimpses of herself in the mirror of the wardrobe and was thrilled by her own beauty—she touched her breasts; so finely shaped, so marvelously proportioned in relation to the rest of her body. And the way her waist came in, and the way her hips curved out—just the right amount! Oh, it was marvelous! She got off the bed and went to the window. The air was clear and fresh, and she could see a long way: in the foreground, shops and office buildings, and behind, the sloping green hills, sprinkled with white and pink villas. She could hear Jim Kae working in the kitchen. She decided to investigate the apartment. Corridor. Several battered leather suitcases covered with a great variety of labels. Fishing tackle. Skis. Bathroom—with a massive device of pipes and gas jets and handles for heating the water. Another door—Jim Kae's bedroom, very simply furnished, very bright and clean and uncluttered. His bed was made. The studio was a large room containing several very low couches and low tables, a number of photographer's lamps, a couple of filing cabinets, several cameras and tripods, a typewriter, and a tray of lenses and filters. Three of the walls were bare, painted plain white. The fourth wall was decorated from floor to ceiling with Jim Kae's pictures: she saw war scenes, infantrymen going over the top, a dead youth lying on a tangle of barbed wire as if it were his bier, and she saw scenes of Africa and China and India, and she saw portraits of Thomas Hardy, of Chaliapin, of Havelock Ellis, of Booth Tarkington, of Marie Sklodowska Curie, of Isadora Duncan, of George Jean Nathan. There were also pictures of film stars like Lon Chaney, Nazimova, John Gilbert, Norma Shearer, Lillian Gish, John Barrymore. She heard footsteps in the corridor and quickly grabbed the only thing at hand— which was one of Jim Kae's sports jackets—to cover herself.

"I was just about to wake you," he said, "but I see you're up. There's a bathrobe in the bathroom which you can use, if you like. I've fixed us some food in the kitchen, so don't be too long—huh?"

When they'd had lunch he went into his dark room and re-emerged, after a while, with the pictures that he had taken of her the previous night. He showed them to her without saying anything. She looked at them in amazement. She had never seen herself in this way. He had brought out her excessive use of mascara and eyeshadow, making her look like an actress made up for a role, but coming through this garish make-up was someone so different from what she thought herself to be—it made her shiver, as if she had run into her double in the street, somebody who looked just like her, but wasn't her.

"That's you," said Jim Kae.

"Is that what I really look like?"

"You don't like yourself?"

"Well, I look kind of sad."

"That's how you looked."

"I thought I was being gay." She liked the picture of herself rushing in late and apparently floating on a blue mist—it gave a great feeling of vitality and optimism. But the other pictures showed her becoming progressively sadder though, as this happened, she tried harder and harder to be lively and gay and sexy—it was a kind of desperate sexiness, as if everything depended on it.

"You can really see things with that camera," she said.

"You're a very good subject. Your face is revealing—even when you don't realize it." He told her that she shouldn't put on any make-up, that she didn't need it, that she looked better without it—a little pale lipstick was all she needed. But no eyeshadow and no rouge and no mascara and no false eyelashes. Some days later, Jim Kae came home late in the afternoon and found her crying. "Some days," she said, "I feel nothing is ever going to happen to me. It's like being on a long, long road that goes on forever without scenery."

"Things are going to happen to you. Things always happen to pretty girls," he told her.

"I don't feel that. I can't seem to snap out of these moods."

She had been staying at his apartment for more than a week and he hadn't made a pass, which puzzled her because all the men who had ever been nice to her did make a pass sooner or later. It was something she had come to expect, and when it didn't happen it bothered her. It was a drag having to wrestle all the time, but at any rate you knew where you were, and in a sense it made her feel more comfortable knowing there was something that was wanted of her. She couldn't figure out what Jim Kae wanted of her, and so the fact that he was being so nice made her uneasy, made her feel she couldn't rely on his niceness, because if a man was being nice to you for no reason—or for some private reason—he could stop being nice just like that, at any time, and she wouldn't be able to do anything about it, not having any card to play. He sensed some of the things she was feeling, and he said: "You know you're the sort of girl it's almost cruel not to make a pass at. You expect it so obviously." She gave a confessional laugh, amazed at his ability to read her. "But I tell you," he went on, "the reason I don't is just because you do expect it, and because you feel that *that* is some way of discharging a debt. Apart from the fact that I don't like taking a girl as some sort of I.O.U., I think you ought to get out of the habit of thinking of yourself as something to be given in return for favors rendered. I know that's hard for you because you don't have any confidence in yourself except as someone a lot of men want to sleep with. That's something that bothers you, I'm sure; on the other hand—which makes it complicated—you can't see what else you've got that anyone might want. That's why I want you to know something about me, which is this. You don't need to have any sort of hold over me—like me wanting to sleep with you—in order to be able to rely on me, within reason. As I said at the beginning, no strings."

She was lying on the couch in the studio, reading the movie magazines. In addition to the current issues there were hundreds of copies of old numbers—many of them containing photographs taken by Jim Kae—in the apartment. She could not understand why he considered this sort of work whoring. She thought they were lovely pictures, and the fact that he had taken them gave her a vicarious thrill, a sense of proximity to the great stars. Copies of *Screenland* and *Screen News* and *Moving Picture World* and *Motion Picture Magazine* and *Motion Picture Classic* and *Hollywood Magazine* and *Movie Weekly* and *Moving Picture Stories* littered the couch. In the magazine she was reading there was a picture of Rudolph Valentino, wearing a belted sports jacket with big, buttoned pocket flaps, at the wheel of an open Voisin four-seater. There was also, by way of contrast, a picture of Mary Pickford cranking a model T Ford, with the caption: "Mary's Starting Something." On another page there was a picture of Gloria Swanson with a peacock, its feathers spread. The caption said: "Lucky Peacock! Who wouldn't spread his feathers for a gal as lovely as Famous Players star Gloria Swanson?" One of the other magazines had an article explaining how Harold Lloyd did his daredevil comedy routines, hanging from parapets and high build-

..... pictures of Tom Mix with a horse, of ....no dancing with Pola Negri at the Coconut Grove, of De Mille on location in the desert for *The Ten Commandments,* wearing jodhpurs, pilot's hat, carrying riding crop and a megaphone. There was a picture of Dorothy Dalton, in the fashions section, described as "wearing a sport tailleur of black Roshanara treco, vestee of plaited Bartholdy linen and vest of brocade accentuating all the grace and daring that characterize her art." An article by Tom Mix on "My Kind of Girl," and by Constance Talmadge answering the question, asked of different stars each week, "What Kind of Girl Am I?"; an article by James Nelson on "What a Woman Expects of Her Man." She read about why King Vidor's marriage had broken up, about somebody called Craig Biddle, Jr., heir to millions, who waited in line at Paramount for an extra job at $7.50 a day! About the chances of a beauty queen—like Mary Astor—becoming a star; about the forthcoming opening of the Seiermann studios; and about the building of the $25,000 Marion Davies bungalow at Metro. She also read that of the 9,973 employees on Hollywood payrolls, 1,800 were girl extras, that they earned an average of $8.64 daily, and that stars were receiving an aggregate of 27,000,000 fan letters a year, which cost Hollywood close to $2,000,000 in answers.

She turned over on her stomach and thought about James Nelson. It would be marvelous with somebody like that. His long, elegant hands. She thought of his long, elegant hands touching her breasts. The thought excited her, and she gave a little shiver. She moved deliberately against the couch, her eyes shut tight—oh, why not? she'd hear if Jim Kae came back. It was such a sharp thrill and it wiped out everything else. She pictured herself with James Nelson—James Nelson undressing her: would he be terribly excited, or calm and debonair as in his films? She pictured him being terribly excited—that calm, slightly remote look quite gone. What if he could see her now? Those men at the Palm Room, they'd give anything to see her like this. She bit her lip and stopped for a few moments, she liked to draw it out for as long as possible. There were so many lovely things to think about. She thought about some of the boys she had actually been with, but in some way they'd been disappointing; they'd been too inexperienced probably. Much more exciting to think about somebody like James Nelson.

181

An older man would know better how to mak̶e̶ ̶h̶e̶r̶
enjoy herself. With the young boys she'd been with it ha̶d̶
always been so hurried, so quickly over. Someone like
James Nelson would know. She heard the key in the door.
Just time to straighten her dress and sit up, but she didn't,
she carried on; she pretended she didn't hear the door opening; then with the realization that he was watching, the
thrill became almost unbearable. He came over, and she
pretended to be startled and embarrassed, and averted her
head. He sat by her on the couch and said, smiling: "Don't
stop on my account." She looked up, and gave him a childish conspiratorial look, and hesitantly resumed the movements, her eyes on him all the time, seeking reassurance
that it was all right. He touched her lightly. "It's a bad
habit, I know," she said with a guilty, little-girlish
smile, "but I never could cure myself of it." "Seems
a hell of a waste," he said gently, smiling. "It cheers me
up," she said, "when I'm low it's the only thing that cheers
me up." He felt the rotary movement of her buttocks against
the palm of his hand. "And with a man?" "I like that
too," she said uncertainly, "but all the boys I've known they
don't care much about the girl enjoying herself."

It was about two weeks later that Jim Kae said he had to
make a trip to New York. While he was away, and he
wasn't sure how long that would be, she could stay in the
apartment. The first few days after he had left she made a
determined effort to get up early, tidy up, do her shopping
—he had left her one hundred dollars to tide her over
until she found a job—and look through the Help Wanted
ads in the newspapers. She replied to some of the ads and
went so far as to see one store manager about a job as a
salesgirl, but the thought of the restrictions on her personal
freedom, of the rules and regulations that she would have to
observe in the matter of dress and speech, so depressed her that she did not bother to telephone the following day, as had been arranged, to find out if she had
been taken on. Rather than work in a place like that, she
would go back to being a taxi dancer. She replied to several
ads from agencies offering "remunerative film work to attractive females between 16 and 29" but none of them were
on the level: they all asked for varying sums (between $15
and $100) for "special tuition," and for enrolling her on

their books. She considered taking a job as a waitress, after reading an article about a girl who served at a lunch counter in a Hollywood drugstore being signed up by a talent-scout. But when Janet turned up at the drugstore there was a line of girls already waiting. It turned out that the girl in question had indeed worked there, several months ago, but there was no vacancy at present.

After a week or so she gave up looking for work and just stayed in bed until the afternoon, and sometimes all day. There didn't seem to be any point in getting up. Nothing nice would happen to her, even if she did get up, so she might just as well stay in bed. She drank innumerable cups of coffee, smoked cigarette after cigarette, had the radio on all the time, and sometimes danced in front of the wardrobe mirror and excited herself by the sight of her own body, and then made love to herself; that was the only thing that kept the depression at bay. It temporarily forced out those dark feelings which she did not understand. Why did she feel so bad sometimes, and other times so high, so very high? When she had a bad thought, she would try to rid herself of it by thinking of something nice, a memory of something pleasant that had happened to her, or else of something nice that was going to happen to her; but it didn't always work.

Jim Kae's hired Packard was paid for until the end of the month and he had told her she could use it until then. She went for long drives. One afternoon, driving in the Hollywood hills, she saw a forest fire. It was a hot July day, and from a distance the smoke of the fire had looked like a fantastic and beautiful cloud formation. It rose in great colored plumes from behind the brow of the hill. It had been very hot driving in the closed car, but as she came nearer to the fire something strange happened: it became cool suddenly, and she gave a little shiver: the smoke from the fire had obscured the sun, and cast a great mile-long shadow over the road and the adjoining hills. As she got closer to the center of the fire, where the smoke was densest, it became still colder: such sunlight as managed to penetrate the pall was transformed, as if by a prism, into extraordinary colors, making everything around look strange and unreal, like in one of those tinted movies. Still she had not seen any actual flames, but as she turned the next hairpin bend she found herself looking

183

down a wooded slope and into the blaze. It was about half a mile below the road, and angry, red, roaring flames, twice the height of the highest trees, were leaping upward. Several cars were parked in the road and people were watching, fascinated by this sight. Janet pulled up too. As she got out, the other cars were starting to move off: the flames were getting too near, and there was no way of telling if they weren't even closer beyond the next couple of turnings in the road. "I wouldn't hang around for long," one driver called out to Janet, as he started his car. Ignoring this advice, she walked slowly to the edge of the road. She shivered, partly from the abrupt drop in temperature, and partly from a profound sense of dread. The cold flames—she could feel no heat coming from them—were leaping up toward her, and she stood staring into them, as hypnotized as a child paying with fire. She knew she should get back to her car and drive away from here. Say it wouldn't start? She would be trapped here with the flames racing toward her. She pictured herself trying to outrun the fire, climbing higher and higher with the great wall of flames behind her. Now she *could* feel the heat of the flames on her face, and little patches of shrub a few yards from her were smoldering from the sparks and burning embers that had been blown ahead of the fire by the wind. It was the sound of a police siren that jolted her out of the hypnotic state; the cop jumped off his motorcycle, grabbed her roughly by the arm and pushed her into her car. "Follow me," he shouted above the roar of the flames. Siren moaning, they made the descent; two bends down the fire was almost at the edge of the road; the dread had gone now, in its place had come a tremendous feeling of exhilaration. The motorcycle cop escorted her all the way back into town, his siren going the whole time, and she felt marvelous, like a celebrity arriving to receive the keys of the city.

That evening she went to see a movie starring Richard Barthelmess who, next to James Nelson, was her favorite male actor. She didn't care for Valentino that much, though she had to concede he was a good actor and possessed a lot of dynamism, but she preferred the gentler, more contemplative type. She liked a man to be firm and masculine, but not rough. The rough, grabby approach did nothing for her. But someone like Nelson, with that wistful, quizzical expression in his eyes and his quiet authority, she found very appealing.

Coming out of her movie, she stood for a while in the noisy and excited crowd waiting for the celebrities to emerge from the première that was being held at an adjoining theater. As the stars started to come out, the cops joined hands and forced a passage for them through the crowd: Janet found herself being pushed roughly back, the weight of the man in front pressing on her, and she in turn pressing on the person behind her. From where she was she could see nothing except the tops of top hats and the feathers of elaborate headdresses.

CHAPTER EIGHT

It was several months since she had been to see her father. For a long time now there had been a great awkwardness between them whenever they met; she had not wanted to see him while she was working at the Palm Room because she was no good at lying, and if she told him what she was doing that look—almost of satisfaction—would come into his eyes, indicating that she had fulfilled his direst predictions. He used to hint that this was how she would end up, and she did not want to prove him right. It was not that she feared his paternal wrath; in a way it wouldn't be so bad if he shouted at her and played the heavy father and demanded she change her way of living. But she knew he would not act that way, it was not in his character; he would simply look at her knowingly, with those distinguished gray eyes, run his fine hands through his silvery hair, and stoically accept the inevitable. The way he looked at her, whenever they had talked about such things, made her feel it was all predetermined, there wasn't anything either of them could do about it—the signs had been there for a long time. He didn't actually say this to her—but she could always tell from his eyes that this was what he was thinking. Still, she wanted to see him. She had happy memories of how it had been between them one time—and then she had done something, had let him down in some way. From time to time she still entertained the hope that it could be like that again, the way it had been. Every time she went to see him she cherished the hope that his attitude toward her might have changed, that her misdeeds of long ago—whatever they were—might have been forgiven.

She parked the Packard round the corner from where he lived (she did not want to have to explain how she came to be driving a car) and climbed the stairs to his second-floor bachelor apartment. She knew he would be in because it was Monday evening, and that was the day he attended to his wardrobe. Tuesdays and Thursdays he went to the Hollywood Athletic Club, and Wednesdays and Fridays to the Hollywood Men's Club. Saturdays he went to a movie, and Sundays—after going to church—he visited his sister in Pasadena. She knocked at his door and heard him call: "Who is it?"

"It's me—Jan."

"Door's open, honey. Come on in." He was pressing a pair of trousers, the steam rising from the damp cloth, as she entered the room; he looked up and have her his distinguished smile. Her heart leaped as she saw, again, how handsome he was with his smoothly chiseled features, his noble brow, his finely molded mouth. "Sorry, baby," he said, "mustn't burn my pants, must I? One second." He gave a final press to the trousers, lifted the damp cloth to examine his handiwork and then, his mouth puckering with satisfaction, tilted the heavy iron upright and came toward his daughter. She thought: it might have been two or three days since he had last seen her—instead of more than that number of months. He embraced her formally, and she noticed again how meticulously he avoided holding her close, how their bodies hardly touched, and how fleetingly and lightly his mouth touched her cheeks.

"How've you been, Dad?"

"Oh fine, fine."

"You look well."

"Feel great. And you? How's my baby?"

"Oh, all right, Dad."

"Good. Good." He gave her that authoritative smile he had given Pola Negri when he had told her, in *The Price of Love*, that she was going to be just fine, just fine.

"Seeing to your wardrobe, Dad?"

"Yes. Clothes are getting more expensive all the time. Got to look after them. Tools of my trade." The room was unchanged; scrupulously tidy and of monastic bareness: a narrow bed with a crucifix hanging above it; two large wardrobes against one wall; a washstand; two armless chairs; a plain white chest of drawers; golf clubs in an umbrella stand, tennis rackets on top of one wardrobe.

"You looking after yourself, Dad?"

"Oh yes," he said, "I look after myself, I keep fit."

"How's work?"

"Can't complain. I work pretty regular. It's been a good year for me. Not like twenty-one—now that *was* a bad year. But since then things have been steadily picking up again. Of course they're always talking about economy waves at the studios, but I think there's a general feeling of optimism. You know there's a fella I ran into the other day, went back East in twenty-one accompanying a corpse, that's how bad things were then. You could get free transportation, from the undertakers, if you rode back with a corpse. . . ." He chuckled. "Well, this fella is back in town, which is a sign things are better."

"They giving you any nice parts?"

"You know how it is, honey. They're all pretty much the same. But I don't have to do any *crowd* work now— they're all *part*s. I had a nice little bit with Vilma Banky couple of weeks ago. Had to put a monocle in my eye— you wouldn't think so, but that's a hard thing to do if you haven't the practice—and give her an admiring look in a restaurant scene. Director was very pleased; said I gave it a lot of distinction. You know, a scene like that *can* be so vulgar."

Now, as often happened after he had answered her preliminary inquiries, there came a gap in their conversation, the silence stretched, making her feel awkward and embarrassed, and she hoped, desperately, that for once he would bridge this gap by asking her about herself. But he seemed not bothered by this heavy, constantly lengthening silence; there was that fixed expression on his fine face, as if he were patiently waiting for the camera to turn. The silence went on and on; if I wait long enough, she thought, he is bound to say something, or would he let this silence go on forever. It became an unacknowledged contest between them—who could remain silent longest. She could stand it no longer; she felt tears coming into her eyes.

"Dad," she said, "I've been so miserable."

"Now, now," he said, "that's not like my baby."

"But it *is*," she said bitterly, "it is like me. I'm miserable lots of times." The tears gushed from her eyes. He pulled his chair close to hers and patted her hand gently, consolingly.

"What a lot of tears! There, there. It's all right."

"But it isn't," she sobbed angrily, "it isn't." Did he realize what a caricature he was of himself, patting her hand and saying it was all all right, as if she were Pola Negri in *The Price of Love?*

"Well, what is it you want me to do, honey?"

"I don't know, I don't know."

"We've all got problems," he said. "Got to face up to them—hmm?"

"I've been working at a place called the Palm Room," she cried, "as a taxi dancer." She saw that look come into his eyes, of satisfaction almost, like somebody getting bad news that he is glad to get because it confirms what he'd been expecting all along.

"You must know what you want to do with your life," he said.

"Dad, what should I do? Tell me. Please, Dad, tell me. I want your advice. I want *you* to tell me what I should do."

"Well, now," he said after thinking a while, his forehead wrinkling in that interesting way, giving the impression that he was about to come out with a statement that was the crystallization of a lifetime's worldly experience. "Well, now. I guess everybody's got to do what they got to do. Nobody else can live your life for you. Now isn't that so? So you see, honey, it's really up to you what you make of your life. . . ."

"But what should I do, Dad? I get so restless, an ordinary job would just drive me mad."

"Yuh," he said, "there's some people have got that restlessness. Your mother was a *restless* woman, always wanting . . . well, I don't know what. *Wanting*. You should get married. You've got looks, you're an attractive-looking girl, you shouldn't have any difficulty. Anyway, come and talk to me about it soon—hmm? Right now, I still got a lot to do. Three suits to press, got to be done before Wednesday. And you know tomorrow night is my night at the Club. I'm on the committee, we got a lot of important things to talk

188

about, the whole future of the Club—whether we should limit ourselves to purely ahtletic activities or take in certain cultural types of activities. I have to make some notes for the committee meeting. Week after next should be less hectic for me, why don't you come round then and we'll have a long talk—huh?"

With a feeling of incredulity, and icy, aching dismay, she realized she was being dismissed. She got up. "That's my baby," he said. She looked at him directly, making no attempt to conceal the feelings that she felt welling up in her, and his eyes met her look and they gave and gave, absorbing her accusation and her disappointment, like rubber taking the shock of a sharp impact.

"Look after yourself, Dad."

"You too, honey." He gave her a peck on the cheek, and smiled his comforting reassuring smile, his professional stock-in-trade. She managed to hold back the flood of tears until she was outside the apartment; then the sobs were wrenched out of her and she ran, crying bitterly all the time, to the car.

She drove without any idea of where she was heading, battered by waves of unhappiness. What had happened to make her father act this way to her, so cold, so unrelated? She could not think what she had done. When she was little, he had adored her, had always made a fuss over her, played with her, told her how pretty she was, and how she was going to be such a beauty when she was bigger, all the boys would be crazy about her. They had had such good times. Such a handsome man, with his silvery hair— his hair had always been silvery—and such a pretty child: people used to stop and look at them, they made such an attractive pair. Everybody liked her father. He had such lovely manners and such a warm—distinguished—smile for everyone. It made people feel good to pass them in the street. "Mr. Derringer and his little girl, such a pretty picture they make. Isn't the little girl just *cute,* with her blonde hair and blue eyes. So *cute.* Such a lovely, sweet child. And can't you see how she just worships her father?" That was before the picture people had come to Hollywood, though there were already a few companies operating in Los Angeles— Col Selig had two rooms and the roof in a two-story business block on Main Street; the Biograph Company's studio was then on Twelfth Street; the New York Motion Picture

189

Company, the Kalem, the I.M.P., the Rex, the Power and the Bison were all in the process of establishing themselves in different parts of Los Angeles. But Hollywood itself was still countryside. You could stand at the southwest corner of Vine Street and Hollywood Boulevard and see nothing but trees. In those days people there acted like country people: seeing the little girl out walking with her father they would come out to exchange the time of day with them—he was then a much-liked employee of a local real-estate firm and known to everyone—and often they would press on them things from their gardens, avocado pears, pineapples, the delicate custard apples, tomatoes. And they would cut flowers for them, and Janet could still remember the smell of the great armful of geraniums that she carried home once when she was very happy and proud, walking at her father's side. People used to say to him, jocularly, that no doubt a handsome man like him would soon be giving up his job in order to become a star of the motion pictures. A go-ahead fellow like him wouldn't want to stick in the real-estate business. Not with his looks and personality. Why, people said, there was a fortune to be made in the picture business. To many people who had talked like that Herbert Derringer had sold lemon acreage at $700 an acre which, within three or four years, had become worth $10,000 an acre. But he hadn't bought any for himself. For a man with his looks—as everyone kept saying—there were more spectacular prospects than dealing in parcels of land, which might or might not appreciate in value in fifteen or twenty years' time. Oh, they could tell he was a young man on his way up.

Driving along Sunset Boulevard, Janet thought about all the times she had been happy with her father. So many lovely, lovely days. She thought about the day of the annual May Day Tilting Tournament and Floral Parade. She must have been about seven or eight then. She had been one of the May Queen's flower maids, dressed in white satin, a garland of flowers on her head. Theirs was a beautiful float, representing a chariot drawn by a bevy of butterflies, and decorated with great masses of Spanish broom and sweet peas. As they were moving slowly along the street, watched by thousands of people who packed the specially erected grandstands, she was looking all the time for her father. And the joy of seeing him, of seeing him stand up on his seat and wave to her, and blow kisses to her! How her heart had swelled with happiness, later, when he told her she was the prettiest girl in the whole parade. After the crowning of the May Queen, the tilting began, and it was her turn to be the spectator and to watch—with such pride—her father's fine display of horsemanship, which had won him a silver cup (presented by the Governor of Nebraska), and had got him his first part in a movie.

She searched her memories of the ensuing years for some clue to the sudden change in her father's attitude toward her—the following year had been all right, and the next, and the next. It was when she was about twelve that the coolness had begun: all those games, the hugs, the petting and the playing had stopped abruptly. That sort of behavior was very childish, her father had said. It would have to stop now she was growing up so fast. And then—soon after —there was that terrible day when he had caught her doing *that* to herself, and she had never seen him so angry, and he had used that terrible word to her. "You little whore," he had said, "that's what you're going to be—like your mother." She didn't know what a whore was exactly, but she knew it was something terrible, and that it had to do with what she had been doing to herself. He had looked at her in such a funny way when he had said that terrible word to her, with a sort of contempt, a very adult contempt, as if by doing what she had been doing she had forfeited all the privileges of childhood.

CHAPTER NINE

The days trickled away like running paint. There was nothing to differentiate one from the other. Outside, the sun shone with monotonous intensity. Sometimes she didn't draw the curtains all day, and when she went out to buy groceries, her eyes, which had grown accustomed to the dimness of the apartment, could not cope with the glare, and she was dazzled and felt dizzy and sick. She took to wearing dark glasses all the time and went out as little as possible during the hours of daylight. Sometimes, in the evenings, she went to a movie, but she talked to no one. She couldn't throw off the depression. She was in the grip of a paralyzing inertia—it was like the day she had watched the flames leaping toward her in the hills above Hollywood and had been unable to move away until that cop had come along and forced her into her car. She ate little and without appetite. She had been living like this for days and days when a sharp sound echoed through her mind: a key being turned in the door. A few moments later Jim Kae came into the room. She ran to him, threw her arms around him, and while the tears streamed down her face covered him with kisses. "I'm so glad you're back," she sobbed, "I'm so glad you're back. I've had such a bad time, I've had such a bad time." He patted and stroked her indulgently, smilingly, as he might a small dog that was leaping all over him and licking him with joy at his return.

"What is it?" he asked several times.

"I'm just so happy that you're back," she said. Until the moment he had come into the room she had not linked her melancholia with his absence. But the relief of seeing him was so enormous that it could not be questioned. She loved him. That was the explanation. There could be no other. "Goodness," she cried, "the apartment is such a mess. Please don't think badly of me, I've had a terrible time, but it's all right now. I'll tidy up, I'll make you something to eat. I'll go out and buy something—what would you like? Oh, dear, I must look a mess." She began to run around the apartment, drawing curtains, clearing up, tidying—all at frantic speed—while he stood watching her, a smile on his face. It was impossible not to be touched by her frantic desire to please. "Now you're not going to do anything," he said. "I'm going to take you out to dinner. Have a bath, put on something that'll knock their eyes out, and I'll take you out to some swank place."

"You know something," she said shyly, "I just found out something. I'm in love with you."

"Now, now," he said lightly, "statements like that should not be made on an empty stomach."

Later that night, after they had made love, he told her gently, but firmly, that he did not love her, and that she must not love him. He told her, again, that the most she could expect of him was friendship, and that she could rely on that more than on grandiose declarations of love.

At the gates, the armed studio cop scrutinized the sticker

on the windshield of Jim Kae's Packard, gave Janet an appraising smile, saluted, and waved them on. Specially erected signs and arrows indicated the direction to be taken; they joined the slow procession of cars making their way along the winding drives, past glass-roofed shooting stages with flashing electric signs above the doors saying "Shooting—no entry," past sprawling, ugly, factorylike blocks, through small piazzas cluttered with lamps and wooden planks and scaffolding and the bits and pieces of various sets—a Doric pillar, hollow and made of plaster; a huge painted back-cloth representing the Houses of Parliament in London; a stagecoach still riddled with arrows; crates full of gold bars, made of wood blocks painted a brassy color; part of a "marble" floor on which several workers were squatting, shooting craps; a winding grand staircase ending abruptly in space. Following the arrows, the procession of cars wound its way around the circumference of the back lot. Janet caught glimpses of various permanent exterior sets: the Main Street of a Western town, meticulously re-created—saloons, sheriff's office, hotel, bank, general store. All façade, with nothing behind the outer wall. A little way beyond it, they passed the ramparts of a medieval castle, its draw-bridge raised, its moat temporarily dried up. Still further on, on a large, shallow, artificial lake, a Spanish galleon, holed by cannon fire, its mast severed and fallen across the foredeck, was picturesquely upended, permanently sinking. Though her father worked in pictures, Janet had never been in a real studio. When, as a child, she had played her small scene in *A Mother's Ordeal,* the filming had taken place in an ordinary room in an ordinary office building in downtown Los Angeles.

Having parked the car in the green parking lot, to which they were designated by the color of their sticker, they strolled in the direction indicated by the arrows, and by the leisurely flow of the other guests. A marquee had been put up on an expanse of well-tended green lawn, fronting a low, white colonial-style building. This was where the executive offices of the studio were located. Guests who had arrived earlier were emerging from the marquee, carrying plates of cold meat and glasses of champagne, and either stood in small groups, talking to each other, or else made their way across the lawn to where rows of chairs and long benches had been arranged facing a wooden platform draped with red, white and blue bunting. On the platform, which consisted of three tiers, there were gilt ballroom chairs, a table draped with the American flag, on which stood a jug of water and two glasses, and a microphone connecting with an amplifier, and with loudspeakers that had been put up all over the lot to bring the ceremony to those unable to be on the lawn. On another platform, a Marine band was providing appropriate music for the occasion, and among the guests on the lawn it was possible to pick out one admiral, three generals, and several other naval and military officers. Most of the guests—though not by any means all—were in formal dress. Decorations were being worn.

At first Janet saw only a blur of strange faces and felt intimidated and out of place, but then she became conscious of the way in which eyes—seemingly accidentally—fastened on her, continued their casual sweep of the packed lawn and then, accidentally again, returned to her. It was extraordinary, and flattering, how many people were really looking at her, while pretending to be admiring the architecture of the executive block, or the roses in the flower beds, or taking in the vastness of the studio. Becoming aware of this—and an exchange of grins between herself and Jim Kae confirmed it—she found herself relaxing and able to enjoy some discreet staring herself. Among the people on the lawn, Janet recognized Monte Blue, Norma Talmadge, Wallace Reid, Anna Q. Nilsson, Buster Keaton and Dolores Costello. Jim Kae identified a number of leading directors for her: Marshall Neilan, James Cruze, Fred Niblo, Raoul Walsh, Frank Borzage, Victor Seastrom, King Vidor. And there was James Nelson—this was a tremendous thrill for Janet—being very attentive to Louella Parsons. In this genteel swirl, a complex ritual was being enacted, which Jim Kae described to Janet. It was an occasion when Hollywood protocol was strictly adhered to, he explained. Maybe it all seemed very easy and relaxed, but if she watched carefully she would see that $7,000-a-week stars only recognized other $7,000-a-week stars. And the bigger the star, the less circulating he did. A great star remained in one spot and waited for everybody else to come to him. When the day arrived that people didn't come to him, it would be a terrible blow. When he had to start circulating and catching other people's eyes, he'd know he was slipping. The picture Jim Kae had always wanted to take of a gathering of this sort

194

was a vertical one, from high up, showing how these gatherings always developed into a series of circles—each with a star figure, whether it was an actor, a financier or a supervisor, at the center. Whoever was hottest at a particular moment had the largest circle around him—and those with lesser circles were seething under their suntans. And how they held on to their own little coterie. The patterns that were formed were almost geometrical in their precise depiction of who was currently where in the hierarchy. And then, by watching carefully, you could immediately spot the climbers and the go-getters. They were the ones who knew instinctively when to detach themselves from the periphery of a minor circle and sidle their way up to the center of a larger one. And then there was all the maneuvering that went on when there was some doubt of the order of precedence as between two people of almost equal standing. It was as ritualized, and as complex, as the courtship of peacock and hen. They might actually look at each other, but neither was prepared to be the first to recognize the other. This might go on for a long time. Then, in a sudden flash of simultaneous mutual recognition—though they may have been standing within feet of each other all the time—they would acknowledge each other's existence. Now came the great trial of strength. Which one would make the first move toward the other? Perhaps one would make a tentative, ambiguous move, but if this did not immediately result in a comparable move from the person he was half approaching, they wouldn't get to meet. The one who made the original move would allow himself to be distracted, sidetracked in another direction. And so it went on. "There are bloody victories and defeats on a day like this," said Jim Kae. "One day a girl walks on to a lawn like this and suddenly there are twenty people clustered around her, and the girl doesn't have to be an expert in Hollywood protocol to know she's arrived. On another day a great figure might walk on to this lawn, and only three people come up to talk to him, and he knows—and maybe it's the first tangible indication of this grim truth—that his star is waning. And then just you watch the rats scuttling away, clutching their plates of cold meats and their glasses of champagne and their ice creams. Watch them as they stare unseeingly into a once-important face— 'Didn't recognize you, baby, you've done something to your hair, you're looking swell. Just getting a drink for somebody. Lovely to see you.' " That was the slippery handshake. And, of course, a trend like that, once set in motion, rapidly gathered momentum, a diminishing circle diminished faster by virtue of the fact that it was diminishing and a growing circle grew faster by virtue of the fact that it was growing. Once the movement had got going—in whatever direction— it snowballed. Now that this had been pointed out to her, Janet could see it happening. And it started a shiver—a mixture of excitement and apprehension—along her spine.

"Of course," Jim Kae continued, "the true Hollywood figure knows and does all this automatically, instinctively, and of course he would be outraged if you told him that that was what he was doing. To be really successful at it you must not even admit to yourself that you are doing it." He grinned at her. "Now having told you what's what, I'm going to throw you in at the deep end and let you fend for yourself. I've got to go take some pictures. Wait, though. Here comes one of the busiest rats—strictly outer periphery, but burrowing his way inward." The man approaching them was Lewis Sholt: he was small and dark, with his hair sleeked down in Valentino style, and his face illuminated by an ineradicable bonhomie.

"Jim Kae!" he exclaimed. "Jim Kae, you old so-and-so. How are things? How's the photography racket?" He regarded him with warm concern. "You're looking great, just great. Listen, you hear the story about . . ."

"This is Janet Derringer—Lewis Sholt," said Jim Kae.

"Glad to know you," said Lewis Sholt formally, and then, pretending that he had not really noticed her properly at first, added with extravagant fervor: *"Very* glad to know you. Those photographers have all the luck." He winked at Janet. "I don't know how he does it—skinny so-and-so. All he's got are looks, money, brains and a camera. Miss Derringer, I suppose I don't need to tell you—I'm sure he's told you himself, knowing Jim Kae—that you are in the company of one of the greats. One of the truly great photographers of Hollywood. Most girls would give their virginity to be photographed by him, and I may add, many have. Am I being indiscreet?—it's a fault I have. Are you in the business?"

"She'll tell you all about herself," said Jim Kae. "I've got to go take some pictures."

196

"You bring this gorgeous creature and then abandon her —to me. I'm overwhelmed."

"I've told Miss Derringer," said Jim Kae, "that if she's going to get anywhere she's got to start at the bottom. So, for the moment, she's all yours, Lewis."

Lewis Sholt emitted an appreciative laugh. "He's a great kidder," he declared. "What a sense of humor. Great guy. Great to see you, Jim. Don't worry about a thing. Of course I'll do my darnedest to steal her from you, but otherwise you haven't got a thing to worry about." When Jim Kae had left, Lewis Sholt allowed himself a long, slow appraising look at Janet. "Hmm," he murmured. "So you want to be a star?"

"I didn't say that."

"You don't want to be a star . . . ?"

"I didn't say that either."

"O.K. You want to be a star. A girl with your looks, it's natural. Take my card. In case I lose you. It so happens I'm in the talent business, I'm an agent for talent. Give me a call. Any time. I guess you can be reached through Jim Kae. I'm on the lookout for talent—and with me, it's first impressions that count. In the presence of talent you get a sort of tingling feeling—you know, that's if you've got a highly developed antenna for that sort of thing. I have. I'll tell you something, baby, you make one hell of a first impression. So if you're interested—just give me a call, and I'll see what I can dream up. I don't make any wild promises like some of these shyster agencies—you know? I don't promise anything. I get results."

A middle-aged, small, sallow-complexioned man, wearing thick-lensed spectacles, was walking past, momentarily lost, trying to distinguish distant shapes.

"Davy, baby," Lewis Sholt called out, at the same time putting an arm around the man's shoulders and gripping him in a sociable vise. "Davy, you're looking great. You been to Palm Springs? There's somebody I want you to meet. Davy, this is Janet Derringer, whom I represent. Janet, baby, you know David Oltram, who made *Flappers*, which was one of the biggest grossers of last year. Incidentally, congratulations on that. I hear it did even better than *The Morning After Eve*."

"Delighted," murmured David Oltram in a middle-European accent, kissing Janet's hand and peering at her through his thick-lensed spectacles. "Mr. Shilto, I congratulate you on your new client. Delighted to have met you, Miss Derringer." He took his leave of them and continued to search for his lost friends.

"A great director," said Lewis Sholt, "and an important man for you to know. You made an impression, I could see that. The way he kissed your hand, you definitely made an impression." Taking her arm, he steered her determinedly into the more densely packed areas of lawn; whenever their further progress was impeded, Lewis Sholt would embrace one of the obstructing individuals, tell him or her how great they looked and how marvelous it was to see them, and in the process tenderly edge him or her out of the way, and push onward, with Janet in tow. By these means, and while lavishly dispensing greetings and tenders of affection and admiration in all directions, Lewis Sholt zigzagged through all the circles, eyes alert, making his presence known to everyone, introducing Janet to someone else every minute, not allowing himself to be detained by anyone he didn't want to talk to, and trying very hard to talk to people he *did* want to talk to but who, most of the time, didn't want to talk to him. He remembered everybody's name; he remembered to congratulate them on their birthday if they'd just had a birthday, on the birth of their child if they'd just had a child, on their divorce if they'd just had a divorce, on the success of their latest venture if it had been a success. And, if it hadn't been a success, Lewis Sholt could always think of something cheerful to say: "That little girl at the beginning is going to turn out to be the best investment you ever made: a million-dollar property," or "In twenty years' time that picture is going to be a classic, and it'll still be making money then."

Janet was dragged around at such a speed from person to person that she was beginning to feel dizzy. But now she was spared any further socializing as the Marine band sounded a trumpet call to signal the start of the proceedings. As the noise of conversations slowly diminished and people took their seats, the stars and key personnel of the new Seiermann-International Studios took their places on the chairs allotted to them on the platform. The last to appear was Willi Seiermann. He came up the steps, two at a time, a squat, round, vigorous ball of a man, who immediately became the focus of all eyes. As he strode rapidly across the platform, straight to the table covered with the American flag, he seemed to be generating energy—he gave it off in a kind of aura. His quick, strange, waddling movements—heavy body so daintily balanced on the small neat feet—gave an impression of great determination, as if he were not so much walking as throwing himself forward. He seemed with every step to be throwing himself into some imaginary fray. As he arrived at the table, without pausing for breath, he raised a hand to silence the band and went straight into his speech.

"First of all," he said, placing the pince-nez on his nose, "I want to read you a telegram I just received from the President of the United States of America." An appropriate hush fell over the audience. " 'On this auspicious day in the history of the motion picture industry,' " Seiermann read solemnly, " 'I send you good wishes.' " He folded the telegram carefully, nodded to the bandleader, pressed his arms firmly to his side, raised his chin high, and then began singing "The Star-Spangled Banner" in a voice that made up in fervor what it lacked in quality of tone, and only a few bars behind the band. The members of the audience, rather taken aback, were a little slow in getting to their feet, but presently they were also joining in fervently. When this was over, Seiermann said, as if addressing somebody actually there: "Thank you, Mr. President. I am appreciative of the honor that you do me." Some members of the audience looked at each other in bewilderment, not quite sure of what honor Seiermann was referring to, but it became apparent that he was referring to the fact that the President had sent him a telegram.

"I make this promise," declared Seiermann, not specifying whether the promise was to the President or to the audience, "while I remain the head of this studio we shall make here the finest pictures, and they will be pictures that the American people will be proud of. If you ask me what is my policy at Seiermann-International, I can give you the answer in one word: the best. That is my policy, and it always will be. To bring the American public the finest there is in entertainment. God willing, I will succeed. Because I think this is the greatest country in the world, and that is something I want to show up there on the screen. There are some people who forget that the people who pay to see the pictures are the ordinary, decent folk who make up the vast

199

majority of the nation. What these fine, ordinary folk want to see is beauty. Yes, beauty. I'm not ashamed to use the word, like some people are. Nature can be beautiful, music can be beautiful, the love of a boy for his mother can be beautiful, and the love of a boy for a girl can be the most beautiful thing of all; sex also can be beautiful, handled with taste. With taste. Ugliness, vulgarity—that is something I will not put up with and I will not tolerate. We will make decent pictures here for decent folk and—we are not prudes —there will be sex in them, but it will be decent sex. Because what is more beautiful than a beautiful girl, and this is a studio that has got more beautiful girls than any other. Also, we got some of the finest actors and stars and directors in the world, many of whom you see behind me. Now I would like to introduce you to some of my principal associates. My brother, Mr. Fred Seiermann, who is Vice-President and Studio Manager. My other brother, Leo, who is Vice-President in charge of theaters." Seiermann paused. "Now some of you, I can imagine, are saying this guy Seiermann sure has got a lot of relatives." This evoked laughter from the audience. "Well, I tell you," he went on, "if that's what you're saying, you never said a truer word." (More laughter.) "It so happens, I'm a man that's proud of his family, and so I would like to introduce you to the rest of them. First, my wife, Sarah. Sarah, my dear, would you stand up so that the nice people can see you." To the audience he added confidentially, "She's not used to publicity, so she's a little shy." There was prolonged applause as Sarah, who was sitting on the platform immediately behind Seiermann, got up, smiled awkwardly, and sat down again. "Now my oldest little girl, Sandra. Sandra, darling, stand up, sweetheart. . . . She's five," he added. Sandra, who had been sitting next to her mother, got up and curtsied. "And our youngest, Esther." He picked up Esther in his arms, made clucking baby-noises at her and held her aloft for all to see. "Esther," he announced, "was four yesterday." This revelation occasioned another burst of applause. "Unfortunately," declared Seiermann, "the rest of my family were unable to be with us today." There was an ironical shout of "Shame" from one part of the audience, followed by titters. "It is a shame," said Seiermann, not in the least perturbed, "because I'm a man who believes in the family, as I think the majority of decent Americans do, and I'm a man who likes to share whatever success I have with those nearest and dearest to me." Some of the bravos that this statement aroused were heavily ironical, but Seiermann was not put out. "And now," he said, "to proceed with the ceremony."

There was another blast of trumpets from the band, and out of the audience emerged two men, carrying between them an enormous golden key. They carried it up the platform steps and, to the accompaniment of the photographers' flashes, handed it to Seiermann, who grasped it firmly in his two hands and then lifted it high above his head like a weightlifter. He stood like that for several moments, the golden key held aloft, while the audience applauded and the photographers reloaded their cameras, and perspiration ran down his face.

The ceremony was over; the stars and directors on the platform got up and after first shaking hands with Seiermann, or embracing him, or both, made their way down the steps. The audience left their seats and made their way back toward the marquee, or accepted glasses of champagne from the waiters.

"An historic occasion," said Lewis Sholt to Janet. Once again Janet found herself being towed back and forth across the lawn, Lewis Sholt holding her wrist so tight it was like being manacled to him. All the time his eyes, keen as a fisherman's, were searching, searching. . . . Seiermann and the studio's contract personalities were now mingling with the guests, saying good-by to those who had to leave, accepting the congratulations of others, holding forth to reporters. Wherever Seiermann went, a group, consisting of his two brothers, his publicity chief, his personal assistant, and his girl secretary, followed, and at their heels came photographers, reporters and various people who were trying to catch Seiermann's eye. When he wished to talk to someone, his minions parted like the Red Sea, so as to give this privileged individual a chance to approach; when Seiermann didn't want to talk to someone, his minions formed a solid and impenetrable ring around him. Lewis Sholt was watching this carefully, waiting for his moment: he saw Seiermann waving to Wallace Reid, saw Wallace Reid acknowledge the greeting and turn to approach Seiermann, saw the group around Seiermann opening to admit the actor into their collective embrace. . . . This was the moment Lewis Sholt chose to rush up to Wallace Reid, wrap one

201

arm fondly around his shoulder, while still towing Janet by the other hand, fall in step with him, whisper congratulations in his ear—and so when the minions again closed the circle, Lewis Sholt and Janet were inside it and in the presence of Seiermann.

"Willi!" Lewis Sholt exclaimed, as if amazed to find him there. "Want to add my congratulations. All the very best to you, Willi. And, incidentally, congratulations on your little girl's birthday, what a charmer she is."

"Thank you, Lewis, thanks," said Seiermann, giving his shoulder a rough, manly squeeze, intended to serve as both a greeting and a dismissal and to exempt him from any further social obligations to the agent; as he turned away, Lewis Sholt detained him by returning the rough, manly shoulder squeeze, and in the process he politely, but forcefully, revolved Seiermann until he was facing Janet.

"Want you to meet somebody, Willi," said Lewis Sholt. "This is Janet Derringer."

"Very pleased to meet you, Miss Derringer," said Seiermann, extricating himself from Sholt's grip. "Lovely to see you, Lewis. Lovely girl." Their moment was over. Now he was embracing Wally Reid. "Won't keep you from your other guests," said Sholt. He seemed pleased with himself as he led Janet away.

"Glad I had a chance to introduce you to Willi," he said. "Willi is an old friend, a great showman and a great guy, and powerful. And I got an 'in' with him. He trusts my judgment. I was the one who made Willi what he is today. I brought him *Arlesia* when he was just a small-time theater operator with a few shabby houses on the Lower East Side. What he is today he owes to me, and Willi is not the sort of guy who forgets an obligation like that. So, you see, I'm very glad he met you because, if *he* liked you, and I think he did, there's no limit to how far you can go."

"I only met him for a second," Janet protested, "and there must be hundreds of people here. He won't even remember me."

"He'll remember you, baby," said Lewis Sholt. "Because I'll remind him. That's what you got an agent for."

Two days later he telephoned her at the apartment. "Listen, baby, I think you made a hit." For a moment she was puzzled.

202

"Who's that?"

"Lewis Sholt. You asleep or something? I was saying—I think you made a hit. With Willi. Talked to him just now. He wants to meet you."

"He wants to meet me? Goodness!"

"Are you free later tonight?"

"Tonight—it's already four o'clock and I haven't. . . ."

"He may not be able to see you tonight, or on the other hand he may. But the thing is to hold yourself in readiness, *in case he can*. He's got a lot on, but he's going to try and fit you in *somewhere*. So get yourself dolled up, baby, and sit tight. Could be he won't be able to see you until late so you better get out your finery—something swish? In case you have to meet him in a restaurant. And, listen, baby, don't eat dinner, he may want you to eat with him, and if you got no appetite it's not polite. On the other hand, don't leave yourself so hungry that you're starving and don't feel at your best, because he may not be able to see you until *after* dinner. I got to hang up now. I'll call you the moment I hear from Willi."

Janet had a bath, and put on her one good dress—sleeveless, reaching just below the knee and draped in loose graceful folds over her body, rather like a monk's cowl. At the waist, she wore a loose hanging sash of black velvet, adorned by a posy of artificial flowers. Underneath, she wore her fine lace panties and silk hose. All dressed up, she waited by the telephone, getting hungrier and hungrier, nibbling at pieces of bread and cheese but not daring to eat a proper meal in case she should be asked to dinner. As the time went by and the telephone didn't ring and her stomach rumbled complainingly, she became more and more nervous. She kept pouring herself drinks to steel herself for the coming interview, and by the time Lewis Sholt rang up to say that unfortunately Willi couldn't make it tonight—he was too exhausted—she was too sloshed to care. For the next four nights Janet was asked to hold herself in readiness, and each night Lewis Sholt rang up to say that Willi couldn't make it. On the fifth night Sholt arrived in person at the apartment. "You ready, baby? Willi's expecting you. You haven't eaten, I hope?"

"I haven't eaten for five nights."

"Good. Willi's a big eater and he don't like to see a girl sitting there picking at her food. He's a gourmet. So when

203

you eat something he's suggested don't just eat it, enjoy
it, and *look* as though you're enjoying it. Incidentally, in
case I didn't mention it when I came in, you look terrific."

"Yes?"

"A million dollars."

"Thank you."

"Don't thank me. Thank God!"

CHAPTER TEN

The restaurant where they were to meet Seiermann was
called Anton's; Janet had never heard of it. She expected a
rather grandly opulent place and was slightly disappointed
when the cab drew up outside a plain door with a modest
canopy above it saying "Anton's." It was very dark inside.
Three or four people were squashed together in a small
room under a huge chandelier that gave virtually no light;
they talked in soft voices which carried no distance at all
but were immediately soaked up by the deep carpets, the
rich upholstery and the heavy tapestries on the walls. When
Lewis Sholt said whom they were joining, the headwaiter
led them up some narrow, carpeted stairs to a room on the
first floor. This was not much larger than the one downstairs. It contained six tables, three of which had been
grouped together, and at which sat Seiermann and three
other men. The other tables were unoccupied. As Janet and
Lewis Sholt approached, one of these men jumped to his
feet and introduced himself as Anton. Seiermann finished
what he was saying before looking round and seeing Janet.
Then he too got to his feet, and the two other men followed suit. "This is Miss Derringer," said Seiermann, and
indicating each of the two men in turn: "Mr. Perce Trope,
Mr. Harry Krantz. Lewis Sholt you know." Seiermann indicated where Janet and Sholt were to sit—Anton held the
chair for her until she was seated and then resumed his
own place next to Seiermann. He snapped his fingers and
a waiter appeared from whom he obtained two huge menus
which he handed to Janet and Sholt. "The gentleman have
already ordered," he said.

The four men were in a row against the wall: Anton, on
the edge of his seat, half sitting, half hovering, from time

to time snapping his fingers to summon a waiter into whose ear he whispered some instruction or other; he was seated closest to the door; next to him sat Harry Krantz, a bony, tough-looking young man with a crew cut; next to him Perce Trope, an oily-skinned, middle-aged man who smiled a lot; and next to him Seiermann.

For the next quarter of an hour, Seiermann finished what he was saying, his face in profile to Janet. What he was saying was meaningless to her. In her nervous state she caught only snatches of it. ". . . decided we ought to have the company listed . . . recapitalized for a million shares of stock . . . only issued half a million at the beginning . . . the A shares have no votes, it's the B shares that carry voting control. . . ." Once or twice during this discourse, which seemed to call for no more than nodding assent or appreciative chuckles from the listeners, Janet put a cigarette in her mouth which Seiermann lit for her while continuing to speak and without looking in her direction: he merely struck the match, and Janet was obliged to lean forward across the table in order to insert the tip of her cigarette in the flame. As she was evidently excluded from the conversation that Seiermann was having with these men, she tried a couple of times to say something to Lewis Sholt, but he immediately shushed her. The oily-skinned man, who was listening so attentively to Seiermann, occasionally allowed his eyes to do a brief circuit of the room and whenever they rested on Janet he gave her a polite smile, which she found it rather a strain to have to return after the fifth time. The other man, Harry Krantz, kept giving her hard, sharp looks from under thick, bunched eyebrows, Lewis Sholt kept punctuating Seiermann's discourse with "fantastic," and "oh great! oh great!" and "well, whad'you know." Waiters were hovering, waiting to catch Seiermann's eye, Anton having indicated by an unequivocal waving of his finger that they were not to interrupt. Neither Janet nor Lewis Sholt had yet been asked to order, evidently for fear this might cause un unwelcome interruption at a vital moment in Seiermann's monologue. Eventually, feeling she had to say something to check the mounting nervousness, she called to the waiter just behind her: "Could I order something? I haven't eaten yet. . . ." Lewis Sholt gave her a disapproving look. But Seiermann immediately stopped talking.

"The lady hasn't ordered yet?" he demanded in astonishment of the waiter. He gave Anton a pained, rebuking look.

"Her order will be taken immediately," said Anton. He snapped his fingers and the waiter obediently bent his head close to Janet's to take her order. She was looking in some perplexity through the vast array of dishes listed on the enormous menu. Seiermann leaned back in his seat and watched her, and now that they were released of their obligation to listen the two other men swiveled in their seats and also looked at her. Anton had taken this opportunity to get to his feet. Having suddenly become the focus of all their eyes, Janet felt herself reddening.

"I think I'd like a steak," she said indecisively.

"And to start, Madam?"

"Have some turtle soup," advised Seiermann.

"All right," she said.

"How would you like your steak, Madam?" Again Janet seemed uncertain.

"Give her a filet steak, medium rare," said Seiermann. "And some asparagus." He looked at her inquiringly and she nodded assent. "And after that some snipe stuffed with *foie gras* like we're all having."

"Goodness," she said, "I couldn't eat all that."

"If you don't want it, you can leave it," said Seiermann, "but I think when you see it you'll want it. What about you, Lewis?"

"I'll have the same," said Lewis Sholt quickly.

"Wonderful," declared Seiermann. He leaned well back in the seat and examined her with unabashed directness for several moments. Janet didn't know what to do with her eyes, whether to look away or to return his look, or to modestly stare at her fingernails. "So you'd like to be in pictures, Miss Derringer?" he said at length. All the men smiled as if he'd said something witty.

"Who wouldn't," she responded.

"Hmm. You have any talent—?" This produced discreet titters from the men.

Lewis Sholt said quickly: "You got to admit, Willi, she's a remarkably beautiful girl."

"Stand up, Miss Derringer," said Seiermann. She gave a little frown, her mouth got halfway to forming a smile and didn't quite make it.

"Stand up, baby, like Willi says," Lewis Sholt urged her

softly. She shrugged and got to her feet; Seiermann's eyes started at her head and moved down, when they got to her waist he leaned round the side of the table to examine her legs; finding his view obstructed by the tablecloth he made an impatient gesture with his hand, indicating that she was to step clear of the table. She did so, and he continued his leisurely scrutiny of her. "Hmm," he murmured, "for once, Lewis, you are not exaggerating."

"May I sit down now?" Janet asked, allowing a slight irony to creep into her voice. The waiter held the chair for her as she resumed her seat.

"Not only beautiful, but proud as well," said Seiermann. "Maybe you'd like us all to stand up so you can look *us* over, and then maybe you'll give *us* a chance in pictures. You want to see *my* legs? Gladly. See, I don't get offended." Without waiting for an answer he got to his feet, placed one foot on the velvet upholstered seat and drew his trousers up a few inches, exposing a hairy calf. The men laughed appreciatively.

"Beautiful," declared Janet.

"You know, I like this girl," said Seiermann, turning to the other men, "She's got a sense of humor and she don't scare easy. She's got spirit. A girl like that could be a star." The men all smiled in a noncommittal way, not sure whether Seiermann was serious or kidding.

"That's what I think," said Lewis Sholt, "I would say she's definitely star material."

"I thought," said Seiermann, "that you had an urgent appointment later this evening, Lewis. To visit your sick mother or something." For a moment Lewis Sholt was taken aback, then he said quickly: "I have got to make a phone call later on."

"Well, then, why don't you make your phone call, Lewis? Maybe your sick mother is calling for you. Young people nowadays got no feelings. His mother is *dying,* and he sits here stuffing himself with food, feeling a pretty girl between her legs under the tablecloth. Why don't you go to your dying mother, Lewis, like a good son, and let *me* feel Miss Derringer between her legs?"

"Willi's a great kidder, a great kidder," said Lewis Sholt, joining in the general raucous male laughter.

"Who's kidding?" said Seiermann. "If you haven't got a dying mother, at least have the decency to invent one when you see somebody is politely trying to get rid of you."

"As a matter of fact," said Lewis Sholt, seriously, "like I told you, Willi, I may have to visit this friend of mine who's . . ." Seiermann cut him short. "Look," he said, "your private affairs is none of my business. If you want to let your mother die all alone while you're screwing some little floozie . . ."

"It's, it's not like that," stammered Lewis Sholt, "it's—"

"A boy!' exclaimed Seiermann in mock horror. "I didn't know you were like that, Lewis. But if that's what you like. GO MAKE YOUR PHONE CALL."

"All right, Willi." Lewis Sholt got to his feet.

"Better still," said Seiermann, "don't make a phone call, take a cab, take a cab to your little friend who's pining his heart out for you."

The grin on Lewis Sholt's face was frozen solid. "Maybe I ought to keep this appointment, baby, it's business," he murmured to Janet. "I'm sure Willi will see you get home all right."

"Get home!" exclaimed Seiermann. "Miss Derringer is planning to go home tonight? A girl is invited to dinner with three charming, handsome men, and already, she's no sooner sat down, she's thinking about going home? Is that polite? Miss Derringer, you want to go home?" The slightly strained chuckles of the others provided a continuous accompaniment to Seiermann's words.

"I also have an appointment," said Janet coldly, her face white. "I think I'd better leave with Mr. Sholt."

"All right," said Seiermann. "Let his mother die alone. Let his boyfriend pine away. Sit down, Lewis. Eat your dinner. It seems Miss Derringer feels more safe with you around." The waiters were now serving the soup; Lewis Sholt sat down. In total silence they all began to sip their soup. For several minutes nobody said a word, everybody concentrating on the soup. Then Lewis Sholt said: "I'm sure, Willi, Janet didn't mean to offend you. I hope you're not offended, Willi."

"Offended," said Willi, "Why should I be offended? You ask me I should see a client of yours, I'm an easy man, I say, 'All right, bring her to dinner.' You want to show me what a talent she is, all right, show me. I'm waiting, I'm listening. So far all I hear is about your dying mother and your boyfriend and that she wants to go home."

208

"Well, this is the way I see it, Willi," said Lewis Sholt. "That she's a stunner you wouldn't deny."

"I don't deny anything, I'm eating my soup."

"What I feel is," Lewis Sholt went on, "that given the chance, she could be built up into star material. She doesn't have much experience, but in my opinion she's a natural."

"It could be, it could be," conceded Seiermann. "What have you got in mind?"

"The usual contract, usual options. I'm not going to hold out for any special deal because what she needs, first of all, is the chance to show what she can do."

"What's that, Lewis?"

"What, Willi?"

"What she can do?"

"How d'you mean?"

"Well, for instance, can she talk? She doesn't talk much."

"Nobody has given me a chance so far," said Janet hotly, feeling the anger rising in her.

"Take it easy, baby, take it easy," Lewis Sholt cautioned.

"Hallelujah! She can talk," exclaimed Seiermann. "What else can she do?"

"I'll be frank with you, Willi, I won't guarantee you she can act because she hasn't yet. . . ."

"So she can't act, she can hardly talk . . . can she screw? At least that she should be able to do?" The men all gave deep male laughs.

"Well," said Lewis Sholt, grinning sheepishly, "that's something I haven't tested personally. . . ."

"I forgot you're only interested in boys."

"Oh, come on, Willi, quit kidding. Give me a break. I'm trying to do something for this kid because I believe in her potential. . . ."

"You're right," said Seiermann, "you're absolutely quite right. Now lets see. There's a little part in the Raoul Walsh picture, we could try her in that. She looks right for it. She could be very good for that."

"That would be great, Willi."

"There are a few little parts coming up. Not too important, you know. It's possible to take a chance on a newcomer. No doubt about it, she looks good. I tell you what, Lewis. I'll give it my personal consideration. Is that fair? Is that fair, Miss Derringer?"

"You mean you'll give me some parts?"

"If you're right for them, why not? Why not? This business needs new talent. We're always on the lookout for new talent. And Lewis Sholt is no fool—are you, Lewis?—so if he comes to me and says 'I've got a girl with possibilities,' it's worth giving it a try."

"Thank you, Willi," Lewis Sholt declared gratefully.

"Say we start her at a hundred a week?"

"That's very reasonable, Willi."

"I get Fred Niblo to shoot a test of her."

"That's very nice of you, Willi."

"That's an improvement on what you been earning before?" inquired Seiermann. "How much can you make in these dance joints?"

"Not much. The girls get half of what the customer pays for each dance," said Janet. "Five cents."

"But she hasn't been doing that for a long time now," said Lewis Sholt. "She quit that a long time ago."

"So for five cents you let them have a quick feel? It's not exorbitant." He turned to the other men. "You wouldn't say that was exorbitant?" He put a hand in his pocket and took out something. "Tell you what," he said, "here's a dollar. . . ." He threw the coin down on the table. "What do I get for a dollar?" Very blatantly, he lifted the table-cloth and put his hand underneath and searched for her knee. There wasn't much room under the table, which was fairly narrow, and it was difficult to entirely avoid his searching hand. "Obviously," said Seiermann, his hand still groping underneath the table, "you don't get much for a dollar. Say I made that ten dollars? No? Fifty? A hundred? Listen, how much does it cost these days to get laid?" The men roared.

"I'm sure you know the price," said Janet, "but I don't. I'd like to leave. My God, I thought people only behaved like this in jokes."

"Now, baby," said Lewis Sholt, "don't get sore. Willi don't mean anything, he's just kidding around."

"I don't like being kidded around," she said, "and I don't like his wet hands feeling up my legs. So I'm leaving." She got up. As Seiermann realized that she was serious about leaving, a look of startled horror came over his face. Lewis Sholt got up too.

"I'm sorry, Willi," he said, "I hope you won't hold this

210

against me. I better put the dumb cluck in a cab. I'll be back."

"Don't trouble yourself," said Seiermann. Janet was already by the stairs, hesitating, uncertain of whether to wait for Lewis Sholt or not.

"Listen, Willi," said Lewis Sholt in a confidential voice, "if you like her—look, I'll fix it somehow. I promise you. I'll have a talk with her. She's just a dumb, raw kid, eighteen years old—she don't know what's what. Look, Willi, in my business, you think I want to antagonize you? Where will you be later on? I'll send her round to you. Look, if it's impossible—I'll send *somebody*."

"So long as I don't have to see your face. . . ."

"Oh, come on, Willi, what you want me to do? Open a vein? Is it my fault? Let me know where you'll be, later, and I'll make it up to you—somehow. Listen, Willi, I got a whole lot of girls on my books and they're not all as dumb as this one. Look, I'll be at my apartment in twenty minutes, give me a little time to make a few calls. I'll call you here within the hour. Within the hour. That's a promise. And if I don't come up with something, you can tread me into the dirt, I'll deserve it."

The next day an enormous bouquet of roses arrived for Janet. With them was a card saying: "I'm big enough to admit when I'm in the wrong." It was signed Willi Seiermann. Later in the morning his secretary at the studio telephoned her to ask if she was free to dine with Mr. Seiermann that evening. She said she was sorry but she couldn't. For the next four days flowers kept arriving from Seiermann, and each day his secretary telephoned to ask if she was free for dinner. On each occasion she said that she was busy. On the fifth day the secretary rang and said, "Just a moment, Miss Derringer. I have Mr. Seiermann for you." Janet waited for ten minutes, and when Seiermann had still not come to the line she hung up. Two minutes after, the telephone rang again. She did not answer. As the telephone kept ringing, at intervals of four minutes, she went out and spent the rest of the day seeing three movies in a row.

That evening Lewis Sholt came to see her at the apartment.

"You certainly messed up your chances with Willi," he sighed.

"I don't care," she said.

"Listen, baby," he said, "I just don't understand you. It's not like you was some kind of pure snow maiden that's never been touched. Willi's an important guy—you have to antagonize him? Can't you be civil to him?"

"I don't like him."

"Did you like all those guys you danced with at the Palm Room?"

"That was different. And I didn't go with any of them. And, anyway, I quit that job."

"Did anyone say you *got* to sleep with Willi? You can't blame him for *trying*—it's a compliment."

"The way he acts is no compliment."

"That's just his way, honey. He never had any education —no upbringing. All right, he's—crude. There are worse things in the world. Listen, baby, be realistic. These guys are not going to put any girl in pictures who don't attract them. If they make a pass, at least it means you've got to square one—they're interested. Now, if you're smart, you keep them interested. This isn't a business like banking. The way these guys operate is: they figure if I go for this chick maybe a couple of million paying customers will too. That's how it works. I don't say you *have* to sleep with them to make it, but what I do say is that if *they* don't want to sleep with you then you got about as much chance as snowballs in hell. With all these good-looking chicks around, are they going to sign up somebody that leaves them cold? Does that figure? You tell me. Let's face it, baby, what are you selling? Brains? Acting? What you're selling is that a guy looks at you and says to himself—'Boy! That's for me.' Sure it's crude, but that's the nature of this business. You're not selling objets de art. So if somebody like Willi gets a yen for you, that's a good sign. Encourage him. If you don't want to go through with it, that's your business. I don't say you got to open your legs to these guys first time round, that'd be just cheap. On the other hand, don't overdo the playing-hard-to-get bit. Play them along—you're not such an innocent I got to tell you how to do that. Willi's flipping for you—don't slap him down. Each time you slap him down you're slapping me too. Do I deserve that? I been working my guts out trying to get something for you, trying to get you started. Once you're a name, baby, you can slap down whoever you like, you can have yourself a ball slapping down every guy who gets fresh. But now you got to play along a little. Listen, baby, you think I would waste my time giving you good advice if I didn't believe in you? I believe in you. I believe in your potential. And I'm not talking about chicken feed. You know how much Mae Murray makes? Seventy-five hundred bucks a week. When you're making that kind of dough you can afford to be a lady, you can spit in their eye—because then they need *you*. You're playing for high stakes, baby. One day they'll come to you with wet palms to get your signature on a contract. They'll get hot pants for you as an *artiste*. That's the day you can spit in their eye. But now—be nice to them. For my sake?"

"Lewis, I don't think I'm cut out for this business."

"What d'you mean? You're a natural. You can be great."

When Seiermann next phoned her she agreed to have dinner with him. Taking her home in his chauffeur-driven car, he drew the curtain on the glass partition separating the driver from the rear compartment. "Oh no," she said. "Please don't do that."

He offered her $300 to spend the night with him; when she refused he started grappling with her. It was difficult to shake him off, he was so strong and insistent. His hands were on her breasts and under her dress, and his lips were on her neck and face. He couldn't believe that she was refusing him. He was as petulant as a child being denied a toy. The next time she went out with him, a few days later, his offer had gone up to $500. When she still refused, he said that he would see to it she was black-listed, that not only would she never work in any picture he made, but she would never work in any picture that anybody else made. The next day he telephoned, apologized profusely for his bad behavior, said that of course he hadn't meant it about the black-listing, and pleaded with her to have dinner with him again that night. She said she was busy all that week and all the following week. After that, he didn't telephone any more. Lewis Sholt also stopped telephoning, and when she called him to ask if he'd been able to get any work for her, he replied that he was working on it, but it wasn't easy, there wasn't a lot of work around, and there were twenty girls for every job that came up. But he'd let her know.

Jim Kae had been away for several weeks, taking stills for a picture being made in Death Valley. When he came back, they had some marvelous days together. Though she kept assuring him that she knew there was nothing lasting in their relationship, it was so good while it was going on she could not believe that it would really end. She was completely unprepared when he told her, late in October, that he was going to Europe, that he was leaving the next morning, and that he did not know when he would be back. There was no need for her to move out. He had renewed the lease of the apartment. Once he had left she realized to what extent she had become dependent on him. Again, she had long bouts of melancholia. From time to time she got some modeling work, posing for pictures in girlie magazines. The men who took these pictures often asked her to go out with them, and when she could not face being alone in the apartment she accepted. Most of these evenings ended with a tussle in the cab on the way home. She developed a variety of techniques for coping with this situation: the most effective one was to be compliant for the duration of the cab ride and then quicky run upstairs while the man was paying off the driver.

November was a bad month. She had very little work and the depressions were becoming worse. At such times, trying to conjure up images to counteract the dark moods, she discovered, by a process of trial and error, that the only pictures that were at all effective in this respect were of those nights when she had been taken out by Willi Seiermann, and had fought with him in the back of his car. She could not understand why this should be because she still thought him repulsive, and she was sure that if he telephoned her now her attitude would be the same; but still it did cheer her up to think of him—of this terribly important man—wanting her so badly.

She was very surprised, on opening the door, to see Lewis Sholt. It was weeks since she had spoken to him, or his secretary, on the phone.

"Just thought I'd drop round and see how you are, baby," he said. As he came into the apartment, his eyes took in the disorder, the stacks of unwashed crockery in the kitchen. "You look marvelous, baby," he said.

"I don't feel it. In fact, I feel like hell."

214

"A bit low—huh?" he said, understandingly. "You need to get out more. A gorgeous-looking girl like you—you ought to be having the time of your life. Tell you what, how would you like to go to a party?"

"Not in the mood," she said.

"No—I mean a real great Hollywood party. I see you need taking out of yourself. Just what you need. At Jamie Nelson's. You ever seen his house pictured in the movie mags? Boy, what a house that is!"

"At James Nelson's?" she said.

"Yuh—I'm invited, I'll take you if you like. You'll meet some people. You'll have a good time."

"You mean you want to take me to a party at James Nelson's house?"

"Yes, sure. That's what I been saying."

She laughed. "James Nelson is my idol. I just idolized him from when I was a kid."

"Yuh, all the dames flip for him. You want to come?"

"You think I look all right?"

"You look great, baby. Just need to tidy up a bit and you look great."

She felt suddenly happy and excited and thrilled. "I'd love to come," she said.

As Janet went out to get changed, he dialed a number. "Oh—hello. Is Mr. Nelson available by any chance? Uhu-uhu. . . . Well, it *is* urgent . . . Lewis Sholt . . . yes, he does . . . Sholt . . . S-H-O-L-T. . . ." He waited, impatiently, for about five minutes. Then: "Hello? Hello? Hello, *Jamie?* Jamie? Is that James Nelson? This is Lewis. *Lewis!* Lewis Sholt. Hello, *Mr. Nelson?* no . . . don't hang up, you remember me, Mr. Nelson? Lewis Sholt, *the agent.* Sure you remember me, Mr. Nelson . . . we had that long talk that time at the Coconut Grove and you said for me to ring you any time. . . . What do I *want* . . . ? You remember we discussed . . . uh, you don't . . . well, all right, I'll be brief, sure . . ." He lowered his voice, looking toward the door through which Janet had left. ". . . Well, you see, Jamie, there's this chick I'm with right now, and I said how I knew you and, well, that there was this party you were giving tonight, I thought maybe I could bring her round there . . . remembering our conversation at the Co-conut Grove . . . Yes, terrific looking . . . Blonde . . . eighteen. . . ." Lewis Sholt gave a slightly awkward chuckle. "Well,

Jamie, that's something I can't guarantee . . . but you don't have any trouble making out as a rule . . . well, I wouldn't waste your time if I didn't feel pretty sure. . . . Oh, definitely. . . . Yes, yes. Oh, we could be there in about an hour. Two hours? Fine. Great. See you then, Jamie. Oh—and nice talking to you again, Jamie. 'Bye." An air of self-satisfaction on his face, Lewis Sholt went into the corridor and called through the bathroom door. "Well, honey, it's all fixed. I just talked to Jamie and he said sure, he'd be charmed for me to bring along a guest." Before they left, he said to her: "Now, just one thing, baby. Let's get one thing clear. With you I have to say this. Now a party is a party. It can happen that sometimes a guy gets a bit fresh. Now you're not going to run screaming out of the room, hollering for ma, if some guy happens to get a bit fresh. Are you? Because if you are, you might as well not come and save me the embarrassment."

"It's going to be that sort of party, is it?" she said.

"Well, I don't know, baby. How should I know?"

She shrugged. "Don't worry, Lewis," she said, "just because I don't like Willi Seiermann doesn't mean I'm against *men*. How do I look?"

"Fabulous."

She gave a pleased, sexy wiggle of her shoulders. "Come on, then," she said, "I'm dying to meet James Nelson."

The driveway seemed to be very long and very dark; looking out she saw the strange huddle of shapes against the sky; the domes and cupolas of the house. They were admitted by a butler into a rather somber hall and asked to wait. It did not sound as if there was a party going on. The silence was inviolable, they felt obliged to talk in whispers as if they were in a museum. She remembered she'd seen pictures of James Nelson's principal bathroom in one of the movie magazines. The bath had faucets consisting of gold dolphins at the four corners, and it was enormous; according to this article she'd read, he had sea water piped into his bath from the ocean. She also remembered reading that he had an aviary, and a cricket pitch where members of the English colony played cricket every Saturday. Or was that at Ronald Coleman's? Standing up, she looked at herself in a very dark mirror. She decided she looked pretty swish. She was wearing a rose-colored evening gown,

216

decorated with patterns of silvery beads. The gown laced up at the back, the laces crisscrossing an area of exposed flesh, narrow at the waist and widening slightly at the shoulders. I do look pretty marvelous, she thought, and the thought made her feel less nervous. Pinned on to the left shoulder strap was a large rose, lying on leaf. Several strings of beads hung from her neck to below her waist. "You think I look all right?" she whispered to Lewis Sholt.

"Great, baby. You look great."

It was twenty minutes before James Nelson came out. He was shorter than she had imagined him to be, well under six foot. And he didn't look the same in a dinner suit— she had always seen him in costume roles. "I *am* most awfully sorry," he said, "but I was expecting you earlier." She looked in puzzlement at Lewis Sholt. "I'm afraid we've already eaten."

"I thought it was a party," she said.

"Yes." He smiled. "A dinner party. I'm afraid you've come just when everybody is leaving." Hearing his voice was a bit of a shock; it didn't seem to fit at all with the image she had always had of him. It didn't go with his exuberant screen personality. It was a thin, rather high-pitched and terribly English voice, though she'd read somewhere that he had actually been born in Lithuania.

"I am very sorry about this mix-up," he said. "Perhaps um . . . Lewis . . . Lewis? . . . you'd bring this charming young lady another evening." With the realization that they were being sent away, she reddened. "Unless that is," he added, "you'd like to stay a little. By all means, if you'd care to. A few of us are having a little poker game. Do you play poker?"

"Not the kind of stakes you play for, Jamie," said Lewis Sholt.

"I *am* sorry," said James Nelson.

"Well, another night maybe, Jamie."

"Yes, indeed. I'll look forward to seeing you both. I'm very glad to have met . . ."

"Janet Derringer," said Lewis Sholt.

"If you would care to stay for a while, you're most welcome."

Janet felt deeply disappointed; it was so humiliating to have got all excited and dressed up and then be sent away.

217

Now she was here she might as well have a drink at least. "I don't mind staying for a *little* while," she said.

"In that case, you stay, baby," said Lewis Sholt. "Poker games are my undoing. If I stick around, I'm liable to lose my shirt. But you stay, baby. Jamie will see you get home all right."

"My driver will take you home whenever you say," said James Nelson, "so if you feel like it, please do stay." She was confused; having said she wanted to stay—naturally assuming that Lewis Sholt would stay too—she didn't know how she could now change her mind without seeming rude, and anyway she did want to stay. She had always wanted to meet James Nelson. "All right," she said.

"I'll see you, Jamie," said Lewis Sholt. "'Bye, baby. Be good."

James Nelson took her arm and led her into "the den" where five men sat around a card table, drinks by them, two of them without their jackets; the cigar smoke made her cough. As the men all stood up she saw that one of them was Willi Seiermann. When she was introduced, he said, "Yes, we met already."

"Ah, you're a sly dog," said James Nelson. He pulled up a chair for her and asked the butler to bring her a drink. For the next hour nobody spoke to her. She might not have been there. Periodically, the butler refilled the men's glasses, and hers; the men relit their cigars when they had gone out; money—large quantities of money—changed hands. Everyone was entirely absorbed in the game, which she did not understand and which nobody explained to her. She had started becoming embarrassed after the first fifteen minutes as she realized they were not just finishing one hand, or round, or whatever it was, but that they were carrying on with their game without feeling under any obligation to take any notice of her presence. The most dignified thing to do, in the circumstances, was to pretend that she was intensely interested in the game and, therefore, was not conscious of their rudeness to her. After an hour and a half had gone by without anyone talking to her, she realized she might possibly have to sit like this all night. The cigar smoke was irritating her eyes. She coughed and said, "I do have to go now."

"I'm so sorry," said James Nelson, "that you have to go. I'll get Hank to take you."

Willi Seiermann got up, stretched himself and pulled at his dead cigar. "Jamie, I'm going to call it a night. I got to be up early in the morning." There were some attempts to make him stay longer, but he insisted that he was too tired. "Well, if you're going, Willi," said James Nelson, "maybe you could drop Miss Derringer home."

"Glad to. My pleasure," said Willi.

In the car he behaved perfectly, said very little, made no reference to their previous tussles; the window on his side was half-lowered and he was breathing in the fresh air with relish. When the car stopped at the apartment, he said: "I got a terrible stomach burn. You don't happen to have some bicarbonate. Or an Alka-Seltzer?"

"I think I may," she said.

"I'd be much obliged," he said. "If it wouldn't inconvenience you." He told the chauffeur to wait, he'd be only a few minutes.

The apartment was very bare now that Jim Kae had taken down all his photographs from the studio wall and removed his equipment. Seiermann sat, his overcoat draped around his shoulders, on a couch, and drank the Alka-Seltzer she brought him. When he had finished it, he handed the empty glass back to her and said, "Thank you very much. You excuse me, I am dog-tired." He got up, patted her cheek in an avuncular way, and left. She went to the window and watched his limousine drawing away. She looked at herself in the mirror, and made a face. It had all been a terrible letdown; she felt humiliated and deeply disappointed.

CHAPTER ELEVEN

Under the impressive letterhead—Hector O. Hesslan Productions—there was just one short paragraph. It read: "Dear Miss Derringer, I have seen some pictures of you taken by Jim Kae. Could you come and see me here at the studio on Monday, 15th, at 4:15?" The signature was a bit of a scrawl, but underneath it were typed the words Personal Assistant to Mr. Hesslan. After a bit she was able to decipher the signature: Alexander Sondorf.

Janet arrived half an hour late for the appointment. The

secretary in the outer office looked dubiously at her wrist watch and pointed out that the appointment was for four fifteen, but she would find out if Mr. Sondorf could still see her. When she came back she said, unsmilingly, "Go in, Miss Derringer." She indicated the frosted glass door next to the paneled, mahogany one. Janet went in. The office, which was small and sparsely furnished—a desk, some chairs, a couple of filing cabinets—was empty. She waited uncertainly; then a door connecting with the adjacent office—presumably the one with the mahogany outer door—opened and a slight youth, carrying a stack of files, came in. He gave her a smile. "I—I had an appointment with Mr. Sondorf," she explained.

"That's right," he said, "I'm Alexander Sondorf."

"Oh!" She had expected somebody older and more impressive looking. This youngster, with his thick black hair and smooth, soft skin, looked as though he was fresh out of college.

"Sit down," he said easily, and put the files away in a drawer. He gave her another smile. He had very nice, intense, dark eyes, and there was a certain shyness in his smile. "I liked the pictures Jim Kae took of you," he said. "He's a very good photographer."

"Yes, he is."

"Do you have an agent?"

"I'm represented by Lewis Sholt."

"Oh yes. Well . . . I just wanted to meet you."

"Oh! I see." Once again, it seemed she was being given the run-around; only this one, having got her there, was evidently too shy and inexperienced to know how to follow through exactly. She wondered whether it might do her some good to play up to him, but decided it probably wasn't worth while. He didn't look the sort of person who could do her any good. She had had high hopes that this appointment, which had sounded so businesslike, might mean that the studio was genuinely interested in her, but obviously what had happened was that this kid had seen her pictures lying around on somebody's desk and had taken a fancy to her. They all wanted to get in on the act: even the office boys.

"I wanted to have a look at you . . ." he said.

"Yes?"

". . . to make sure I hadn't been taken in by Jim Kae's

photographic skill." He smiled again. People who were going to do something for you didn't smile so much. "How are you fixed tomorrow?"

"Tomorrow?" Surely he wasn't trying to make a date with her as clumsily as that.

"I'd like you to be here at two-thirty. Can you do that? You'll have to be on time." This last was said firmly, but his smile softened it.

"Why do I have to come tomorrow again?" she asked suspiciously.

"To have a screen test."

"Oh, I see," she said feebly.

"Well, can you be here at that time?" There was a slight sharpness in his voice.

"You mean I might get some parts?" she asked. She still thought he must have an angle. Screen tests were dangled tantalizingly in front of girls by men who wanted something in return, they weren't handed out just like that.

"I don't know," he said. "We test a lot of girls. But I wouldn't waste the company's money, or my time, if I didn't think you had something. When you come tomorrow, *please,* a little less make-up, and bring a change of clothes and a bathing costume. Don't try and look like anybody you've seen in movies. Bring what you would normally wear. All right?" He opened the door for her and was showing her out. She couldn't think of anything to say except, "Thank you very much—tomorrow, two-thirty?"

"That's right," he said kindly. "And don't lie awake all night thinking about it. I want you to look your best. If you are nervous, it doesn't matter. It'll be our job to make you feel relaxed. Good-by, Miss Derringer."

The next day when she arrived at the studio she was directed to stage G. There she found Alexander Sondorf, the cameraman, and a make-up girl, already waiting. After she had been made up and the cameraman had arranged the lighting to his satisfaction, Sondorf said gently: "Remember, everyone is nervous when they're being tested, so don't worry about it. You'll forget about it after a while." He gave her an encouraging smile.

On this stage there were several rather shabby permanent sets: a hilltop with an apple tree in full blossom: part of a grand staircase, the steps of which had been paint-

221

ed to look like marble: two walls of an elegant drawing room: and an exterior set representing a section of a cobbled Paris back street. Sondorf asked her to sit on the hilltop, under the apple tree. "I'm going to talk to you," he said, "I don't want you to act or pose. Just be yourself." She nodded vigorously; the strong lights made her blink, made it very hard for her to relax her face into a natural expression. "I want you to tell me about yourself," he was saying. "How old are you, Janet?"

"Eighteen," she gulped, addressing the bright dazzle of light which obscured him from her sight.

"Where are you from?"

"I'm from here. . . ."

"From Hollywood?"

"Los Angeles."

"A local girl?"

"Yes."

"Why d'you want to be in movies, Janet?"

"I-I-I suppose it's . . . well, I guess I want what everyone else . . ." Her voice trailed off. "I'm sorry, Mr. Sondorf —I'm making a mess of this . . . the lights are in my eyes . . . oh gosh! Is the camera going already? Oh, I'm sorry . . . I *am* making a mess of this. . . ."

"Why d'you think that? Don't look *into* the lights, look over here. That's right."

"What? Pardon—I am sorry, I didn't catch . . . ?"

"I asked why you think your making a mess of this."

"Well. . . ." She took a big breath. "I don't seem to be able to think of anything *intelligent* to say."

"Some girls might be more concerned in this situation about how they look—that they look pretty."

"Well, I know I look all right," she said with a little laugh.

"You're sure of yourself in that respect?"

"Is that wrong?"

"No, no. Not at all."

"Do I have to sit under this tree?—I feel so silly, sitting under this tree. Mr. Sondorf? Mr. Sondorf, are you there?"

"Yes," he said, "those sets are pretty silly and unconvincing. Just treat them as what they are—sets. You don't have to pretend you're sitting under a real apple tree."

"Oh, I see. I didn't know that."

"Janet, while you're talking, turn your head so that we

see you in profile and full-face. Will you do that? In your own time. Tell me something, Janet, do you think it would be glamorous being in movies—is that what appeals to you about it?"

"I should think it'd be *exciting*," she said. "I like to have lots of things happening around me, I like things to be going on all the time. I don't like the quiet much. I guess the quiet frightens me. Don't like sitting still—" She gave a little giggle. "I guess you noticed that."

"Walk about if you like, but don't go over that white line or you'll be out of camera."

She got up and gave the apple tree a disdainful look, examined some of the blossoms critically. "Doesn't look very real," she said.

"It photographs real. They say it photographs more real than real apple blossom—that's movies for you!"

"Well," she said, "what I like about movies—you wanted to know, didn't you?"

"Yes."

"Well, what I like—about being *in* movies, I mean—is . . . is you don't have to be the same person all the time. I mean, you can get so sick of yourself, being always the same. Sometimes I get awful bored with being me. Don't you? Don't you get bored with being—oh, I'm sorry, I didn't mean it like that. To be one person one day and somebody else the next, that must be exciting. I imagine you couldn't get bored with that. Is this the sort of thing you want me to say?"

"Say whatever you feel like saying."

"Aren't I suppose to be trying to *act?*"

"All right. I will give you something definite to do. Come down from that hilltop, you don't really like it up there, I can see. Go over to the Paris street." When she had got there, he said: "What I want you to do is to walk along the street. That's all. All right? Start walking. Now— up there, looking out of one of those windows, there's a boy watching you. Just a boy watching you, that's all. But you've noticed him before and the way he's watching you makes you feel good, attractive. You're just beginning to be noticed by boys and this makes you feel very good. When you get to the lamppost look up at him, give him a smile—not a vamping smile, a nice, warm, grateful smile, because you feel happy and pleased to be admired. Just a quick smile, and then walk on." When she had done this, he said: "I'm going to change the situation. Stay where you are by the lamppost. You're a whore. There's a man coming along the street toward you and you're trying to pick him up. He's seen you, he's looking at you. Give him a look that will stop him. To make it more difficult, this is your first time on the street, and you're frightened . . . it's got to be a bold, provocative look, but it's also got to have some of that frightened feeling in it."

When she had done as he had asked, he said, "All right, all right," and came out from behind the lights. He stood looking at her as if searching for words. "I'm sorry," he said eventually, "but I do think it's kindest to be blunt. My advice to you is get yourself a nice job some place with regular hours and regular pay. I don't think you have any talent that could be used in movies. I'm sorry, Miss Derringer." The disappointment which clouded her face was heart-rending. Tears came into her eyes despite all her efforts to hold them back. He stood watching her, making no attempt to console her. Then he smiled. "Now *that*," he said, "was good. You see, when you *feel* something, you can show it. But if you don't *feel* it, you don't know where to start, and you make all sorts of horrible grimaces to express something very simple. I'm sorry I had to do this to you just now, but I had to get some spontaneous reaction from you. I kept the camera going. You were good."

"I was?" Her face glowed with sudden happiness.

"And you looked very pretty, even crying." The way her face had lit up with pleasure was quite affecting. "There you are," he said, "and now you've given me the scene with the boy looking at you from the window. That was exactly what I wanted to see: that look of pleasure at being wanted. Well, that's all I'm going to ask you to do. They will want to do some routine stuff with you. Glamour poses—bathing costume stuff. All that should be easy for you."

"Do I have a chance?" she asked.

"Yes," he said, "I think you do. I'll be in touch with you as soon as I get some kind of reaction to this test. Good-by, Janet."

She was very elated when she left the studio: she knew that the bathing costume stuff and the glamour poses had gone well, because by the time she had finished there were twice as many technicians on the set as when she had started, and Mr. Sondorf, in his reserved way, had been definitely encouraging. He had liked her, she felt sure. The way those technicians had looked at her. It was thrilling. Her imagination took wild leaps and she pictured herself as a great movie star. I'm Janet Derringer, she thought, Janet Derringer, the movie star, in the flesh. She drove straight to Lewis Sholt's office, and burst in to tell him the good news. He listened quietly to her story of what had happened, and then said: "Well, that's great, baby. That's just great. But just one thing, honey, don't tie up too many hopes with this—huh? You know, Alex Sondorf isn't exactly a power in this business. I knew him when his name was Sondorpf and people spat in his eye trying to pronounce it. Look, I got nothing against the kid. He's a nice kid. But he's nobody. He's Hector Obadiah Hesslan's personal assistant, which means he's a general dog's body, a messenger boy. He's a nice kid, so I guess he conned somebody to let him test a few girls—you can get to meet some terrific-looking chicks that way. I don't blame him. Why not? But I don't like to see you get all steamed up about something that's got about one chance in a thousand of turning out. *I* know this business, and I know what's on the level and what's not. Maybe you'll be lucky, maybe some executive gets to see that test and likes what he sees . . . maybe, but don't count on it, baby. Anyway, you need Alex Sondorf? I introduce you to Willi Seiermann, who is the boss of a big studio, who really can do things for you, and you get all worked up because Obadiah Hesslan's office boy—that's all he is, baby—says a few nice things to you. . . ."

"I thought he was very nice," she said, looking crestfallen.

"Sure he's nice. A real nice kid. A nice nothing."

PART THREE

CHAPTER TWELVE

The interoffice memo was headed: "From Studio Manager to Mr. Hesslan's Assistant." It read: "Have had no response from Mr. Hesslan to my memos of 20th, 21st, 22nd, 23rd Jan. I emphasize again that it is imperative we get some decisions from Mr. Hesslan on the urgent matters raised in these memos. I urge you to use all your endeavors to locate Mr. Hesslan in Europe immediately. Cables should be addressed to all foreseeable stops on his trip so as to ensure that *one* of our messages reaches him. Please give this top priority." It was signed Saul Jessup. Alexander called in the secretary from the outer office, Miss Pearce, and dictated a reply: "From A. Sondorf to Studio Manager. All your memos to Mr. Hesslan have been cabled to him the moment I have received them. Unfortunately, the stops on Mr. Hesslan's honeymoon itinerary are *not* easily foreseeable. His cable of Jan. 19, from Athens, said he was leaving that day for Rome, and consequently your memos were cabled to him there . . ." He was interrupted by the ringing of the telephone; it was Saul Jessup's secretary, asking him to come up. Alexander picked up a bulging paper folder and walked up to the Studio Manager's office on the first floor. The corridor outside had linoleum flooring, and the walls were hung with framed photographic portraits of some of the Hesslan contract stars. The Studio Manager's office had wall-to-wall beige carpeting, a dark brown leather settee, several dark brown leather armchairs, a large desk; on the walls there were oil portraits of some of the studio's principal stars and a huge colored graph showing the varying box office returns of the studio's products over the past five years: the graph had been dipping steadily during the past three years. Off this room there was a shower and toilet.

"Ah, Sondorf," said Jessup as Alexander came in. "You got my memo?"

"I was just replying to it."

Jessup stood up behind the desk; he was a large, ruddy-complexioned man with a paunch that he carried aggressively, as if it were some kind of battering ram with which obstacles could be pushed out of the way. He came from behind the desk, the jacket of his dark blue shantung silk suit open, his lips pursing and unpursing; he had a nervous chracteristic—whether sitting or moving about—of doing little agitated movements with his legs, as if resisting an urgent desire to urinate. While pacing, which he did in minuscule steps that seemed inappropriate for so large a man, he had a disconcerting habit of doing a sudden knee bend, as if about to embark on a morning's physical exercises. He was unconscious of doing any of these movements.

"Look here, Sondorf," he barked, "how the hell am I supposed to run this studio if I can't get an answer to my cables? Do we have *any* idea where Mr. Hesslan is now?"

"The last cable from Cairo said he was en route for Rome. He didn't say by *what* route."

"From *Cairo!* Did you check all the possible routes?"

"There are quite a few, especially allowing for the new Mrs. Hesslan's passion for travel."

"You mean to tell me that a man like H. O. Hesslan can just disappear—for days—and that nobody can reach him? What about New York—how do they keep in touch?"

"They don't. Like us, they receive *his* messages, but whether or not he receives theirs is in the lap of the gods. I have a feeling that Mr. Hesslan may choose not to receive some of those messages. There are times when he doesn't want to be bothered with details. I was working for him the last time he went on a honeymoon trip to Europe. It was the same then."

"Details!" exploded Jessup. "I have a cable from him here . . ." He picked it up from the desk and read it " '. . . Staupitz not to go another cent over budget.' How does he expect me to stop Staupitz going over budget? Staupitz won't even talk to me, he won't even let me on the set, he

227

maintains that his contract specifies that all his dealings are to be with Mr. Hesslan personally."

"I know," said Alexander sympathetically.

"Well, what am I to do? There are four pictures due to go on the floor within the next three weeks that need his final O.K. If we don't get it immediately we're going to have studio space standing idle, overheads mounting up, salaries being paid, and nothing to show for it. What does he expect me to do? You're sure he appreciates the urgency of the situation—the need for specific decisions?"

"Oh, yes."

"Then why doesn't he make them?"

"He *has* made his feelings known on a number of these points." Alexander opened his folder and leafed through some of the cables. "For instance, on December fifth he cabled to express his enthusiasm for a new novel, *The Rich, Full Life*. 'Grab it if still available' are his actual words."

"I know, I know," said Jessup wearily, doing a knee bend. "They want fifteen thousand dollars for it, and Mr. Hesslan's instructions are that we are not to spend more than ten thousand dollars on any story property without his specific approval."

"I would say that his cable constitutes approval of the higher price," said Alexander.

"You would say, *you* would say," Jessup raged quietly. "But *he* doesn't say. I have no *authority* to spend fifteen thousand dollars. There's that Vice-President and his staff of efficiency experts from New York breathing down my neck, making me take out the 'regards' and the 'best wishes' from cables. What are they going to say if I spend five thousand dollars more than authorized on a story property?"

"I don't think Mr. Hesslan expects their suggestions to be taken too literally," said Alexander. "As far as I am aware, they are here purely as a sop to a minority group of shareholders."

"Mr. Hesslan has given instructions that all their suggestions are to be given the most careful consideration. Those are his actual words. The most careful consideration."

Alexander smiled. "I think he expects you to consider them, and reject them. Mr. Donaldson is not *his* nominee. I think he wants Mr. Donaldson placated, but I don't think he wants too much attention to be paid to any of his ideas."

"That's *your* interpretation of it, Sondorf. In the last four years there have been five Studio Managers who are now ex-Studio Managers because they made the wrong interpretation of Mr. Hesslan's wishes."

"I can only tell you what I think," said Alexander. Jessup's left leg described a nervous pirouette. His eyes stared blankly at an oil portrait of Zasu Pitts. He breathed noisily in and out several times as if doing a deep-breathing exercise.

"Tell me something, Sondorf," he said, his voice becoming confidential and inquiring. "You've been with Mr. Hesslan for how long—three, four years? Have you formed any opinion as to his . . . his uh . . . attitude toward . . . his executives?"

"I don't follow."

"Well," he said, unable to entirely repress the irritation from his voice, "people arrive from New York with fancy titles—Vice-President in Charge of Production, Studio Overseer, Chief Production Supervisor. Every month a new batch arrive with newer and fancier titles. They all have their own ideas of how the studio should be run. Does Mr. Hesslan *intend* them to run the studio?"

"What did Mr. Hesslan say to you?"

Jessup gave a painful laugh. "Mr. Hesslan can be very cryptic when he chooses. His reply, whenever I've broached this matter, has usually been to the effect that I'm the Studio Manager and he expects me to manage the studio. But my position has never been *precisely* defined, you see."

"I guess that's what he wants you to do," said Alexander, "manage the studio."

"Yes, yes," said Jessup, withdrawing behind his vague air of authority, a little shamefaced at having exposed his doubts to this youngster. "You understand, I've been speaking to you in confidence."

"Of course."

"I'll send my girl with today's messages for Mr. Hesslan. Send them to him in quintuplicate or whatever—to every possible place he could be. Why all the messages have to go through you I cannot fathom. I would have thought it was much simpler . . ."

"I think *Mr. Hesslan* considers it simpler to send one set of instructions, which I can then pass on to the appropriate departments, rather than have to repeat himself all the time."

"Quite. Quite. I understand that. Do try and impress on him, Sondorf, that we require definite instructions."

"I'll try."

Jessup gave a wry smile. "Let's hope," he said, "that this marriage of Mr. Hesslan's lasts. I don't think I could survive another of his honeymoons."

In the evening Alexander went for a walk in the hills above Hollywood. Tomorrow, he decided. The sense of readiness in him was a quiet passion. He was very calm. Everything was possible. He was a little awed by himself. He no longer daydreamed, as he used to do when he walked by himself, projecting himself into imaginary situations. That was not necessary now. It was going to happen, and it was not necessary to think about it. He had no definite plan beyond the opening move, after that he would have to act quickly and decisively, and he knew he could rely on his inner ear to tell him how to play it minute by minute. There was no need to rehearse anything in his mind. He was pleased with the way his heart beat so steadily. He went back early to his room at the Hollywood Hotel, and he slept deeply without dreaming.

As on previous days, Alexander arrived at the studio at fifteen minutes past nine, and Miss Pearce handed him the mail and the cables from Mr. Hesslan. In his own office he extracted the Western Union envelopes from the rest of the mail, and without opening them locked them in a drawer. On his way out he told Miss Pearce that he was going on the set—he did not say which set—and would not be available all morning.

"Say if Mr. Jessup should want you?" she said.

"I'm not available," he said.

He walked unhurriedly along the corridor, past the long row of doors with the supervisors' and directors' names inscribed on brass plates, past the Chief Accountant's office, past the Publicity Department, and left the executive building by a side door marked Emergency Exit. He cut through the carpenter's shop, exchanging greetings with some of the men working there, and came out at the back of one of the smaller shooting stages; from there he continued along the

230

network of narrow alleys at the back of the shooting stages until he came to stage J. On the high, padded door there was a sign giving the name of the production: *Night of the Fête*. Under it was a notice which said: "This set is closed to all visitors including studio personnel not directly concerned with the production. No visitors will be admitted without Mr. Staupitz's personal—signed—authorization." This was signed Walter Staupitz. Alexander pressed down the handle and pushed open the heavy door with his shoulder. He had come in at the back of the big Monte Carlo set. Carefully stepping over cables, he made his way along the perimeter of the set until he came out in the brightly illuminated square in front of the casino and the Hotel de Paris. Several dozen extras, meticulously outfitted in the styles of 1905, were standing about awaiting their instructions. Outside the Hotel de Paris, whose frontage and lobby had been painstakingly reproduced, several carriages were drawn up, and some of the horses had become restive and were being calmed by the coachmen. Alexander saw James Nelson, wearing the white uniform of a captain in the Austrian Dragoons, his peaked cap set at a rakish angle, in a huddle with Walter Staupitz, who was wearing riding breeches, black leather riding boots and an open-necked shirt. He was a large, heavily built man with a harsh Prussian face and a Prussian army officer's haircut: close-cropped on top, and almost clean-shaven at the back and sides. He was holding in his arms a beautiful black cat, which he kept stroking with great tenderness, while he gave instructions to Nelson, and to the key members of the unit grouped around him.

"Right, we go," he called, having apparently made his requirements clear.

"Crowd—get ready, please," an assistant director called through a megaphone. "Right. Start promenading on the count of three. Coachmen, on action, please." Staupitz was casting a critical eye over the set to insure that everything was as it should be. Satisfied, he gave a commanding nod to the assistant director, who began to count through the megaphone: "One, two . . . three." At the count of three the crowd artists started to move, in accordance with the detailed instructions they had individually received from Staupitz—talking, smiling, exchanging looks and greetings. Staupitz called "Action," and the first of the coachmen urged his horses forward. Then James Nelson came running out of the hotel lobby, hailing the waiting fiacre; as he strode toward it an assistant director, standing out of camera, released the black cat and urged it forward. It ran obediently across Nelson's path and then stopped at more or less the prearranged spot, between him and the cab. The camera, mounted on iron tracks, tracked into a close shot as Nelson, a fearful expression on his face, stopped as if to stroke the cat. At this point another assistant director, also out of camera, whipped off the cloth cover from a small cage to reveal a fierce-looking dog, which immediately began to bark menacingly at the cat. The cat took absolutely no notice. After about a minute of this, Staupitz wearily called: "Cut." The extras, like toy soldiers whose mechanism has run down, stopped promenading, talking, smiling, bowing, exchanging greetings, and resumed their natural bored, listless postures, immobilized wherever they found themselves when the camera had ceased to turn. It was the twenty-third attempt to get the cat to bristle, and it was the sixth cat that had been tried. In rehearsal it had bristled every time the dog had barked at it, but, perversely, it refused to do so on the actual take. Some of the other cats had bristled as soon as they were released by the assistant director; others which had bristled at the right moment had done so in the wrong place, running under the coach, or out of camera. This one had invariably stopped in the right spot, but wouldn't bristle! Production had already been held up for two days on account of this one shot.

"We try the Persian cat," Staupitz called. At this point he caught sight of Alexander. "I expressly have forbidden for anyone not connected with this production to come on to my set," he shouted at Alexander. Staupitz had the sort of voice that always sounded as if it were coming through a megaphone. "I will not have these front-office toads and lackeys snooping around my set," he continued to rage, bristling in a manner that the cat had so far refused to do. Alexander calmly continued to stroll toward him, his body relaxed, his eyes alert. "Well, what have you got to say for yourself?" Staupitz blustered in a strident voice. For a great man, Alexander reflected, he was curiously incapable of controlling his temper, but probably the recalcitrance of the cats had made him mad, even more mad than usual. When

232

he got close enough to make himself heard without having to raise his voice, Alexander said gently: "I'm sure there's some perfectly straightforward explanation, but I don't seem to have had a reply to my memos."

"I don't reply to office boys," said Staupitz brutally. "Nor do I have time to waste talking to them. Will you please leave my set at once, which you have entered in defiance of my strict orders."

"This production is already more than one hundred and seventy thousand dollars over budget," said Alexander softly. "And I understand you have asked the wardrobe department to remake four hundred and sixty uniforms because the crests are incorrect in some detail."

"That is so."

"Well now," said Alexander easily, "is that absolutely necessary? Surely one or two uniforms could be altered for close-ups. In a crowd scene it's going to be impossible for anyone to notice a minor inaccuracy in four hundred and sixty uniforms . . . in any case there can't be many people who will be familiar with the exact design of the crest of the Austrian Dragoons in 1905. . . ."

"I am not in the habit of giving explanations of my methods. . . ."

"I'm sorry about that," Alexander cut in. He spoke quietly, factually, without emotion. "I wanted to give you the opportunity of making the necessary economies yourself. But as you are not prepared to comply with reasonable requests, I'm taking you off this picture . . ."

Staupitz was so amazed by this statement that for some moments he just stood there, his mouth hanging open, his incredulity so great that he could not frame sentences to express it. Then he began to roar with laughter, his entire body shaken by the violent convulsion, the laughter forcing the spittle out of the corners of his mouth. As if in response to a signal, the members of his unit—who had been as staggered by Alexander's words as Staupitz himself—joined in the raucous laughter, and presently the laughter began to spread all around the set, the nervous tension everyone had been feeling finding release in this sudden orgy of laughter. Even some of the extras joined in, and all over the set grips and electricians were looking at each other inquiringly—what was the joke? When the hilarity had abated somewhat, Alexander looked up to the gantry and called out in a strong, firm voice: "You can save the lights . . ."

The laughter dried on Staupitz's face like mud. "Get off my set," he yelled at Alexander, "before I personally break your neck which, I can assure you, is something it would give me the greatest pleasure to do. Don't strain my patience, boy!"

Alexander beckoned to the assistant director. "I'm afraid my voice is not quite as strong as Mr. Staupitz's, so would you please announce that I am closing down this production temporarily, until a new director is found. Dismiss everyone, and tell them to hold themselves in readiness to recommence shooting this afternoon, by which time I hope to have a new director." The assistant director gave a weak smile, as if somebody was playing a practical joke whose humor was lost to him. "Well, as you seem to have lost your powers of speech," said Alexander, "and seem incapable of understanding very clear instructions—you'd better give me that megaphone." As he reached to take it from him, Alexander again looked up to the gantry and repeated in a low, firm voice: "I said you can save the lights."

In the next few moments several things happened simultaneously. First, one of the electricians, in response to Alexander's instructions, extinguished the arc lamps in his charge, which had the effect of considerably darkening the set. At the same time, Staupitz, no longer able to contain his anger, leaped at Alexander, gripped him by the throat as if to strangle him and started striking him about the face with the back of his hand. And as he leaped for Alexander, one of the grips leaped at Staupitz, trying to pin the director's arms to his sides. While the three men were struggling, with members of the unit looking on, undecided about whom to support in this situation, the other electricians took their lead from the first one who had extinguished his lights and followed suit, plunging the set into semidarkness. The effect of this was dramatic and almost magical; the fact that the electricians had responded to Alexander's orders automatically gave him, in the eyes of the others, the authority to act as he had done. The fact that Staupitz had leaped at him and struck him also seemed to put the director in the wrong, and now the other members of the unit joined the grip in pulling Staupitz off. Held back by three members of his unit, Staupitz screamed at Alexander: "I will sue you for this, I will destroy you, and those of you who went to his help will never work for me again."

Alexander ignored these remarks and addressed himself to the men holding Staupitz. "I should be obliged," he said to them, "if you would escort Mr. Staupitz out of the studio."

"On whose authority are you acting?" Staupitz screamed, having apparently reconciled himself to the fact that he could not break loose and smash his fist into Alexander's face, as he would have liked to do.

"On my authority," said Alexander, smiling faintly.

"Who are you to . . ."

"I'm the person who's taking you off this production," said Alexander, by way of providing his credentials. He turned to the assistant director and gave him instructions. The assistant director took back his megaphone and asked for quiet. The set became hushed except for the sounds of carpenters working in the background. "Everybody, please," he called. "This production is closed down temporarily. Mr. Sondorf asks that you reassemble here at two-thirty, by which time it is hoped that it will be possible to recommence production. Mr. Staupitz has been relieved of his duties in connection with this production, and all further instructions will come from Mr. Sondorf."

Alexander thanked the man who had leaped to his aid and noted his name, Frankie Brendano, and he thanked the other members of the unit for their attention and co-operation. As he was leaving the set James Nelson came up to him. "That was well done, and it needed doing. You can count on me to support you, if you need support."

"Thank you, Mr. Nelson," Alexander said. "I appreciate that."

"Come for dinner one evening," James Nelson said.

"I'd like to do that."

"That Prussian bastard needed teaching a lesson."

"I was sorry to have to do it," Alexander said. "He's a great director."

"Twenty-three takes to make a cat bristle! He's out of his mind, and he was driving all of us crazy too."

"It would have been a great shot if he'd got it," said Alexander.

In the corridor outside his office, Alexander saw Miss Pearce looking for him. "Oh, Mr. Sondorf," she called, "Mr. Jessup has been asking for you. It's very urgent. He says you're to go to his office immediately."

"I can't see Mr. Jessup now," Alexander said, opening the mahogany door of Mr. Hesslan's office and going inside. Just then the phone rang, and Miss Pearce picked it up. "It's Mr. Jessup," she said. "He wants to know if you're back."

"All right," said Alexander, "put him through." He went inside and sat down behind the big desk with the green leather top. He picked up the telephone, a 1905 model of brass with an ivory handle. "Yes?"

"Sondorf? What the hell's been going on? Somebody's just told me you went on the set and got in a row with Staupitz. . . ."

"I fired Staupitz," Alexander corrected him.

"You what!"

"Jessup," Alexander said, "I don't have time to talk to you now. I'd like you to be in my office—in Mr. Hesslan's office, that is—immediately after lunch. I'm calling a meeting of heads of departments for two-thirty . . ." A moment of fragile silence.

"I presume you have Mr. Hesslan's authority for what you're doing . . . ?"

"When Mr. Hesslan says he wants something done," declared Alexander, "he expects it to be done at once."

"Look here," said Jessup plaintively, "I never received any *precise* instructions . . ."

"I have a great deal to do this morning," Alexander said, cutting him short.

"I—I'd like to know exactly what my own position is," Jessup demanded with a faint show of asserting himself. "I'm entitled to know . . ."

"Mr. Hesslan," said Alexander, "has a high regard for your experience and knowledge of studio affairs, and so have I. I'd like to have you stay on, and I hope you will. Let me know what you decide." Alexander replaced the receiver. He got up and looked slowly around him. Unlike the other offices at the studio this one was furnished and decorated to look as little like an office as possible. It had a huge open fireplace with marble jambs, in which logs were laid out in readiness for a fire that had never

236

yet been lit. One wall consisted entirely of library shelves on which were arrayed complete sets of the works of Dickens, Shakespeare, Balzac, Goethe, Zola and others, the titles and the authors' names printed in gold on leather spines of varying colors, but closer examination revealed that these were only spines—without pages or words to go with them. The whole wall was an elaborate fake: by pressing a button behind *David Copperfield* the wall swung open to become a well-stocked bar. The other walls were of paneled mahogany. There were various niches in which stood bronze statues of semidraped women, some of whom had been converted into lamp bases. On a pedestal, in the shape of a Doric column, stood a bust of Hector Obadiah Hesslan, and there was a portrait of Mr. Hesslan above the elaborately carved mantel. On the desk, which was bare of papers, stood a brass inkstand surmounted by an albatross, and a leather portfolio with the initials H. O. H. embossed in gold on it, but all it contained was the menu of Mr. Hesslan's fifty-fifth birthday lunch. The other furnishings included a long conference table, two buttoned leather settees, and some library steps by the non-existent library. Presumably they were used for getting at the drinks on the upper shelves.

Alexander called in Miss Pearce and dictated several memos. When he had done this he told her that he was not to be disturbed, and that he would take no calls, and see nobody, until after lunch. As soon as she had left, he lay down on one of the leather settees, closed his eyes, and concentrated on relaxing all his muscles. There was nothing to do now except wait—wait for the news to circulate. Hector Obadiah Hesslan would not hear of what had happened for at least two weeks. Alexander was the only person who knew that Mr. and Mrs. Hesslan had gone on a big-game-hunting safari to Central Africa.

CHAPTER THIRTEEN

At two twenty-eight the heads of departments started to file into Mr. Hesslan's office, holding folders, files and brief cases, looking at each other questioningly, exchanging whispered jokes of the gallows-humor variety. They were all highly paid men with wives and families and mistresses and mortgages; some of them had survived several successive new régimes; others had earned their promotion as a result of the previous reorganization of the studio; all, on having learned of this latest upheaval, realized that their futures hung in the balance. Dependent on how they played their cards, this latest change might benefit them or otherwise. Those who had made themselves agreeable to Alexander, on the theory that you could never know, were tentatively congratulating themselves on their foresight; those who had been less farsighted were now frantically trying to remember exactly how they had acted toward him, and hoping that if they had slighted him in any way he might not have noticed, or that he might have forgotten. This was the first time in years that a conference had been held in Mr. Hesslan's own office and this lent a kind of additional awesomeness to the occasion and to the man who was now taking charge. When Saul Jessup came in there was a somewhat exaggerated display of friendliness toward him, all of them being anxious to prove that they could be nice to a man even though he no longer had power. When Alexander came in, at two-thirty exactly, some of those in the room started to get to their feet, but he quickly waved to them to remain seated, and himself sat down behind the big desk with the green leather top. His entry had cut a path of silence through the packed room.

"First," said Alexander without any preliminaries, "the question of the production program for the next two months. We shall go ahead with *The Time of Night, Oooh La La and All That, Heaven's Fury, The Girl Who Said No to Bluebeard, The Eagle's Wings, 1,001 Nights, The Ideal Husband, The Pasha,* and *Give Me the Moon. The Time of Night* is ready to go; all the others need a considerable amount of working on. I am calling production and story conferences on each of these films in the next two or three days. I hope we can get the problems straightened out. From what I have said, you will have gathered that we are not going ahead with *A Girl's Folly, Evil Sisters, Man Crazy, Black Garters, Beautiful Passion, Silk and Satin, Little Bertha, The Bank Robbers, My Son,* nor with *Romeo and Juliet.* If you have any comment," added Alexander, "please make it now."

238

"I have a comment." The speaker was a thin, white-haired man with very fine, delicate features.

"Mr. Donaldson," said Alexander, "I should be glad to have your views."

"As you know," said Mr. Donaldson in his oratorical manner, "I represent a substantial body of shareholders in H. O. Hesslan, Inc. Unfortunately, I have not had an opportunity of discussing these new plans with Mr. Hesslan himself who, as you all know, is in Europe on his honeymoon. However, while being fully cognizant of all the difficulties of evolving a program that will secure the approval of the paying public, I must—representing, as I do, the interests of the shareholders—protest at the abandonment of projects for which substantial payments have already been incurred."

"Your point is taken, Mr. Donaldson," said Alexander. "But I think you will find that in the long run it is better to cut our losses than to go ahead with productions in which I have no faith. . . ."

"If I may say so," said Jack O'Halleron, a supervisor who had just heard that three of his productions were to be scrapped, "we mustn't lose sight of the fact that we are producing two pictures a week at this studio, and at this rate we can't afford to be finicky."

"That's exactly what we are going to be," said Alexander toughly. "Finicky. We are going to be very finicky indeed. We are going to stop making pictures because we made them three years ago and they were a success then. We are going to stop making pictures because *something* has got to go on the floor next week. If it's unavoidable, we are going to have idle studio space. I want all of you here to get out of the habit of thinking that anything will do simply because we are committed to making something like a hundred and five pictures a year. Anything won't do. None of you who are supervisors should take it for granted that because you have been making one sort of picture for the last four or five years you can continue to do so. Now, in place of the pictures that I have shelved, we are going to acquire the following, and I want all the supervisors whose schedules have been reduced to familiarize themselves with these properties, and to have some ideas on casting and directors by tomorrow morning. These are the properties we are going to acquire:

The Rich, Full Life; The Trembling Earth; A Girl in a Million; Mirella; Galileo; and *Nobody's Choice.*"

Again Mr. Donaldson got on his feet. "While I would not criticize the choice of subjects on artistic grounds," he declared, "I am familiar with some of these titles and I believe that the price being asked, for two of them at any rate, exceeds the ten thousand dollars limit that has been set on the acquisition of story properties."

"That is true," said Alexander. "I propose to pay the higher amount being asked on the simple principle that it is better to pay fifteen thousand dollars for something that is worth making than to pay ten thousand dollars for something that isn't. If fifteen thousand dollars is the genuine market price for a property today I am inclined to think that it's probably worth it, and we cannot afford to lose worth-while properties simply because we have set an arbitrary limit on the prices we are prepared to pay. That would put us permanently at a disadvantage to all the other studios." He looked around the room. "Are there any questions?"

"Yes," said one man, whose name Alexander did not know, "what is happening to *Night of the Fête?*"

Alexander looked at his watch. "It is now being directed by Dak Strohmer."

"We had one fine picture in production at this studio," said the unknown man, "and now we haven't got even that. In the circumstances, I have no alternative but to offer my resignation." Now Alexander remembered who this man was; he was—theoretically—the supervisor of *Night of the Fête,* a fine man no doubt, but so totally ineffectual in curbing the wilder excesses of Staupitz that hardly anyone could even remember his name.

"I am sorry you feel that way," said Alexander. "But *Night of the Fête* will still be a fine picture, and with Strohmer directing we shall bring it in at a reasonable cost. You had already allowed the picture to go one hundred and seventy thousand dollars over budget. I consider that inexcusable, and had you not offered your resignation I should have felt obliged to ask for it. From now on supervisors will be responsible to me on a day-by-day basis. I hope it is understood that no production is so important that it is exempted from my attention, and no production is so trivial that it does not merit the expenditure of my time on it. If we make five pictures a year, or a hundred and five, they are going to be the best that we can make. Thank you, gentlemen, that's all for the time being."

"Scene 1. Ext. A lonely stretch of country. Iris in close shot, Sally, a little girl of seven. Iris out. Subtitle: 'Little Sally, mute since birth . . .'"

Alexander looked up.

"This is an example," he said, "of what I don't like about this script." The director, Brad Sheenan, a tough movie veteran, his laborer's face baked hard as pottery, gave a grunt of incomprehension, and shot a despairing glance at the writer, a dumpy, chain-smoking, masculine-looking woman who had written dozens of scripts of this sort.

"Seems fine to me, Sondorf," he growled. "Babs knows what she's doing."

Barbara Doone, her eyes narrowed against the permanent smoke signals rising from her lips, asked in a hoarse voice: "What exactly were your thoughts apropos the script?"

"Well," said Alexander, "here we have a story about a little girl, a mute, who happens to overhear a plot to murder a rich, eccentric spinster living with her brother in a lonely old house. She tries to communicate what she has found out but the old lady being very eccentric and withdrawn and unfriendly, and the little girl being a mute, it is very hard for her."

"You've got it absolutely," said Brad Sheenan with a hint of sarcasm.

"It seems to me," said Alexander, "that this is the sort of story that should take advantage of our own limitations . . ."

"I don't follow you."

"We can't speak to the audience any more than the little girl can speak to the old lady. What we have to do, and what the little girl has to do, is to *show* the danger, without using words. All the way through the script you're using subtitles to tell us, first, that the little girl is a mute, then you keep telling us—in words—what she is thinking, how she is trying to warn the old lady but can't. I think all that should be out. I think we should make the audience suffer a little, we should make them think: what is she trying to tell us, what is it? You're with me?"

241

"Yes . . . ?"

"Let's see the danger in the little girl's eyes—without verbal explanation—and let's put the audience partially in the shoes of the old lady, thinking: 'What on earth is the child up to, what is she trying to say?' This way we can get across the desperateness of the child's plight, of trying to communicate danger without recourse to words. If we use words, in the form of subtitles, we're cheating."

"I don't see how it can be done," said Barbara Doone, "without hopelessly confusing the audience."

"I'll give you an example of how it can be done," said Alexander. "Let's take the scene where the little girl comes to the house and the door is opened by the brother whom she identifies as one of the people in the plot. She runs away in terror. Then you have an explanatory subtitle: 'Miss Drayton's own brother in the plot! How can Sally warn her of the terrible danger?' Instead of that title why don't we actually show Sally trying to warn her of the danger? What could she do, not being able to speak? Her problem is the same as ours. All right. No subtitle. She runs away from the house in terror. . . . We take it from there."

"Why is she in terror?" put in Brad Sheenan. "Without the subtitle the audience won't know."

"That's good," said Alexander. "They're thinking: she's seen something that has utterly terrified her, made her run away instead of going through with her plan to get to the old lady. What is it that she's seen? The audience is right there with you. They'll wait for their answer—in fact, the more you draw it out, the bigger the suspense. Right, what does the little girl do? She runs into the grounds. She sees the old lady watching her from an upstairs window. She can't shout to her—what does she do? She's on a gravel path so she gets a stick and she starts to write in giant letters: 'DANGER—YOUR BROTHER . . .' The old lady is watching, she's nearsighted, can't make out the words, she goes for her spectacles, puts them on, slowly. Meanwhile, the brother is coming down the drive, the little girl sees him and runs away, the brother starts to rub out the words with his feet. The old lady at the window has put her spectacles on—she can just make out the word 'Danger,' but no more. But the brother can't be sure exactly how much she's seen." Alexander stopped and looked at them

242

both. "I'm not a writer," he said, "I'm not saying that is the best way of doing it, but it is a way of doing it without using a subtitle. I think you could go through the script and eliminate eighty per cent of the titles and I think that would make it a more exciting picture."

"I can see that it's more visual that way," conceded Barbara Doone grudgingly.

"It's more of a *movie*," said Alexander with a smile. "Before you start the rewrites, get them to screen *The Last Laugh* for you. A German movie with not a single subtitle in it. Today's Thursday—I'd like to see the rewrite by Monday."

Alexander spent the rest of the day going over the budgets of the pictures due to go on the floor during the next four weeks. Supervisors, having had the budgets of some of their pictures slashed, were surprised when Alexander actually insisted on increasing the budgets for others. "It's not a question of slashing costs," he explained, "it's a question of spending the money on something that gives us value on the screen." In one instance he told a supervisor: "We had to pay a lot of money to get Vilma Banky for this role, there's no point in economizing on her wardrobe. We want her to look gorgeous and the clothes we've got for her are, frankly, tatty." He told another supervisor: "Mick Denton is suffering from a Staupitz complex. He thinks that unless he goes over budget his standing as a director is going to be diminished. That's something we've got to stop—this idea that there is some sort of distinction in going over budget. Nobody is going to get away with it from now on. It's just nonsense to say that he needs to build the whole of that ballroom. To say that the players won't *feel* they're in a ballroom unless they *are* in a ballroom is ridiculous. They're supposed to be actors. Two walls and a section of floor is enough. We will not hire real chandeliers—they make no story point whatsoever. And we do not need one hundred and fifty extras for that scene —half a dozen of the same ones going in and out of camera are sufficient to suggest a big ball. If the central situation between Rod la Rocque and Mae Murray holds, nobody will be looking that closely at the faces of the couples in the vicinity. In any case, by using those half a dozen well, Denton should be able to create the impression of a hundred."

While Alexander was holding these conferences, Staupitz had tried to gain admission to the studio, accompanied by his lawyer. The studio cop, who had firm instructions from Alexander that Staupitz was not to be admitted, barred his way. Staupitz lost his temper. He started to shout and threaten. Finding his bluster of no avail, he sought to force his way past. The studio cop stopped him. There was a fight. A press-agency photographer was around—nobody knew who had given him the tip-off—and that evening the newspapers carried pictures of Walter Staupitz in a fight with the studio cop. Alexander issued a terse statement, through the publicity department. It said: "Walter Staupitz has been replaced as director of *Night of the Fête* by Dak Strohmer. This is as a result of differences of opinion between Mr. Staupitz and the studio." However, the story of Alexander's scene with Staupitz on the set leaked out, and most of the papers carried their own highly colored versions of what had happened. A great deal was made of Alexander's coolness, reasonableness and youth in contrast to Staupitz's Teutonic arrogance and aggressiveness. Some of the papers carried items asking: "Who is Alexander Sondorf—the new power at Hesslan studios?" And some of them answered their own question with brief, if somewhat fanciful, résumés of his career to date. In their files they found one or two pictures of Alexander, most of them taken in the company of Hector O. Hesslan or one or another of his stars, and these pictures were printed big on the front pages of all the Los Angeles newspapers. As most of the pictures were two or three years old, they made Alexander look even more improbably boyish than he was in fact, and so added to the dramatic value of the story —that this mere youth should have succeeded in ousting the formidable Walter Staupitz.

The conferences would start at 9 A.M., during breakfast, in Alexander's small suite at the Hollywood Hotel, continue in the limousine that drove Alexander to the studio, and not stop until well after midnight. Even then, supervisors, studio executives, directors and writers could not count on remaining undisturbed. Often he would telephone someone at three or four in the morning, and after a nominal apology—"I hope I didn't wake you"—would outline an idea he had just had. He seemed incapable of realizing that other people might need to sleep, make love to their wives, pursue their private lives. From the first day, he had laid down that supervisors and executives must always leave a telephone number where they could be reached at any time of day or night; when they went from one place to another, they were required to telephone the studio and establish their whereabouts. One supervisor, who neglected to do this, discovered, on arriving at the studio the following day, that he had been replaced by someone who *had* been available when Alexander wanted to talk. There was no rancor in Alexander's actions. He explained pleasantly to the replaced supervisor: "This is an emergency period for the studio and it's easier for me to replace you than to tire myself looking for you. I can't afford to get tired just now. But I have every confidence in you and I'd like you to hold yourself in readiness: there are one or two productions I'm considering that may suit you, and I shall want your advice."

The breakfast conferences were usually with writers. Sometimes Alexander had very definite ideas which he outlined while he drank cup after cup of strong black coffee and nibbled at some toast and honey; if he had no ideas he listened to the writers' ideas, and decided which should be pursued and developed and which abandoned; if these particular writers had no ideas that fired his imagination, other writers were put on the same subject—sometimes he had four or five writers working, simultaneously, and unbeknown to each other, on the same story.

Wherever Alexander went, one of a relay of four stenographers went with him, and transcripts of the highlights of every conference were sent to all those who had taken part in it. During the morning, at varying intervals, studio personnel that Alexander wanted to see were shown into his office. Sometimes Alexander brought the discussion to a conclusion in two or three minutes: "That sounds fine. Go ahead." But even if there were big problems, no single conference, in the mornings, was allowed to go on for longer than half an hour.

At twelve forty-five Alexander took a light lunch—fruit juice, steak and salad, black coffee—in the commissary, at a table large enough to seat twelve. Each morning, from six to ten people working at the studio were invited to take lunch with Alexander. He found this a convenient way of eliciting, at first hand, small pieces of information. Set-dressers, publicists, assistant directors, cameramen, art directors, cutters and junior writers were asked to these lunches. The exchanges that took place could hardly have been described as conversations. Alexander asked questions, and received answers. These lunches gave people, who might not otherwise have had access to him, the opportunity of taking up something with him directly. He believed in being accessible. If they had something important to say, and could catch his interest in the first minute or so, he was always responsive. He was ready to listen to anybody's ideas, and if they were good he acted on them.

Immediately after lunch he spent an hour or so in the projection theater seeing the previous day's rushes. There were usually anything from two to eight—or even more—takes to choose from, and he expressed his preference and added such comment as he considered appropriate. If he really disliked something he saw, he explained precisely what it was that he disliked, and asked the director to reshoot the scene. But his comments were designed to avoid the necessity of retakes; when he was talking about the previous day's rushes, he was thinking about the effect of his words on that day's shooting—it was a matter of encouraging what he considered to be the right tendencies and discouraging the wrong ones. He knew exactly how much weight to give to each utterance to make it effective: "I love the way that girl moves. She's a bit wooden in close-ups, though. I'm glad you're shooting around her in the emotional scenes, she can't handle those. Keep her moving, keep her moving, doing physical things all the time. That's the only way she expresses herself, in movement. If you can think of some more *physical* things for her to do, in place of some of those tearful close-ups she can't handle, that'd be great. When the guy runs out on her, why not have her play a really mean game of squash with some poor guy that she's taking it out on, and practically hammering into the ground. I think that'd be good. I think that's the sort of girl she is. Not the sort that sits moping by a window. Otherwise, I think the stuff is looking great."

"I don't think you're getting as much out of Colman as you could," Alexander told the director. "You're holding him back too much. In his case, his mannerisms are what

246

the public wants to see. They want to see that slow, wistful smile coming into his eyes. It's not too slow. Don't worry about it being too slow. Colman is a *slow* actor, he doesn't do lots of quick, sharp, abrupt things, but it's not slow in terms of the audience because there are those lovely things going on underneath all the time. You can stay with that smile for quite a while longer before he makes the lunge. Let them almost think he's not going to do anything, and then surprise them. And let's keep that smile going throughout the sword fight: he's an English gentleman, educated at Eton, the audience expects him to smile at his adversary. That smile, during the sword fight, is something kids will remember when they're old men. It's a romantic picture, let's not be afraid of being romantic."

"There are some scenes," Alexander said, "when not seeing the actors' faces is more effective than seeing them. We must get rid of this idea some of our lighting cameramen still have that it's their job to make every object on the set clearly visible. Here you have a couple of people sitting by a candle, and the amount of illumination provided is equivalent to what three or four massive chandeliers would give. In that scene, the only thing I want to see clearly is their hands touching, the audience will supply the happy look on Tessa Bowden's face, and their imagination will make a better job of it than Tessa Bowden could ever do."

Immediately after rushes, Alexander held the big script conference of the day. This was the only meeting that was allowed to go on for as long as two hours, if necessary. At this conference the basic conception of the film was hammered out, the story line was determined, the key scenes were blocked out, and ideas on casting were thrown back and forth.

Between six and nine, on certain days of the week, Alexander returned to the projection theater to see the rough-cuts of completed productions together with the director, the supervisor and the cutter of each picture in question. Then he expressed himself on the subject of the editing and indicated where he felt that titles contained in the shooting script could be left out in the final editing. He was all for leaving out titles wherever possible.

Sometimes he had dinner at the studio and then stayed on in his office reading scripts and synopses and books that the story department was proposing should be acquired. While reading, he dictated ideas and suggestions into a dictaphone or—which he preferred to do—rang up directors or writers or actors he had in mind for a particular subject to try his ideas on them. He hardly ever got back to the Hollywood Hotel before midnight, and then he spent another couple of hours in bed doing more reading and telephoning. Two or three times a week this routine was varied and he spent the evening seeing the première of a new film.

He hardly ever ran out of ideas in these first weeks, but when he did he never wasted time sitting around brooding. "We've gone a bit stale on this one," he'd say abruptly. "Let's all drive out to the ocean." All the people involved in the conference would be bundled into cars and driven out to one of the more secluded beaches. He loved the ocean, and swimming was the only form of exercise he took. People working at the studio learned to always have their swimsuits with them: a decision to go swimming might be taken at any time of day or night. Half an hour's vigorous exercise of this sort could have a reviving effect on Alexander, and driving back to the studio his ideas would start to flow again.

Sometimes he went alone down to the shore, and it gave him a great feeling of calm to look out across the great, grayish-black expanse of water, and he felt involved in the ocean, as if he could contain all of it within himself. He felt a great peacefulness then, and everything inside himself was as still as leaves on a windless night.

CHAPTER FOURTEEN

Five weeks after Alexander had taken over at the studio he received a cable from Hector O. Hesslan, saying: "ARRIVING TUESDAY STOP BE GOOD ENOUGH TO HOLD YOURSELF AVAILABLE FOR QUESTIONING." Later that morning Jessup came in, looking like a red-faced schoolboy who has caught the headmaster swiping the sports trophies. His feet were more agitated than ever. "I've just learned, Sondorf," he said, his mouth twitching, "that you had no authority to take charge of production. I've been asked to insure that you are available when Mr. Hesslan arrives with the Assistant District Attorney."

"That's all right," Alexander said, "I wasn't planning to go anywhere on Tuesday."

When Hector Obadiah Hesslan marched into what had previously been his office, accompanied by his lawyer, Judge Dyson, and the Assistant District Attorney, Mr. O'Day, Alexander was lying on the black leather settee, having the brief nap that he usually took in the middle of the morning.

"I beg your pardon," said Hesslan sarcastically, "maybe I should have knocked."

"That's quite all right," said Alexander easily, getting up. And then: "Sit down, gentlemen."

"Well, that's real civil of you," said Hesslan with irony. He was a tall, deeply sun-tanned man, as sparsely built as a sailing boat, with pale, almost transparent eyes. Both he and Alexander had started to move at the same time toward the chair behind the desk: Alexander got there first and sat down in it. He indicated chairs where the three men could sit. Judge Dyson, whom Alexander had met frequently while working for Hesslan in New York, was just under five feet high, totally bald, and a dandy. Today, as always, he wore an elaborate boutonnière in the lapel of his jacket—his suit was a Prince of Wales check—a cream-colored silk shirt, white spats and reddish brown shoes; two diamond rings glittered on his small, fat fingers, which he had a habit of flexing repeatedly, like a pianist before a concert. The skin on his face was as smooth as a baby's and he reeked of Lavender water. O'Day, a pale, bony man of about fifty, with thinning gray hair and nicotine-stained fingers, had an obviously deferential attitude toward Judge Dyson. Having had his chair stolen almost from under him, Hesslan sat himself on the edge of the desk, his back to Alexander.

"Judge," he commanded brusquely.

"Alexander, you can offer us an explanation," said Judge Dyson sternly.

"What exactly is it you want explained?"

249

"It's no use bluffing, Alexander," Judge Dyson said solemnly, "we have a complete report of your activities. . . ."

"There's something you're not satisfied with, Mr. Hesslan?" Alexander asked.

"Hell!" Hesslan exploded. "It's misrepresentation, it's a clear-cut and obvious case of fraudulent misrepresentation. Isn't that so, Judge?"

"It certainly is. It's probably conspiracy too, very likely."

"Mr. Assistant District Attorney," Hesslan barked, "I expect some action from you."

"You shall have it, you shall have it," the Assistant District Attorney assured him obediently. "Just as soon as the facts have been established we shall not hesitate to . . ."

"I gather," said Alexander, "that what is bothering you gentlemen is that I have taken charge of production here . . ."

"Without any authorization, and by means of a blatant and unscrupulous and . . . and impertinent deception," thundered Judge Dyson.

"That's a matter of interpretation . . ." Alexander began, but was interrupted.

"Interpretation, crap!" Hesslan let fly, wheeling round and pointing an accusing finger at Alexander. "I trusted you, Alexander, I gave you opportunities that no kid your age ever had, and what d'you do when my back is turned —when I'm on my *honeymoon*—?"

"It's quite true," agreed Alexander, cutting in, "that I took charge of production here without being officially entitled to do so."

"Well, I'll be damned!" said Hesslan.

"He admits the felony, he admits it," cried O'Day in high-pitched triumph.

Ignoring the interruption, Alexander continued, "Moreover, I think you should know the exact extent of what I have done these past five weeks, without, of course, as you point out, being officially entitled to do so. First of all, as you know, Mr. Hesslan, I fired Staupitz. At the rate at which Staupitz was filming, *Night of the Fête* would have come in $295,000 over budget. As a result of my replacing Staupitz, the picture is only $170,000 over budget—that is to say, the amount it was already over budget when I replaced Staupitz."

"Dammit, boy, what authority had you? A . . . a . . . a

250

kid of your age—to fire one of the great directors . . ."

"As I've been explaining to you, Mr. Hesslan, I had no *authority*, I used my own judgment."

"Nobody had put you in the position where you were entitled to use *your* judgment. You were never called upon to use your judgment. Your job, as my secretary and personal assistant, was to *liaise* between me and company executives. That's all, to pass on my instructions."

"I don't deny that," said Alexander quietly. "But, as I was using my own judgment, I came to the conclusion, Mr. Hesslan, that your instructions would not be implemented unless I implemented them personally. If you will bear with me a while I'll tell you exactly what I did. *Night of the Fête* is completed and ready for release. *The Rich, Full Life*, which, again using my own judgment, I bought for fifteen thousand dollars, is in the final stages of editing, and I'm very pleased with the way it has turned out. In addition, I bought eight other properties at a total expenditure of one hundred and twenty thousand dollars, which is less than the amount saved on the Staupitz picture. Three of these properties are now on the floor, the remaining five are in an advanced stage of preparation and can go on the floor within the next couple of months. Of the properties that were already scheduled by the studio, I approved nine, and two of them, *The Time of Night* and *The Pasha*, are now in production, which means we have a total of five pictures shooting at the moment, bringing the studio up to full production capacity. I shelved ten productions on the schedule because I had no confidence in them."

Alexander had spoken in quiet, factual tones, overriding the various attempts by Hesslan, Judge Dyson and the Assistant District Attorney to interrupt him, ignoring the indignant snorts of Hesslan, the incredulous gasps of the Judge, and the solemn frowns of the Assistant District Attorney. When he had finished, there was a moment of amazed silence. Then the Assistant District Attorney, drawing himself erect and mustering the full authority of his office, declared solemnly: "From what I have heard this certainly does sound to me like a *prima facie* case of fraudulent misrepresentation . . ."

"Can you give me any good reason," demanded Hesslan of Alexander, "why I should spend one more moment of my time talking to you instead of handing over the whole matter to the Assistant District Attorney?"

"For one thing," said Alexander, "there are at this moment more than twenty subjects in varying stages of preparation, production and completion—representing a total investment of about three million dollars. I'm the only person who knows exactly where we are going with these productions, and I am in daily contact with writers, directors and supervisors who are relying on my guidance. I think if you removed that—if you removed me, that is to say—some of them would find themselves pretty much at sea because they have been trying to fulfill my conceptions, and I think it would throw them if they now had to fulfill somebody else's. What's more, you haven't got anybody else who could run this studio for you." Alexander paused. "My authority for taking charge of the studio," he said, "is that I can run it better than anybody else."

For a while after Alexander had finished talking everyone remained silent; Judge Dyson was flexing his fingers, the Assistant District Attorney was frowning, and Hesslan was feeling the rough stubble on his chin. Eventually the Assistant District Attorney cleared his throat and said in his pedantic courtroom voice: "It seems to me that we have here a case of a young man seeking, by means of the perpetration of a gross piece of misrepresentation, to uh . . ."

"To . . . uh . . . what, Mr. Assistant District Attorney?" Alexander asked pointedly.

"To—uh; well, the assumption is—and this is no doubt something that can be substantiated once we have gone through the books—that this action, this misrepresentation, was done for purposes of personal gain."

"Well, let me tell you something," said Alexander. "At no stage in the last five weeks have I signed a single document or check. All that has been done, quite properly, by Mr. Jessup. I have sent out a large number of memos, but they have all been signed by me in my capacity as Personal Assistant to Mr. Hesslan. At no stage have I used any other title. Whenever any action has been taken, it has been put into effect by Mr. Jessup or whichever department head was responsible. It is true that invariably they acted on my instructions, but they were responsible for implementing the action."

"Whatever you actually said in so many words," Judge Dyson declared, "you cannot deny that you created the impression of having the authority to do what you did."

"I was not aware," said Alexander, "that it was an offense to be authoritative."

"In my opinion," said the Assistant District Attorney, "the misrepresentation is inferred once unlawful gain has been established."

"But Mr. O'Day," said Alexander, looking more innocent than ever, "I have made no gain. As Personal Assistant to Mr. Hesslan I continued to draw my normal salary of a hundred dollars a week . . ."

Hesslan had begun to chuckle, the sound starting deep inside him, as a series of tremors, and then forcing its way upward until it was expelled, violently, in staccato exhalations: Hah! Hah! Hah! Hah!

"You didn't draw expenses?" Judge Dyson demanded.

"I drew expenses," said Alexander, "on the same scale as before."

Hesslan was still laughing: Hah! Hah! Hah!

"In that case," said the Assistant District Attorney, "can you explain to me how, earning a hundred dollars a week, and drawing no expenses, you were able to stay in a hotel suite costing fifteen dollars a day?"

"On the expectation of future earnings, Mr. O'Day."

Hesslan had only just brought his laughter under control. "Well, I'll be damned," he said. "Well, I'll be damned. A snotty-nosed kid of twenty-three or twenty-four, or whatever it is, is earning a hundred dollars a week, fires one of the country's top directors, a man earning seven thousand dollars a week. He initiates a three-million-dollar production program. He bosses around executives and supervisors twice his age, earning ten, twenty times his salary, having ten times more experience than him. A snotty-nosed kid, whose only education is a few months at stenography school, does this. And they take it from him. The whole bunch of them—they take it from this kid! What do you conclude from that, gentlemen?" Hesslan was looking sharply from the Judge to the Assistant District Attorney, both of whom seemed uncertain of what answer was expected of them. "I tell you what I conclude from that, gentlemen. Either my studio is run by a bunch of fools and idiots, or the snotty-nosed kid is a snotty-nosed boy genius.

253

That is what I conclude, gentlemen. And as I do not like to think so badly of myself as to allow the possibility that I could have appointed a bunch of fools and idiots to run my studio, I am forced to accept the latter explanation, *much* as it goes against the grain for me to do so. Judge, you can go back to New York. I don't envisage any legal action. Mr. O'Day, I'm sorry to have troubled you, we shan't require your assistance after all. Alexander, maybe you could use your influence around here to see that an office is put at my disposal during the next few days, seeing that my own office seems to be occupied."

"I'll do that, Mr. Hesslan. And—oh—Mr. Hesslan. The question of my salary."

"I guess you're entitled to a raise. What do you think you're worth?"

"I'm worth more," said Alexander, "but I'll take five hundred dollars a week for the time being."

CHAPTER FIFTEEN

There were some strange houses in the mid-twenties in and around Hollywood. There were copies of French châteaux, colonial mansions, English castles, Spanish haciendas, Cape Cod "cottages," Italian villas and Arizona cattle ranches, all seeking to be the apotheosis of whatever it was they were copying. But in addition to these houses, which were famous primarily for the scale of lavishness with which they imitated the recognizable styles of other places and other periods, there were some houses that were not recognizable as being of any previous period or any known place, and the style in which they had been built could only be called Hollywood-phantasmagoric. There were houses that had indoor waterfalls, bathrooms that resembled the hothouse of some botanical gardens, and one star had recently bought a carved oak and ebony bed inlaid with gold, at a cost of $200,000. There were houses here that dispensed with geometric lines and sought to represent organic, growing things: ironwork imitating ivy tendrils, garden lamps shaped like plants; stone treated to resemble flesh and bone. One star had a private chapel (overlooking her swimming pool), the gables of which were covered in imitation snow carved out of stone, defying the sun to try and melt it. The towers and turrets and domes and castellations and parabolic cupolas and arched entrances of these houses were the sights that visitors on sight-seeing tours associated with the mad eccentricity and the reckless extravagance that were more or less expected of the great Hollywood figures.

The house that Alexander had rented was by these standards a fairly modest place. What he loved about it was that there were views of the ocean from all the principal rooms, and there were stone steps leading down through the rocks to a small, private jetty from which he could swim—in complete seclusion—in a tiny bay not much larger than some Hollywood swimming pools. This was the first time he had lived outside of a large city, and to find trees growing outside his windows, and nameless flowers proliferating on the trellis of the terrace and the walls of the house, continually amazed him and delighted him. The ocean enthralled him—it could look so dark and deep and cold, and yet consoling in its immensity. Sometimes the night smelled as if all the perfume bottles had been left open, and sometimes the strong, harsh smell of the ocean pervaded everything.

Dear Paul (Alexander wrote), Your telegram of congratulations meant more to me than I can tell you. I have thought about you a great deal these last months—even though I have not written—and of our time together in New York and of our long talks which meant so much to me. I have been meaning to write to you for a long time, but somehow did not dare. I did not know whether I had your approval and so did not know if I should write you a defensive explanatory letter or a boastful triumphant one. I am still not sure which it should be, but I am encouraged to think, from your telegram, that you are still on my side, even if perhaps you don't *entirely* approve.

First, let me say that not everything you have read in the newspapers is true. In the business with Staupitz, there was no rancor on my part. I still consider him a great director and admire him enormously as an artist, and I do not pretend for one moment that *Night of the Fête* will be, *artistically*, the film it would have been had Staupitz been allowed to finish it in his own way and in his own

255

time. I often think about the fact, and I find it ironical, that my present position should have been achieved at the expense of a man I have so admired, and whose work you and I have spent hours discussing. But what I did was unavoidable. You will have to take my word for that, it is something I can only explain in person.

Before acting as I did I had been thinking a great deal about a talk we had one night in New York, sparked off by an article Stephen Raille had written. I was very much struck by something you said then, paraphrasing Raille: that those of us who thought as we did would always lose out against the Willi Seiermanns because we were hindered by all sorts of scruples that they—the Seiermanns—didn't have. I seem to remember that your attitude was that we were all too lily-livered, too innocent, too virginal: that, as a result, in the end, the Willi Seiermanns *did* take over, and in the end we would have to submit *anyway* because *they* would have all the power, and that all we did by refusing to become involved in commerce was to relinquish, without a struggle, the right to say *how* commerce should dictate to art. We agreed, I think, that commerce would increasingly dictate to art since art was now a matter of mass communications, and mass communications were either politics or business; and I think we agreed that, given these circumstances, the only sensible course was for people like *us* to try and grab hold of the reins of power.

I realize that when we had these talks you said these things dialectically; that, in a sense, you were propounding an idea in order to test whether it would stand up; I don't think we came to any definite conclusion about the validity of that particular argument then. What I have done is take the argument a step further, put it into action, and all I can say is that the proof will be what I do. Whether it's worth it, whether the theory stands up, can't be endlessly discussed in the abstract. It may be that if you sing the devil's tunes you become the devil's man. This is something we have to find out. What induced me to act as I have done is the conviction, which has been building up inside me, that I *know* how pictures should be made, and that I can get them made my way, and that it is better for people like me and Thalberg to be controlling the making of pictures than to leave it to the Louis B. Mayers and Willi Seiermanns. I hope this doesn't sound either like an apologia—or like bravura.

I miss you very much, Paul, I miss your insight, your understanding, your wide and deep and detailed knowledge of things—so much wider and deeper than mine—your advice and your help and your friendship. My dearest wish is to be able to persuade you to come out here. I would love to have you working at the studio—say, as story editor, or as a staff writer, or in any other capacity that might appeal to you. Really, I would be glad as hell to have you here, and we could have a great time. This really is a marvelous place. The climate is fabulous—I swim two or three times a week, even in February. And if you want to go skiing, there's snow in the mountains just a few hours away. As for girls, they are almost too abundant. One gets spoiled. Come out here soon. Alexander.

The group in the projection theater waiting to see the rough-cut of *The Rich, Full Life* consisted of the director of the film, David Watterton; the supervisor, Sam Frobe; Saul Jessup; the studio casting director, Mo Pearlman; and the studio publicity director, Pete Fenton, who had just finished telling a new joke about Alexander Sondorf. A fog of cigar smoke filled the small and rather shabby room, and the nervous tension could be measured from the amount of unmelodious laughter that crackled back and forth like static on a heavy day. Alexander came into the projection theater accompanied by the cutter, a hard-faced blonde of about fifty called Lorna Driscoll. "Everybody seems to be in a pretty good mood," he said, catching the residue of laughter still in the air.

"Yuh, I been telling slanderous jokes about you," said Pete Fenton.

"I hope they were funny," said Alexander, sitting down in the place reserved for him. "Right. Let's go."

"Alexander," said Jessup, "there are some tests Mo would like you to see. Do you have the time?"

"I'd appreciate your opinion," said Mo Pearlman.

"Sure. After the picture. We'll run them after the picture." He looked at his watch. "How long's the film run?"

"One hour fifty-five," said the director, David Watterton. "You think that's a little long?"

"Not necessarily. Let's look at the picture and then we'll decide."

The story of *The Rich, Full Life* was of a working-class New York boy, with looks and charm, who works as a bell-boy in one of the big hotels and dreams of being a part of the rich life he sees going on around him. He finds a benefactor in a rich, well-bred and cultured man about town—played by Adolphe Menjou—who takes a liking to him and gives him a job as his social secretary. By meticulously modeling himself on his benefactor, whom he admires tremendously, he acquires the polish and grace and the air to gain acceptance for himself in this world, which he has always longed to be part of. In fact, he makes out with a rich girl who is very much a part of that world. With all this within his grasp, it emerges that his benefactor, for whom he had had such respect, is a high-class confidence man.

The essence of the story was in the basic tenderness of the phony relationship between the boy and the confidence man, and the film depended on the latter's being always completely convincing in his pretense before his exposure, and remaining sympathetic after it. At the end, when the lights came on, everybody looked toward Alexander. There was a couple of minutes' complete silence while Alexander arranged his thoughts, watched intently by the others. "You've got a wonderful performance out of Menjou," Alexander said, eventually. "In the beginning he's everything you expect him to be, amusing, debonair, sophisticated, but at the end he's also moving—it's very moving, the comedown of a great confidence man, who in his day has conned the crowned heads of Europe, now reduced to conning the saloon-keeper's daughter in some hick town. It's funny, and it's moving at the same time."

"You liked it, Alexander?" David Watterton inquired.

"I would say we have a big success on our hands," Alexander declared. "The fact that the boy is a bit wooden, and the sex interest is rather dragged in, will be commented on by the critics, but it's not going to worry the public. I think if we cut anything, we should cut the boy—all the scenes in which he's on his own are slow."

"But you liked the picture, Alexander?" David Watterton repeated again.

"It's going to be a famous film," said Alexander. The

general relaxation of tension which this declaration produced could be felt; it was as if, Alexander having said it would be so, it already was so.

"How do I sell it?" demanded Pete Fenton sourly; "basically it's the story of two men."

"You sell it," said Alexander, "tastefully. That's the first thing. This is a quality picture. As for the actual angle, we'll have to work out something. Best-seller. High Society —Menjou. I think the publicity should emphasize that this is the story of a bellboy's transformation into a high-society buck. That always goes. But under no circumstances do we even hint at the twist—that Menjou is a phony. All the publicity should lay it on about how well-equipped Menjou is to play the role. And let's keep in mind what we're saying in this picture; that Society, the social whirl, is so phony that the person most at ease in it, most qualified to shine and sparkle in it, is a *professional* phony." Alexander paused, and for the first time since the picture had finished, smiled. "Congratulations, David. It's a fine piece of work."

"Buying the property was your idea, Alexander, and casting Menjou," conceded David Watterton, feeling able to be generous. Alexander turned to Mo Pearlman: "I'll see those tests now." Lorna Driscoll asked Alexander if he needed her, otherwise she had some things to take care of. Alexander said sure, it was all right for her to go. The others said they would stay around for the tests. In the mood of elation that Alexander's words had created there was no better way of shedding the day's tensions than by looking at tests of some new girls.

The first four girls elicited some pretty savage comments; one girl was said to have the expressiveness of a potato pureé; of another, with a somewhat forbiddingly austere expression, it was remarked that it would require an electric drill to deflower her; the third girl was conceded to have good legs, but there were horrified groans when she started to "act"; the fourth girl was considered a carbon copy of Gloria Swanson. The fifth girl was thought possible, and Mo Pearlman was proposing to give her the usual seven years' contract with six-monthly options on the studio's side. While all these tests were being shown, Alexander was not joining in the general, schoolboyish ribaldry, but holding himself a trifle aloof from all that. The sixth test to be shown was the one he had made himself of Janet

Derringer. He had not seen it before. He had forgotten about this girl, and he felt a little guilty, remembering how anxious and hopeful she'd been. He shifted in his seat to a more attentive position. The girl's nervousness and awkwardness in front of the camera, dazzled by the lights, was immediately apparent, but occasioned no sarcastic remarks. As he saw her mouth moving, Alexander remembered her actual words and smiled to himself. Asked to do definite things, she was unnatural, but once or twice—when she was talking about not liking the quiet, when Alexander told her that she had better forget about a career in movies, and immediately afterward when he reassured her and told her she was good—something happened in her face, something that was not acting, but was a very direct and vivid communication of what she was feeling at that moment. The absolute—and formed—rightness of her expressions was somehow moving, the way a child is moving who has got a certain look or expression just right, though these moments were so fleeting you could easily miss them. Immediately after the scenes Alexander had done with her came the cheesecake stuff. Traditionally, this consisted of girls disporting themselves in various stereotyped poses in swim suits, but in this case Janet's co-operativeness had evidently fired the cameraman to try some innovations and there were shots of Janet taking an imaginary shower, her hands folded across her chest, the nipple of one breast rather deliciously exposed, of her lying on an inflatable mattress sunbathing, of her doing the shimmy. In these scenes she was quite relaxed and unself-conscious.

"The boys had themselves a good time with that one," remarked Sam Frobe.

"You can tell the kind of scenes *she's* been rehearsing," said Pete Fenton.

"What does everybody think?" asked Alexander. "Mo?"

"She's a doll to look at, Alexander," he said noncommittally.

"David, what's your opinion? Could you get a performance out of her?"

"Hard to say, Alexander. She has a certain quality, I think she has this quality of getting people rooting for her, which is unusual for a girl with her looks. But she's a complete neophyte, isn't she? She'd have to learn from the beginning."

"Pete? Could you get publicity on her?"

"You can always sell cheesecake, sure. But isn't everybody forgetting something—that's Janet Derringer." There was a small pause, but the significance of the name did not register with anyone. "You guys don't know about Janet Derringer? She's Willie Seiermann's girl."

"Yuh, that's right. Pete's right. I know about this chick," said Sam Frobe. "She's the one. Oh, sure. I know about her."

"Beats me how we came to make this test," said Mo Pearlman.

"*I* made it," said Alexander. "I think she has something."

"She certainly has looks . . ." Mo Pearlman agreed.

"I don't feel that she's outstanding," said Saul Jessup.

"There's a certain sadness that comes through the dazzle —it interests me, and I think it'll interest audiences," said Alexander.

"What's so special about sadness?" demanded Pete Fenton. "This town is lousy with sad-looking girls."

"I think this girl feels things strongly, and I think she can be got to express what she feels," said Alexander.

"The thing is," said Jessup, "is Willi Seiermann going to thank us if we offer her a contract? If what Pete says . . ."

"I'm not interested in Willi Seiermann's thanks," said Alexander. "Mo, write to her agent, offer her a contract. Usual terms." He got up and left.

Three days later Mr. Pearlman came into Alexander's office with a reply from Lewis Sholt, which said that, unfortunately, Miss Derringer could not accept their offer as she was already under exclusive contract to Seiermann-International.

Several times Alexander changed his mind about the type of automobile in which he would go to meet Paul at the station. First, he had decided to go in the chauffeur-driven Lincoln which the studio put permanently at his disposal. Then it occurred to him that maybe it was a bit formal to meet his friend in such an official car and the presence of the chauffeur might have a dampening effect on their reunion, and he decided to go in his own Hispano-Suiza two-seater, the 1919 model he had bought only a couple of months ago from James Nelson. He loved this car, with its romantic name, its silver stork poised on the great, shining hood, its marvelous performance—getting up to 50 m.p.h. nothing could touch it, even these days—but then he thought, changing his mind again, that it might seem showy turning up in the most fashionable and admired car of the period. It might emphasize, in an unpleasant way, the change in their relative positions. He thought perhaps it would look best if he took a cab, and got his secretary to book one, and then became angry with himself for being so concerned about what impression he made on Paul and, at the last minute, canceled the cab and went in the Hispano-Suiza.

When he saw Paul running down the platform toward him, his arms spread exuberantly to embrace him, the grin on his face as warm and unrestrained as always, his apprehensions vanished in a moment of pure elation. "You look fantastic, fantastic," said Paul, thumping Alexander's shoulders roughly and joyfully. "My God, you have grown. In less than a year you have *grown*. Fantastically. But where's the red carpet? Where's the brass band? Where are the dancing girls? I heard in Hollywood you do *everything* big!"

"I didn't know you cared about such things," said Alexander, "or I would certainly have laid it on."

"You really lay on dancing girls?"

"For you—anything, Paul. It's wonderful to see you. I really mean that."

"And it's wonderful to see you—and to see you such a big success. I predicted it. Didn't I predict it? I always used to say, didn't I?—that quiet little one, he's the one who's going to outshine us all. While we sit around *talking*, he's doing things."

Paul loved the car. He walked around it, feigning swooning admiration. He caressed it playfully as if it were a beautiful girl. And when Alexander got into the driving seat, he murmured incredulously: "It *goes* as well. I thought it was just something that Michael Arlen dreamed up." All the way to Hollywood, Paul kept talking, as he had always done, in his extravagant, uninhibited way, turning in his seat to look at girls they passed in the street, taking in everything with the relish that was characteristic of him. Alexander had booked a room for him at the Ambassador. The room, he thought, was just fantastic, and so was the view, and so was the chambermaid, of whom he caught a momentary glimpse in the corridor.

That night Alexander gave a small supper in Paul's honor, to which he invited James Nelson, David Watterton and his wife, Adolphe Menjou, Irving Thalberg and Norma Shearer, and the two nicest girls he'd been able to find among the studio's contract players. Paul charmed them all. At 4 A.M., after they had seen the two girls home, Paul and Alexander strolled together along Wilshire Boulevard, dizzy from talk, dehydrated by the outpouring of their respective news, all of which they had felt they must impart there and then. For the first time since Paul's arrival, there was a moment of quiet, each feeling a little guilty about having burdened the other with so much information in one massive, unassessable lump.

"They wouldn't publish your novel?" said Alexander after some moments of silence in which he realized that this had been the evening's most serious news, and had not really been given the proper amount of attention.

"No, not one of them," said Paul.

"I can't imagine it's bad," said Alexander, "from what I read of it and from all the things you told me, it can't be bad."

"Bad?" roared Paul. "It's a fantastic masterpiece, that's why they won't touch it, it scares them. They say the book is obscene. How can you get through to them? If the sexual act is obscene to them, then of course the book is obscene, but that is their fault, not mine. To them it's fine as long as you suggest that procreation is achieved by the intercourse of euphemisms, or even by the meeting of burning lips, or some other discreet form of parthenogenesis. But the idea that sex isn't just a good bang, that it can be tragic—that it can be the tragic, destroying factor in somebody's life and relationships—and therefore has to be described as honestly and in at least as much detail as, say, a landscape or a dinner—that they will not allow. Look at the outcry against Lawrence in England, aaginst Staupitz in America. It will take fifty years before what I'm saying is accepted.

"I'd like to read it, Paul."

"You will read it, but there is nothing you will be able to do about it, Alexander."

"Let's see," said Alexander. "Look, we're both just about dropping. What time do you want the car to pick you up tomorrow? You'll come out to the studio?"

"Sure."

"After lunch?"

"Fine."

"I tell you what. I'll have a studio car at the hotel at midday—you won't get up before then? If you want to go anywhere before coming to the studio, just tell the driver to take you. And don't pay for anything. Sign for everything. It'll be taken care of."

"You are looking after me like a Jewish mother," said Paul.

Alexander loved showing Paul round the studio, and Paul seemed delighted by what he saw, was charmed by the people he met—or appeared to be—and uncritical of studio methods. Alexander had been afraid that Paul, with his trenchant views and hypercritical attitude to everything, might be derisive of the picture business, but not at all. This bothered Alexander rather, and eventually he asked Paul outright why he had not criticized anything he had seen. Paul smiled his engaging smile and placed an arm fondly on Alexander's shoulder—the paternalistic gesture irritated Alexander slightly. "My dear Alexander," he said, "if you are in a whorehouse you do not complain to the madam because the girls are unfamiliar with the works of Baudelaire."

"You are comparing this to a whorehouse!" said Alexander.

"Come on now, Alexander—you must not take my metaphors too literally. I would never dream of calling Hollywood a whorehouse—I have far too much respect for whorehouses."

"Then you really despise us? And, by implication, me?"

"Really, I don't know what you want me to say, Alexander. There is a lot I despise about America, but I live here. There is a lot I despise in myself, but I continue to live. From what I have seen of Hollywood so far—and, remember, I'm a newcomer—there isn't much to admire about it. Don't misunderstand me, Alexander, I don't particularly *admire* an electric power station, but I'm most grateful for the amenities it provides me with. You mustn't take offense; what I say doesn't mean I don't intend to enjoy myself while I'm here."

"Let me ask you something, Paul. What did you think of my getting rid of Staupitz?"

"Alexander, I have no personal feelings for Staupitz, whereas I *have* personal feelings for you. In your position I might have done exactly the same, but I still can't say that what you did was right."

"Have you forgotten our talk in New York? Look, Paul, my father hated the movies because they were not as cultural as the theater. There are people who hate skyscrapers because they shut out the view from their back garden— but the skyscrapers have formed a new view that nobody could have foreseen until they were built, and it's probably as impressive as the view they despoiled from anybody's back garden."

"Why do you feel you have to justify yourself to me, Alexander?"

"I don't," said Alexander shortly.

CHAPTER SIXTEEN

Alexander was driving fast, the needle was steady at eighty; it was a beautiful engine, and its delicate responsiveness was very satisfying to him. Driving fast, obtaining the maximum performance out of the Hispano-Suiza, invariably had a soothing effect on him. He loved the sensation of speed, he loved being able to provoke the gentle night breeze to a controlled fury as he squeezed down on the pedal. Ahead of him, a dark shape appeared in the tip of the headlamps; he braked and prepared to swerve if he should not be able to bring the automobile to a halt in time to avert this obstruction, which he now saw was a man— signaling with his arms. For him to stop? There must have been an accident, he thought, pushing down hard on the brake pedal.

"What is it?" he shouted to the man as the car came to a stop, its wheels smoking. The man had leaped to the safety of the side of the road, and could no longer be seen. The headlamps illuminated nothing but empty road: there was no sign of any vehicles that might have been involved in an accident.

"Mr. Sondorf?" a voice called from the darkness.

"Yes?" There was complete silence. "What the hell is going on?" Alexander demanded, getting out. Then, with sudden shocked comprehension, he saw the shadows become tangible and come toward him. It flashed through his mind that one of the men had known his name. "What do you want?" he demanded. He tried to get back to the car, but there was one of them behind as well. "I have no money with me," he cried.

"It ain't your money we want, Wonder Boy," said the one who had spoken before. And then they started hitting him. The blows seemed to be delivered by the darkness, as if there was no human agency involved; only from the pain could he tell that men's fists were smashing into his face and chest and stomach. The first few blows had knocked him to the ground, and now they were dragging him off the road, into a thicket. His mouth was full of blood, and the blows in the stomach had made him gasp for breath, making him choke on his own blood. Hands were gripping him by the necktie, pulling him to his feet and holding him upright, and while he was held like this, fists were using him as a punching bag. They were working almost soundlessly, smashing up his face with precise, unhurried thoroughness. His hands were being held and he could not free them, and his attackers carefully kept beyond the range of his flaying legs. As he felt himself going under—felt the start of the sickening, headlong fall, felt these tearing, breaking sensations in his limbs and bones, as if his whole body were breaking up—he gasped: "Why d'you want to kill me?"

"Oh we're not going to kill you, Wonder Boy. This is just the first installment."

The pain on recovering consciousness, and the attendant panic, were almost worse than the actual attack. He was retching violently and the light in his brain was flickering feebly, like the filament in a bulb before it finally burns out. He had no sensation of what was up and what was down, he seemed to be trying to climb upward, up a vertical cliff face, and when he fell back, it felt as if he were falling from a great height with the ground constantly receding beneath him so that the impact, for which his whole body was fearfully tensed, was constantly postponed. He lost consciousness for a second time.

When he had been brought in by the highway patrolman

who had seen the empty car, its headlamps blazing, he had been pretty much of a mess, his face swollen, covered in blood and dark mauve bruises, but he had not been gravely injured. The men had done an expert job of beating him up without running any risk of killing him. The police found no clues as to who his assailants might have been, but guessed they were probably professional hoods, and they could suggest no possible motive for the attack except that he must have enemies who wanted to get even with him. All the time Alexander kept remembering the sneering voice: "Oh we're not going to kill you, Wonder Boy. This is just the first installment." Who were they? Why had they attacked him? Could it be that they had been hired by Staupitz? He had a big grievance against Alexander, but it hardly seemed in character for him to hire others to do his fighting. He was said to have punched Louis B. Mayer on the nose on one occasion, and he was known to have fought duels in Austria, but he was not the sort of man to hire professional gangsters to do his dirty work. If not Staupitz, who could it have been? There must have been dozens of people, Alexander decided, whom he had offended since taking charge of the studio. There must be all sorts of unlikely people—people he had never heard of possibly—who had grievances against him. As his body mended, and the physical pains diminished, he realized with mounting horror that he would probably never find out who his attackers had been.

At night he dreamed again of the man with the knowing expression on his face, the "him" whose face Alexander did not know but of whose *presence* in the crowd he was so chillingly conscious, the anonymous "him" who knew Alexander and followed him always. The beating he had taken, the mysterious threat that this was only "the first installment," had the same flavor as the nightmare: the one seemed a continuation of the other, it was almost as if these figures out of his own mind had acquired a real, physical existence in order to overcome his one remaining defense, that he could wake up.

He *had* woken up, his nerves screaming voicelessly for Nembutal, to the awareness of some indefinable fear. What was it? What had happened a moment ago in the dreaming state to make his body twist inside itself, as if trying to run away from itself, it was running without motion but with all the strains and stresses of running; he caught sight of his face in a mirror and the agony on it was that of an athlete after some great, self-transcending effort. He reassured himself—there is nothing there, only empty darkness; but there is something there, something the electric light bulb can't reveal, the something that the running body is running away from, he could know what it was only from the trail it had left inside him. Whatever had happened in the dream, whatever terrible confrontation had occurred, he was left now only with the echo of his own scream, without the source of it or the cause of it.

At the studio he was conscious all the time of the fact that any one of those deferentially smiling faces might mask the identity of his enemy, sometimes a deferential smile seemed to become transformed into a knowing leer, and Alexander did not know if this was an optical illusion, the result of trying too hard to decipher the secret meaning in a smile, or a moment of penetrating insight. He became cool and suspicious toward anyone who had not actually proved his loyalty. Paul he could trust, and he could trust James Nelson, he felt, and David Watterton—they were people who had benefited from his take-over. But the hundreds of others he came in contact with? He was forced to suspect them all. And living all the time with this threat which he could not pinpoint, of which he could never be sure he had rid himself, his nervous reserves were slowly being eaten away. Often he had to go home in the middle of the day and lie down and try to regain enough energy to enable him to keep up with the essential work.

The mounting feeling that, in his present state, he could not cope with things added enormously to his terrors. Worst of all was the sudden feeling of exhaustion that came over him at times, and the panic attack this could produce. It would happen suddenly, without warning, in the middle of a conference: the terror spreading through his limbs, making his mind go blank, his heart beating irregularly; everybody would be watching him, waiting for his pronouncement, and he would have to hold on to the desk with sweating hands to keep himself from falling. The only way out was to resort to extreme curtness: "We're not getting anywhere. We'd better wrap it up for today. That's all, gentlemen." And with a supreme effort, he would get to his feet and march out—ignoring the startled expressions on the faces of the people in the room—and stagger to the toilet where he would sit with his head between his knees, trying to compose himself, to quiet the frantic beating of his heart and to accept the imminence of death. Only when he was able to do that did he start recovering again. He had consulted several doctors, none of whom had been able to find anything organically wrong with him. It was the result of overwork, they said, it was all in his mind. The horrible thing was that there was no way of telling when such an attack might occur, it seemed unrelated to any external situation; it might come in the middle of watching a movie, or at a cocktail party, or during a story conference, or in the middle of the night. Desperately seeking to find some underlying pattern in these attacks, it seemed to him that they usually occurred—though not always—when he was in some situation from which it was difficult to escape. For this reason he avoided public events, refused all invitations to speak at dinners, or to sit on the platform at some big function. At premières he always insisted on having an inconspicuous seat near an exit, so that he could slip out unnoticed. He did nothing to correct the impression he was creating of being arrogant and off-hand and ungracious on social occasions; it was better that people should think this of him than that they should know the real reasons why he would suddenly have to cut short a conversation and leave. Similarly, his grim silences, which were interpreted as an expression of boredom, could serve to mask a sudden inner tumult. There were certain places that he considered safe places, where he nearly always felt happy and at peace: by the ocean, in a moving car, in his own house, knowing that there were servants downstairs who could be summoned by pressing a bell. He did even more of his work than usual by telephone, or by dictaphone, and he had a projection theater fixed up in his house, and sometimes, when he could not face going to the studio, he had the day's rushes shown to him at home.

"Well, how's the invalid?" said Paul cheerfully. Alexander was sitting in a rocking chair, under a striped sun-umbrella by the pool, speaking into a dictaphone. From inside the house came the low, slightly distorted sound of Alexander's voice as the typist transcribed the cylinders Alexander had made the previous night.

"Not too bad," he said, smiling weakly and removing his sunglasses. Seeing Paul always raised his spirits. Sometimes they argued fiercely, but he always felt safe with Paul. His presence was tremendously reassuring. Since appointing him Story Editor, he had come to rely on him a great deal.

"What did the doctor say last night?" Paul asked.

"The same as all the others. That there's nothing the matter with me."

"You got a bad beating up," said Paul.

"What terrifies me is that I don't know who did it. That it could happen again, any time, as they threatened."

"Listen to me, Alexander," Paul said, "if you are afraid of being beaten up again, why don't you take on a body-guard? I'm serious. I don't think for one minute that he will ever be called upon to do anything, it's entirely for your own benefit and peace of mind. Take on a *personal* chauffeur. There must be plenty of tough ex-cops around who can drive a car."

"It's a fabulous idea," said Alexander, jumping up from his chair excitedly, the blood—and vitality—returning to his face as if in response to smelling salts. "Why didn't I think of that? It's a fabulous idea. There's that grip at the studio, who came to my rescue when Staupitz jumped on me, Frankie Brendano, he looked strong enough. Paul, you're a genius. I feel better already. What a simple solution! I'm sure I could get a license for him, in view of what happened to me."

"A license?"

"A firearm license."

"You want him to be armed?" Paul gave a surprised laugh.

"Why not? There might be three or four of them. If it gets around that he's armed, they will think twice about trying anything again." Paul was looking at him in quiet wonder. "Why d'you look at me like that, Paul?"

"You never cease to amaze me, Alexander. A moment ago you were a delicate, pallid youth, nursing your symptoms, too fragile to look at the sun or the world, and suddenly you're a gun-toting . . ."

Alexander cut him short with a chuckle: "I have a way of vacillating between extremes," he said. "You know, suddenly I feel much better. He can even be with me when *I* want to drive—it's perfect."

As often happened with Alexander, the liberation from some fear released in him a great flood of energy and ideas, an unstoppable flow. He was pacing the terrace in a transport of making plans.

"*The Rich, Full Life* has got to have a big opening," he said. "That's why I've been holding it back. It's the first film to come out that is mine from beginning to end, that I conceived and brought to fruition. It's got to make a big impact. Everything depends on that. A so-so success would simply mean a confirmation of my present position, and that's not enough. I'm still tied down. I can't spend more than fifteen thousand dollars on a story property without getting Hesslan's O.K. Every picture with a budget of over two hundred thousand dollars has got to be okayed by Hesslan. Half the people under contract are dross, worthless, but I can't get rid of them, and while I can't get rid of them I can't sign up better people to replace them, which means I am working all the time with inferior material. . . . All those properties you have been urging me to buy, do we have anyone to put in them, to write them, to direct them?"

"No, I agree we haven't."

"That is why *The Rich, Full Life must* be a success—for me, personally, so that I can get carte blanche. I know, we'll open it at the new Seiermann theater, it's a four-thousand seater. I'll speak to Willi. His own studio has got nothing big enough at the moment to open that theater. *The Rich, Full Life* is just right for it."

Alexander continued to talk on like this, his mind leaping from one subject to another, his thoughts racing ahead of his words. "The other thing I'm going to do, Paul, is I'm going to see Henry Kabe. It's at his behest that we get these stupid economy waves—cutting out the 'regards' in telegrams—putting an arbitrary ceiling on the budgets of pictures. I'm going to talk to Henry Kabe myself."

Two weeks later Alexander, accompanied by Paul, set off on the trip east to see Henry Kabe and to finalize arrangements with Willi Seiermann for the première of *The Rich, Full Life*. It was very cold in New York. The day they arrived they lunched at the Ritz, and all sorts of people—some of whom Alexander was sure he had never met—came to their table to offer congratulations on *The Rich, Full Life*, about which word had evidently got around. Jesse Lasky and Adolph Zukor, who had been lunching at an adjoining table, stopped on their way out to tell Alexander what great things they had been hearing about him, and suggested he give either of them a call if he ever wanted to "talk." When Alexander introduced Paul to one of the table-hoppers, the man asked: "Your aide-de-camp?" Alexander was embarrassed at having their respective positions spelled out in such an unequivocal way and murmured, "Mr. Krasnor is a very brilliant young writer," but Paul brushed this explanation aside with the interjection: "Brilliant and largely unpublished."

"The idiot," Alexander muttered when this man had left, but Paul seemed unperturbed. "My dear Alexander," he said, "I have no objection to being described as your aide-de-camp. I might object to the word 'stooge,' but aide-de-camp seems a nice way of putting it."

By tacit mutual agreement they went to none of the places they had frequented before Alexander's departure for Hollywood, when he had been working as Hesslan's secretary. "We had some good times together," Alexander said once, thinking back to the times when Paul had been taking him around. "Yes," said Paul, "though I don't know how we managed to make do without *poussin paysanne*. It shows what the human being can put up with." Alexander smiled a little sheepishly; these remarks of Paul's were always made good-humoredly, but none the less he resented, slightly, being made to feel guilty about his success, or—at any rate—having his success denigrated by means of such facetiousness. The best attitude, he discovered, was to anticipate Paul's mocking little remarks, and get them in first. Addressing the headwaiter, he would say, for Paul's benefit, "Oh not *poussin paysanne* AGAIN!" and then both would burst into uproarious laughter, completely mystifying to anyone not in on their secret joke.

At the hotel—Alexander had a suite and Paul an adjoining room at the Waldorf-Astoria—Paul would make a thing of ordering *pêches flambées* for breakfast and then complaining lengthily to Alexander for having taken him to such a hick hotel, where it took them half an hour to prepare a simple little breakfast of coffee and *pêches flambées*. And once, when Paul tried to bring an obvious whore up to his room, and was politely told that ladies were not allowed in gentlemen's rooms after 10 P.M.—unless the gentleman had a suite with a sitting room, that was—he

272

insisted on getting Alexander down into the lobby and complaining to him in a loud voice that this lousy hotel would not allow him to take his own mother up to his room, as if he would try to interfere with his own mother! After a tearful farewell to the whore—"Good-by, mother. Pray for me, mother!"—he quickly anticipated Alexander's anger with a profuse and sincere apology. He was drunk, he explained abjectly, otherwise he would never have dreamed of doing anything so outrageous as to try to take a whole to the Waldorf-Astoria. "I know, I know," he said, "if I go on like this—if I don't pull up my socks—you're going to have to get yourself another aide-de-camp."

"Oh, quit fooling, Paul. I'm tired."

"All my life," he went on, "I dreamed of being Alexander Sondorf's aide-de-camp. And now, having made it, I ruin it all. Ruin it with my stupidity and coarseness! It's drink. Drink is what is to blame." Alexander put him to bed, and in response to Paul's heartfelt plea, "Forgive me, mother!" simply grinned good-naturedly. He couldn't get really angry with Paul, ever.

"Sorry, Alexander." The words were spoken when the lights were already out.

"Oh what the hell!" said Alexander, going into his own room.

The financing house of Kabe, Linder & Co. was ostensibly run by a man called Stafford Deems, but Alexander knew that all major policy decisions were still taken by old Henry Kabe. Kabe had tried to avoid seeing Alexander, saying that at his advanced age, he was now in his eighties, he could no longer concern himself with the day-by-day running of the company's affairs. But Alexander, playing on the old man's well-known love of intrigue, sent him a message saying that what he had to discuss was highly confidential, and that if he talked to Stafford Deems it would certainly get back to Hesslan. This had the desired effect, an invitation to come and see Kabe.

In the two weeks prior to this meeting Alexander spent a considerable amount of time with a financial journalist—a friend of a friend of Paul's—finding out as much as possible about Kabe. He was one of the original masters of the technique of creating great industrial combines. By the process of bringing together a dozen or more companies operating in the same field, and providing the finance for the amalgamation, he would invariably end up controlling the resultant combine. Once created, this combine would be powerful enough to eat up most of its smaller competitors who had resisted the initial move, or force them, in turn, to combine. Sometimes the second combine, formed to fight the first one, was financed by investment houses, commercial banks or insurance companies which, it emerged later, were also controlled by Kabe. Kabe had never concerned himself with mining copper, building railroads, drilling for oil, or making cars or movies, but once companies were established in these fields and required fresh capital for expansion, he provided that capital and in doing so often—if it seemed useful to do so—acquired control of the companies.

CHAPTER SEVENTEEN

Henry Kabe lived in a fifteen-room apartment that occupied the entire top floor of a tower building on Park Avenue. He had his own entrance hall on the ground floor, where a doorman and a private detective were always on guard to scrutinize visitors, and to ensure that they were "expected," before pressing the button that opened the elevator doors. One of Kabe's private secretaries provided whichever doorman was on duty with a list of "expected" visitors, and anyone not on that list was not admitted. When Alexander arrived and gave his name, he was immediately shown into the elevator which was large enough to take fifteen people at a time and furnished like a salon, with French chairs and sofas, carpets, antique mirrors, and lit by a crystal chandelier. When the elevator came to a stop, a butler opened the doors from the outside and took Alexander's hat and coat and placed them, temporarily, on one of two fifteenth-century coffers which stood in a small alcove in the hall, on either side of a Greek Bacchus holding his winebowl and his grapes. Alexander followed the butler across the marble hall, glimpsing nothing but empty sky through the windows along one side, and experiencing the almost physical sensation of being at a high altitude, as if the air actually were more rarefied up here. He was shown straight into Henry Kabe's study, without fuss, the butler announcing him in a soft murmur: "Mr. Sondorf," and then quietly closing the door behind him. Kabe was standing behind a high, narrow, stand-up desk, and he was in his socks; he finished something that he was writing rather laboriously, the effort making him grimace slightly, before looking up. "Sondorf," he expostulated, "you're the fellow that's been pestering to see me. *What* is it you do?"

"I run the Hesslan studios in Hollywood," said Alexander.

The voice was surprisingly strong and grating coming from this thin, frail old man, with his almost feminine features: thin, prissy lips, small, delicately made nose, white hair brushed flat and lying on his head like a fine rug, piercing blue eyes, skin as pallid as a dead man's. The room was terribly overheated, it was like a hothouse, and Alexander had the impression that Kabe was some rare plant that would immediately shrivel up and die if exposed to the normal atmosphere. But this impression was immediately belied as Kabe crumpled up some papers on the stand-up desk, threw them onto the floor, which Alexander saw now was as littered with ticker tape and crumpled and discarded papers as a newspaper office, and strode vigorously across the room to a settee, sat down, and started pulling on his shoes. There was nothing feeble about the way he pulled on his shoes. The only sound, while he did this, was the intermittent stutter of a tape machine, spewing out the stock market quotations.

"What was it you wanted to see me about?" demanded Kabe, when he had laced up his shoes to his satisfaction. His dangling hands encountered a crumpled-up piece of paper, uncrumpled it, regarded it critically for a moment, and then crumpled it up again and threw it behind him.

"I wanted to get your support," said Alexander, "for spending more money."

Kabe sat up abruptly. "You want to spend more money, do you?"

"Yes."

"Picture people spend far too much."

"That's a matter of opinion, Mr. Kabe."

"What makes you think, Mr. Sondorf, that I have anything to do with how much you spend out in California?"

"I think these economy waves are largely inspired by you."

"You think that, do you?"

"And I think some of the things that are being insisted on are not very sensible. For instance, the ruling that the 'regards' should be left out of cables."

"Picture people are much too verbose," declared Kabe. "Should be possible to conduct business without wrapping up everything in endearments."

"The endearments are necessary, Mr. Kabe. When you have to send a tough cable to a director on location, saying what you didn't like about the way he handled a certain scene, you must wrap it up with love and kisses and assurances of your continued belief in him, otherwise you risk throwing him completely. At five cents a word, the love is worth putting in. Leave out the 'regards' from even the most routine cable and you make it sound harsh. 'Regret can't offer you more than ten thousand dollars' is off-putting on its own, possibly even offensive. But if you add 'love to Hermann and the kiddies,' it takes the sting out of it."

"You've made your case, Mr. Sondorf. You can have the love and kisses back. Anything else?"

"Yes. There's a picture I want to spend a million and a half on."

"That's quite a jump. From five cents a word to a million and a half dollars."

"I thought I'd give it to you in easy stages, Mr. Kabe."

"I don't think any moving picture can earn that kind of money back."

"*Birth of a Nation* did, and so did quite a few others."

"And a lot of them lost it."

"I know. But even if we lost money on such a picture, making big pictures—with the best talent available—is worth while, it expands our potential market for other pictures by increasing our audience. Every big picture, Mr. Kabe, even if you lose on it, if it's a good picture, makes the people who've gone to see it want to see others."

"I've always believed in letting the other fellow expand the market," said Kabe.

"I know. But I don't agree with that. I don't have time to wait until somebody else has expanded the market."

"You're a young fellow. Very young, I'd say—in your

twenties? Why are you in such a hurry, Mr. Sondorf? I don't think I was ever in a hurry."

"You must have known you were going to have a long time, I'm not that sure."

Kabe got up and walked across the room, kicking crumpled bits of paper out of his way, until he came to a glass door, which he slid open, and stepped out into a glassed-in roof garden, circumventing the entire apartment. This was where Henry Kabe took his daily walk, three times around the periphery of the apartment, breathing in the fragrance of the painstakingly cultivated plants and flowers which blossomed here, so surprisingly, twenty-four stories above the sidewalks of Manhattan. There were no neighbors here to observe him, and nothing to see except the pinnacles of a handful of other buildings of equal height—the Heckscher Building, the Ritz Tower, the Hotel Shelton. When the weather was good, he would put on his overcoat and some of the glass panels overhead would be opened to admit precisely calculated amounts of fresh air or sunshine. But today it was too cold. For Alexander it was a strange sensation, walking through this meticulously-laid-out garden, heated to hothouse temperature, with nothing but sky and space all around.

"D'you mind walking?" asked Kabe.

"Not at all."

"Good."

For a while Alexander walked silently at Kabe's side. The old man seemed totally oblivious of the flowers cultivated so painstakingly for his benefit, or of the lighthouse view of the sky, or of the almost tropical heat that brought no hint of perspiration to his face.

"Why didn't you put these proposals to Mr. Hesslan?" demanded Kabe at length.

"I knew there was no use getting his agreement, if your support was lacking."

"I'm a minority shareholder."

"You could exercise your influence."

"Why should I do that?"

"I should think because you . . . enjoy exercising your influence."

Kabe gave a thin laugh that sounded like somebody playing a tin kettle. "You think I enjoy power, do you?"

"If you didn't, I can't imagine why you've bothered to acquire so much of it."

Kabe laughed again, appreciatively. "I'll tell you something," he said in a confidential voice, "it doesn't give you the gut-ache." He continued to walk in silence, his own silence just one layer in the many layers of silence in which he was wrapped; the rooms in the apartment must have been soundproofed because not a sound came from any of them, and not a sound came from the city far below. Alexander said nothing while they completed the first circuit of the roof garden. Then Kabe said, "I'm glad you don't feel you have to talk all the time. Nervous people feel they have to talk all the time." After the second time round, Kabe said: "I do this three times. Does it bore you?"

"No. If it doesn't bore you."

"It bores the shit out of me, but at my age I don't have many alternative recreations." He looked sharply at Alexander. "Too hot for you?"

"It *is* hot."

"You know what people say about me and this place? They say: old Kabe, he keeps that apartment heated to furnace temperature to acclimatize himself. For that place he's going to." This was followed by another tin-kettle laugh. "Had you heard that?"

"No, I hadn't."

"People think that when you're old you can't mind that much about dying. I mind like hell, Mr. Sondorf."

"I'm sure."

"Well, it was good of you to accompany me on my walk. I've enjoyed talking to you. If you want to talk about anything else ever, come and see me. I'll think about your suggestions. Good-by to you now."

In the remaining ten days before the première and the opening of the Seiermann Theater (Willi had decided to bestow his own name on his new super cinema), most of Alexander's time was taken up by publicity. The New York offices of both Seiermann-International and H. O. H., Inc., had been spending vast sums on a joint national advertising campaign to launch the new theater and the new film. A great deal of excitement had been generated. Alexander's youth and good looks and extraordinarily rapid success, together with the fact that all sorts of highly fanciful

278

stories and anecdotes about him had gained circulation in the past year and a half, made him a natural subject for the newspaper and magazine writers. Up till then he had declined all requests for interviews, and this had given him an aura of mystery that made him even more attractive to the newspapers. But now, in order to get the maximum amount of publicity for the film, he was obliged to make himself available to the press. He got Pete Fenton over from Hollywood to handle this side of things in conjunction with Willi's own publicity man, Terence Rowley. Willi, never averse to talking about himself, was also getting a tremendous amount of publicity, and it was impossible to open a newspaper without seeing pictures of him —usually together with one of his glamorous stars—and interviews with him and stories about the marvels and wonders of the Seiermann Theater, and even statements by Willi about what was wrong with the world. Alexander was much more reserved in his interviews; he was cordial and hospitable to the journalists, but not excessively communicative. He answered their personal questions obliquely and did not allow himself to be pressed. He would not confirm or deny any of the many versions of how he had taken control at Hesslan's. He would reveal nothing of his personal life, evaded questions about girls, smiled noncommittally at jokes about him being a mother's darling, and talked forcefully about the picture industry, and with carefully restrained enthusiasm about *The Rich, Full Life.* Very few of the journalists who came to interview him had much in their notebooks—in the way of sensational quotes —by the time they went away, but most of them went away liking him. The women journalists adored him and devoted most of their space to describing his dark good looks, his extreme youthfulness combined with great forcefulness of personality, his beautiful manners, his touchingly "shy" evasions when they asked him about girls—Alexander now knew how to make "shyness" serve his purposes. To the more serious interviewers, he talked fluently about the conflicts between art and business in picturemaking, paid tribute to the genius of Walter Staupitz, but added "the fact that a man is a genius doesn't mean he's always right." He posed for photographs, and the fact that most of them were taken in fairly opulent surroundings inspired the caption writers and the headline writers to use innumerable variations of the phrase "the rich, full life of Alexander Sondorf." (In the ensuing months it became a catch phrase throughout the United States. When a boy wanted to ask a girl to the corner drugstore for a milk shake, he'd say: "Come with me to the rich, full life." And when a girl was being taken on the town by a young blade, people would say: "Ah, he's giving her the rich, full life routine." And when doctors had to warn middle-aged businessmen to take it easy, they'd say: "A bit too much of the rich, full life—eh?" There were innumerable other applications. Cole Porter incorporated the phrase in one of his songs, sociologists used the phrase ironically, satirists used it satirically, and moralists and reformers thundered it from platforms and pulpits with withering scorn. It was one of those phrases on everybody's lips in the mid-twenties. Even before the opening, Alexander's prediction that *The Rich, Full Life* was going to be a famous film had proved right.)

The day of the première, a girl phoned to say that she was speaking for Mr. Kabe. Mr. Kabe wished to thank Mr. Sondorf for the tickets for the opening, but unfortunately he hardly ever went out these days and therefore would not be able to make use of them. Would Mr. Sondorf mind, the girl wanted to know, if she used one of the tickets herself—as she very much wanted to see the film. No, not at all, said Alexander. In that case, she continued, if she might ask a further favor, as it was rather late and she had not make arrangements for anyone to take her, would he mind dropping by and picking her up. Alexander said he wasn't sure that he could do that, he had a lot to take care of, and drop by *where* exactly? The apartment, she said. Which apartment? "My grandfather's apartment," she said, "you were here the other day."

By 8 P.M. the crowds, which had been gathering behind police barriers at the intersection of Seventh Avenue and Forty-ninth Street since late afternoon, were no longer controllable and were spilling over into the streets, slowing down the procession of Marmons and Minervas and Pierce-Arrows and Lincolns and Checker cabs and Rolls-Royces to a stop-start, stop-start crawl through the slush and the rain. Some of those arriving for the opening had abandoned their automobiles just outside the congested area and, with chauffeurs and footmen forming the spearhead and holding the umbrellas, were making the dash toward the marquee entrance of the Seiermann Theater. Periodically, a roar would go up from one part of the crowd, and spread rapidly through the forest of umbrellas, as somebody thought he had spotted somebody. "It's Charlie, Charlie . . . Charleee . . . Charleee!" or, "It's Gloria Swanson, it's Gloria . . . oh it's Gloria . . . oh, Gloria . . . *hey, Gloria.*" Wet faces from the crowd were pressed unabashedly right up against the windows of slowly moving automobiles, ecstatically staring inside, seeking to identify the dazzling shadows. Flood lamps played on the crowd, illuminating different sections of it in sudden shafts of warmth and brightness, while newsreel cameramen, in various points of vantage, filmed the excited faces before swiveling round to catch the arrival of some celebrity.

Struggling through the blaze of white light at the entrance, people looked suddenly flattened, their features ironed out. The swinging away of a flood lamp provided an only momentary letup from this third-degree lighting. Inside, in the packed lobby, the air was thick with the smoke of photographers' flash powder, and people stood about emitting whews of relief that they had finally made it, shook the rain off their coats, and stamped the slush off their shoes, and stared at each other, and women examined themselves in hand mirrors to see if any irreparable damage had been done to their coiffures and make-up. Just inside the entrance it was all coats and Inverness capes and furs and opera cloaks and Homburgs and crushhats and overshoes, but a little deeper into the theater, in the circular area formed by twelve great marble columns, bare shoulders and large plume fans and dainty gold slippers with rhinestone heels, and patent-leather shoes of unblemished shininess, implied a magical imperviousness to climatic conditions outside.

Under a vast crystal chandelier, on an enormous oval rug with the golden monogram ST at the center, and backed by a massive floral display, the centerpiece of which consisted of the name SEIERMANN spelled out in red and white carnations, stood Willi Seiermann, in tails, flanked on one side by his wife and two daughters, and on the other by two brothers and one brother-in-law. He was beaming pinkly through his pince-nez at the incoming guests. Every time a celebrity was presented to him—his staff had strict and precise instructions about who was to be presented and who wasn't—he posed for the photographers in the attitude of welcoming these especially privileged guests. As the photographers' flash powder went off, it was invariably into the cameras, and not at his guests, that he was beaming his heartfelt welcome. Harold Lloyd's hand was vigorously pumped, Gloria Swanson was embraced and kissed while her husband, the Marquis de la Falaise de la Coudraye, looked on tolerantly; Mrs. Otto Kahn received a formal handshake, Texas Guinan was not presented, but the kiss she blew to Willi as she swept past was extravagantly returned; Mayor Jimmy Walker had his shoulder slapped and his hand firmly squeezed in both of Willi's.

At eight-thirty, five minutes before the program was due to start, Alexander arrived with a party that consisted of Adolphe Menjou, David Watterton, his wife Deborah, Paul, and Susan Kabe. Seeing them arrive, Willi urged his whole family forward, like a star performer sweeping his company toward the footlights for the final curtain call. He grasped Alexander's head with rough, paternalistic pride, and demanded rhetorically: "Who discovered this boy genius? *I* did. Who saw the talent blazing in him like a holocaust when he was just a shaver? *I* saw it." Alexander introduced his party. When he came to Susan Kabe, Willi beamed and said, "I am very pleased to meet you. I had once the privilege to do business with your grandfather. Now take good care of her, Alexander, she's a lovely girl, you're a lucky man. You're joining us afterward?"

"Sure, Willi," said Alexander, "sure," and moved his party on, steering them up the marble steps, and then on past the Maharajah (Smoking) Room. They were all looking all the time, as everyone else was doing, marveling at the great dome, its periphery molded with high-relief figures of charioteers and cornucopias and lyres, gasping at the size of the principal chandelier, commenting on the lavish use of gold leaf, which covered virtually every exposed surface not of bronze or marble or glass, pausing at various places in the gallery of the mezzanine floor, and leaning over the marble balustrade to look down into the great lobby, as vast and glittering as a state ballroom, admiring—or loathing—the statues and busts that stood in niches between the entrances to the loges.

It was eight forty-five before all the 4,174 red plush seats, each bearing the monogrammed ST on the back, were occupied, and the house lights went out. First, there was a newsreel showing the emergence of the Seiermann Theater out of rubble to its present magnificence—oohs and ahhs and a certain amount of ironical applause were elicited by the statistics of its magnificence. Then darkness again, so complete and surprising that some people thought the power must have failed. But now a thin beam of light cut through the dark spaces of the theater and discovered the chubby face of Willi Seiermann on the stage, and Willi was declaiming in a resounding voice: "Ye portals bright, high and majestic, open to our gaze the path to Wonderland, and show us the realm where fantasy reigns, where romance, where adventure flourish. Let ev'ry day's toil be forgotten under thy sheltering roof—O glorious, mighty hall—thy magic and thy charm unite us all to worship at beauty's throne. . . . Let there be light . . ." Whereupon the stage was dramatically flooded in waves of colored light, out of which there rose, as if out of the ocean, a symphony orchestra of 110 musicians, which proceeded to play "The Star-Spangled Banner" while Willi, alone in the foreground, stood stiffly to attention, and a picture of the President of the United States was projected onto the screen. This was followed by the projection on the screen of messages of congratulations from the President and from civic notabilities. Then came a spectacular ballet, depicting the invention of the cinematograph by Thomas Edison, and the growth and development of Hollywood. The climax of this was when a dozen horses thundered backward and forward across the stage, and ballet dancers, as Indians, balletically bit the dust. After this came the film. As Alexander's name came up on the credits, Susan Kabe turned a smiling face to him, and Alexander said: "Don't hold the preliminaries against me. I'm only responsible for the film." As the film unfolded, Alexander glanced from time to time at Susan Kabe to elicit her reactions, and she smiled back at him encouragingly, and once she gave his hand a reassuring pat. As she felt him becoming aware of her, she put her mouth close to his ear and whispered playfully, "How do you do, Mr. Sondorf. I'm so glad to meet you at last. . . ." He gave her a puzzled look. "This is the first time you've *noticed* me," she explained.

283

"Oh, I'm sorry."

"Well, you did have a lot of important other things to think about." The way she said "important" was mocking him very slightly.

"Yes," he agreed, laughing.

With the varying amounts of light of the screen playing on her features, she was a few bold charcoal strokes—so much left out, so much implied, so much to wonder about. Her eyes, amused, curious, casually flirtatious, seemed to know—oh! such a lot, but she wasn't telling. The bone structure of her face had a definite line, a sort of swagger cut; she would look good in a slouch hat; she had the slightly mannish look of somebody who doesn't need to trade on her femininity. There was, too, a hint of toughness about her that he liked. There was nothing about her you could be sure of, as you could be sure of the girls he took out in Hollywood. He realized there was a sort of battle going on, quietly, between them, as to who was going to be impressed most: he by her, or she by him.

You couldn't tell from the applause at the end, this sort of audience had even applauded the "Hollywood ballet" with enthusiasm, but looking at the faces of the people around him Alexander could tell that they hadn't been bored, they had that not-quite-here look still, which meant that the emotional ties with the story had not been broken the moment the film had ended. That was a good sign, it indicated that they had been involved.

"It was very good," said Susan Kabe. "How clever you are to have made such a *good* film."

"I didn't direct it," he explained, but this seemed a mere technicality. It was clearly his film. Such a lovely legend was being born, and nobody wanted to spoil it by raising hairsplitting quibbles. David Watterton had never done anything outstanding before—he was just a competent and colorless Hollywood director. The *new* name, the thrill-name, was Alexander Sondorf. As they made their way out, he could feel the excitement swirling and eddying around him. In the lobby, Willi—alone now, having dispatched his family home—was perspiring with enthusiasm. "We have a table at the Ritz-Carlton Roof," he called to Alexander before becoming submerged in congratulatory embraces. All the way out, Alexander had to run a gauntlet of back-slapping hands and avid eyes and demanding clasps; he saw little huddles of people, ostensibly talking to each other, but all surreptitiously looking him over, and looking over this girl who was with him, who seemed to set the seal on his success. At the Ritz-Carlton, there were more photographers waiting; it had got around whom he was with—"He's with Susan Kabe," people said to each other, staring, craning necks. Before the cameras they grew toward each other, linked and joined in the dazzling flash, wedded on the photographer's plate; pressed together by the excitement all around them they shone in unison. She did not taste the same as other girls when he kissed her, she tasted of privilege, of rarity, her kiss was the bestowal of grace on him, the millions behind her had given her this fine flavor, this blending of exquisite things—it was not like kissing just any girl. After they had eaten, and been charming to a thousand people, and had said witty things to each other and everybody else, and were together, alone, in the cab, he said lightly, "Come back to my hotel." Her humorous eyes were delicately, gravely, considering the invitation, playing with it daringly, this exquisite offer—such a delicate taste. This leaping ahead of strangers to the possibility of such a startling intimacy. Such a fine, rare taste!

"I'd like to." Her words, lightly spoken, cutting through all preliminaries and all the stages leading up to, arriving breathless and surprised. Their smiles leaped ahead, soaring over all the intermittent stages, and for a moment the agreement, the verbal agreement, made the anticipation for both of them such a sharp thrill that it seemed impossible anything later could equal it. They didn't touch all the way up to his suite; taking her coat off was like unwrapping some priceless gift. She murmured appreciatively as he held her lightly, while they discovered each other. "Oh-oh-you make me feel so . . . so . . ." she said. "You make me want to do such things." Still the smile hovering on her lips as her mouth formed an oval. "Would you like that?" He nodded, and very gravely, very carefully, she dropped to her knees, lifting her dress enough to avoid kneeling on the fine material. "Do Hollywood girls do this?" she asked, looking up at him with her grave eyes.

"Yes," he said, "but it's not like this."

She understood that for her to do this now, when they were still strangers to the closer intimacy, would be something that could not be equaled later on. "I *want* to do that with you," she said.

"And you?"

"No, first let me—I like to wait."

All the time her grave, and somehow still slightly remote, eyes watched him. He felt his body come into a sharp focus of impossibly concentrated sensation. Nothing could be as sharp and sweet as this moment which was already over and was another kind of moment as it was happening. After a while she stopped and said, laughing at herself, "Now I don't want to wait any longer." He started to fumble with her dress, but she told him not to bother, and, very roughly now in contrast to the carefulness of her movements before, pulled up the material of the dress and, raising herself slightly off the carpet, deftly pushed something small and flimsy down her thighs and legs and kicked it away, spreading herself in the same movement. Even like this her expression was still a little haughty and a little amused. He lay down at her side and her eyes watched him, smilingly, as his hands moved upward, and she laughed with pleasure at the sudden urgency that came into his eyes as his fingertips discovered her readiness. "Oh, yes," she said, "oh, yes, like that, like that. That gets me. That really gets me—hot." She propped herself up on her elbows so she could see better. "Oh, it's marvelous," she sighed, "it's like petting in a parked car. No. No, go on, go on, I want to like this the first time. Just with your hand." And as her excitement grew, she pulled at the bodice of her dress and bared one breast for him to see, and squeezed it through the circle of her fingers, making it taut, and when it happened it was such a quick little spasm, and she said: "Oh! Oh! Oh! This almost happened while we were dancing. I've been on the edge of this all evening."

And, a little later, she asked him if he liked to play games, and he said what sort of games? "Pretending games," she said. "Pretend you're going to leave—that you don't want to any more. Then I have to *make* you stay—you see? Then I have to beg you. Now say you're not going to— go on, say it. Use the word. And then—I have to beg you to—you see—" She was already deep in the pretense and very excited. "Go on," she said, "say what I said."

CHAPTER EIGHTEEN

"I'm sorry, Mr. Fenton," said Miss Pearce, who was becoming more officious in her manner every day, "but Mr. Sondorf still can't see you. He's talking to New York. I will call you just as soon as he's free."

"I'll wait. Say, tell me something. Does she call him or does he call her?"

"That's none of your business, Mr. Fenton."

"Oh, come on, honey. You wouldn't want to deprive me of the vicarious thrill of being in on the Wonder Boy's platinum-plated romance. Now don't deny it. I bet you listen in sometimes. You're blushing, Miss Pearce. Oh, *that's* what they talk about."

"You're a crude, prying man, Mr. Fenton."

"Can't help it, baby. My newspaper training. Tell me, you get a bang out of it—listening in?"

"I refuse to have this kind of conversation with you. If you don't mind, *I* have some work to do."

Paul came into the outer waiting room and looked questioningly at the secretary. "Oh, Mr. Krasnor," she said, "Mr. Sondorf does want to see you, but he's on the phone at the moment. Do you mind waiting?"

"I'll wait. Pete Fenton, how is it in publicity?"

"Publicity! Spend all my time denying reports of his romances. *I* don't even know if I'm lying or not. Say, you hear the story about the Hollywood star trying to explain to his little boy about Jesus Christ?"

"Even if I had, that wouldn't stop you telling it," said Paul, smiling.

"Well, see, this star is showing his little boy a huge crucifix in a church, and he's explaining that Christ is love and that He died on the cross so that all of us sinners could be redeemed. . . ."

"Yes," said Paul, "I hope it's not going to be blasphemous, you know Miss Pearce's susceptibilities . . ."

"It's a very moral story," said Pete Fenton. "Well, see, this guy, this star, is saying that Christ died for all of us. 'For *all* of us?' asks the little boy. 'Sure, for all of us,' says his dad. 'Did He die for the President of the United

States?' asks the little boy. 'He certainly did,' says his father. 'Did He die for Mr. Henry Ford?' asks the little boy. 'He sure did,' says dad. 'And for the King of England?' 'Oh, yes.' 'And for Louis B. Mayer?' 'I guess He died for Louis B. Mayer, too,' says his father. 'And for Willi Seiermann?' demands the little boy, looking up in utter awe at the figure on the cross. 'Well,' starts the movie star. Whereupon a voice from the cross calls out, 'Somebody get me down from here. I've changed my mind.' "

Miss Pearce gave a little disapproving snigger; Paul gave a rich chuckle.

"*Get me down from here, I've changed my mind,*" repeated Pete Fenton with relish. The door of Alexander's office opened and he put his head out.

"Didn't we have an appointment at twelve?" he asked Pete Fenton.

"I've been here all the time. You were on the phone."

"I've been off the phone for three minutes."

"I'm sorry, Mr. Sondorf, it's my fault," said Miss Pearce, giving Pete Fenton a dark look.

"That's all right, Miss Pearce. Come in, Pete. Paul, will you come in too?" Even before they were seated, he said, "Now, Pete, you say I've seen all the publicity on *The Rich, Full Life.*"

"Everything of importance," said Pete Fenton. Alexander sat down behind the desk and opened a large artist's portfolio containing photostats of dozens of articles and notices; he leafed through these, a slight frown on his face. "They're great notices," said Pete Fenton, "with one or two exceptions. Not so good on the boy, as you expected, but marvelous for Menjou and for the picture. They're selling notices, Alexander. *I'd* want to see this movie after reading those notices."

"The picture has had a fantastic reception," said Paul.

"Yes," Alexander said, "it's doing very well." He handed a sheet of paper to Pete Fenton. "You can do a release on this. Takings at the Seiermann."

Pete Fenton scrutinized the sheet. "$57,838 in the first week. And the fourth week is up on that! Wow!"

"That may be partly the theater," said Alexander, "the test will be how it does in the sticks."

"All the sneaks have been great, Alexander."

"Yes, it's a good sign. Pete, you say I've seen all the publicity . . . ?"

"Well, there may have been some *unimportant* pieces that I felt you didn't need to be bothered with."

"Is this what you call unimportant, Pete?" Alexander reached under a stack of papers and produced a copy of *Vanity Fair*, which he threw across to Pete Fenton, who stared at it glumly.

"Yes, I know about this," he confessed.

"Why wasn't I shown this? Because it's adverse?"

"Look, everybody knows that Stephen Raille is a left-wing agitator who don't have a good word for anything or anybody. He's a lousy writer, what's more."

"I'm not interested in your literary judgments, Pete. I want to know what you were proposing to do about this article."

"I was proposing to ignore it, like it deserves to be ignored," said Pete Fenton with emotion.

"That's what you propose, is it?"

"Yuh."

"All right. Give it back to me. Let's go through it together." Pacing calmly, Alexander began to read out the article in a flat, unemotional voice: " 'Hollywood is a place where geniuses are less rare than you might suppose from seeing its films. Only the other day there were five of them in town. Seeing that I was given a choice, I decided to interest myself in one called Alexander Sondorf, not only because he's the youngest—having gotten into the same class as Leonardo da Vinci, Goethe and, all right, Edison —before he's hardly out of his teens, but also because he's being offered to us as a *literate* genius, and this does sort of single him out because that isn't a claim made for just any old run-of-the-mill Hollywood genius. I was also interested in him because some friends and colleagues, whom I had not previously suspected of sycophancy or insanity, had joined in the general hysterical stampede to acclaim *The Rich, Full Life*, the first film to be made under Sondorf's auspices in Hollywood, and now being shown at a mausoleum that Mr. W. Seiermann has put up at Seventh Avenue and Forty-ninth, and which for me would be redeemed, partially at least, if it already entombed its progenitor. The film is based on a pretty good novel by Harland Stahl, has a screenplay attributed to four writers, was directed by David Watterton, and stars Adolphe Menjou. Quite a few others had something or other to do with it, and if you look carefully at the list of credits you'll find the names of the people who were responsible for the hair dressing, the costumes, the camera work and the shifting of pieces of equipment from one place to another, but nowhere will you find exactly what Sondorf did for, to, or in, this picture. Yet on the front of the Seiermann, there is a gigantic illuminated sign which says: "Alexander Sondorf's *The Rich, Full Life*," though it refrains from mentioning the authors, the director, the star and the people who shifted pieces of equipment from one place to another.

" 'Ah, but I'm not being absolutely fair. There is a definite contribution that Sondorf, according to reports, made to this film. He provided the ending. In Stahl's novel, the exposed confidence man commits suicide in preference to facing a life without the glitter and the glory that he's had in the past, and the boy who was his protegé—and idolized him as a genuine exemplar of upper-class wit, style and charm—cynically sets out to emulate his mentor and teacher, being by now unfit for any career other than conning. What happens in the film? In the film, and this is where Sondorf's genius presumably manifests itself, the con man shrugs off his exposure and disgrace and, after first insuring that he has set his young protegé on the path of virtue and reformation, goes on conning away, on a less elevated scale perhaps but no less charmingly or endearingly. Sondorf has another claim to fame. He is the man who, while working as a mere Personal Assistant to H. O. Hesslan, took it upon himself to sack Walter Staupitz, and had him thrown out of the studio and beaten up by a studio cop; after which he brought in another director to finish *Night of the Fête*. If this sort of thing entitles you to be called a genius then we must all start calling Mussolini's black-shirted strong-arm men geniuses. The fact that Sondorf is apparently a personable young man, reputedly kind to his mother, and possessing the ability to charm, seems to have dazzled a lot of people only accustomed to meeting the cruder kind of Hollywood mogul. His background is reassuringly ordinary . . . ' " Alexander paused. "We'll skip my background," he said, "as he says, it's reassuringly ordinary. Now here we are. 'Moreover, he knows whom to talk to about what. In a long interview with *New Republic* he talks feelingly, and even intelligently, about the art of motion pictures, and not a mention of money. Then, if you pick up *Variety,* you will find his views, also feelingly expressed, on how the box-office yield of films can be increased, and not a mention of art. In both interviews he gives the impression of being well-informed on his subject, and he is as fluent, in the former, in quoting what E. M. Forster said about the novel as he is, in the latter, quoting the box-office returns of *The Ten Commandments.* The truly horrifying thing about Sondorf is not that he is doing exactly what every other film mogul is doing, namely making money for himself and his shareholders, but that he should have succeeded in deluding some people into thinking that he is some kind of cultural trail blazer and that he stands for a new spirit in Hollywood. If this slender youth is the sole repository of our cultural hopes in the field of the mechanized arts, then the outlook is black.' " Alexander put down the article, and looked up. "Well, Pete? That's the article you propose to ignore?"

"Like I said, Raille is just a left-wing agitator."

"Is the article justified, would you say? Is it fair comment?"

"Justified?" Pete Fenton repeated uncertainly.

"That's not fair," put in Paul. "He works for you. Do you expect him to tell you that article is justified?"

"What do you think, Paul?"

"I think he makes some valid points."

"Valid points," exploded Pete Fenton, *"Jesus!"*

"Such as, Paul?"

"Taking sole billing outside the theater."

"Uhu. What else?"

"Changing the ending."

"Is there any part of the article you think is not fair?"

"He probably doesn't know all the ins and outs of the Staupitz situation. And the tone of it is—well, unsympathetic. He is making a particular case and he's marshaling the facts to fit that case. You could use the same set of facts and make a different case. It depends where your own sympathies lie."

"From beginning to end," said Pete Fenton, "that article is a string of distortions and misrepresentations, it's a slur

on your personal integrity, it mocks your contribution. . . .
It's libelous, we could sue . . ."

"We're not going to sue," said Alexander.

"You could have him black-listed," said Pete Fenton,
"that's what Willi wants to do. He's a writer, he'd never
sell a story to Hollywood. That's the way to deal with
these bastards."

"What we're going to do," said Alexander, "is invite him
here as our guest."

"That *bum* . . . you want to invite that bum . . . ?"

"Listen carefully," said Alexander, cutting him short.
"When we're attacked by a man of Stephen Raille's stature
we must take notice. He's right about the billing, and he's
right about the way you boys in publicity bandy around
words like genius; his whole article is based on the fact
that people have been making exaggerated claims on my
behalf. It's my fault, I should have stopped it. He's wrong
about the ending of *The Rich, Full Life*, and he's wrong
about Staupitz, and he's wrong about one or two other
things. But his is a legitimate point of view, and when
we're attacked by a man like that we must take notice,
we can't shrug it off. I don't want you to keep these sort of
things from me, Pete. I want to know who is attacking us
and why, and when the attack comes from reputable newspapermen and writers I don't want them to be blacklisted
or barred or anything like that. On the contrary, I want
them to be given every facility to see exactly how we work
and what we do and what our problems are and what
we're trying to achieve. And if, after they've seen for themselves, they still attack us, that's their privilege. I want you
to see to it that words like genius and boy wonder are
not applied to me in any material emanating from this
studio. And I think it would be a good idea to prepare a
release explaining the function of a studio chief so that
people have some idea of why my name is up there on the
billing." When Pete Fenton had left, Alexander turned to
Paul. "Dammit, the one man who could really hurt me
with an attack like that is Stephen Raille. It hurts because
I've admired him for years, as you know. That *he* should
have so completely misunderstood what I'm trying to do,
that's what hurts."

"You're serious about inviting him here?"

"Yes."

"What makes you think he'd come?"

"Maybe he won't. But I've written to him that I respect his attack, and that I consider it would be valuable for a man of his standing to see what goes on in Hollywood at first hand, without any restrictions, and to write about it on the basis of what he has seen."

"That implies he didn't know what he was talking about in that article."

"I tried to avoid that implication. You can read the letter, if you like." Alexander called in Miss Pearce and asked her to fetch a copy of the letter to Raille. When Paul had read it, he said: "Yes, a good letter."

The reply from Stephen Raille, which came about a week later, read: "Dear Mr. Sondorf, Your letter intrigued me, as it was meant to do. When one attacks somebody as toughly as I attacked you, and receives in reply a courteous and well-reasoned answer, one is inclined to be a bit put out—at least I am. After getting your letter, I very carefully went over every word I had written about you, thinking that maybe I had been unfair. I have to say that I came to the conclusion, after a lot of thought, that what I wrote was both justified and called for. What does intrigue me (and it bothers me a little too) is that, after what I wrote, you should want to invite me to Hollywood and offer to let me sit in on all your activities with absolute freedom to go away and write exactly what I like. This is the sort of offer one can't turn down—you must have realized that when you made it. All right, I accept. But for obvious reasons I don't want to come as the guest of the studio. I hope there is no misunderstanding about the basis on which I am accepting your invitation. In my newspaper days people realized that because you took a drink with them it didn't mean you had become their blood brother (or if they didn't realize it, it was just too bad), but nowadays I find I have rather to spell this out."

Stephen Raille was a tall man, with a shock of curly gray hair, and a permanent stoop that must have been the result of always having had to bend slightly to avoid hitting his head against things. His face was as full of interesting lines as a map, and these lines gave weight to all his expressions, as if even his smile was something arrived at only after a lot of thought and struggle. In contrast to his writing, his manner was unassertive, almost diffident. When he propounded ideas, it was always in a very tentative way. He had no difficulty listening, and for the first twenty minutes of their meeting he let Alexander do most of the talking and politely but firmly refused to be drawn into talking about himself. He sat listening very attentively, though frequently shifting his position, curling and uncurling his long legs, moving his weight from one elbow to the other, as Alexander reminded him of what he had said in that *New Republic* article a few years back. He let Alexander finish, and then said, "Well, yes . . . I think I did say something like that and I still think that artists are too squeamish about exercising power, but you see what I have against you" (and he gave a smile as he said this) "is that I don't think you are an artist, and that's why I objected to your taking credit for *The Rich, Full Life*."

"I agree about the billing," said Alexander, "and you may have noticed I had that put right."

"Last time I walked past there," said Raille, "your name was still up, twice the size of Menjou's and about three times the size of Stahl's."

"That's because it is my film. I know that's difficult for you to accept, considering that somebody else wrote it and somebody else directed it, and I didn't even shift the scenery. But in a way I did all these things; I made all the important decisions affecting those things. It's like with Willy Randolph Hearst, maybe he doesn't set up the type himself, or tap out the editorials himself, but they're his papers."

"I see you're not overmodest about the people you choose to compare yourself with," said Raille, smiling. "I've worked on Hearst newspapers and I can assure you that I never expressed Hearst's point of view."

"Maybe not consciously. But you can be pretty sure that he picked you because he knew that there were certain areas in which what you wanted to say and what he wanted you to say happened to coincide, and by limiting your activities to those areas he, in effect, got you to express *his* attitude. When he was gunning for the trusts and the big-business racketeers for his own reasons, it suited him to have you do the muckraking for him. But do you think he would have let you write against a war in Cuba that he'd set his heart on?"

"I have to give you that."

"When I say that it's my picture, it doesn't mean I necessarily have to bend people to my point of view; it means I've put together the people in such a way that they will give me the result I want."

"You think doing that, exercising that sort of judgment and power, makes you an artist?"

"I don't know what it makes me. Head of the factory? Chief turner of the sausage-machine handle, which is what Staupitz calls me? Producer? There isn't a word for it really. Because what I do is not describable in one word— it's not what Seiermann does or what Zukor does or what Griffith does or what De Mille does. What I have is—I have an instinct about what is possible. When I was a lot younger, I thought pretty well everything was impossible, everything seemed much too difficult—to learn lessons, to get to be older, to kiss a girl. And then I discovered that things—all sorts of things—were possible. When I realized this, I had to make these possible things happen. It's like if you're the guy who's realized the possibility of making a clock; naturally you want to *make* the clock—or at least have the clock made. Maybe I don't actually know how to make a clock, that is to say I don't know how to make the component parts, how to put them together, how to make them work. My contribution is that I have realized that a clock is possible, that it can be something other than an hourglass or a sundial. What I have is—an instinct about what *can* be. Other people have to actually make it happen—they have to make the pictures—but I know what is possible. When you complain about my changing the ending of Stahl's novel, you are complaining that a clock isn't an hourglass. You may find this difficult to accept, but I actually think that my ending works better than Stahl's *for the picture*. I think my ending is subtler, more moving, and more in character. I think, in a picture, the suicide would have looked melodramatic and phony."

"And the reformation of the boy?"

Alexander smiled. "In the book he's corrupted, in the picture he's reformed. Either could happen. Mr. Stahl is obviously more pessimistic than I am. I couldn't see why we shouldn't give the kid the benefit of the doubt."

Raille laughed. "You want to tell me, Mr. Sondorf, that in choosing that ending you were not a little guided by thoughts of the box office?"

"I was guided," said Alexander, "by what I wanted to see happen. And"—he smiled—"naturally I hope that what I want to see happen is what millions of paying customers will want to see happen."

During the next few weeks, Stephen Raille sat in on all of Alexander's conferences, was given the run of the studio, came to rushes and to sneak previews, went on the set with Alexander, took lunch with him every day in the commissary, and even stayed in his office when he took private telephone calls. (Alexander did not want to give him the impression that there was any aspect of his work that he was trying to conceal.) After one of these calls, Alexander said, "You know, at the end of this you're going to know more about me than I know about myself."

Raille said, "It puzzles me that you don't mind exposing yourself so completely to a stranger."

"I don't feel you're a stranger," said Alexander. "I'll tell you something that I felt I couldn't at the beginning because then it would have sounded like I was trying to soften you up. But I think I can tell you now. When I was a kid my father took me one day to have lunch at Holland House, and you were there, and he pointed you out to me as a journalist who had exposed the corruption in one of the city councils, and I remember being very impressed by this, by this picture created in my mind of a man using words to fight—to fight the judiciary and the cops and the legislature, and winning. After that I read everything you wrote, and I got to know you, and I used to measure things I wanted to do against your hypothetical reactions . . ." Alexander smiled. "That's why it hurt when I read your article about me. You were probably the only man who could hurt me then. Because I felt that if I had lost you, your approval, I'd gone wrong somewhere."

Raille looked grim, and didn't smile. He said, "I wish you hadn't told me that."

"I'm sorry," said Alexander, "maybe I shouldn't have."

"When you're writing journalism,' said Raille, "there's such a thing as knowing too much about your subject."

"Forget what I said," said Alexander. "You don't need

to have any compunction about attacking me. Remember, I sacked Staupitz, and he was a man I admired. You can sort of half like a man, or half dislike him, but when it comes to taking action you can't sort of half sack him or half attack him in print. Writing your kind of articles is *action,* and as far as I am concerned it's understood that what you feel about me is probably more complicated than what you can express in a magazine piece. As for having your approval, it wouldn't be worth a damn to me if I felt it had been obtained by some sympathy-winning trick."

Raille nodded and said nothing. Alexander could not tell what his feelings were. During a conference, when he had been laying down the line, he would sometimes shoot a quick glance at Raille to catch his reaction, but his eyes were always quite noncommittal, they gave away nothing. Raille never talked about himself, and if the conversation turned to something controversial he might state his own attitude in a few words, but if people disagreed with him he never argued. He just gave one of his hard-won smiles and let the matter pass. He was so silent and unassertive much of the time, making his huge frame as inconspicuous as possible, scribbling notes on scraps of paper and the backs of used envelopes, that it was possible for Alexander to almost forget that he was there.

The conference had been called to discuss a script that three writers had been working on, under Paul's supervision. As usual, Raille sat a little apart from the others, on the leather settee. Alexander was telling the writers what he considered wrong with the script. "What we have failed to do in the present version of the script," he said, "is to find a visual equivalent for the verbal wit of the play. It isn't funny because it relies too much on titles. There's too much for the audience to read."

"It's not slapstick, Alexander," said Paul.

"I know that. But still we've got to *think* in pictures."

"You want us to go back to cave-man language?" said Paul sarcastically. "Big-man-empty-belly, see-good-eat-lion, kill-good-eat-lion, fill-empty-belly. Good."

"As it happens," said Alexander, "that's pretty good picturemaking. It's visual. It can be done. You see, abstract thought can be visually conveyed. Take this passage from the Old Testament. I don't know my Bible very well, but

297

this is a passage I remember: 'I returned, and saw under the sun, that the race is not to the swift, nor the battle to the strong, neither yet bread to the wise, nor yet riches to men of understanding, nor yet favor to men of skill; but time and chance happeneth to them all.' Now that's an abstract thought, but see how it is conveyed in images. That's what movie making is about. What I'm complaining of in our script is that it contains too many abstract ideas that have not been translated into pictures, which is why you have to have so many titles to get across essential information."

"I felt," said Paul irately, "that even the minuscule intelligence of *our* audiences would not be unduly strained by giving them a few hundred simple words to read in the course of a film running an hour and a half."

"I don't know about our audiences," said Alexander quietly, "but you lose *my* interest in the first five minutes."

"If you insist on playing the philistine," said Paul angrily, "there's no use arguing with you . . ."

"Come on, Paul," said Alexander, "this is something we've been over a hundred times. Picturemaking is not putting some illustrations to words, and it's not theater with dialogue printed on slides. It's got to have its own language or it's nothing. Even when we get sound, the story will have to be told in pictures."

"That's what's called progress, is it?" said Paul. "Back to communication at the level of the cave man." He gave a snort of disgust, and pushed back his chair, as if about to get up and walk out.

"If I might butt in at this point." It was Stephen Raille who had spoken from where he was sitting on the settee. "As a writer, I couldn't help being interested in the problems you are talking about," he said. "If you'll excuse me butting in—I sympathize with Paul Krasnor's point of view, of course. It's tough, after all this time, to find that word language, having been developed and refined over thousands of years so as to be capable of expressing a whole lot of pretty delicate shades of meaning, has got to be thrown out the window and replaced by cave-man picture language. It would be pretty hard to discuss Kierkegaard in picture language. But then that's not what you're setting out to do, when you make pictures. What Mr. Sondorf says makes

298

sense to me. Pictures, if they're to amount to anything, must have their own language."

That evening, Alexander made a point of driving Paul back to his apartment. After they had been silent for a while, Alexander closed the glass partition separating them from the driver's compartment. "I'm sorry if I seemed to be lecturing you today," he said.

"I must have needed it," said Paul, "even Stephen Raille is on your side now. Perhaps Γ don't understand about picturemaking; perhaps I don't understand about writing either. Perhaps you should let me go, Alexander. I'm not of much use to you here."

"Don't be ridiculous, Paul. I rely on you tremendously."

"That's rubbish. You're carrying me. Not one subject that I've developed has gone ahead."

"I rely on your advice and your judgment and your friendship, Paul. Come on, snap out of it, Paul. You've told me that often enough. Your confidence is at a low ebb today. The only reason you don't grasp immediately what picturemaking is about is because you *are* capable of thinking in abstract terms. I have the advantage over you because I never *could* do that. Always had to think in pictures."

Paul said wryly: "It has occurred even to me that I might be wrong. Supposing, after fifty years, one finds out that actually one was always fifty years behind the times—that's a nightmare thought, my God!"

"Why wait?" said Alexander. "The thing about making pictures is that you can't wait for the verdict of posterity. You get your answer quick, unmistakably. I like that. I think you would get to like it, Paul. Come on, I always thought of you as such an optimist."

"So I am," said Paul. "So I am. You will see. In no time at all I will have learned to write like a cave man."

By the end of Alexander's first year in charge of production at Hesslan's, the studio had grossed $13,000,000, an increase of $2,633,000 on the previous year—and the first time in four years that the grosses were up. *The Rich, Full Life* alone had taken $800,000 in its first year, and it was estimated that its eventual world gross would amount to around $4,000,000. It had cost just over $200,000. Despite these results, Hesslan was still refusing to allow Alexander to spend more than a maximum of $250,000 per picture; moreover, Alexander could sign up new talent only to replace artists whose contracts were expiring and not being renewed. Hesslan was insistent that the overheads must not be increased. Alexander's talk with Kabe had apparently had no effect. He kept bombarding Hesslan with memos pointing out that while these arbitrary restrictions were in force, they could not compete with spectacular productions such as *The Big Parade* and *Quo Vadis,* which were expected to gross $10,000,000 each. But these memos had no effect. Nor did Hesslan think that this was the right moment to draw up a new contract with Alexander and increase his salary which was still $500 a week. Considering that Alexander had been earning a fifth of that only a year ago, Hesslan considered it was adequate pay. He didn't deny that Alexander was making a good job of running the studio, but on the other hand all the film companies had had a good year, and he wanted to wait and see if the upward trend was maintained before committing the company to increases in expenditure. These restrictions made Alexander restive, and he let word get around that he might be prepared to consider offers from other companies. Zukor had asked him to come around and have a chat any time, and William Fox had been very flattering and had indicated that Alexander could always come to him, but neither had made a definite offer. Alexander knew that if he went to these men and said that he was available, and what were they prepared to offer him—he might get a good deal, but it was unlikely that he would get the deal that he wanted. To get that, he would have to arrange things so that they came to him; then he could name his terms. Therefore Alexander arranged for items to be planted in various of the columns to the effect that he was considering a unique offer from Metro; this he immediately denied, before Metro could deny it. He also telephoned Irving Thalberg to apologize, personally, in case the story had caused him any embarrassment as production chief of the studio; he didn't understand how the story had got into the papers, Alexander said, because in point of fact the deal he was negotiating—and he was telling Thalberg this only because he felt he owed him an explanation and he must ask him to treat the information as confidential—was with United Artists. By such means, in a matter of a couple

300

of weeks, Alexander had got enough contradictory rumors started to make it quite impossible for anyone to determine the exact truth of the situation. Now he began to get invitations to lunch or dinner from Fox, from Louis B. Mayer, from Zukor, from Mary Pickford, from Harry Warner, and others. Alexander accepted all these invitations; Fox made him an outright offer of $800 a week and "no unreasonable ceilings" on production costs, and Alexander said he would think about it. His seeming disinterest, which in some cases he maintained throughout three or four successive lunches or dinners, created the impression that he was already fixed up. When Willi Seiermann telephoned and invited him to dine *that* night, Alexander felt pleased because it indicated that at last a sense of urgency was becoming apparent in the approaches to him.

CHAPTER NINETEEN

When Alexander arrived at the Montmartre, which was where Willi had proposed they should meet, he discovered that eleven other people had been invited too. If Willi had betrayed a degree of eagerness by insisting on seeing Alexander immediately, he was now skillfully countering this impression by turning the occasion of their meeting into a formal dinner party. He had gone so far as to have place cards on the long table. Alexander saw that he had been placed on Willi's right.

"Willi, how are you? You didn't tell me one had to dress."

"You look beautiful just like you are, Alexander. I am happy you could come."

"It was nice of you to ask me, Willi."

"It was my pleasure, Alexander. My pleasure. You're looking wonderful, Alexander."

"So are you, Willi."

"I feel it, Alexander. You know what we took at the Seiermann this week? $108,377! It's an all-time record."

"Congratulations."

"Thank you. Thank you, Alexander. I appreciate that." Willi had a way of interpreting every routine social courtesy as a sort of oath of allegiance. "You know everybody

301

here, I believe," said Willi, indicating the other guests in an offhand way, as if they were extras, merely there to dress the set. "You met Miss Derringer?"

"Yes, I have," said Alexander, smiling at her and giving her a slight bow. He saw that she had been put at the other end of the table with Terence Rowley, Willi's personal publicity man. This was a well-known Hollywood device. When a prominent man, who was married, wanted to go out in public with his mistress, he provided her with an escort, known as a "beard," who was ostensibly her companion for the evening. Everybody knew that Janet was Willi's girl, but as he was never seen alone with her, scandal was averted. Terence Rowley, not being interested in girls himself, was ideally suited for the role. The general public, not aware of his real function, or of his own inclinations, regarded him as one of Hollywood's most successful Casanovas because he was always photographed in the company of gorgeous girls. He was in his forties, English by birth, and though superficially charming, could be very boring. Alexander felt sorry for Janet. Having been put at the bottom of the table with Rowley, and Willi's offhand attitude toward her, made her status quite clear to the other guests. Their heads were all turned toward the focal point of the table, which was where Willi was standing with Alexander. Alexander had been to enough such dinner parties to know that all those heads would remain at that angle all evening, that all eyes would be on Willi and himself, that all ears would be striving to catch what they said, and that Janet, in view of her situation apropos Willi, would be denied even the normal attention that a girl of her attractiveness would normally get. The other guests were all connected with the business in various capacities. A man called Gower, an attorney who did a great deal of film work, had found his place card next to Janet. He was quite an important man, in some respects, and he evidently felt it was demeaning to be sat next to Willi's girl at the bottom of the table, where he would probably have to spend most of the evening looking at the back of the neck of the person next to him. He stared for a moment at his card, exchanged looks with his wife who had been placed almost opposite him, and, incited by the faint sneer on her lips, mustered enough courage to inquire gruffly: "Isn't there some mistake in the seating plan?"

"Mistake?" said Willi. "Mistake?" He pretended not to understand although everybody else around the table understood quite clearly. There was a moment of embarrassed silence, during which Gower was seen to redden, and his lips twitched.

"Yes," said Alexander, breaking the silence. "You're right. There has been a mistake. I particularly asked if I might be sat next to Miss Derringer. You should be sitting here—Mr. Gower, isn't it?"

"Yes, that's right," said Gower. Alexander indicated his own chair, next to Willi, and beckoned to Gower, who approached to take his place, with the air of a man who knows his rights and sees to it that he gets them. Alexander held the chair for him, insured that he was comfortably seated before making his way down the table to take the vacant place next to Janet, who turned her face up to him and murmured a low "Thank you." For a couple of moments Willi sat absolutely still. Then he got up and marched quickly down the length of the table. He stopped by Alexander, and snapping his fingers at a waiter, ordered: "A chair!" When the chair came he indicated with a perfunctory wave of his hand that all the others were to move up their chairs one place to enable his to be placed next to Alexander's. As soon as this had been done, he sat down, and Mr. Gower discovered, to his evident consternation and embarrassment, that he was once again at the bottom of the table, every head having now swiveled the other way, facing toward the new focal point provided by Willi and Alexander.

"How very nice of you, Willi, to come and sit next to me," said Alexander. Willi, having been compelled to show his hand by coming to sit next to Alexander, now saw no point in concealing what was on his mind.

"Alexander," he said, "you know I always had a great belief in you, from the beginning. Now I hear you're going to leave Hesslan's, naturally I'm interested. Tell me, you fixed up already?"

"Willi," said Alexander, "I had no idea you wanted to talk business."

"With us," said Willi, "there is no need for fencing. Am I right? We've known each other a long time. What is Fox offering you?"

"You couldn't meet it," said Alexander.

"Why not let me decide, Alexander? I'll be open with you. Sure, I want you. I got a lot on my shoulders. I got the theaters to run, a lot of my time I got to spend in New York. I need somebody out here to run the studio that I can trust."

"I'm sure this must be boring, Miss Derringer," said Alexander, giving her a confidential smile.

"Miss Derringer will not get bored," said Willi, authoritatively.

"What's your offer, Willi?"

"You tell me what you got in mind?"

"You're approaching me, Willi. I'm all fixed up bar the signing. But if you want to make an offer, I'll consider it. For old times' sake."

"I prefer you say what you're asking," said Willi. "If you leave it to me, I'll offer something ridiculous."

"Don't be bashful, Willi. Try me. Offer."

"One thousand dollars a week," said Willi.

Alexander laughed: "That *is* ridiculous."

"So you tell me what you had in mind."

"What interests me," said Alexander, "is to have a free hand."

"Within reason," said Willi. "Everything within reason. The day-by-day running of the studio I leave in your hands. But I got to keep for myself the final say."

"The signing of talent, selection of story properties, casting, budgeting of pictures you'd leave to me?"

"Within reason," said Willi. "You know I'm not an unreasonable man."

"Uhu . . . uhu."

"A deal like this," said Willi, "can only be arrived at on a basis of mutual trust. Not everything can be put on paper."

"I remember we had that problem once before, Willi."

"You going to bring up that old matter? I tell you something, Alexander, you won't get a fairer deal from anyone. I guarantee you, whatever Fox says now, you get a fairer deal from me because I always looked on you more like a relative than an employee, than a business associate I should say."

"It's something I'll have to think about."

"And the compensation. What you had in mind? Be frank with me, don't be embarrassed, we known each other a long time—I'm not an unreasonable man. If we can come to an understanding . . ."

"What I had in mind," said Alexander, "is twenty-five hundred dollars a week . . ." Willi made the pained expression of somebody being squeezed dry. ". . . and twenty per cent of the profits of the pictures with a guaranteed minimum annual compensation of three hundred and fifty thousand dollars." The look that had come over Willi's face was of someone who had been kicked in the crotch by somebody he had previously regarded as a friend.

"That is a deal?" he said. "That is grand larceny. People have been put in jail for less."

"I told you you couldn't meet Fox's offer," said Alexander.

Willi's appetite throughout the rest of the dinner was definitely impaired. After sulking silently throughout the first two courses, he tried to reopen the discussion, but Alexander was talking to Janet and didn't seem very interested. "Let's forget about it, Willi," he kept saying. "You don't really need me and you certainly can't afford me, so why upset yourself?" The amount of attention that he was paying to Janet also annoyed Willi; he was encouraging her to talk, and listening to what she said as if she were important; you might have thought he wanted something from her. The way he was being ignored, by both of them, at his own dinner party, made Willi feel as if he were crashing their date.

After dinner as Willi, Janet, Terence Rowley and Alexander waited for their cars outside the restaurant, Rowley made the usual, tactful offer to withdraw: "Willi, there's a couple of the press lads I said I might have a drink with . . ." This gave Willi the alternative of offering to drop Miss Derringer, or else of ignoring the remark and leaving it to Rowley to see her home. Willi was looking at Alexander, wondering if there was any point in taking the discussion with him any further that night. Alexander said, "I'd be glad to see Miss Derringer home, if Mr. Rowley will allow me." Rowley gave Willi a startled look. Everybody knew the way it was. "I don't think we should keep Mr. Rowley from his work," added Alexander. "Do you, Willi?"

"He can come back. I'm sure the press boys will still be there," said Willi.

"Oh, why put him to all that trouble?" said Alexander blandly.

"It's no trouble for him," said Willi. "It's what he's paid for."

"What is what he's paid for?" said Alexander, innocently.

"To maintain good press relations," said Willi, shortly.

"Oh, I see. But it's no trouble at all for me to see Miss Derringer home."

"It's none of my business," said Willi, "but I don't call that politeness." He was trying to control his anger.

"I am sure Miss Derringer will excuse him this once," said Alexander.

"Don't worry on my account," said Janet, "if it's not taking Mr. Sondorf out of his way . . ."

"Not at all." Both Alexander's and Willi's cars had drawn up and their respective chauffeurs were holding the doors open.

"Do what you like," said Willi, and got into his car. Alexander indicated his own car with slightly exaggerated gallantry, and Janet, struggling to stop from laughing, got in.

It was a mild winter night, the kind of night that still could surprise Alexander, and give him a sense of great forces holding back, holding themselves in check, as a form of courtesy almost. He opened the window and enjoyed the cool breeze on his face. The landscape did not look hostile, and the mountains seemed very near and accessible. He turned to the girl. There was something very appealing about her; he would have liked to use a little of his power for her. It was like having the only team of huskies in some frozen wasteland when the beautiful girl happens along, and just has to make it to the trading post by nightfall—that was when you appreciated having the only team of huskies. "Why did you sign up with Willi?" asked Alexander.

"You never called me," she said, gently reminding him, "and my agent said men who give you screen tests are not to be trusted."

Alexander laughed. "I had a lot on my mind just then, but I did call eventually, at any rate the studio contacted your agent—you'd already signed with Willi."

"You wanted to give me a contract?"

"Yes. Didn't Lewis Sholt tell you?"

"No."

"Your test was good."

"Was it, was it really?"

"If you'd like to see it, I'd gladly arrange that."

"I would like to." There was a kind of underlying—

almost secret—rhythm to her, the hidden meter in a piece of free verse; it was something you only just caught sometimes. And there was that faint sadness, like the shadow of a memory, that touched up her face, even at a time like now when she was not unhappy, and gave such nuances to her expressions.

"Why did you sign with Willi?" Alexander demanded, and realized that his voice sounded harder than he had intended.

"Why? You mean, why am I *with* Willi?"

"Yes."

"I guess . . ." She was trying to work it out, her brow puckered worriedly. "I suppose somebody being that *sure*, like Willi is . . . you know what I mean. I'm never *that* sure . . . no belief in my own judgment," she laughed. "I always had to have somebody *tell* me I was right before I could be sure. Like in school, I never was very good because, though I often had a hunch I knew the right answer I wasn't certain ever, so I was never the one to put my hand up and say, 'I know, I know.'" She laughed again. "Well, I imagine Willi must have been what I needed because he's so sure about everything, isn't he?"

"I wish . . . I wish," said Alexander, "I'd made that call before you signed with Willi. Is he going to do anything for you?"

"Oh, yes. He says he's going to make me a star."

"I don't think I could have promised you that," said Alexander. "I could only have promised to try you in some small parts."

"You don't have to *worry* about me," she said, laughing to see such concern on his face.

"I do, though. That's something you have. One director who saw the test said you have the ability to make people root for you."

"I can look after myself," she said.

"With Willi?"

"Are *you* going to sign with him?"

"Maybe, if he meets my terms. But I *can* look after myself. Why d'you laugh?"

"Because you said that so toughly and yet you have such a gentle look, as if you couldn't say boo to a goose."

"It's deceptive."

"I know, I heard you tonight, and I heard stories about you."

"Seriously, what are we going to do about you? Will you let my lawyers look over your contract at least? I don't trust Lewis Sholt. And please think of me as somebody you can always come to— You need . . . a little—"

"Yes, Mr. Sondorf?"—playfully.

". . . looking after."

"Are you a looker-after, Mr. Sondorf?"

"I don't know. Would you like me to be?"

"Now I don't know what sort of offer that is?" They both laughed; he felt responsible for her; he felt he wanted to make sure she cleaned her teeth regularly and didn't smoke too much and watched how much she drank and drove carefully. It's quite ridiculous, he thought.

"Where is it you live?" She felt that he had deliberately broken the mood.

"At the Mecca Hotel."

"You live in a hotel?"

"Yes, I love hotel life. Actually, the Mecca is more of a hotel-apartment building, and it has room service and I never was much good at cooking." Alexander gave the address to the chauffeur.

The Mecca turned out to be a sprawling mock-Eastern building, with bulbous domes, keyhole-shaped windows decorated with fancy wrought-iron grilles, and a large courtyard full of aging palm trees and parked automobiles. It looked like a film set, the kind Alexander would have had struck. The car drove into the ungated courtyard and drew up in front of the hotel entrance. He wondered if he should kiss her, and felt momentarily awkward: she must have had to do a lot of tussling in the backs of cars. "Well," he said, "please remember—that you *can* call me . . . I mean that."

Her eyes were laughing, reading him; then they became almost solemn. "You were going to kiss me then," she said.

"Who said you weren't bright?" he responded, mocking her gently.

"Why didn't you?"

"I hate corny situations."

"Oh." She looked slightly offended.

"What I mean," he said, "is that after what I've been saying it would have looked as though I had an angle all along."

"And if I asked you in for a coffee, would that be corny?"

"Who cares!" he laughed, opening the door for her and following her out of the car. He told the chauffeur to wait. They went in by a side entrance, to which she had a key, avoiding having to pass the desk clerk who sat in the front lobby. Her apartment was on the first floor, at the end of a dim corridor. As she fumbled in the dark with her keys they both heard the telephone ringing inside. Having opened the door she dashed to the wall phone and inquired breathlessly, "Yes?" It seemed a rather one-sided conversation for she said nothing for the next two or three minutes, simply making noises of assent or disagreement. The apartment consisted of a suite of connecting rooms, an unused-looking kitchen and a bathroom. The furnishings were in keeping with the outer appearance of the hotel. A low couch heaped with cushions, an armchair covered in a fabric of imitation ocelot skin, a red velvet pouf with a cigarette burn on it, an octagonal table with a mosaic top and lion's paws legs, a hand-painted screen depicting birds in flight, a pair of standing lamps in the form of bare-breasted Negro slave girls holding torches of contorted, smoky-colored glass. An overhead lamp of filigree brass-work with a fringe of tiny colored beads, and four smaller lamps hanging, like bells, from the beaks of four birdlike heads. Vases of smoked glass, and various dark bronze objects. The sitting room was divided from the bedroom by wrought-iron gates through which he could see a large, unmade bed, curiously canopied—rather like a howdah.

Janet was talking in a low voice into the wall phone. She hung up and said, "Sorry," and then started going around switching on lights, which did not make the room perceptibly any brighter but gave a sort of dull glow to various parts of it. Whatever pseudo-ideas of film star opulence the Mecca had once aspired to had evidently been abandoned some time ago; the apartment had the slightly chipped and used-up look of a place where too many people have been careless with their cigarette ends. Still, as Janet put a record on and the phonograph began emitting hootchy-kootchy music, Alexander felt agreeably like a blade. "You like it?" she asked, meaning the apartment.

"Yes," he said, "*yes . . .*"

"I'm sorry about the mess, the chambermaid only comes

in every other day and today I guess was the day she doesn't come."

"Don't worry, it's fine."

"You want a drink or a coffee?"

"What are you going to have?"

"A crème de rose."

"What's that?"

"Third gin, third dry vermouth, third Dubonnet. And a cherry."

"Sounds wonderful. I'll have one of those, too."

She brought him his drink, clinked his glass with hers, picked the cherry out with her fingers and put it in her mouth—"Sorry, no cocktail sticks, I'm out of them," she apologized—and then sipped her crème de rose appreciatively. "I can't get over," she said, "that you're so young."

"I used to be even younger," he said, smiling. Her attitude to him was uncertain, curiously respectful; he was such an important man. "And then, on the other hand," he said, laughing, "I was never young." She wanted to give him back being young, she wanted to be for him what very young men dream about. Without having to talk about it they were conspirators, plotting together—to restore a mood. He felt what he had missed, growing up in such a hurry.

"Dance with me?" she invited, raising her arms and starting to move to the music.

"I'm sorry," he laughed. "Can't. Never learned."

"Everybody can dance."

"On a very crowded dance floor, I can shuffle a little. But those steps you're doing are much too difficult for me."

She was laughing delightedly. "I'm so glad there's something you can't do."

He looked at his watch, saw her face cloud, and said: "My driver *is* waiting down there." Then, after a pause: "Janet, I want you to look after yourself . . . and to remember what I said about calling me any time."

"Stop worrying," she said. She came and stood near him, looking up into his eyes, and he took her hands in his and leaned toward her and kissed her tentatively on the lips, as if they were very young and he was very unimportant, as if she might refuse him, drawing back after a few moments to look questioningly into her eyes. Seeing her intense expression made him smile, as if he were now much older than her; again, unhurriedly, with studied calm, he leaned toward her and resumed the kiss—only their lips and hands touched. She kissed unambiguously; this one contact being all for the moment, she gave herself to him at the lips with a readiness that was touching and childlike. Like a complicated argument pared down to one startlingly simple point, their kiss clarified things. There was suddenly nothing still unresolved between them. There was no hurry; he felt sensual and tender, wanting it to be sweet without being cloying, wanting the sharp blood-quickening things and also wanting it to be *nice*—undesperate. He slid up her dress carefully, while she stood still, and he delighted in her unceremonious transformation—from formal dress to erotic vision: frilly suspenders, fine panties, bare thighs, stockings. There were plenty of girls he could have now as easily, but it wasn't *now* in their conspiracy, it was then, when nothing was possible; and the thrill of surprise was of then. The mood was strongly woven between them and he touched her as if it was all absolutely new to him; the mind-stopping feel of silky underthings and—petal-soft flesh, it had the taste of a first-time experience. She was pushing the panties down, like somebody in a desperate daydream of long ago, letting them remain awkwardly around the knees, and she leaned against the wall and made it possible for him: they had held hands on many dates, and laughed together, and kissed a little, and had thought long about each other, and had spoken about the future, and had danced in a crowded place, and now the thing they had both thought about so much, with such hot anticipation and fearful foreboding, was happening. That was how it was. Her face had such freshness, and every sensation seemed to take her by surprise. It wasn't elegant, like that, but it had the urgency and the beauty of true hunger. For both of them it was a matter of a minute or so. The letdown for him was greater than usual: the present reasserting itself—the barebreasted slave girls with their torches, his automobile and chauffeur waiting outside, Willi, Rowley, the vulgarly intrusive thought—"What is her angle?" Sensing his feelings a hurt look came into her eyes; for her there had been no letdown; he felt again a dispassionate tenderness toward her, and also gratefulness. She had given him something very strong—a memory of a vision. She was only partly satisfied, and she wanted him again, immediately. He took her to the bed and undressed her. He was very conscious of everything now: that absurd, howdah-like canopy above, the rings of many glasses which had stained the wood of the table by the bed, the carefully calculated softness of the lighting, the heavy-smelling perfume, the ornately frilly corset hanging over a screen, an open drawer full of a disorderly heap of underwear. This time he made love to her with detachment: her passion touched him like a performance on the screen—her face so intent, so absorbed in what she was feeling. In love-making, even more than at other times, everything she felt showed. Again he felt quite romantic about her, she had such joy from bodily things. He waited as long as possible before saying, "I do have to go."

"Ohhh," she cried.

"I'm afraid so." He dressed quickly, conscious of her watching him all the time, as if trying to commit him to memory.

"Will I see you again?" she asked.

"Of course. I'll call you."

"Don't call us, we'll call you?"

"No, no. Anyway, as I said before, you *can* always call me, whatever happens. I mean that. But I will call, and I'll see you again. I want to."

At her insistence he took her number, and wrote it on a scrap of paper. "You might lose that," she said anxiously.

He laughed. "You know it wouldn't be all that difficult to find out your phone number."

"Even if you lose the number they'll put you through if you ring the hotel and say who you are."

"I'll remember that," he teased her. He kissed her lightly.

"Oh, don't go, don't go," she pleaded.

"Look after yourself now," he said as he left.

Two weeks later, in a small town just across the Mexican border, Alexander and Susan Kabe were married. Paul was best man. The only other witness was somebody picked off the street. The news did not break until the newlyweds were on the *Mauretania* sailing for Europe. Then, for several days, the papers were full of the story, and at Southampton they had to give a press conference for the reporters who were waiting for them.

BOOK THREE

CHAPTER ONE

The procession of cars came to a halt at the foot of the hill. Looking back across the flat land, the route they had come along was still marked for several miles back by the wake of dust that they had stirred up and which had not yet settled. It was very hot. The sun was like a blood orange. Alexander was in the lead car—his new, black Bugatti "La Royale" coupé-de-ville, with the enormously long hood, open driver's compartment and delicately curving fenders which swept back, as gently as a girl's flowing hair. Frankie jumped out of the driver's compartment and opened Alexander's door. The others were also getting out of their cars. "The rest we have to do on foot," Alexander called to them. Some of the New York financiers looked dubiously at the steep, narrow, rocky path that curled up the side of the hill, and one of them dabbed his brow with an eau-de-cologne pad and demanded, "Aren't there any donkeys to take us up?"

"We weren't calculating on entertaining visitors," said Alexander briskly. "It's not very far." He was wearing a kepi, Levis tucked into riding boots, and a British army officer's tropical tunic; field glasses were suspended from his neck. He began the climb, followed by Frankie carrying a small alligator document case. Halfway up, he stopped and looked down. The New York financiers had taken off their jackets and undone their high, tight collars, and were being helped up over the rocks by some of the drivers. Willi Seiermann, wearing a bush jacket and shorts, and disdaining all help, was making rapid headway, hurling his big, broad body up the steep incline. Alexander waited until Willi had caught up. "Somebody," he said, "could have told those New York financiers what to wear."

"I thought you were going to make provisions," said Willi reproachfully. "If any of them have a heart attack don't make me responsible, that's all."

"They're the ones who're demanding economies," said Alexander smiling. "They're the ones who accuse us of wasteful extravagance."

"A couple of donkeys wouldn't have broken us," said Willi.

"It's bad for morale," said Alexander. "This is a hard location. Nobody gets preferential treatment."

"All right, Alexander. All right." From over the brow of the hill came the sound of many voices, of great activity.

"There is an easier way up," confided Alexander, "but this way it's more dramatic, they'll appreciate it more. *They* wanted to see how we make pictures. A little exercise won't hurt them. After they've had a drink they'll feel like men of action."

The sweat was pouring off Willi by the time they got to the top. They were on a wide plateau overlooking a shallow valley with a river running through it. Below them, but not all that far below them, more than three hundred covered wagons were drawn up on the near side of the river; three of them were actually in the river, about a third of the way across, one had been overturned and was secured against the pull of the current by means of ropes tethered to steel spikes on the bank. When the time came these ropes could be loosened, by the grips who now stood guard over them, so as to allow the wagon to be swept downstream at a controlled speed. Squatting, sitting, and lounging around the wagons were several hundred men, women and children, the women in gingham dresses and some in headscarves, the men in rough trousers and waistcoats and collarless shirts. Girls from the make-up department moved among them, rather like nurses, carrying small, neat boxes, delicately applying dust and dirt, and mud, and sometimes "blood" (mineral oil with vegetable coloring), with little pads, or spraying already sweaty faces with "sweat" that would look more real than their own. To the right, a couple of hundred head of cattle were bunched tightly together in an improvised corral. From a smoke machine, contained inside one of the covered wagons, and suitably camouflaged, feeble little puffs of grayish-white smoke were rising to hang pathetically in the almost windless air until dispersed by the wind-machine. "It's got to be blacker and thicker—*thicker*," somebody was shouting to the men frantically working inside the wagon to correct the defective mechanism. The Indians were nowhere to be seen. They were being organized by an assistant director on the other side of the river, behind the ridge of the hill;

they would first appear outlined against the sky, and then come charging down. Five cameras were to be used. One was mounted on a dolly track that curved between the wagons to the river's edge. Another was mounted on a steel platform. The third was placed in a kind of fortified dugout on the other side of the river, and would photograph the Indians charging down the hill and, it was hoped, would get shots of the underbellies of the horses as they leaped over the dugout. These horses would be ridden by stunt riders, but none the less there was an element of danger for the cameraman in the dugout. A fourth camera was mounted on a platform that had been built in the river, and would shoot the action in the water. And the fifth camera was up on the plateau, where it would get panoramic shots of the whole battle. On the plateau there were several tents and marquees which were being used as dressing rooms for the principal players and as offices for the production unit. A line of canvas chairs had been provided for the visitors, not far from the edge of the plateau, which would give them a fine view of the action. The director, George Larson, was on a white mare, and dismounted as he saw Alexander and Willi approach, handing the reins to the groom in charge of the horses.

"How goes it, George?" Alexander called out.

"I think we're getting organized." The two men stood next to each other and surveyed the scene, Alexander looking through his field glasses. A messenger on horseback, an assistant director carrying a huge megaphone, a continuity girl carrying a copy of the script, and a secretary followed the director wherever he went.

"It looks good, George, it looks good. Can I see the map?" A large colored map was produced by the secretary and unfolded on the ground. It showed the exact positions of the various groups that would be taking part in the action and gave the lines of their movements in relation to the cameras. The pioneers were shown in blue, the Indians in red. The exact positions of the principals at different times of the action were marked with their initials. The disposition of the extras was shown by means of arrowed lines. Those who were to die were indicated by little crosses of blue and red. How they would die was described in the script, but the map gave the overall picture: where the main slaughter would occur, where there would be iso-

317

lated fatalities, and the places where nonfatal wounds would be sustained. A thick cluster of crosses in red ink indicated that some fifty or so Indians were to die as they came up to the edge of the river on the far side; in the river itself these crosses were more widely dispersed; a series of arrowed red lines showed the attackers who would survive. The blue crosses, on the near side of the river, were fewer and more widely spread out. Two ambulance trucks were standing by, which could get anyone who was injured to Los Angeles Hospital in forty-five minutes, and a doctor and two nurses were on hand at a casualty post set up just outside the battle area. Alexander lowered his field glasses and turned to George Larson: "It looks good," he said. "Looks *dangerous.*"

The New York financiers had now arrived, breathless and panting and sweating. They looked pleased with themselves for having made it. There were five of them: two bankers, a member of a New York investment house, a director of U.S. Telephone & Radio, which had an interest in Seiermann-International, and a director of the Wisdom Assurance Corporation of New York, which also owned a substantial block of shares. They made appreciative noises as iced drinks and caviar canapés were brought round on trays by white-coated waiters from the Ambassador. Later, they would be served with picnic lunches of *pâté de foie gras,* cold salmon, grilled chicken, champagne, and ice cream. As they flopped down in the canvas chairs, they were provided with field glasses and opera glasses through which they could get a better view of the location. They made impressed noises, asked humorous questions of Pete Fenton, who had been designated to look after them and explain anything that needed explaining, expressed mock-disappointment at the absence of female interest, made various ribald jokes, guffawed, chuckled, and agreed that it was all most impressive and enjoyable, and when were they going to see some action?

Alexander had been joined by Paul and Stephen Raille, who had come in the last car. Alexander offered his glasses to Raille, who took them and examined the scene. "Should be effective," he agreed. The technical adviser, Major Dextor, came up to confer briefly with the director. "How's it look to you, Major?" Alexander asked.

318

"Very real, sir. Very real," the Major said, verbally jumping to attention on being addressed.

"All the details correct? Details are important."

"Could be the real thing. Yes, sir. Could be. Makes you quite itchy to get your hands on one of them sabers." He gave a bellowing laugh, which terminated abruptly. He looked nostalgically down into the valley. "Of course you never saw it like this," he said, "being in the thick of it. But this is what it *would* look like. Yes, sir. What you might call a view from the gods. Up here."

"Do we have enough ammunition?"

"Seventy thousand rounds, plenty."

"Let's go on down and take a look round," said Alexander. "You want to come, Stephen? Paul?"

"I'll stay up here," said Paul. "I'm not that good on a horse."

Stephen Raille agreed to accompany him; two horses were brought round to them and they mounted, assisted by the groom.

"I'd like you to come along," said Alexander to the director. "And you, Major." The four of them, accompanied by the messenger on his horse, rode slowly down the gently sloping hill. In every part of the valley final preparations were now being made for the shooting. When they came to the wagons, alongside the river, Alexander dismounted and walked among the actors playing the pioneer families. He stopped to talk to Sam Shaw, a big, red-faced, white-haired man who had been a variety comic before Alexander had brought him to Hollywood.

"How goes it, Sam?"

"Practicing my funny faces for the death scene," Sam said.

"There won't be a dry handkerchief in the house," Alexander assured him.

"I keep telling those bum script writers that I'm too young to die," said Sam Shaw, "but you think they have any compassion in their stony hearts? No, sir. I really would have liked to make it to the end of the picture, having gotten this far."

Alexander and his group went on, pausing to examine the dummy carcasses of dead oxen and the dummy corpses of pioneers, looking at blanket rolls and at ancient carbines and pistols and cooking utensils, laughing at the attempts

319

of a member of the props department to catch a pig that had escaped, squelching through the thick mud until they came to the wagon containing the smoke machine. This had now been repaired and was emitting thick black smoke to everyone's satisfaction. Everywhere, grips, some stripped to the waist, were working with saws and axes and wrenches, huge flies buzzing around their sweaty faces and crawling unhindered over their chests and backs.

"How long before we're ready to go?" asked Alexander.

"We're pretty well ready now," said Larson. "Half an hour maybe."

"Good. It all looks fine to me." The plan of the action had been worked out in meticulous detail at conferences between Alexander, the director, the art director, the writers and the technical consultants during the past two months. Satisfied that everything was as it should be, Alexander and his group rode back up the hill where the financiers, who were feeling peckish after their recent exertion, were wondering whether luncheon was going to be served before or after the battle. They said they could wait until after if the battle wasn't *too* long.

At five minutes to twelve Larson was satisfied that everything was ready. By now there was a readily discernible tension that seemed to link everybody in a human chain, as if they were all going to cross the rapids together. Nerves were tightly strung. Everybody was intensely absorbed in his own particular function to the exclusion of everything else. The financiers momentarily stopped masticating as Larson nodded to one of his assistant directors who thereupon fired a starter's pistol which reverberated startlingly through the valley and surrounding hills. The scene began with some of the pioneers driving the cattle into the river —over their bellowing you could hear the yells of the herd master and his men urging them on. Alexander had remained on his horse and was watching intently through his field glasses.

"They should look round more," said Alexander to Larson, "those hills hold danger for them, I want more feeling of danger." Larson took the megaphone from the assistant director and shouted into it: "Look up into the hills—let's feel the danger in the hills. More urgency, everyone. You're working against time. Your lives depend on getting those cattle across fast."

Through his field glasses, Alexander saw the herd master's face, saw him framing obscenities with his lips in response to the director's instructions. "That's good," Alexander said, "get them riled, it looks good."

"Come on," Larson shouted into the megaphone, "don't mollycoddle them—drive them, drive them hard. Get that herd moving, get it moving. Let's see you work up some sweat . . ." When the herd was halfway across the river, the starter's pistol was fired twice, the signal for the wagons in the water to start moving, and for the pioneers and their families on the bank to start going about their tasks in preparation for the fording. The whole scene was slowly beginning to come alive now as families lashed down their belongings on the wagons, drivers attended to the harnesses, women hung on to their children, men on horses galloped up and down the length of the wagon train to inspect the state of readiness of individual wagons, periodically looking up anxiously into the surrounding hills, while others checked rifles and ammunition. Now the whole wagon train was on the move, the dust rising, the lead wagons swaying precariously as they entered the water, the oxen moving heavily. Larson was looking inquiringly at Alexander. "I think now."

"Not yet," said Alexander, "this stuff will play like a dream. Not yet." Some of the cattle had been separated from the main body of the herd and were being swept rapidly downstream toward the wagons, making the oxen rear up in the water and emit fearful noises. The herd master did not have to act now as he yelled at his men to keep the herd together. Things were beginning to happen that were not in the script. One of the herdsmen was thrown from his horse and narrowly averted being hemmed in by the struggling, bellowing animals in the water. A wagon became separated from the oxen as the harness broke and a girl extra gave an unscheduled scream as she was precipitated into the river; she was rescued by a stunt man.

"Now," said Alexander. Larson turned to the assistant director who fired his starter's pistol three times. For a while nothing happened. Then, against a blood-red sky, the first Red Indian appeared.

"Let's have some reaction," Larson shouted into the megaphone. "Pioneers—first reaction. Check guns. Uncertainty.

321

Not too much, not too much yet. Wagon drivers, rein in your oxen. Mothers, hold your babies tight, hold them tight —apprehension! Just apprehension. Not panic. No panic yet."

On the plateau, the white-coated waiters were refilling the financiers' empty glasses and Pete Fenton was explaining the plan of the battle. The man from the telephone company was saying: "Isn't some of that pretty dangerous?" Paul, who was sitting in one of the canvas chairs, said: "We try not to kill anyone if we can possibly help it." There was a gasp from the financiers, followed by slightly sheepish chuckles, as they saw the horizon become darkened with the figures of hundreds of Indians on horseback, as if a forest had suddenly sprouted into the sky. "Impressive," said one of the bankers.

"Now," Larson screamed into the megaphone, "everyone turn back, everyone in the water—turn back. Let's have some panic. Confusion. Panic and confusion." With yells and whoops, the Indians started to charge down the hill. On the bank, the wagons were being formed into a protective enclosure, several were overturned to provide a barricade, and men with rifles grimly took up their positions behind them while the women and children huddled together further back. The first shots rang out, fired by the Indians as they thundered down toward the river. The fire was returned by the herdsmen in the water, sheltering behind the frightened animals. As the first wave of Indians entered the river, the pioneers in the wagon enclosure opened fire: horses reared up, painted bodies fell by the dozen into the river. The pioneer families whose wagons had already started the crossing were now swimming desperately for the bank. The ropes holding the overturned wagon were loosened and it began to drift downstream, a woman and her child clinging to it, three Indians in pursuit. Arrows were flying through the air, some of them burning, and falling into the enclosure. The smoke machine emitted thick clouds of black smoke. Many of the Indians had succeeded in crossing the river and there was hand-to-hand fighting between them and the pioneers. Sam Shaw, after making a brave stand, was felled by a blow from a tomahawk and dragged by his son under a wagon where the death scene was played out. (The close-ups would be shot later in the studio.) Every time it looked as though pioneers had succeeded in throwing back a wave of attackers, more Indians thundered down the slope and across the river. The battle lasted just under an hour; on the screen it would run, with studio-shot inserts, for about fifteen minutes. When it was all over, the valley looked as if a battle really had taken place there; tired extras were sprawling on their bellies and backs, smoke was still rising from the smoke machine, the ground was littered with bloodied dummy corpses. Over the megaphone, an assistant director announced: "Corpses and wounded, do not remove your wounds. *Repeat:* do not remove your wounds until instructed. Everybody stay where you are, please." On the plateau, Alexander and Larson had dismounted and were huddled together in conference; with them were Paul, Major Dextor, Stephen Raille and other members of the unit.

"I think it was all right," said Larson. "What do you think, Alexander?"

"I think it was good."

"There were some slip-ups, but I don't think they hurt us any."

"How did it look to you, Paul?"

"Bloodcurdling," said Paul.

"We were trying to make it a little more than that," said Alexander quietly. "Stephen?"

"I think it got the right feeling. I think it will look real."

"Can I tell them they can break for lunch?" an assistant director asked.

Alexander was looking thoughtful. "There's something that bothers me. There's one thing that's phony."

Major Dextor repeated his assurance that it was all as authentic as it could possibly be. "No, I don't mean on the technical side, I mean phony dramatically. And I think I know what it is, what's been bothering me all the time I was watching—it's Sam Shaw's death scene."

"I thought it was great, Alexander," said Larson. "He plays it beautifully."

"Yes, he does. That's just it. He plays all of it beautifully." A pause. "I don't think he should die."

"He dies in the book," Paul said.

"I know. But in the book he wasn't played by Sam Shaw, and Sam gives the part a great quality, he gives something to the picture that I don't want to lose two-thirds of the way through. The audience is going to feel cheated losing him at this stage."

"That's good," said Stephen Raille. "Because he plays it so well, because they're rooting for him, they will *feel* his death. That makes it stronger."

"Yes, I know, that's a good argument, Stephen. But my hunch is that he shouldn't die. *I* don't want him to die. I have to go by that—I can't explain it to you, Stephen, but I know I'm right. His death is quite arbitrary. It has no purpose . . ."

"That's what's good about it. That's the story you're telling. Some of them died, and some made it, there's no rhyme or reason to it."

Alexander thought for a while. Then he said, "George, I want you to reshoot that part of the scene. Sam Shaw doesn't die . . ."

"That's ridiculous," said Paul, "that's . . ."

"I appreciate your advice, Paul," Alexander said, "but I've made up my mind."

"So be it," said someone.

"*Amen,*" said Paul.

Willi drove back to town with Alexander. He was all in favor of Sam Shaw not dying, but he was worried about the impression it had made on the financiers when they had learned that a part of the battle was to be reshot because it had been decided that one character shouldn't die. If Sam Shaw was going to be spared, couldn't this have been decided before the battle? Alexander said it was something he had only felt during the battle. He had to go by his feeling, and before the battle he simply hadn't had the feeling that Sam Shaw should live. He said the retakes wouldn't cost all that much, only one part of the battle would need to be retaken. "You should have seen how grateful Sam Shaw was," said Alexander, grinning, "when he heard we were going to let him live."

"It's an extra four weeks' work at four hundred and fifty dollars a week."

"No. It's not the money. Sam doesn't need it that bad. No, he *feels* that part. That's why I was sure it was wrong for him to die."

Before going home, Alexander stopped at the studio to check through the day's memos. There was a pile of them, succinctly phrased, on one sheet, in accordance with his instructions, waiting for him. They ranged from a lab report on a color process they were experimenting with to a director's "highly confidential" misgivings about the lack of sex appeal of a certain actress assigned to him. Alexander called in Miss Pearce and answered all the memos—more than twenty in all. He had made it a rule that all memos would be answered immediately. He did not believe in leaving people in a state of waiting uncertainty. He arranged a meeting for the following day with the lab technicians to discuss the color process, he told the worried director that the actress in question had enough sex appeal for the part, and if it turned out that she hadn't, he, Alexander, would take full responsibility for the deficiency. He answered all the memos decisively and unequivocally. If he had any doubt about the correct approach to a particular problem, he did not express it. He did not believe that anyone in doubt was helped by having his doubts confirmed. He knew, for instance, that the director's misgivings about the actress were justified, but he also knew that it would be too costly to replace her at this stage of production, and by expressing his faith in her Alexander was relieving the director of an anxiety that could affect his handling of the whole picture, and have the effect of making the girl come over even less sexy than she was.

When he had finished dictating the answers to the memos, and Miss Pearce had left the office, he poured himself a large brandy and lay down on the couch and closed his eyes. Whenever possible, he tried to take a half-hour's nap before going home. He was getting to need this in addition to the half hour he took in the middle of the morning. He knew that when he got home, Susan would almost certainly have invited a minimum of a dozen guests for dinner, and he would be expected to sparkle. That was the trouble with having a reputation for being inexhaustible and the "Boy Wonder," people expected evidence of it all the time. What made things worse was that he could not afford, ever, to reveal signs of tiredness to the sort of people who were liable to be at Susan's dinner parties, or to people at the studio, or to Willi's New York financiers. They were all watching him all the time for signs that the strain of running the studio was too much for him, that he could not keep up the pace at which he was driving himself. The brandy was beginning to work. Drunk neat, at times of great tiredness, it did not have an intoxicating effect. On the contrary, it seemed to sharpen one part of his mind at the same time as dulling another part of it, and it provided him with an infusion of pure energy. He had brought the bottle with him and placed it on the floor by the couch, and now he poured himself another large drink, calculating the dose as carefully as a doctor administering a drug. Two large ones now would see him nicely through the rest of the evening; at the party two or three glasses of wine would keep him feeling good; he would not need to drink any more than that. Now, as the brandy did its quick work, he felt rather pleased that he would come home to a house full of people who would wring the last drops of that day's energy out of him; already, in anticipation, he was rising to the occasion. This was when Susan loved him most, he felt: when he was at the high tide of his charm and persuasiveness, when the magic flowed in him and communicated itself, effortlessly, to everyone around him. He sometimes felt that Susan invited some of these people for the specific purpose of matching them against him, so that she would be able to enjoy the thrill of his victory or experience the delicious *frissons* of fear if it seemed that he might be defeated. These nights were all battles. The brilliant and the ambitious came to challenge his supremacy—to fire their polite conversational darts at him and see if they could pierce his seeming invulnerability. He did not know why it was that he had always won so far; in the three years since their marriage many clever men had come to their house and matched their superior wits against his, but none had scored a decisive victory. Only Stephen Raille, of all the guests who had so far been to his house, had seemed to Alexander to possess the power to defeat him. He was apprehensive of what Raille could do to him, if he chose. But he did not choose. He never chose to press his advantage when he had scored a conversational point over Alexander; always, at such moments, he chose to withdraw behind an enigmatic smile, feeling no compulsion to take the argument to the point at which Alexander would be defeated. Only Alexander knew how vulnerable he had been at the moment when Raille chose not to press his point. It puzzled Alexander that Raille should show him such consideration, almost friendship, when in his everyday dealing with Alexander he remained cool and uncommitted, like

326

someone trying on a suit of clothes. It disturbed Alexander that he had had to go against Raille that morning on the question of Sam Shaw's death. Though he knew he was right. Alexander felt disturbed by the thought of what Raille might be thinking of him at this moment. Raille was always so . . . so ambiguous in his attitude toward Alexander. His acceptance of the offer to remain in Hollywood, as a sort of super script adviser at Seiermann-International, had amazed Alexander. Certainly Stephen Raille did not need the money; he lived modestly, and his books and journalism gave him a more than adequate income. This year, moreover, he had a play running on Broadway, which must be making some money for him. It was precisely because Stephen Raille was totally independent of him that Alexander attached so much value to his approval. There were a dozen of his closest associates whose true opinions of him meant nothing to Alexander—they were paid to agree with him—but Stephen Raille was an honest man, that was indisputable, and he was the only man working at Seiermann-International whose regard Alexander knew he could not buy. According to Paul, who had got to know Raille well, Raille had accepted the offer to stay on in Hollywood because he had marital problems and welcomed a genuine excuse for being out of New York. But to Alexander this seemed too simple an explanation. If he had simply needed an excuse for leaving New York, there were plenty of very good ones available to him, he could take his pick. Some of his early plays were being performed in Europe, where they were having considerable success, and he would have had even more excuse for going on a trip to Germany or France or England than for coming to Hollywood. But for some reason he had chosen to accept Alexander's offer, and even though he argued against some of Alexander's decisions, he invariably accepted them once they had been made. Paul, on the other hand, was becoming increasingly obtuse. Though Alexander had never actually expressed this, he felt irritated that whereas a distinguished and successful author like Stephen Raille was prepared to accept his decisions, Paul— whose novel nobody had wanted to publish and whose sole professional achievement prior to arriving in Hollywood was that he had had one story published in the *Saturday Evening Post*—was always argumentative and even derisive. It wasn't that his personal feelings for Paul had changed in any way; Alexander still felt closer to him than to anyone else, and Paul was the only person he knew he could go to in an emergency. He felt free and relaxed with Paul—under no obligation to shine or impress—but he was annoyed by his querulousness.

The flashing lights under his eyelids were slowly diminishing in intensity; he felt his pulse at the neck and was glad to discover that his heartbeat had settled down to a slower, calmer rhythm. Soon he would be able to go home. While this nightly ritual of burying his tensions worked, he had nothing to fear. He knew that he could not be defeated unless his own body let him down. That was the only real danger. He wondered whether he should have another brandy to obliterate this disturbing thought. Frankie still accompanied him everywhere he went, the loaded pistol in the holster under his arm, or in the secret pocket under the dashboard of the car. He decided against having another drink. The dose he had taken was medicinally just right. Today had been a very tiring day, coping with those financiers, shooting the big batttle scene; it was to be expected that he should feel a little more tired than usual. There had been moments during the battle that had reminded him of something, touched chords of memory, almost as if he had actually been in that valley once with the Indians appearing on the horizon. Had he dreamed such a scene? The thought of Frankie waiting outside in the car, and of the secret pocket under the dashboard, reassured him. He smiled sheepishly to himself on catching himself out in such a thought, as a rational man might smile on finding himself touching wood. Perhaps he should tell Susan to cut down on the entertaining. It would be a relief not having to shine all the time. In a way, though, the dinner parties were the easiest way of keeping Susan adequately entertained—at least the burden of keeping her amused and stimulated was spread among several people whereas, when they were alone, he had to assume all of it himself. She was only happy when something was going on, preferably when several things were going on at the same time. Ideally, he reflected, she would like to have sex, listen to brilliant talk and eat all at the same time—with violins playing in the background!

Some days he found himself wondering what it was there had been between him and Susan in the first place. She had been a sort of prize for him, Henry Kabe's granddaughter, and—he reflected—he must have been a sort of prize for her. They had won each other, against fierce competition, and for a while, a very short while, the thrill of that had been enough. But, he thought wryly, they couldn't sit at home and gloat over each other, over their winnings. He tried to think when it had begun to be over. In Venice? As early as that? In the second week of their honeymoon—when the newspapermen were chasing them and everyone talked of their "brilliant" marriage? As if it were some kind of a public performance. A royal alliance, some of the papers had called it: Henry Kabe's granddaughter, and the "Boy Wonder" of Hollywood. It wasn't merely that her sexual tastes, which had seemed charming and exciting at the beginning, had palled on him once they were married. It wasn't only that, though the discovery that the *sanctioned* sexual act meant little or nothing to her, that it was only the playing and the petting and the pretending that could excite her, had come as a shock to him. Seeing them together in those first weeks, everyone said how obviously in love they were. Their undisguised desire for each other was so sweet, people said. The darlings, they could hardly wait. It was a shame they had such a lot of social obligations to fulfill when clearly they just wanted to be alone with each other. Susan would whisper in his ear how much she wanted him—right there and then—and couldn't they go somewhere, just for a moment, she didn't care what people might think seeing them creep away. In dark vestibules, or on a momentarily empty terrace, or in their cabana on the Lido beach—with their friends just outside—she would take his hand and press it between her thighs and in this way achieve a quick and thrilling satisfaction. But when they were in bed together, naked, she was not very passionate. Only by resorting to elaborate pretenses—that she was a chambermaid who had come to clean the room when he had dragged her onto the bed, that she was a stranger whom he had picked up in a café only a few minutes earlier—could she work up any enthusiasm for the actual act. At first he had found these games exciting, but as it became clear that there was to be nothing between them except games, he began to feel that he, Alexander, did not exist for her, that he was many men for her, and this was fine as long as he was not himself. Even when he was ostensibly himself, when they went out together and dazzled her friends, it was the public image of him that she so ostentatiously adored. She was in love with what the newspapers had written about him, and when he attempted to explain to her that some of those things were exaggerations, or downright lies, she would turn on him fiercely and say, "Why have you got to spoil things? Why have you got to spoil what's lovely and beautiful?" What had really spoiled things for her was the night in Venice when he had had the panic attack. It had been a very close, heavy evening; they had had very little sleep for the past few nights, and he suddenly felt he was choking. He went to the window and opened it wide, but there was no air outside either. He began to make choking, gasping sounds. The city, with its tightly packed buildings, its meager shreds of sky, seemed to enclose him—if he could have seen the sea he would have been all right, but there was only the canal to look out on, and the width of the canal did not give him enough space to breathe. He was holding his chest and making terrible gasping sounds. "Are you sick?" Susan demanded. "Oh my God, is it your heart?"

"It'll pass," he muttered grimly. "Don't *you* get panicky, that's the worst thing for me."

"You look so sick," she gasped. "I'll call a doctor."

"No. There's nothing a doctor can do. Oh my God, I feel I'm going to die. I can't breathe, I can't breathe . . ."

"Oh Christ, oh Christ, oh Christ!" The panic in her voice spread to him like a leaping flame. With a violently shaking hand he poured himself a huge brandy and gulped it down, the liquid spilling out of the side of his mouth and over his clothes. Making a great effort, he said, "Look, please, *please* don't panic. It's a nervous thing. If you panic too, it makes it worse. Do you understand that? It's in my mind—I feel I'm going to die, but I'm *not* going to . . ." The words were uttered in a series of desperate gasps.

"It's just nerves?" she said. He nodded his head vigorously.

"Oh for God's sake, you know the scare you gave me!"

"It's quite real for me," he managed to gasp.

"Well, what am I supposed to do?"

"Just keep calm."

"Keep calm! If you know it's just nerves, can't you pull yourself together? My God, you look terrible." Her words, spoken with barely concealed resentment—such a lovely dream, such a lovely trip that he was spoiling by giving in to this nervous thing, whatever it was—made him feel worse. He looked at himself in the mirror. His face seemed almost purple, his pulse was beating so fast he could not distinguish the individual beats, maybe he *was* dying, how could you know it wasn't the real thing this time? The look on her face, at seeing him like this—of disgust almost! That was how people looked on death, it disgusted them. Maybe he *was* dying. He began to sob, the sobs going through his body like electric shocks.

"I'm going to fetch somebody. I'm going to get a doctor," she said, going to the door.

"Please don't leave me," he gasped. "Don't leave me alone."

"I've got to get a doctor," she said.

When she had left, he thought he was going to pass out. Making an enormous effort he went to the phone and asked for the concierge. "Is there a motorboat available?"

"Yes, sir. When—when will you require . . . ?"

"Right now. I'm coming down."

"Yes, sir."

He staggered down the stairs, holding on to the banisters to keep from falling. He went straight to the hotel's landing stage, without looking for Susan, and almost toppled into the back of the motorboat. "Let's get going," he said. *"Subito—* huh? *Molto presto.* That way. *Da questa porte."* When they got to the Basin of San Marco, where the Grand Canal opened out spectacularly to join the sea, he began to feel calmer. Now the motorboat was able to get up speed, and as the wind whipped his face he stood up in the boat, his mouth open, gulping the air into his lungs, becoming drenched by the spray. The bitch, he thought as he began to feel better, the rotten, lousy, spoiled bitch! All she is good for is playing games. He was perfectly all right the next day. "My God, what a scare you gave me!" she said several times. "You scared the life out of me." He apologized for having scared her and was sweet to her for the remaining few days of their honeymoon. It wasn't her fault that she couldn't cope, he had decided; he couldn't really blame her. He'd just have to make other provisions.

When they got back to Hollywood he went to see a doctor friend of his, Edgar Fellowes, whom he knew he could trust and who had some knowledge of psychiatric matters.

Alexander explained that he did not wish to subject his wife to the ordeal of having to cope with him when he had one of his attacks. It would be much better if some professionally qualified person were around at such times. As a result of this conversation it was arranged that Mrs. Irene Brown, who was working for Dr. Fellowes as a nurse-secretary, should come and work for Alexander, as soon as the doctor could find a replacement for her. She was a middle-aged English widow, with a reassuringly matter-of-fact attitude to life. Alexander had had several talks with her on the occasions when he had been to see Dr. Fellowes, he had approved of the unfussy and efficient way she had given him injections, and of her slightly bossy attitude to him—she was certainly not overawed by Alexander. Officially she was coming to be his private secretary; she would live in the house, be part of the household. Nobody would need to know that she was also a trained nurse. And —if she was called upon to act in this capacity—it was arranged that she would not mention the fact to anyone.

For the first few months of their marriage, Alexander—now that Mrs. Brown was available in case of emergency—quite enjoyed Susan's games. They had separate bedrooms because she thought it was much sexier to have to come to each other rather than just be there together. Susan loved to leave little notes for him on his bed, saying how much she was longing for him and saying where to meet her and when. In the beginning it had been romantic to creep out of the house and through the grounds to keep these assignations, to make love to her on a bed of pine needles with the danger always present that one of their gardeners might discover them. "Where can we go?" she'd demand, absolutely absorbed in the game. With fourteen bedrooms in the house he found it difficult, sometimes, to act his part with conviction. "Let's go in the bushes," she'd say; there weren't really any bushes on their grounds, only meticulously clipped hedges, but the word bushes had some special erotic meaning for her, as had certain other words which she kept using, almost as a kind of ritualistic chant, during their love play. She would beg him to enter her, but when he attempted to do what she asked he discovered that this was not what she wanted: she wanted to use the word, she wanted to beg, that was what excited her. When, on one occasion, she asked him to keep her panties, because if her

332

husband found them he'd be able to tell what she had been up to, Alexander felt that their games had reached the point of ultimate absurdity. "Oh you're such a spoil-sport," she said when he told her he was too tired to play. The only way out was to make a game of turning her down. When she asked him to meet her in the woods, he'd slip a note under her bedroom door saying, "Can't tonight. My wife has returned home unexpectedly." This quite pleased her sometimes because it enabled her to write him long, erotic letters, saying how much she longed for him, how she would lie awake all night aching for him, etc., etc.

To the outside world their marriage seemed ideal. Everybody who came to their house liked her. She was such a good hostess. To Alexander's great surprise, Stephen Raille got on very well with her and always seemed pleased to be asked to their house. For a man who expressed himself so forcibly in print, and Henry Kabe had been the subject of some of his most virulent attacks, he was extraordinarily polite in private. He could not have approved of many of the people who came to Susan's dinner parties. His most scathing novel, *The Manipulators*, had been about such people —the puppet masters who controlled America. When challenged to explain how he could stand to be in the company of people he condemned in his books, he would reply, smilingly, that policemen had to be in the company of criminals, and missionaries in the company of pagans, and if Christ did not object to taking bread with whores and thieves what right had he to be any more particular? This always produced chortles of laughter. Somehow, without softening his point of view, Stephen could say such things, to people's faces, without causing offense. Alexander came to certain conclusions about Stephen: that he was a lonely man who found it difficult to make friends; that he had still not recovered from the break-up of his marriage; that he considered himself, in the deepest sense, a failure. There seemed to be some great internal debate going on in him all the time. Why did he choose to stay on in Hollywood? "My God," he'd replied, doing his painful smile, "you ask some difficult questions. Why do I stay? Partly because I think that to ignore the movies is like being a writer at the time of Caxton and ignoring the printing press; I don't believe in art for the privileged few, for the cognoscenti. I

333

don't believe in the possibility of 'pure' art; come to that, I don't believe in the possibility of pure anything. And what appeals to me about movies is the immediacy of their effect, and that they can reach such a lot of people. As for my other reasons, well . . . when I've found out what they are I'll let you know." This was the nearest Stephen had come to revealing himself. The answer dissatisfied Alexander. He liked to know where he stood with people and Stephen, although always pleasant and courteous to him, simply wouldn't commit himself. It irked Alexander that he could not know for sure whether Stephen thought well of him or just considered him one of the "whores and thieves." The articles he'd come to Hollywood to write had never been written. "I stayed too long," he told Alexander. "A reporter has to go down into the deep, that's his occupational hazard, so he can come up and tell what he's seen. But if he stays down there too long, he can lose the desire to come up again and tell about what he's seen."

CHAPTER TWO

The sun, coming through the Venetian blinds, struck the glass top of Lewis Sholt's semicircular desk, causing Janet Derringer to be dazzled. She averted her head, and he got up and adjusted the blinds, bringing a comforting darkness to the mahogany paneled office. "Listen, baby," he said, resuming his seat, "I'm not talking to you as your agent now, I'm talking to you more like a friend."

"Yes, Lewis."

"Sure you can break the contract. There's no contract been made that can't be broken. If you want to go be a stenographer in New York—if that's your *ambition*—I say to you break the contract. Let Willi sue. But you want to be a stenographer in New York—thirty bucks a week, *maybe?* You can't even type. Look, I don't want to interfere in your personal life, but you got it *bad?* I look at you; I see a beautiful girl, well-dressed, her own car, a diamond ring on her finger. Is that *bad?*"

"I just wanted to know," said Janet, "if the contract is watertight."

"As far as this business is concerned, it's watertight.

Another four years to go. If you broke it, they couldn't *kill* you. But nobody in Hollywood would give you work. A girl who breaks a contract is a pariah. It's reasonable, they've got to safeguard their interests."

"You couldn't get the contract changed? So I could work outside. In over three years, I've done maybe four weeks' work."

"You get paid."

"I'd like to work, Lewis."

"Listen, baby, we have this conversation, regular as clockwork, once every three months. Right? You know Willi. You're a bit closer to Willi than I am. He don't want you to work outside."

"What would it hurt him if I took that singing job? How could that hurt my 'career' or the studio?"

"You're asking *me?*"

"You're my agent. You got me into this contract."

"Listen, baby, I made a contract between you and Seiermann-International. What your arrangement is with Willi is none of my business. I don't ask and I don't want to know."

"All right, Lewis. I'm sorry I've taken up your time."

"*Baby,* you know that's what I'm here for. Any time. You're looking marvelous. Really swell." He came out from behind his desk. His manner toward her was almost paternal, though he could not have been more than a few years older than her. They all became bloated-looking with success, even the thin ones. Lewis Sholt still had a thin face. It was just around his waist that his success showed in those extra folds of flesh. "Listen," he said, putting his arm around her, "one day you may thank me. One day you may end up being *Mrs.* Willi Seiermann. It's not impossible. It's been going on how long? More than three years? Listen, baby, it's a good sign he don't want you to work outside. He's *jealous;* he don't like the idea of all those men gawking at you in some cheap night club."

"And the records he wouldn't let me make? And the stock company offer I had to turn down? He won't even let me have drama lessons."

"He loves you."

"Oh, Lewis, you're such a fool."

"Maybe I am a sentimental fool. But to my mind the way Willi acts is like a man who's in love."

"Yes?"

"You don't agree with me?"

"Lewis, *I* know how Willi acts."

Driving home, she thought: why do I go to Lewis Sholt, as if he would think of *my* interests? Nobody is going to risk antagonizing Willi by helping me. That was the situation she had got herself into. Everybody knew that Willi didn't want her to work—why should anyone stick his neck out by giving her a job? It wasn't as if she had such a blazing talent that people would consider it worth while to take a risk for her. It was hard enough persuading people to give her a chance; the moment they found out she was with Willi, and under exclusive contract to Seiermann-International, the offers were invariably withdrawn. "Sorry," they'd say, "but it'd be an infringement of your contract." Even if she left Willi, while he chose to hold her to the contract she could do nothing: just loaf around and collect one hundred dollars a week. There were times when she might have been prepared to take the risk and clear off, change her name, and try to get a job somewhere in show business where Willi had no power. But she knew that if she did that her father would suddenly find it impossible to get work. When Willi wanted to be nasty he'd tell her how he would put her *and her father* on the black list if she ever did something against his wishes; in a more benevolent mood, he'd claim that he only talked of the black list to frighten her, that no such thing existed. But she knew that the black list did exist. There was a story about a character actor called Ed Sayler who had apparently known Willi years ago; he'd been getting small parts in movies when he made the mistake of going up to Willi one day and saying, "Remember me?" Willi remembered him, and Ed Sayler didn't work again. The only person who put any work her way was Alexander—he didn't seem to mind crossing Willi—and as she was under contract to Seiermann-International, Willi could not offer any convincing argument why she should not be in some of the company's films, if she was suitable for them. At any rate, Janet assumed that it was Alexander who was putting the work her way, she felt sure that nobody else would have dared to go against Willi's known wishes. But she had not actually seen Alexander since that night before he got married. She remembered that he had said she could always call him,

336

but presumably his marriage had automatically canceled that offer. Besides, people were always making extravagant promises. The person who made them had no intention of keeping them, and the person who received them never expected them to be kept. This was understood. It was the etiquette, as ritualized as a litany. People were really rather offended if you had the bad taste, or the innocence, to remind them of their promises, to expect them to be kept. A man putting his hand under your dress was expected to offer you the world, and you were expected to thank him for it, but you were not expected to believe him. Of course if you were smart you knew how to play this game: you offered yourself as readily as he offered you the world, but you didn't *give* until the deal was signed and sealed. It wasn't whoring, it was just the way things were done. It was the girl who gave herself without getting anything in return who was considered a tramp. When Lewis Sholt had shown her the contract he had said, "Listen, baby, it's a standard contract. They have to put in all that stuff to protect themselves. But Willi is not going to hold *you* to it, if you want out." Even her private life was controlled by the contract. There was a morality clause which said that not only must she not be guilty of immoral behavior, but she must not conduct herself in such a way as to give rise to the impression that she might be guilty of immoral behavior. Of course, all the contracts contained that clause, but it was up to the studio to decide if and when they wanted to exercise it. If she had wanted to leave Willi for somebody else they could immediately drop her contract—invoking the clause and thereby blackening her name. Her day-by-day movements were controlled by the studio, even though they hadn't given her any work for months. Willi could insure, quite legally, that she was there when he wanted her. The studio simply instructed her to "hold herself in readiness," which meant she had to stay on call, by the phone. Willi could—and frequently did—phone up and say, "I'm coming round in half an hour." If she wasn't in, she had to have a pretty good excuse. Willi did not seek to keep her entirely imprisoned, not entirely. He appreciated that she might want to get out sometimes when he was too busy to see her. That was what Terence Rowley was there for. She could always ring him and ask him to take her to a movie or somewhere for dinner. When Willi was in New York, the arrangement was that Terence Row-ley took her out Tuesdays and Saturdays. The studio didn't approve of her going out alone nights, it created a bad impression, and they had to safeguard their investment. However, they didn't object to her dropping into a movie in the afternoon, or having tea with a girlfriend. She had often thought about how she could free herself. There were two alternatives. She could break the contract, by just going away, in which case probably neither she nor her father would work again in the movies. Or she could behave in such a way that the studio would be obliged to drop her, in which case her name would be blackened by rumor and gossip about why she had been dropped, and, even if she survived that, the black list could still be used against her and her father. She had only one card to play against Willi: that he didn't want to drop her. There was the night he had come to the apartment in a towering rage, having discovered that she had been seen out with Paul Krasnor on three successive nights. He was powerless to do anything against Paul, because of Paul's special relationship with Alexander, and this had exacerbated his fury. He had called her a whore. If she wanted to act like a whore he knew how to treat whores. He took her in a rage of passion, afterward throwing dollar bills all over her. A few days later the vaguely threatened reprisal happened. He arrived at the apartment late at night, unannounced, accompanied by a tall, thin, blond young man with the emptiest eyes she had ever seen and a knowing grin slithering all over his face, like somebody out of control on an ice rink. He was smoking one of Willi's enormous cigars with the air of a man who appreciates a good thing. He had a rather femi-nine laugh. "Well," said Willi, plonking himself down on a couch and indicating to the young man that he should do likewise, "what you think of her?"

"Very nice," said the young man, slyly looking her up and down, and then emitting a little giggle. Janet looked wonderingly at Willi. He had never before brought anyone to meet her. This young man had not been introduced, even. They had evidently dined together and were both a little high. Willi, as was often the case, was suffering from dyspepsia and his high, stiff collar was cutting into the flesh at his neck; he asked her to bring him an Alka-Seltzer and undid his collar and the top button of his trousers. "You like the look of her?" said Willi to the young man.

"Oh yes. Yessirree. Yes, I do." This was followed by another little titter, repressed before it could become a laugh.

"Nice pair of tits—huh?" Willi demanded rhetorically.

"Oh yes, very nice *indeed*," the young man agreed. "Exem-mmm-plary pair of tits." He had a slight stutter. He choked back another giggle.

"Good legs too," said Willi, crossing to Janet and pulling up her skirt to display her legs to the young man, who responded with the expression of somebody tasting wine, considering carefully, and coming to the conclusion that he approved. Janet was stunned. She was looking at Willi disbelievingly. For the next twenty minutes or so the men kept up a form of cross talk akin to a very blue act in a low burlesque show, supplying their own laughter—Willi emitting great guffaws, the blond boy tittering in accompaniment, taking his cue from Willi to become increasingly ribald. The talk was about Janet and what Willi claimed were her sexual tastes. Then the jokes came to an end. Janet was sitting absolutely still, her face expressionless. "So you like her?" said Willi, looking at the young man, who nodded, passed his tongue over a dry lip, and poured himself another glass of soda water which he gulped down. "You like her?" he repeated again. Taking the young man's elbow, he gave him a small shove in Janet's direction. "Be my guest," he said. "Go on. Be my guest."

The blond young man's face hung open in an expression somewhere between a grin and a stutter. He sat down at Janet's side, scratched his chin thoughtfully and then looked uncertainly at Willi, who nodded encouragement to him. Mustering all his courage, he started, clumsily, to feel her breasts through the material of her blouse. Janet sat unmoving for some moments, then she turned and smashed the back of her hand across the blond young man's face. He seemed startled, put his finger to his mouth, examined the blood from his lip and again looked inquiringly at Willi. "You're frightened of her?" Willi threw at him. As if her blow had cured him of his hesitancy, he grabbed hold of her, and succeeded in pinning down one of her arms with his knee while he struggled to keep the other one pressed down on the couch behind her head. His free left hand was under her skirt. After a little she stopped struggling. This so surprised him that he released his hold of her, but she made no attempt to break away from him. Disbelievingly, and trembling a little, he began to unbutton her blouse, wincing at her slightest movement in anticipation of another blow. But she remained quite still as with mounting excitement he undid the blouse and fumbled to undo her bra; she made no attempt to stop him; his hands went over her breasts, they were pointed and taut. "All right," she said. "All right." She stood up and undid her skirt and pushed it down over her hips. "Come on. Come on, loverboy, let's see what you can do." The tall, blond boy again looked inquiringly over his shoulder at Willi. "Go on," said Willi gruffly. He started to undo his buttons, but she took over from him. Willi sat unmoving on the couch, enveloped in cigar smoke. The thin, blond boy had thin, strong arms, cruel fingers. His lank, blond hair kept falling over his eyes and he kept having to stop momentarily to push it clear. The sensation inside her was racing, like the flame of a fuse, toward the point of disintegration. If only there were nothing left of her afterward. She longed —to be nothing and no one. If only the moment—like a heat flash—would leave nothing of her. In his paroxysm he had the face of a stuttering idiot. His fingers were bruising her, she did not feel it as pain, nor the other as pleasure. Her mind had lost the knack of distinguishing. She felt the panicky rush of feelings to their only exit. A stampede in the dark. Only the moment of release mattered. The spasm emptied her, as if her whole being had been scooped out. She saw the little piles of their clothing on the floor, they were like dead bodies, she thought. The tall, thin, blond boy had collapsed and was another discarded pile of something or other on the floor. He hardly stirred as Willi came to her; and she hardly stirred as Willi took her, in great excitement, whispering "whore" into her ear.

When they went out together, accompanied, of course, by Terence Rowley, Willi was much nicer to her than he had been in the past. At times he was almost gallant. Having been Willi's girl for so long had given her a sort of status. The gossips speculated about whether he would one day divorce his wife and marry Janet Derringer, and conscious of these rumors, Willi treated her in public with the courtesy and deference due to someone he might conceivably marry one day. He was very fussy about the way she dressed: she must not look cheap or flashy: Willi wanted her to look dignified when she went out with him. The rumors which kept reaching him that he was going to marry Janet one day had gained such force and apparent conviction that he had come to almost believe them himself. The subject had never been discussed between them, but the *New York Graphic* had speculated whether Willi's fling would lead to marriage; and as he hadn't sued, this was considered, by some of the gossips, as tantamount to a proposal. Janet had also read the article, and though she hadn't talked to Willi about it they both understood that the fact that he hadn't sued meant the idea wasn't quite as outlandishly absurd as all that. And his public behavior toward her seemed to confirm her new status. He seemed to enjoy the speculation about his private life, and though Janet was always officially "with" Terence Rowley, Willi of course knew that everybody else knew that she was with him, and the way he acted indicated that he knew that they knew. Willi, somewhat to his surprise, discovered that he had become very attached to her. He could talk more freely to her than to anybody else. He felt completely at ease with her. He would sometimes tell her stories of what his enemies were trying to do to him that made him weep with self-pity.

"They're so full of jealousy," he'd say to her, "one day it'll choke them. They want to destroy me. They say to themselves—what right has he got to run an empire? That I built it myself—that don't give me the right in their eyes. Did he go to Princeton or Harvard or Yale? What is his family background? Those lousy bastards with their boutonnières and their fine talk. Business they'll do with me, but you think they'll invite me to their homes? They look down their noses at me—they think I don't know. They'd like to carve me up between them. All those bankers and financiers. When it was a risk, this business, they wouldn't risk a cent of their lovely clean money, but now they like to grab the whole business. But I'm not such a fool. I can look after myself, with *all* the enemies I've got. I was always a scrapper, and if they think they can beat Willi Seiermann they're going to get the surprise of their lives. They want to take over my business, they got a surprise coming. I'll take *them* over."

Janet had no idea what he was talking about when he talked in this way, and she did not try to find out. Since she had known him there had always been enemies who, according to Willi, were trying to destroy him. And there were always people who slighted him, by not inviting him to their homes, or by not responding warmly enough to his overtures of friendship, or by declining his invitations, or by forgetting about his birthday or wedding anniversary. On his birthday, at Christmas, and on his wedding anniversary, he received hundreds of telegrams and presents and congratulatory cards: on each occasion two of his secretaries were entrusted with the task of sifting through them and making lists of the people who had sent good wishes and of those who had sent presents. When these lists had been made, another list was made of all those people from whom he had felt entitled to receive congratulations or gifts who had forgotten or neglected to send them. Anyone who figured too often in this list became, if he was powerful, an enemy, or if he was an employee was put on the gray list: that is to say, he wasn't actually fired—he would be given the opportunity of redeeming himself—but he was not presented with any opportunities for self-advancement. Willi considered that it was a sure sign of incipient treason if one of his employees forgot his birthday.

There were times when Janet thought of killing Willi, and at other times she almost loved him: he absorbed her, the way blotting paper absorbs ink, and she was glad to have everything decided for her. If she broke free of him what would she do, what would she be? It was too difficult. People said he was despicable and how could she stay with him? But, in his way, he looked after her. It was horrible, of course, being controlled and spied on, having to ask permission before she could do anything, having to resort to elaborate subterfuge if she wanted to see somebody he— or "the studio"—might disapprove of. She was not faithful to Willi, but when she went with another man, the fact of deceiving Willi—the knowledge of the punishment she might incur if he found out—made the thrill additionally sharp. She hardly ever saw the same man twice, and she never gave any of them her address or telephone number, but when she felt the black depression threatening to engulf her, that was still the only way of saving herself—the sex thrill starting up in her was like all the lights suddenly coming on at dusk.

Lately, Willi had been taking fewer precautions to prevent himself being seen coming out of Janet's apartment. Instead of using the small staircase leading to the side door, he would often come down in the elevator and cross the main lobby on his way out. The bellboys and the doormen and the desk clerks all knew him, though they were discreet enough to call him "Sir" and not "Mr. Seiermann" as he went by. He always tipped them all handsomely. Tonight, as he strode purposefully across the slightly dingy lobby, through the undergrowth of drooping indoor plants, to a chorus of "Good evening, sir," he felt, as he often did when he left Janet, that nothing could go wrong for him. He caught sight of himself in a mirror: I've got a funny walk, I'm a bit of a funny-looking character altogether, he thought, but there wasn't a smirk on anybody's face as he went past. Deferential bows, slightly envious, knowing looks in their eyes—but not a single smirk. His gray fedora set at a rakish angle, his light, camel-hair coat draped loosely around his shoulders, a cigar projecting from his mouth, he felt gratifyingly raffish. I'm really a pretty disreputable character, he thought with satisfaction. Still, I'm entitled. I deserve it. I worked hard—I built up an empire. I'm entitled to a little enjoyment. It's fair. What did I have as a young man—Sarah, and occasionally a prostitute. Now I can take my pick. I don't kid myself they do it because of my beautiful blue eyes, but they got respect for me, even if they hate me they got respect for me. I'm a man who's made something of himself. Waiting for the cab, he thought about Janet. He would hate to give her up. She gave him more pleasure than any of the others he had from time to time. Maybe he should marry her. She didn't have airs, she wasn't difficult and demanding like some of them were, she was no trouble at all. All women were whores basically—except the ones like Sarah who were no good at all—so he might as well be married to a good one, one who did it with enthusiasm. At least if he married her she'd have no excuse having other men, as he suspected she did. He couldn't stand thinking about her doing those things for other men. That made him so mad he preferred not to

343

think about it. The cab had arrived; feeling unusually generous he gave the doorman a couple of Havanas in addition to the dollar tip. All the way going home, he had a pleased, self-satisfied grin on his face; it was wiped from his face the moment he entered his own house.

It was not yet eleven, but the house was dark. This infuriated him. What was Sarah trying to do, save on the lights? As he handed his coat to the butler in the marble hall, he bawled: "Sarah! Sarah! You saving on lights again? What goes on in this house, I have to come home to a dark house? Sarah, where are you?" To the butler he said, "Go switch on the lights. All of them. In the future I don't want a single light switched off without my permission." Then, addressing the marble emptiness: "Maybe somebody wants to give the impression nobody lives here any more. I'm a rich man, I can afford the electricity bill. You hear that, Sarah? Where the hell are you, woman? I want to see lights on in this house when I come home—I don't want to have the impression I come home to a grave." As the three French rock-crystal chandeliers came on in the hall, giving out a diamond blaze of white light, Sarah could be seen shuffling along the upstairs gallery, wearing the dreadful dressing gown and nightdress that he had ordered her a hundred times to get rid of. She was yawning.

"I was resting, Willi," she said in a small voice that seemed pitifully inadequate for the vast spaces of this house.

"What? What you say?"

"I said I was resting, Willi."

"Oh."

"You've eaten?"

"Yes. Listen, how many times have I told you to get rid of that *shmatteh* you're wearing? Anybody would think you were married to a pauper."

"It's comfortable, Willi."

"Comfortable! It's a disgrace. My wife should wear such a rag, such a *shmatteh!* Sarah, you look terrible."

"I know, Willi, I haven't been well."

"Always you're not well. What's the matter with you? Didn't I have the best specialists for you? None of them could find anything the matter with you."

"I don't *feel* well."

"You know sometimes, Sarah, you make me so angry I could, I could . . ."

"I know, Willi, I know, I'm sorry. Willi, do we have to have an argument throughout the whole house . . .?"

"What you nervous about? The servants? I pay them I shouldn't have to lower my voice for them. It's my house, if I like to shout, I'll shout."

"Yes, Willi."

"Will you do me a favor, Sarah, will you burn that dressing gown and that nightdress and those slippers and buy yourself some new ones or else I swear to you I'll do it myself, I'll tear them off your skinny body—in front of all the servants—and I'll burn them myself. Have I made myself clear? Has it sunk in what I'm tell you?"

"Yes, Willi."

"Yes, Willi," he mimicked. "How many times have you said that and still not done anything about it?"

"I know, Willi, I know. I'm sorry. Oh—I must tell you something. What is it? Oh yes—Alexander called."

"Alexander called? Why didn't you tell me?"

"I am telling you."

"He's at home?"

"Yes."

"All right, Sarah. You're tired, go and rest. You got anything else to tell me?"

"No, Willi."

"All right, go and rest, Sarah." Willi went into his study and sank into the maroon leather chair with the side-wings behind his desk. He picked up the phone and dialed Alexander's number. As usual his secretary, Mrs. Brown, answered. "I'd like to speak to Alexander," he said. She knew his voice; he did not have to say who he was. As he waited for Alexander to come to the phone, he put his legs up on the desk and breathed in deeply. He loved talking to Alexander. This was one of his great pleasures. To work out with Alexander the details of running the studio gave him some of the purest pleasure he knew. The boy was a genius, and to work with him—to feel the force of his ideas, the power of his imagination—gave Willi a thrill that he could only compare to the thrill of sex. In a way it was better than sex, because there was no letdown after the moment of climax: to feel the interplay of his own ideas with Alexander's, to watch them being translated into pictures, and then to wait—like somebody waiting for the roulette wheel to stop turning—as the results came in in the

345

form of box-office returns; this, to Willi, was the great and exalting pleasure of his life. Sometimes he thought, as he studied the magical figures of what his pictures were earning and what his theaters were taking, that this must be the sort of sensation one got out of being truly religious.

"Willi?"

"Yes, Alexander."

"Willi, I've had those damn financiers on my back all day. I can't work with them sniffing around."

"Alexander, take no notice of them. That is my department. I handle them—I know how to deal with them."

"I wish you would get them off my back."

"Tomorrow I come to the studio. You leave it to me. Otherwise everything is all right?"

"Yuh, everything is great. But they scare me with their demands, economies, restrictions, retrenchment. It's getting worse. I can't make pictures that way."

"Alexander, you doing anything now?"

"Susan has got some people here."

"I got some ideas to talk over with you, maybe we have a nightcap together."

"I don't know that I can get away."

"I come round to you. I'm not sleepy, I'd like to talk to you because I got a great project that could solve all our problems with New York. It's such a fabulous idea, if I don't tell you I'll burst. Believe me, if we can swing it, we got no more problems. It's simple and it's beautiful."

"Willi, I'll go along with anything to get those bastards off my back. Come on over, I'll give you a nightcap."

"Wonderful. I come over straight away." As he marched out of his study and into the now brightly illuminated marble hall, he called out in a loud voice from which he could not exclude the pleasure he was feeling at having a legitimate reason to leave: "Sarah . . . Sarah, darling, I got to go out to see Alexander. I don't know what time I'll be back, just rest, my darling, just rest." In the car, as it drew away from the house, he noted with satisfaction that the blaze of light now beaming out could be seen for miles around.

CHAPTER THREE

There was a message for Willi when he arrived at Alexander's house. The gatekeeper said Mr. Sondorf had just telephoned through to say he would meet Mr. Seiermann in five minutes by the oval fountain on the lower north terrace. Further along, where the drive broadened into a semicircular forecourt, there were perhaps forty or more automobiles and their chauffeurs waiting. Willi got out of his Pierce-Arrow and started to walk hurriedly toward the north terrace. He was feeling a bit piqued. To come to somebody's house and be told to meet that person by a fountain! Like a salesgirl! What made it doubly irritating was that he couldn't be *sure* it was a slight; maybe in these circles it was done; maybe it made a difference that it was Alexander's own fountain. On the other hand, whether it was done or not, Willi did not consider it good manners . . . but Susan had never liked having him in the house, she always seemed uneasy when he came to dinner, as if he was going to blow on his soup—usually she only asked other movie people when he came to dinner. She was probably an anti-Semite, even though she was married to Alexander.

He walked quickly down the wide steps at the side of the house, his feet curiously nimble and almost dainty for a man of his build, holding on to the balustrade for support, and glaring occasionally at the statues of magnificent male figures that lined the coping. Greek gods! he thought to himself, sourly studying their proportions, well in one respect they were all smaller than he was. This thought made him feel good. At the fountain, Willi lit a cigar, stuck his hands deep into his pockets and began to pace, occasionally looking up to the house which was blazing with light the way Willi considered a house ought to blaze with light. On the upper terrace, the French windows were all open and guests in evening clothes were strolling and admiring the gardens. From up there they had a fine view of the three swimming pools, two rectangular ones and a circular one in the center, and of the parallel lines of single jet fountains which, illuminated as they now were, gave an impression of naked swords forming a guard of honor. All this he's got thanks to me, Willi thought with pride and satisfaction, and seeing Alexander coming toward him down the steps forgot all about whether or not it was a slight being asked to wait in the garden.

"I'm sorry, Willi," Alexander said, "but Susan had asked all these boring people I was sure you wouldn't want to meet. And, anyway, Helder was there."

"Helder? Of U.S. Telephone and Radio? Who's making all the trouble for us?"

"Yes."

"He said anything?"

"We didn't discuss anything specific. But he made himself clear. Too much extravagance in Hollywood, he said, it had got to stop."

"Well, in that respect, Alexander, I don't altogether disagree."

Their problem was that although the previous year Seiermann-International had had a gross income of $87,200,000, their profits had fallen to $9,000,000. This was said to be due partly to Alexander's extravagance. In addition to spending large sums on individual pictures, which he could justify on the grounds that by and large these pictures made their money back, and sometimes made huge profits, he was also spending a colossal amount on experimentation: new wide-screen processes, new color processes, and on the development of various talkie systems. All this was costing many millions each year, and whereas the pictures could always be counted on to make *some* money, the experimentation could conceivably turn out to be a total loss. Alexander insisted that no major company could afford *not* to spend money on experimentation. In the next few years sound was bound to be universally introduced; color processes and big-screen processes must play an increasingly more important part in picturemaking. A company that had done no experimentation, and owned none of the relevant patents, would find itself forever after paying out millions in license fees. Whoever owned the patent to a basic sound process, for instance, would be able to hold the rest of the industry up to ransom. It would be disastrous, Alexander maintained, if the ownership of such a patent fell into the hands of one of the giant corporations, such as U.S. Telephone & Radio, which was not basically interested in picturemaking as such, though it had interests in many picturemaking companies, including Seiermann's. He had pointed out to Willi that the pressure to cut expenditures at the studio could be traced back to U.S. Telephone & Radio, which was itself—through its subsidiaries—developing various sound processes and was naturally eager to eliminate potential competitors in this field. The fact that the pressure for Seiermann-International to abandon research projects, as an economy measure, was now being stepped up indicated to Alexander that the processes he was developing represented a threat to U.S. Telephone & Radio. "Either we hold out," he told Willi, "or we end up working for U.S. Telephone & Radio, taking our orders from New York." Alexander had succeeded in persuading Willi that the right thing to do was for them to keep their nerve and resist all the pressures. Voting control of Seiermann-International was vested in 400,000 B shares. When the company had been formed these shares had been divided in the following way. Willi's associates, consisting of eight principal groups, held 200,050 voting shares between them; Willi himself held 199,950. In effect this meant that Willi controlled the company for all practical purposes. Only the combination of all eight groups—who between them had only 100 more shares than Willi—could outvote him. The assumption was that such a thing would not happen unless Willi pursued a policy so obviously indefensible as to unite all eight against him. The extraordinary situation which had now developed (and which had made Willi and Alexander believe that there was a definite purpose behind these moves) was that five of these groups had indicated their opposition to Willi's current policy and were demanding slashing economies. The threat that hung in the air was that the remaining three might also be brought round to voting against Willi. He therefore had the alternative of acceding to the demands, or to take the risk that he might be outvoted and ousted from his own company. Alexander felt sure that this ganging-up was the result of pressure from U.S. Telephone & Radio, a great $3,000,000,000 octopus whose tentacles extended everywhere, and which had power to put pressure on the other groups of shareholders to make them toe the line.

What none of the eight groups knew was that Willi had

foreseen such an eventuality. Even while the company was being set up, Willi had found one man in one of the eight groups who had agreed, secretly, to sell Willi 150 of his shares for $10,000, which was more than ten times their market value. Thus throughout his long poker game with New York, Willi held the secret trump—that he, in fact, had voting control of the company. This was something that only he—and the man who had sold him the shares— knew; not even Alexander had been told. It was useful to Willi to be able to disclaim personal responsibility for certain decisions, to be able to say that they were forced on him. Though he was inclined to agree with Alexander that U.S. Telephone & Radio was behind the ganging-up of the shareholding groups, and that T. & R. was doing this in order to serve its own interests, Willi was also worried about the fall in profits and the rise in expenditures. In the next few years the situation would become worse. Silent films could be released anywhere in the world: but it was unlikely that talkies would have the same universal appeal. Why should Finns and Japs change their language to suit Hollywood? There was bound to be a big fall in foreign earnings. Moreover, going over to sound was going to hit Willi hard—in addition to having to convert his studio, he would have to re-equip his chain of 800 theaters. For months he had been pondering how expenditures could be reduced; he had gone over the figures again and again; he had studied the reports of efficiency experts; he had considered a whole range of economies, including sweeping salary cuts. But however he juggled with the figures, no really substantial reduction in expeditures could be achieved without cutting down on output and experimentation. Then it had come to him, and for several minutes he had just sat there, murmuring "Beautiful, beautiful . . . *beautiful*." He could have kissed himself with joy. Without there and then going into all the ins and outs of the plan that had just come to him, as a kind of revelation, he knew that it would work from its beauty and its audaciousness. The solution was not to spend less, but to spend more. During the next few weeks he worked out the details of the plan, and the more he went into different aspects of it the more beautiful did it seem to him. Now he was ready to tell Alexander about it. Alexander was the only person he could trust implicitly. He approached the subject in this way. He asked Alexander to consider the positions of Seiermann-International and Hesslan's. Both organizations had rental agencies in practically every country of the world. Both organizations were spending vast sums on research and experimentation, and obviously a good deal of this work was being duplicated. These two organizations owned cinemas which were run in rivalry with each other; competed with each other for stars and story-properties, thus sending up the prices; maintained two sets of executives and staffed rival offices in all the principal cities of the United States. Willi had worked out that the amount of money lost by the two organizations on the duplications of their basic work amounted to something like $19,000,000 a year. Or, to put it the other way round, if Seiermann-International and Hesslan's were to combine it would mean a saving of $19,000,000 a year, which would more than make up for the losses expected as a result of the diminution of the foreign market when sound came; it would, in addition, pay for the initial cost of converting the theaters and studios. Once this work had been paid for, and it was a nonrecurring expense, the annual saving of the combined organizations—even allowing for a substantial fall in foreign earnings—would within three or four years show in the form of greatly increased profits.

Alexander agreed that this was so, but as Hesslan had shown no indication of wanting to sell, how was he to be taken over? Willi now outlined the second part of his plan. Henry Kabe, as Alexander knew, owned one third of the shares of the Hesslan organization; Hesslan personally owned less than one-quarter of the total number of shares. Anyone who could buy Henry Kabe's shares would obtain effective control of the company, provided it could be shown to the rest of the shareholders that such a move was in their interest. Furthermore, it was known that several of the other large shareholders were in various ways indebted to Kabe and could be relied upon to support a move that had the old man's approval. Henry Kabe's shares were valued on the stock market at $40,000,000. "Supposing," said Willi, "that I go to Henry Kabe and offer him $60,000,000 for his shares. I give him $20,000,000 in cash and $40,000,000 in stocks of the new combined company. He makes a straight profit of $20,000,000 and his holding in the new company is more valuable because it is a bigger company whose profit potential is infinitely greater. What reason would he have not to go along with a deal like that? He can't lose on it. And as far as I'm concerned, the $20,-000,000 it costs me is practically made up in the first year's saving on operational costs."

"It would mean that Henry Kabe no longer had behind-the-scenes control, his holding in the combined organizations would be too small for that."

"I know," said Willi, "but is that such a big thing for him to give up? At his age? Considering the amount he controls already. Considering he never exercised his control very much. Considering the profit he would be making on the deal. Considering that his grandson-in-law would be the Vice-President and Chief of Production with a very big say in the running of the whole outfit." Willi beamed at Alexander. "I happen to know he has a very high opinion of you, Alexander."

"You realize, Willi, that if Kabe told Hesslan, Hesslan might be able to get his friends to buy up enough shares to give him overall control? A lot of people who might not be prepared to do that now would be prepared to do it to stop you getting control."

"Is Kabe going to do that, Alexander? Double-cross his own grandson-in-law?"

"You're relying on that, are you?"

"Listen, Alexander, family is family. If you want to know what your own profit will be on the deal, Alexander, I gladly discuss that. Any time you say. I tell you now: I'm prepared to make you a bonus payment of a million dollars if the deal goes through. In addition, we tear up the old contract and . . ."

"Take it easy, Willi, take it easy . . . we're not that far. Let me think. It *sounds* feasible. And it would certainly get us out of our present difficulties. No more interference? No more having to fight financiers?"

"You deal with me. And you know we have always got along."

"I would want the studio side to be autonomous. If I lose money on the pictures, you can get rid of me. But otherwise no interference."

"I agree that the pictures you personally make will be

your pictures and there will be no interference. But you can't personally make ninety-five pictures a year."

"All right—then the deal is this. I have my own production group inside the company. To make up to eight films a year. Complete autonomy. No interference. The financial aspect we work out later. In addition, I run the combined studios and supervise the overall production program in conjunction with you, as now."

"Agreed."

"You agree to that?"

"Alexander, I have complete faith in you, you know that."

"There is one other problem," said Alexander. "Aren't you going to run into the Sherman Anti-Trust Act?"

Willi gave a self-satisfied smile. "The Sherman Anti-Trust Act," he agreed, "is a big stumbling block. But in a funny way it's also to our advantage. It's what is going to stop anybody else doing what we are going to do. Because for anybody else it would be a very big stumbling block. You know how it works, Alexander. If you're a beef man and you want to buy up a rival chain of butcher shops you got to go to the Attorney General's office and get permission. Maybe you get it, maybe you don't. That's when you find out if you got friends. That's when it counts having backed the right man. Now I tell you something that you don't know about . . ." Willi paused dramatically; he had the air of a conjuror who, having already dazzled his audience with his consummate skill, still has one more rabbit to pull out of the hat. "If Coolidge had got the Republican party nomination and been re-elected I don't mind telling you, Alexander, I would have had to think twice about doing what I am aiming to do. But when it was a question of backing Coolidge or Hoover for the nomination, the man I backed was Hoover. I have a great respect for Mr. Hoover, and the moment I met him I said—that is the man I back. And I don't mind telling you, Alexander, that in Republican party circles my support don't exactly count for nothing. I'm a big contributor to party funds, so what I say has got some weight. But I did more than that. When I met Mr. Hoover and came to the conclusion that he was the right man to be President, I gave Mr. Hoover a personal promise. I have newsreels, I told Mr. Hoover, that go into all my theaters and reach a minimum of ten mil-

353

lion people, and I gave Mr. Hoover my personal promise that my newsreels would be devoted in his interest. For him getting the nomination and for him winning the election. And I kept my word. Mr. Hoover is a fine man, and a great human being, and when he is inaugurated on March fourth he's going to be a great President, and Mr. Hoover is not a man who forgets who his friends are. I already had talks with Colonel William J. Donovan, who is going to be Hoover's Attorney General, and I have sounded out 'Wild Bill' Donovan on various matters, and though he can't make a definite promise—because he's not *yet* Attorney General—I think, Alexander, we are not going to have to worry about the government."

"Then it looks like we're in business, Willi."

"You say the word, Alexander, and we're in business."

"Tomorrow I'll get my lawyer to draft a letter of agreement between you and me, Willi. Let's say—two million dollars if the deal goes through, twenty per cent of the gross . . ."

"Of the *gross*, Alexander, that's . . ."

" . . . and autonomy for my own group, making up to eight pictures a year, with no ceiling on the budgets. Overall supervision of the rest of the program on the same basis as now . . ."

"If you got one failing, Alexander," said Willi with a weary smile, "it's that you love money."

Alexander smiled. "That's a failing, Willi, you should be able to sympathize with."

Willi paced for some minutes in absolute silence, like a man tussling with his conscience. "All right, Alexander," he said at length, "I agree. I think you're robbing me, but the way I feel it's not like giving the money to a stranger, the way I look on you, Alexander, it's like giving the money to a member of the family. That's why I agree." And he embraced Alexander with rough tenderness to settle the deal.

The meeting with Henry Kabe took place in his New York apartment one week later. All the time Willi was talking, Alexander was watching Kabe's eyes—they were like crocodile's eyes, deeply buried in layer upon layer of hard skin: at times his eyes were so covered by these concealing layers that little more than the pupils were visible.

He was such a very old man. His skull seemed to be of no more than eggshell thickness, his hold on life was by means of a thin and delicate thread. At times it seemed to Alexander as if Kabe had already departed and was looking at the world of the living through a periscope from the place that he so confidently expected to enter. Why should a man like this, aged eighty-eight, care about making another twenty million? He already had more millions than he could possibly have days left to him; why should he care about the struggle for power between picturemaking companies? Probably he had never seen more than two or three movies in his life; considering that he had lived in virtual seclusion—hardly ever going out—for the last twenty years this was quite possible. As Willi talked—and sweated in the overheated atmosphere of the apartment—Kabe's eyes, what little could be seen of them, gleamed with a kind of posthumous lechery. When Willi had finished talking, Kabe said in his startlingly firm and forceful voice: "How are you going to find the sixty million dollars to pay me?"

"I was hoping," said Willi, "that it would only be twenty million dollars. That you take the balance in the shares of the new company."

"I'm only interested," said Kabe, "if it's a cash deal."

"Sixty million dollars is a lot of money to raise quickly," said Willi.

"It is," Kabe agreed.

"I think I maybe can do it," said Willi, "if that's your absolutely final word."

"It is, Mr. Seiermann."

"Then I have to go and see what I can raise."

"I will help you, Mr. Seiermann. Your companies are good solid companies. You are good for sixty million dollars. I will tell you where you can find the money. I will give you a list. Tomorrow call on my general manager, Mr. Stafford Deems. He will give you a list of banks and investment houses whose friendship I can rely upon. They will provide you with the sixty million dollars you need."

"That's very handsome of you, Mr. Kabe. I appreciate that."

"It's in my own interest," said Kabe, smiling; when he smiled his features rearranged themselves in a violent and unexpected way. "How is Susan?" he asked before they left.

"She is very well," said Alexander.

"I'm pleased to hear it," said Henry Kabe, "I like that girl."

During the next few days, while Willi was calling on the various banks and investment houses and corporations Kabe had suggested might be willing to loan him the money, Alexander was thinking all the time: why should Henry Kabe insist on getting his sixty million dollars in cash, and then send Willi to raise the money from banks and companies that Kabe either controlled in fact, or controlled by virtue of being able to put pressure on them as and when necessary? With one hand he was going to take sixty million dollars for his shares, and with the other hand he was loaning Willi the sixty million dollars. Maybe, thought Alexander, when you got to own and control as much as Henry Kabe, this was the only possible way of doing business. He could think of no other explanation that made any kind of sense. In a way, of course, it made very good sense. Not only would Kabe collect sixty million dollars, but—through the companies that provided the money—he would also share in the interest on the loan. This seemed to Alexander a typical Kabe deal. The interest on the loan would run at around three million six hundred thousand dollars a year, an amount much greater than what he could expect to earn in dividends during the next few years, if he had kept his forty million dollars invested in shares of the combined companies. Moreover, whereas dividends were subject to fluctuations in earnings, the interest on the loan was guaranteed and both the capital and the repayment were secured by the tangible assets of the company. Thus Kabe, as usual, had managed to extract the utmost for himself, without taking any risk whatsoever.

CHAPTER FOUR

The transfer of the Hesslan shares from Kabe to Seiermann took place in July 1929. It produced a great outcry of protest, and many of the newspapers carried articles demanding that the government should act to force Seiermann

356

to divest himself of these shares which, they claimed, gave him a monopolistic hold on the industry. At the same time, articles of a more personal nature appeared about Willi, imputing that he was a man of dubious moral character, and implying that he should not be permitted to wield such a fearful amount of power. To counteract this adverse publicity, Willi's own publicity machine—in association with those sections of the press friendly to him—concentrated on building up Alexander, presenting him as the most enlightened and farsighted of the studio chiefs, as the man who was doing more than any other to bring taste and culture and artistry to picturemaking, and as an administrator of scrupulous honesty and fairness. Some of this publicity embarrassed Alexander, but he appreciated the necessity of going along with it. Astutely, Willi kept in the background, gave no interviews, and let all the glory that was going be heaped on Alexander.

Late in September the *New York Daily Graphic* announced a series of articles by its Hollywood correspondent, Martha Hall. Recalling the scandals of the early twenties, such as the notorious "Fatty" Arbuckle case, it promised a frank and searching look at "Hollywood after Hays." (Will Hays was the man who had been brought in by the industry itself to administer a censorship code designed to placate those religious and other bodies that had been attacking Hollywood for the low moral standards purveyed in its films and practiced by its inhabitants.) After the scandals of the early twenties, Hollywood had made a great show of putting its house in order, and now, the *Daily Graphic* promised, it would reveal to what extent this had been done. The banner teasers were: "Is Hollywood Still the 'Sin City' of the U.S.?" The first article made it quite clear that the answer was going to be decidedly in the affirmative. It was by nature of an introduction and spoke rather vaguely, and without mentioning names, of talent agencies that were actually a cover for call-girl rackets, of producers' casting-couch habits, of "actresses" who had been convicted in the courts of prostitution—as any girl who had ever had a bit in a movie felt that this entitled her to describe herself as an actress, it was not difficult to find a number of such girls (who were and always had been prostitutes) willing to talk about the wild parties they had been to at the houses of "the greats." "The greats" were not identified by name. The first three articles were of this nature, and though they caused a certain amount of annoyance, they were sufficiently vague and unsubstantiated for the industry's spokesmen to be able to dismiss them as "the *Graphic*'s usual scandalmongering." To counteract the effect of these articles, stories were put out about the number of happy marriages in Hollywood, the number of churches in the community and the serious, hard-working nature of most of its citizens. Hollywood was no better and no worse than any other American town of comparable size. Then Martha Hall's fourth and final article appeared. It purported to be an account of a wild party that had been held in the house of a famous movie idol at which "some of the most famous names in the land" had stripped down to nothing, at which "actresses" had given depraved displays for the entertainment of the guests, and which had culminated in a general free-for-all orgy. First reaction was to dismiss this article as yet another piece of lurid invention, and this story—like so many others about Hollywood—might have been quickly forgotten but for what happened a few days later. Another newspaper, more reputable than the *Graphic* and friendly to Hesslan— it had been one of the most vociferous voices in opposing Seiermann's take-over—revealed that the wild party had taken place in the house of Seiermann-International's biggest star, James Nelson.

This revelation came at the worst possible moment for Willi. He and Alexander were in Washington having talks with the Attorney General's office. That office was maintaining that the Administration, far from giving its tacit consent to the acquisition of the Kabe shares, had always made it quite clear to Seiermann and his lawyers that such an action constituted a contravention of government policy and was a clear infringement of the Sherman Anti-Trust Act. Seiermann was to divest himself of these shares forthwith. This was serious, but it was not yet calamitous. Feeling that perhaps the Attorney General's office had not been adequately briefed, Willi sought an interview with the President. He was gratified to receive an immediate answer, inviting him to lunch the following week. It was the day before his meeting with Mr. Hoover that the story implicating James Nelson had appeared.

Throughout the early stages of the lunch no reference

358

was made to Willi's problem. The President was glad to make the acquaintance of Alexander, about whom he had heard a great deal, and was most gracious in expressing his thanks to Willi for all the loyal and much-valued newsreel support rendered by the Seiermann organization. It was not until coffee had been served that Hoover broached the subject of Willi's problem. "Well now," he said. "What is the problem that's on your mind?" Willi explained that with the coming of sound, and the inevitable fall in foreign earnings that this would bring about, an organization such as his was going to find itself in serious difficulties. He did not think it was excessively boastful of him to point to the great things he had done in establishing the motion-picture industry in America, and he felt sure the President did not need to be reminded how vital it was for the nation to maintain the industry in a healthy state. With Sondorf running the production side he felt he could safely claim that his organization was second to none in the world. He explained that it had been necessary to spend huge sums on research and experimentation, and as a result of this work America would be able to maintain its world supremacy in the field of motion-picture making. However, the taking over of Hesslan's, and the resultant saving of $19,000,000 a year in overheads, was absolutely vital to the continuation of the industry on a sound and profitable basis. For this reason he had been most distressed to find that the Attorney General's office was now insisting that he must divest himself of the Kabe shares.

Mr. Hoover cut him short. "Don't worry about it," he said, "I'll talk to them, and I don't think you'll have any further difficulties there." Willi was profuse and fulsome in his thanks. "However," Mr. Hoover added, "there is one thing I must add. If this deal is allowed to go through, my Administration is going to be subjected to criticism. I'm not complaining about that. In politics—as in your business, I'm sure—you get used to that. But I must tell you, Mr. Seiermann, that it would place me, personally, and my Administration, in a most embarrassing position if the opponents of this deal were able to say that the running of this great combine was in the hands of people who were not, in every respect, *the right sort of people*. Do I make myself clear, Mr. Seiermann?"

"Mr. President," said Willi, "you make yourself absolutely clear. And I give you my personal assurance that there is not a word of truth in any of the vile stories that have been printed by some sections of the gutter press, who also happen to be gunning for me."

"I accept your assurance, Mr. Seiermann. But I would add this. For a public figure it is sometimes not enough that the rumors are untrue, they must also be seen to be untrue."

"Mr. President," said Willi, "you can rely on me to take firm action to squash these rumors and show them up for the filthy lies and libels that they are."

"Good," said Hoover, getting up. "I'm glad to have had this opportunity of meeting Mr. Sondorf, and of expressing to you, Mr. Seiermann, my appreciation of the valuable and loyal services you have rendered the Republican party."

"I am honored to have done it, Mr. President," said Willi.

At Chicago, Willi and Alexander changed trains, from the Twentieth Century to the Santa Fé, for the final three-day journey across Kansas, New Mexico and Arizona to Los Angeles. Usually Alexander made use of the time spent on the train to read books and scripts, but on this occasion he was in no mood for reading. In Chicago the papers had been full of the James Nelson scandal: a great hue and cry had been started up, and was growing all the time, with reformers and self-appointed guardians of public morality demanding a clean-up of Hollywood, describing the town as "a modern Sodom," a "hotbed of vice and depravity," and in other such terms, which naturally made all the headlines. So far James Nelson had refused to make any statement to the press, and there were stories that he was beseiged in his house with reporters waiting day and night outside the grounds. From Chicago, Willi had called Pete Fenton to say that Nelson was to remain incommunicado and say nothing for the time being. He had also instructed Fenton to issue a statement that there was no truth in any of the current rumors; that the studio insisted on the highest standards of morality on the part of its contract personnel, and that anybody found to have infringed against those standards "would be dealt with." Throughout the three-day journey, not knowing exactly what was going on minute-by-minute in Hollywood, Willi was in a state of near hysteria. Sometimes he was in tears as he sat with Alexander, bemoaning the unfairness of fate in subjecting him to such an ordeal at such a time. How could God treat him this way? What had he done to deserve it? Just because some son-of-a-bitch actor liked to play with girlies! His whole empire was threatened. "Everything I built up," he moaned, the tears rolling down his cheeks.

"Come on, Willi, it's not necessarily as bad as that," Alexander consoled him. "It's a situation we can deal with."

"You know, Alexander," Willi said, "sometimes I get a dread in my heart I can't describe you. I'm an emotional man, you know that. It pierces me here . . ." And he rapped his heart with his clenched fist. "Sometimes I see myself a pauper. Sometimes I see myself I haven't got a stitch of clothing to wear and my enemies ground me into the dirt. I see them grounding me into the dirt. Wiping their boots on me. I tell you, I have dreams. I wake up sweating from the dreams I have. You think I don't know that they hate me—I got enough enemies to fight a world war. Who can I trust, Alexander? Tell me that. A man in my position, I can't trust nobody. You know what has been the great happiness of my life? That I had the good fortune to find you. One person I can trust."

Willi became increasingly maudlin as they neared Los Angeles. Chain-smoking cigars, chewing them into a messy pulp and discarding them half-smoked, tears periodically welling up in his eyes, he was grotesque and comical. This absurdity, Alexander thought, rules an empire. People actually go in terror of this ridiculous, fat little man. Whenever he could extricate himself from Willi's company, he walked the corridors of the train alone, thinking. It was worth saving the Seiermann empire. Willi he could deal with, he had vanities and weaknesses that could be played on, and his feelings for Alexander, ludicrous as they were, could be utilized. The alternative to Willi was infinitely worse. U.S. Telephone & Radio didn't have personal vanities and fears and weaknesses that you could play on.

At Los Angeles station, the reporters were waiting for them. As had been agreed, Alexander did the talking. "We have laws in this country," he said, "and I think we ought to stick by them. If some breach of public morality has occurred, it's for the law officers to take action. I don't hold with trial by rumor or with the blackening of reputations to serve the political and financial interests of certain groups and individuals. We also have laws to protect people against that sort of thing, and we shall take full advantage of these laws as soon as I have been able to ascertain the facts. That's all I can say for now."

They drove straight to the studio for a conference with Pete Fenton and the lawyers. Pete Fenton looked badly rattled, more sour than ever and despondent. "I haven't been able to get anything out of James Nelson," he said. "But my information is that the story is substantially true. There was a party. Girls did strip—there was one babe who sat in a bathtub of champagne while guests came and filled up their glasses. Some of the papers have got hold of that. There was also some kind of *exhibition* involving two girls. As far as the general orgy is concerned, it seems that people did retire to various rooms, and they didn't lock any doors."

"Was James Nelson personally involved? Did anyone see *him?*" Alexander asked.

"The word is that lover-boy Jamie prefers to watch."

"Were there any other of our people involved?"

"I haven't got the full list of who was there."

"Get it. We've got to know."

"That son-of-a-bitch," Willi raged, "that son-of-a-bitch— we got two million dollars tied up in unreleased Nelson movies."

"James Nelson is not to blame," said Alexander meaningfully, "if he gives a party and his guests get out of hand. What's he to do? Call the cops? Have his guests arrested? He's an English gentleman. As long as he, personally, didn't participate we can beat this rap."

"That's going to be hard to prove, Alexander," said Pete Fenton glumly.

"He's got to face the press and make a frank statement," said Alexander.

"That's right," said Willi, suddenly inspired, "the whole thing could've been a plant—an organized smear by people interested in blackening me . . ."

"Not too fast, Willi," Alexander cautioned. "First, let's find out from Jamie Nelson exactly who was there and what did happen. Then we'll know how to play it. Pete, call Nelson and say I'm on my way over to see him. No, I better talk to him first . . . see if you can get him now, Pete."

James Nelson's house was one of the acknowledged show-places of Hollywood. It had been widely publicized as having cost over half a million dollars to build, and had been described by one columnist as "a cross between Mesopotamia and megalomania." Another well-known, and in these circumstances unfortunate, joke about it was that "it instantly brought the faithful to their knees, and put the unfaithful on their backs." It was approached from one side by a great avenue of gently ascending steps that rose between tall, shaped cypresses. From the bottom you could just see the tops of the Byzantine-style towers and castellations which surmounted the house. As you walked up the steps the house became revealed, progressively, arousing, as someone had put it, "the same gee-whizz reaction as a James Nelson movie." From the top of the steps you looked across an artificial lake, in the center of which there was a large fountain consisting of a huddle of ecstatic stone nymphs, to take in the wide horizontal sweep of the house. In the center there was a colonnaded rotunda surmounted by the largest of the Byzantine-style domes while clusters of lesser domes and turrets rose from the east and west wings. However, it was rare for anyone to approach the house from this side because it meant a longish climb up the steps. The more usual approach was by driving on beyond the steps, along the walled periphery of the estate, and through the domed gateway which led to a straight, mile-long carriage drive. The first part of this drive was through wooded grounds, affording a view, as if through a telescope, only of the rotunda. Then, after about three-quarters of a mile, the woodland ended and in its place there was a rectangular expanse of lawns and flower beds. At this point the occupants of an approaching car were treated to a sudden, dramatic, wide-angle view of the east to west spread of the house.

When Alexander's car arrived at the main entrance gate, he saw that there were over a hundred reporters and photographers waiting there. They were noisy and belligerent and resentful—some of them were spending their fourth or fifth day in a row hanging around outside the grounds, and their mood had not been improved by the fact that Nelson had requested, and been given, police help to keep them under control. Some were squatting on the ground playing cards, but mostly they were just lounging around: bored, weary, impatient, resentful. After all this hanging around, whatever was going to happen had better be big! That was the unspoken threat in the air. Like the reporters Alexander had already encountered at the station, they were, collectively, pretty fearsome in their determination to get a story—*any* story—as long as it would justify all this waiting, and make up for the indignity of being pushed around by cops, and forced to be perpetually maneuvering for positions so that when something did happen they would be in the right place to observe it happening. The grandness of the house, the fact that there were servants with dogs on the other side of the gate to see that if anybody did slip past the cops he didn't get far—all this, over a period of days, had served to make their resentment ferment dangerously. A few days ago, reading of the Nelson scandal, their reactions had probably ranged from mild disapproval to slightly grudging admiration. But now they were guardians of public decency. Alexander was sitting in the front of the Bugatti coupé-de-ville, next to Frankie. Yahoos and catcalls and ribald jokes and questions greeted him as the automobile made its way through the crowd of reporters toward the gates. Alexander told Frankie to stop, and stood up in the front seat.

"I just want to thank you boys," he called through the noise, "for all the free publicity you've been giving one of my biggest stars. I sure appreciate that," he added, laughing, and one or two of the reporters joined in the laughter. "Now," Alexander continued, "I can't promise you a story, but I don't see why you should have to hang around here. We'll see if Mr. Nelson will give us all tea. I can get a few of you in my automobile, the rest of you who haven't got automobiles can either follow on foot. Or—it's about a mile's walk—I'll have cars sent for you from the house. I promise you nothing will be said until you're all there. And please accept my apologies for you having been kept hanging around like this—it must be that Mr. Nelson is scared of the press. Fortunately, he's even more scared of me." This produced more sympathetic laughter. Alexander got out and opened the doors of his car and squeezed half a dozen reporters into it. Seeing that this was causing a fierce crush, which could develop into a stampede, because reporters at the rear were afraid they were being kept out of something, he decided to walk to the house with those who didn't have transport. This seemed to satisfy everybody and

364

had the effect of calming them all down. The gates were thrown open, the car went ahead, and Alexander went in, preceded by pressmen in cars and cabs, surrounded on all sides by reporters and photographers, some shouting questions at him as the great disorderly phalanx made its slow progress up the long drive. "I don't know any more than you do," he replied to all the questions, "but I'm damn well going to find out. I think you have the right to know, and I know I have the right to know, and I'm going to see to it we get some answers. All right?"

The reporters trampled through the flower beds, crushing tenderly nurtured plants underfoot, and across the croquet lawns, somebody threw an empty beer bottle into one of the swimming pools and somebody else demolished a cactus plant with a savage kick. Outside the house, the reporters who had been in Alexander's car, and those who had gone ahead of him, were waiting to be let in. Alexander made his way through them and rang the bell; first, a spy hole opened, and then the door was opened by Nelson's butler.

"There are some gentlemen to see Mr. Nelson," said Alexander. "Look after them, Hank."

As the reporters poured into the house, the impressiveness of the entrance hall had the effect of quieting them. The domed skylight of stained glass filtered the sunlight of its dazzle and created the kind of churchlike gloom that automatically makes people lower their voices. The butler, Hank, led the way to the principal reception room, throwing open gold-lacquered doors on which there were designs of intertwined dragons. Tea had been prepared on a long banqueting table and there were many plates of canapés and little sandwiches. Servants handed these to the members of the press as they came in. The intimidating opulence of the room made some of the reporters, who were a little grubby after their long vigil, feel self-conscious and ill at ease. They looked around, some with unconcealed awe, others with slightly contemptuous expressions on their faces, made notes, accepted the tea or coffee or beer offered them, squaffed down the delicate little sandwiches and canapés two or three at a time, plonked themselves in gondola-shaped settees supported by gilded dolphins, felt the rich material of the drapes. For a while they were appeased, then somebody demanded: "When do we get to see lover-boy?" And a chorus of voices took up the demand.

"I'll go fetch him," Alexander promised, and returned five minutes later with James Nelson and a young, good-looking woman. Most of the reporters did not specialize in movie stories and had never seen James Nelson before, in the flesh: they were surprised to find that he was considerably shorter than they had expected and serious-looking: he had put on a pair of heavy spectacles. Alexander held up his hand and called for quiet. "Mr. Nelson will be glad to answer your questions," he announced, "if you'd all be kind enough to give him a little room so all of you can see and hear. Right. Now, first question."

"What have you got to say about the 'Party'?" a reporter demanded immediately and aggressively.

"I had a feeling you weren't going to ask me about my new picture," Nelson responded lightly. This caused some laughter, and also evoked some incredulous titters. Nelson had a most unexpected high-pitched voice, terribly English, almost lordly, not at all the sort of voice that people would associate with the kind of parts he played on the screen. "First," he said, "I'd like to introduce you gentlemen to my fiancée." And he indicated the young woman at his side: "Delia Colpayne." He took her hand, and squeezed it tightly as they looked into each other's eyes for a long moment like innocent lovebirds.

"Fiancée?" one or two voices demanded in surprise.

"Yes, we've been keeping our engagement sort of private. Miss Colpayne is from England." Delia Colpayne gave them all a warm, though aloof, smile, as if she had come among them to do relief work. "I'm not entirely used to your American ways, as yet," she conceded modestly, "but I hope I shall soon become acclimatized."

"A couple of Jamie's parties should do it," a reporter interjected. She gave a pained frown, and ignored the remark.

"When's the wedding going to be?" somebody asked.

"Just as soon as Delia's family can get out here," said Nelson. "Sir Arthur Colpayne, Delia's father, is hoping . . ." He was cut short.

"Let's leave that for the Society Section—huh? Now about the party."

"Ah, yes. The party. Well, it was a humdinger of a party, all right." This produced some sympathetic laughter. "As it

366

happens, I didn't see all that much of it. I was seeing a movie at the time."

"A blue movie?" Bawdy male chuckles.

"No. Black and white."

"You went out to see a movie with a house full of guests?"

"I have a projection theater right here."

"Must have been a pretty gripping movie, considering what was going on."

"I honestly don't know. I must admit I slept through most of it. It was one of my own movies. I always sleep through my own movies."

"You trying to tell us you didn't know what was going on, that you didn't take part?"

"I confess I did have an inkling of what was going on. And—no, I didn't take part. I was with Miss Colpayne all evening. Some gate-crashers—at any rate they were people I had never seen before and certainly hadn't invited—evidently decided the kind of party they wanted it to be."

"You made no attempt to stop it?"

"I should have stopped it, of course. But have any of you ever tried to stop people determined to—what shall we say —whoop it up?"

"What about the girl in the champagne bath? Didn't you invite her—you must have provided the bath?" More raucous laughter.

"You've heard of the young lady who brought her harp to a party. Well, I can only assume that this young lady brought a bathtub, and, presumably out of consideration for her feelings, somebody *did* ask her to play. But it wasn't me. I don't care greatly for champagne." The laughter of the reporters was becoming more sympathetic, more of them were now laughing with Nelson than at him.

"Who was the girl in the champagne bath?"

"I have no idea. The only time I saw her she had no obvious means of identification about her. One girl looks pretty much like another in a champagne bath."

"She was the same girl, wasn't she, who later took part in a perverted display with another girl?" This question, toughly put, silenced the room.

"I wouldn't know about that," said Nelson. "If that did happen it must have happened while I was fast asleep during the movie. The projection theater is sound-proofed."

"That's a pretty easy way of getting out of it," one reporter declared. "How do we know you're not lying?"

"I tell you how you know," Alexander put in. "If you've seen any of James Nelson's movies you'd know he's not that good an actor." That caused more laughter and served to dissipate the tension. "And now," Alexander continued quickly, "I think you'll agree that Mr. Nelson has answered your questions very frankly. He's due at a meeting. If there are no further questions, would you all excuse him." There was a certain amount of protest at this, but some of the reporters were already rushing out to get their stories to their papers, and the others seemed momentarily undecided between staying on and possibly getting some more quotes, or making it to the nearest phone as fast as possible. As Nelson was already starting to make his way out of the room, and the chance of getting any more out of him seemed to be diminishing, most of them decided to settle for what they had got. Now, with a few exceptions, they were all rushing to get out, and presently the huge banqueting room was empty except for three or four members of the press whose deadline was evidently not so urgent, who remained to finish off what was left of the canapés.

On arriving back at the studio, Alexander got Pete Fenton to issue a statement to the effect that the police were being asked to find the people who had gate-crashed James Nelson's party and had been responsible for what had happened. This statement, in conjunction with Nelson's press conference, had the desired effect. The hue and cry was still on, the reformers were still demanding action and the newspaper editorials were still thundering about the depravity and perversion rife in "this 20th-century Sodom," but the main force of their censure fell now on Hollywood in general. There was considerable doubt about whether Nelson had been telling the truth at the press conference, but the way in which he had handled the situation had earned him the benefit of the doubt with many people. The suave way in which he had faced his accusers was counted in his favor. During the next three or four days, though the anti-Hollywood campaign continued to build up and was becoming increasingly hysterical, Alexander and Willi began to feel that they were going to be in the clear. Indeed, they were being congratulated in some sections of the press for the frank and decisive way in which they had dealt with the situation, not seeking to cover up for their star, but on the contrary exposing him to frank press questioning. Just when it seemed as though everything was going to be all right after all, Pete Fenton barged into Alexander's office with a copy of a Los Angeles evening paper which he put down on the desk without a word, but with a look that foretold calamity. Alexander read the story which had been ringed in. The headline was: "Girl in Champagne Bath Talks." There followed an interview with Joan Torthe, who confessed to being the girl in the champagne bath at the James Nelson party and also to being the girl who had, later, given the exhibition with another girl. Then came the bombshell: "Joan Torthe, an 18-year-old movie extra, said that she had been taken to the party by Seiermann-International Story Editor, Paul Krasnor, who had promised her $500 if she would give an exhibition with another girl. She had got to know Krasnor, with whom she had had a number of dates, as a result of working at the Seiermann studios." There followed a long, detailed and lurid first-person account by Joan Torthe of the party. The paper which carried this story was one that had all along been vociferous in opposing Willi's takeover of the Hesslan Studios, and in the course of Joan Torthe's confession no opportunity was missed to identify Nelson and Paul Krasnor with Seiermann-International. Joan Torthe's confession ended with the words: "I know that what I did was wrong. But I am telling what I know to protect other girls from being misled and corrupted, as I was, by evil men." Pete Fenton said that, according to his information, Joan Torthe had been paid $2,000 by the paper in question for her confession. This was considerably more than the current market price for such stuff. Alexander picked up his phone and asked for Paul Krasnor, but he was not in his office. He then tried Paul's home number; there was no answer. He told Miss Pearce to keep ringing at intervals of three minutes. He called Willi and Stephen Raille on the internal phone and told them what had happened, and suggested they both come to his office. When Willi arrived—just after Stephen—he said: "*Your* friend, Alexander. Your friend has done this to us. There is only one thing to do. We fire him, disassociate ourselves from him entirely, and invite the cops to take the appropriate action."

Alexander said: "Before we do anything, I want to hear what Paul has got to say."

"What can he have to say? Sure, he'll deny it. But I been making inquiries and it's true he's been dating her, and it's true she worked for us in a couple of pictures. That's enough to crucify us. What difference does it make what *he* says?"

"Let's not lose our sense of proportion on this," said Alexander. "What hurts us most on this is that she says he offered her five hundred dollars. The implication of that is that he was functioning as a procurer for profit, that he was using his position here to meet girls, and that what happened at the party, instead of being a spontaneous and voluntary act on the part of the girls involved, was in fact organized and paid for. Now that hurts us badly, if it's true."

"You doubt it's true?" Willi demanded.

"So far we have only the word of the girl, reported in a paper with a vested interest in maligning this studio."

"And if it turns out it is true—what you propose?" asked Willi.

"I don't know. What are your views, Stephen?"

Stephen Raille thought for a while, worriedly. Then he said, "You oughtn't to be put in the position of having to decide what to do. It shouldn't be for you to decide how another man should live."

"I know that, Stephen. But *knowing* it is not going to get me out of having to do something."

"I suppose you could say that the private life of one of your employees is not your concern."

"Not his concern," exploded Willi. "Not *our* concern. Forgive me, you don't know what you're talking. The President of the United States is concerned, and we shouldn't be?"

"I agree with you in principle," Alexander said to Stephen. "But the way the situation has developed there is no way for us not to be concerned. The morals thing has become an issue."

Willie said, "If he wants to go in for that sort of thing, couldn't he have had the sense to be—discreet. At a party of James Nelson's! He might as well have taken the Hollywood Bowl for it."

"The point about Paul is that he's not discreet," said Stephen quietly.

"I know. What the hell am I supposed to do?" Alexander asked.

"I wouldn't like to be in your shoes, having to decide," said Stephen.

"Oh come on, Stephen," said Alexander with some anger. "Don't be so goddamn removed from it all. He's your friend as well."

"The reason you're doing what you're doing is because you feel capable of taking decisions of this sort. I don't. I'm sorry, Alexander, but you're stuck with it."

CHAPTER FIVE

It was after midnight by the time one of the many messages left for Paul at the various places he was known to frequent reached him. On the phone to Alexander he sounded cheerful and a little high. He agreed to go back to his apartment straight away and wait up for Alexander. "From the look on your face," he said blithely, as Alexander came in, took off his coat and threw it on a settee, "I surmise I'm in for a lecture."

"A lecture!" Alexander said grimly. "It's a bit more serious than that."

"Oh come on, father," Paul said, mock-pleadingly. "I'm sure you used to go with girls yourself when you were my age."

"Are you sober?"

"It's going to be that sort of a conversation, is it? Look, Alexander, it does not worry me what some newspaper scribbler says about me. My reputation is not that precious to me."

"It isn't a question of your reputation, Paul. It's the damage to the studio."

"Oh, dear," said Paul. "The good name of . . . and all that. It seems that having gone to considerable lengths to lose a family, I have gained a studio. What do you propose to do, father? Cut me off without a credit?"

"I wish you wouldn't kid, Paul. This is serious. What I want to know from you is—is the story true?"

"I'm going to be cross-examined, am I?" Paul asked in a straight voice.

"It's going to be thrown at us that you used your professional position to procure girls for depraved perversions."

371

"Well, first let me say—and I think you, Alexander, are in a position to know this—that I have never experienced any great difficulty in finding girls, for 'depraved perversions,' or whatever you like to call it, even before I was privileged to work for this great studio of yours."

"That's not the point, Paul. You *are* working for us now, and as an executive of the studio your actions reflect on us. I'd like an answer to my question, Paul." The lines of Paul's face had tightened.

"In a minute," he said, "I'm going to get very angry. I'm not going to have anyone, not even you, Alexander, come into my apartment and subject me to an inquisitorial cross-examination about matters that concern me and nobody else."

"I thought I was putting it politely, Paul."

"I don't feel I owe you any explanation, Alexander. What I do is my own concern."

"Not entirely."

"Yes, entirely, damn you—you're making me very angry. I won't answer to anyone, and especially not you, for my private life."

"You may have to answer to the cops."

"What!"

"Procuring is an offense."

"God Almighty, I'm a procurer now."

"I'm not saying what you are. I'm talking about the impression created and as you refuse to answer . . ."

"I'm trying to keep my temper, Alexander. You're a very old friend otherwise I'd have kicked you out of here when you first started this line of questioning. All right. I will give you an answer to your impudent and offensive question. I did take Joan Torthe to the party. I did—in what you might call the heat of the moment—encourage her to do what she did, but she didn't need all that much encouragement. I did not pay her, and I did not offer to pay her."

"That's all I wanted to know."

"If you want my resignation, it'll be on your desk first thing in the morning."

"No, that would be the worst thing you could do. Tantamount to an admission. We shall have to sweat it out. If you'll just quit getting all steamed up for a moment, I'd like to tell you what is involved. The Seiermann-Hesslan merger will not be allowed to go through if our opponents are able to make us out a bunch of moral degenerates. That's what they are trying to do. If this one charge against you can be made to stick, the implication is obvious, isn't it? You did meet her through her working at the studio, and it will appear that we are the sort of people who corrupt innocent young girls who come to us for work. Whatever the truth of the matter, that's how it looks. In those circumstances, the Administration is not going to allow Seiermann to take over another studio and so expose even more innocent young girls to such a fate. Does that spell it out for you?"

"And what is the verdict of you all?" said Paul mockingly.

"I don't know, Paul. I'm not sure how to play it. Any suggestions?"

"I have no suggestions, Alexander. I can't play these sort of games." He was silent for a while. Then: "I'm sorry, Alexander—that I got mad at you."

"It's all right, Paul. It happens in the context of friendship."

"Whatever you decide," said Paul, "is all right by me."

"I take it there are no letters from you to this girl to indicate that you ever paid her money?"

"We didn't correspond."

"Well, that's something. *Did* you ever give her money?"

"Well, yes. But only cab fare basically. These girls are always broke. I'd sometimes give her a few dollars—cab fare home. One doesn't ask for change."

"I see. Well, we'll have to play it by ear. Don't talk to anyone about it. Don't talk to reporters. Don't come to the studio tomorrow, wait here until I call you. It may be a good idea for you to take a vacation for a few weeks. We'll see."

"You should have got rid of me. Right at the beginning. When I said."

"It wouldn't have been any fun running the studio without you, Paul."

"It's reassuring to know," said Paul, "that I served some purpose, if only amusing you."

The following day Paul was arrested and charged with procuring. Willi called an emergency meeting of chief executives in his office at the studio. In an impassioned speech, during which he was often close to tears as he repeated again and again how much was at stake, he urged that the only course of action open to them was for the studio to

373

disassociate itself from Paul Krasnor, and the only effective way of doing this was for Alexander to announce that Paul had been fired.

In reply, Alexander said: "To fire Krasnor now is to prejudge his case. It is not only morally wrong, it is also—I suggest—politically inexpedient. To fire a man *after* he's been arrested on a morals charge is not going to impress anyone of our moral integrity. On the other hand, by standing by him, we can get him off. The procuring charge is ridiculous—it's a panic action on the part of the District Attorney. He's under pressure from all sides, and he's got to find somebody to take the rap. He can't make the procuring charge stick. I am sure that Krasnor did not take money and did not pay money to this girl, or promise to pay her. Are we going to take her word against his?"

"Don't you see," Willi interrupted, "that whatever actually happened it's going to look . . ."

"It's going to look bad," Alexander agreed. *"Whatever* we do, it's going to look bad. That's something we can't avoid. But throwing Paul Krasnor to the wolves is going to look a lot worse. Let's at least have the courage to stand by a man to whom we have given a responsible post. If we have so little faith in our own judgment that we abandon this man even before he's tried, how is *that* going to look? I think we are going to have to make a pretty subtle moral distinction—and make it stand up in public—between a man acting as a pimp and procurer and a man indulging his own maybe unconventional sexual tastes. I think this is an example of the latter, and I think we have to say that a man is entitled to behave as he chooses, provided he keeps within the law. I think that whatever Paul Krasnor has done, he has kept within the law. I think we have to resist the pressure on us to join the mob in crying for *somebody's* blood. Therefore I have to make it clear to you, Willi, that I will not fire Paul Krasnor, and that if he is fired over my head this will automatically result in my own resignation, and I would make it quite clear why I had resigned."

"You're putting a pistol to my head," Willi cried out emotionally.

"Not a pistol, Willi. A cannon."

"All right, Alexander. Do it your way. You know so much better than everybody else. I wash my hands of the matter. He was your appointment."

"That's right, Willi."

"So what do you propose to do?" demanded Willi.

"I propose to get an acquittal for Paul."

The day Paul had been let out on bail, he was attacked in the street by a man who had recognized him from the pictures in the newspapers. He was quite a mild-looking man and had come up to him calmly, and then had unleashed at him a barrage of foul words: "Filthy pervert ... pimp ... filthy foreign pimp ..." Paul had just grinned and ignored him, and attempted to walk on, whereupon the man had struck him on the side of the head with his clenched fist, muttering: "That's what decent Americans think of people like you. Go back to your own country." Telling Alexander of this incident, Paul seemed fairly matter of fact. "It's extraordinary," he said, "the fury one triggers off in people. They resent you, not because you've done something they disapprove of, it's not that basically. It's that they feel so deprived. How can they continue to put up with their dumpy, dreary wives when somebody like me actually does what they'd all like to do? It upsets the equilibrium of their whole existence. The fury of the sexually underprivileged is a terrible thing, Alexander. That's why I'm not going to get off. They'll excuse James Nelson because he's a movie star, and they've accepted that movie stars are different, but not me. D'you know who wrote those articles, the exposés? I thought the name was familiar, and I checked up. You remember that little newspaper girl we picked up one night in New York, who wanted to come along to Madame Menocoulis's? That's the one, Martha Hall. It's fantastic to think about it. Has she been waiting all these years to get even with me? For what? For not taking her? It seems incredible, doesn't it? She probably doesn't even realize it herself."

"We'll get you off, Paul. You mustn't get despondent. I want you to be confident and assured in court. We'll beat them."

"I suppose if I am convicted, they'll deport me. It'll make them feel better if they can blame it all on filthy foreigners—get rid of them, cleanse the American nation of its impurities!"

"If you are convicted, and I don't think for a moment you will be, we will fight the case all the way to the Su-

375

preme Court. We would contest any deportation order all the way. You can be sure of that. You have a lot of people supporting you."

"Ah well," said Paul, "I suppose that's something."

The public fury against Paul continued to mount; the newspapers, using him as the pretext, as if he had already been convicted, became even more virulent in their demand for action, for a clean-up, for the end of what they called casting-couch rule in Hollywood. James Nelson, in his role as the innocent whose house had been invaded by sexual hooligans, supported these demands. Alexander saw Paul most evenings and was gratified to note that he was remaining calm in the face of all the violent abuse being unleashed against him.

The day before the trial was to open, they drove up into the hills—they were alone, Frankie had been given the afternoon off. Alexander had left the studio early and now, together, they stood watching the lights coming on in Los Angeles: the signs jostling each other above the buildings: Jesus Saves: Chevrolet: and the one that advertised an indigestion cure, its electric bubbles effervescing into the sky. It had been one of those hot, sticky September days when just to breathe is an effort, but it was cooler in the hills. The trees, projecting at curious angles out of the sides of the hills, seemed anachronistic in this setting, seen against the electric growths on the distant rooftops. The searchlights had not come on yet, or perhaps tonight nothing world-shaking was on to require heralding.

"What a strange place this is," Paul said. "What dreams they must have had when they came here, across two thousand miles of desert and mountains. What a dream it must have been to keep them going. Gold and freedom— and now the sky promises them instant relief for nervous dyspepsia and, if that should fail, the divine intervention of Our Lord. Tell me, Alexander, have you ever tried to think of yourself in a nonmaterial context? I tell you, it's very good for the soul. Try to create a picture of yourself that is completely divorced from job, position, setting, possessions—in fact, all the trappings by which everybody recognizes you, and by which you recognize yourself. It's hard to do, but very interesting. If you can peel all that stuff away and there's still something left, then you can congratulate yourself."

"I think you should get some rest, Paul."

"Don't worry, Alexander, really."

Alexander drove him back to the small house in Beverly Hills that he had rented for Paul (it had become impossible for him to remain at the apartment where he was pestered all the time by reporters and threatening anonymous callers). Before getting out of the car, Paul said: "Alexander, it moves me very much the way you are backing me up. Americans find it very hard to express strong feelings as between men—on the Continent we are not quite so inhibited, but in this respect I've rather fallen into American ways. So this will have to do . . ." He put out his hand and gripped Alexander's in it tightly, then he was gone before Alexander could think of anything to say. He got out of the car and watched Paul walking rapidly along the short drive, open the door of the house, switch on the lights; he waved to him, and Paul waved back before closing the door. Alexander got back into his car and drove off; there was a kind of steady ticking in his mind that was accelerating as he drove faster; he had a feeling of unease that he could not decipher. It was dark now. Coming round a bend in the road he suddenly saw the moon—it was very near and low, just clearing the brow of a hill; it was full and yellow—a great yellow, unblinking, venomous eye in the sky. Another bend in the road, and it was gone—and the momentary feeling of profound dread passed—but two turnings later it was there again, this horrible yellow eye, veined with shadows . . . Without thinking, he felt in the secret compartment under the dashboard: at such moments of irrational apprehension it was somehow reassuring to touch the gun. Nothing. It wasn't there. The compartment was empty. His first thought was that Frankie had forgotten to leave it there; when he drove he carried it in the shoulder holster. Then the other possibility occurred to him, making his whole body tremble, making the fear spurt inside him like blood from a deep wound. He slammed on the brakes and then, hooting continuously to warn the oncoming traffic, turned the long car in the narrow road. He drove back at great speed, throwing the car around the curves in the road with a deeply implanted skill that was not dependent on his conscious mind. Each time the car went around one of the hairpin curves, the whole of its long body trembled from the centrifugal force pulling on it.

From time to time, Alexander caught glimpses of the yellow moon in his driving mirror: it revolted him so much that he adjusted his mirror to avoid seeing it. Throughout the drive back he felt like a man in the moment—artificially prolonged—of losing his balance on the edge of a cliff. If only he were wrong. If only Paul would come to the door and say, "What is it, Alexander? Did you forget something?" he would kiss him with joy. He would bridge that distance that separates men; he would hug him so tightly, so unashamedly, so lovingly. "Dear God," he said out loud, "please don't let Paul be dead, please don't let Paul be dead." He was a child again, entrusting himself to unidentified forces. As he drove, the sobs were being wrenched out of him. "This is reality," he thought. "Up to now it was just playing. This is real. I can feel the hard cutting edge of reality. It cuts into you." Reality was the grating of steel against bone, the tearing, breaking, *physical* sensations. All the rest had been phantom fears, dressed-up fears.

He was coming up the short drive of Paul's rented house. The lights were on. Everything was quiet and still. Surely, if something had happened . . . somebody would have heard, there would be fuss and commotion. Perhaps he was in time. "Please, dear God, let me be in time," he prayed. Then he heard the sharp, flat thud, which made his bowels move and his head turn as if he were going under gas. He staggered to the door, his body shaken by violent retching. The door was locked or bolted. He had to force a window. It gave into the kitchen and set off a burglar alarm as he entered. He had very little breath in him as he opened the door. He was surprised that he did not collapse when he saw the sight in the living room. He had never seen so much blood. He had not known that a human being had so much blood in him. The walls were spattered and running with blood, as if the place had been used as an abattoir. Paul had put the pistol in his mouth and pulled the trigger. The whole back of his head had been blown off. What remained of him was so ghastly—so much a breaking-up of the conventional concepts of a human being—that Alexander threw up, almost without being aware of it, as a kind of automatic reflex action. Immediately afterwards, he felt a steeliness come into him, as if everything inside him had closed tight in self-protection. He stepped around the body

378

and looked on the desk. There were several letters there. One was addressed to him, another to Paul's mother in Czechoslovakia, another to the District Attorney, and one to Janet Derringer. Alexander put them all in his pocket. He bent down over the body and looked at the gun which, in death, had become joined to the fingers in an unbreakable grip. All at once he could not stop the tears, and he kneeled there, sobbing helplessly, until the police, summoned by the burglar alarm, turned up. Alexander's letter read: "I know this is ridiculously melodramatic, but really the vultures want blood and I'm not prepared to let them suck me dry at their leisure. This is far the best way. Sorry to use your gun, hope it doesn't cause any difficulties with the cops, but pills are too slow and entail the risk of resuscitation. My God, how it has all turned out! Don't feel too bad about this—it will upset you, of course—but believe me it's not as terrible to me as it will seem to you. It pleases me to think that there has been at least one moment in my life which I controlled entirely. One can't allow oneself to be pushed around by the furies all the time. Believe me, I love you as a friend, Paul."

Within half an hour Pete Fenton arrived, and shortly after him came Willi, and soon after him came the reporters. They wanted a statement. Pete Fenton urged him to say nothing, but Alexander went outside the house and spoke to the reporters. He spoke in a flat, weary voice from which all the surplus emotion had been drained: "Paul Krasnor," he said, "was hounded to his death for being a womanizer. A good many of you here now took part in that hunt. He was not a procurer, and he was not a pimp, whatever the law might eventually have decided, and he did not corrupt anyone. He was a sweet man, he was my closest friend, and I am proud to say that. He was charged with this trumped-up charge of procuring because the public needed a scapegoat; its sexual envy had been fanned by the newspapers and the so-called reformers to the point where it needed a scapegoat the way that flames need firewood. That was Paul Krasnor's role. Somebody had to pay dearly—and be seen to pay dearly—for all the fun and games of Hollywood, which have so aroused the anger and the envy of the nation. The public had to be given a victim: Paul Krasnor, conveniently, was at hand, a custom-built scapegoat. He was a foreigner, an artist, a Bohemian, a known womanizer. If the public could be made to believe that all the sexual excesses they had been reading about were the filthy contrivance of artists, foreigners and Bohemians, their envy and resentment could be conveniently drained off. So the buck was passed, with expert sleight of hand, and Paul Krasnor was the unfortunate bastard who couldn't get rid of it to somebody else. Paul Krasnor didn't kill himself because he was a procurer who couldn't face exposure; he killed himself in disgust at the hypocrisy of the people all around him. He killed himself because he was disgusted. Paul Krasnor died because he practiced what others only dream about guiltily, and their envy was too much to put up with."

The reporters had listened in silence while Alexander said all this: but when he had finished one of them spoke up and said, "What did you do to save him?"

"Not enough," said Alexander, "I'm ashamed to say, not nearly enough."

CHAPTER SIX

Alexander was in no state to drive home; Willi took him in his car, shaking his head all the time and muttering, "The poor bastard, the poor bastard. But you mustn't blame yourself, Alexander. You did everything that could have been done." Alexander remained silent. His exhaustion was such that he could not form words. At home Susan was entertaining guests; he could not bear to see her; helped by Willi he went straight up to his room and rang for Mrs. Brown who gave him an injection and telephoned for Dr. Fellowes. At Alexander's insistence, Willi left. Alone with Mrs. Brown he was able to let go, and he sobbed like a child, gripping her arms, hanging onto her with the desperation of a man clinging to a handhold on a sheer cliff face. By the time Dr. Fellowes arrived the injection had begun to work and he was calmer. What had happened was explained to Susan when she came up to rebuke him for having forgotten his birthday dinner party. That day he was twenty-nine years old.

While Alexander was ill, Willi was obliged to take charge of public relations. He called a press conference at which he said: "Ever since I been in Hollywood I have urged the tightening up of moral standards. Recent events have shown the terrible consequences of loose and licentious living. We must put our own house in order. And I make you this undertaking. While I have anything to do with the running of studios, I shall make it my personal duty and obligation to see to it, God willing, that the sanctity of family life is respected, both on the screen and off. The morality clauses in all contracts will be rigorously enforced. I don't care how important somebody is—or how much money he makes for the company—if he or she can't live decent they will be dropped and ostracized from the studios. The scandals which have been shaking Hollywood, and which lose us the respect of decent, ordinary people, are going to stop, and if the scandals don't stop the people who make them are going to stop."

Willi's statement was generally welcomed by all sections of the press. He was commended for giving a lead to the whole industry with his promise of the strict enforcement of moral standards. But, many of the newspapers said, talk was all very well; they'd heard all this before; it remained to be seen if, in fact, Seiermann and the other leaders of the industry would now take the appropriate action. One or two papers did express doubts about the propriety of employers interfering with the private lives of their employees, and warned that this might constitute an encroachment of the individual's liberty, but these voices were decidedly in the minority.

Immediately after making this statement, Willi made a trip to Washington to have further talks with the Attorney General's office. He had had no word from the government, but he was reassured to find himself described by the Washington papers as the man "who was going to put Hollywood's disorderly house in order." He had brought Sarah and his two daughters with him to Washington, and all newspaper pictures showed him in the bosom of a happy family group.

The conferences with the Attorney General's office were inconclusive. It seemed that nobody was prepared to commit himself one way or the other. The negotiations dragged on and on, and each day questions that had apparently been settled days earlier were brought up again. Willi knew enough about the technique of stalling—he practiced it himself when it suited him—to recognize the signs. He was not being given a definite no, and on the other hand he was not being given the go-ahead. He was being given the runaround, and from his own use of this ploy he knew it must mean that there were some unrevealed factors affecting the negotiations. He was not the only person who had pull in Washington, and the others—whoever they were—were obviously pulling hard. In addition, everybody seemed nervous and tense, and they had reason to be. The headlines of the past few days had been ominous—"Acute Weakness in Market," October 17th; "Wave of Selling Engulfs Market," October 20th; "Continuation of Selling Wave," October 22nd. Willie decided to break off the discussions and return to New York.

On the evening of October 24th he attended a banquet in honor of Colonel Claudius H. Huston, the new treasurer of the National Committee of the Republican Party. It was a distinguished occasion. Among the guests were several members of the Cabinet and Party leaders from the Senate and House. Also there were the heads of all the principal financial groups: the Morgans; the Rockefellers; the Chase Bank; the Kabes; Kuhn, Loeb; Goldman, Sachs; Hayden, Stone; Dillon, Read; Halsey, Stuart; the Equitable Trust; the National City Bank; and others. They heard a speech by Secretary of Commerce Lamont which painted a dire picture of the state of the economy. No nation, he said, could continue when its citizens refused to buy bonds. All great nations were built on the public's willingness to buy bonds. Unless a great market could be created for bonds, and the speculation in common stock terminated, the nation was threatened. That day the newspapers had carried headlines of "a paper loss of four billion."

The next morning, Friday, October 25th, Willi rang the nine brokers with whom he had stocks, in corporations that he did not control, to a total value of $15,000,000, and instructed them to sell. By Monday they had all been disposed of. By Tuesday their value had fallen to less than $4,000,000. His shares in Hesslan's, for which he had paid a total of $60,000,000, and which he had not sold in the general panic, were now worth rather less than $30,000,000. Most of these shares were with the banking houses, nominated by Kabe, as partial collateral against the loans which they had made to Willi to enable him to pay Kabe his

$60,000,000. Unbeknown to Kabe, Willi, to protect himself, had bought a further $20,000,000 of stocks on the open-market, in the names of relatives, so as to insure control for himself. These shares had been bought through brokers on a 50 per cent margin, which meant he had actually put down $10,000,000.

On Tuesday, the 29th, Willi was in his New York apartment on Park Avenue. Soon after ten, the telephone rang. It was one of his brokers to say that the market was still falling, the Hesslan shares were continuing to decline and Willi would immediately have to send $300,000 to cover his margins. As soon as he had hung up, the phone rang again and a second broker came on with the same story and a demand for $200,000. Ten minutes later the first broker was back on the phone to say that the amount now needed to cover the margins was $600,000. Willi sat down at his desk and started to make out checks from his personal account. He had just finished making them out when, in rapid succession, the remaining seven brokers called, each demanding sums varying from $200,000 to $700,000. He totted up the total and found that his margins were short by $8,000,000. He tore up the checks. Sarah came into the room, and saw immediately from his face that this, now, was a serious calamity, and not the kind of imaginary calamity that Willi was always anticipating.

"It's serious?" she said.

"It's worse than serious," said Willi. "Don't anybody answer the phone until I say. I got to think."

"Don't upset yourself, Willi," she said feebly. "The main thing is your health."

"Upset myself?" he said. "I'm not upset. Look"—and he extended his hands—"steady as a rock. You think I scare so easy? I tell you something, Sarah, my darling, the test of a general is not in peace, it's in war. If I can't save myself, then I deserve it. But God has been good to me so far, why should he let me down now—tell me? Why build me up, just to kick me down?" He was quite calm, almost cheerful. "Whatever happens, Sarah, one thing you can be sure. I don't throw myself out of any windows. You don't have to worry. I'm not that kind of a fool. Everybody is in the same trouble, the ones who'll come out of it are the ones who keep calm and don't panic and use their brains."

"How bad is it, Willi?"

"Bad?" He laughed. "I need by tomorrow eight million dollars that I don't have. By this afternoon it could be twelve to thirteen million dollars. If I can't pay the brokers, they put the shares on the market which will drive the price down to nothing. And I got shares with the banks that cost me sixty million dollars—that I owe them still. By tomorrow, they could be worth practically nothing. So how do I pay them? They could wipe me out, Sarah. Sarah, would you be so kind to ask the maid to bring me some coffee? And don't worry yourself."

When she had left, he picked up the phone and rang, one after the other, all the banks with which he had ever done business or where he had had accounts, and he explained his problem and that he needed about $13,000,000 by tomorrow. He offered as security those of his assets that were not already hypothecated, and also his personal possessions. But the answer from all of them was the same. They were in trouble themselves, they had no spare cash to loan him, they were very sorry. Then he rang Stafford Deems, of the Kabe organization, and after explaining his plight asked if Kabe would make him a secured loan of $13,000,000. It did not seem to him an unreasonable thing to ask, considering he had just recently paid Kabe $60,-000,000 for his Hesslan shares. Deems said he would take up the matter with Henry Kabe immediately and ring back. Half an hour later he returned the call to say that Mr. Kabe was sorry but he needed all the cash he had to support his own companies. Willi then rang U.S. Telephone & Radio which, as one of the main shareholders in Seiermann-International, would surely be interested in saving Willi. Its resources were vast. It could either make the loan out of its own funds, or by exerting its influence could induce one of several banks, with whom it had great sums on deposit, to make the loan. Gregory Helder, of Telephone & Radio, said that certainly he would take up the matter and he was hopeful of being able to come back with an affirmative answer. By midafternoon he was on the phone to say that Telephone & Radio could not see its way to making an unconditional loan. However, in the circumstances, as a special favor to Willi, they were prepared to pay $5,000,000 for the patents that Seiermann-International owned in a sound process being developed at the studio, and if he agreed to this sale they were prepared to loan

384

him the balance of the money that he needed to see him through. Willi replied, angrily, that he had already spent more than eight million on developing this sound process, that its potential value was incalculable, and that he would not take a cent less than $20,000,000 for the patent. Helder said he was very sorry, but they could not do business on that basis and, if he felt that way, he should go elsewhere for the loan. Willi hung up. Of course they were in a strong position to dictate terms: if Willi could not meet his financial obligations, and Seiermann-International was to be dismembered by its creditors, U.S. Telephone & Radio, with its cash resources, could step in and, by paying off the debts, acquire control of the tottering empire at a cut-rate price. There was nothing to stop them waiting for this except the thought that Willi might be able to raise the money elsewhere; and, of course, if they made it clear that they did not wish him to be able to raise the money there were not many banks, even in good times, who would be prepared to help Willi at the risk of incurring the displeasure of the mighty U.S. Telephone & Radio. This was the situation that now faced him. How could he save himself if his principal shareholders were bent on destroying him, and if they were going to use their influence to prevent others from helping him? The first necessity was to appease the brokers. Accordingly, Willi now telephoned each of them and asked them to come to an emergency meeting at his apartment that day, after the Stock Market closed.

When they had all assembled—their weariness after the day's calamities very apparent in their faces—Willi said: "Gentlemen, I have done a little arithmetic and I find that I owe you $11,736,000. What I have to tell you is that I haven't got it." This resulted in uproar: different faces registered anger, dismay, fear, resignation. "Now," Willi continued, "though I haven't got the money right now I have hopes of getting it. What I want to persuade you gentlemen to do is to declare a moratorium for twenty-four hours to give me time to find the money." This evoked a considerable amount of protest; how were they to know that he would *have* the money in twenty-four hours? "Let me put it to you like this," said Willi gently, "if you don't accept my proposal for a twenty-four-hour moratorium, and you start to sell the Hesslan shares that you hold, I shall

385

put *my* Hesslan shares on the market and very quickly they will be worth nothing, and your shares will be worth nothing. So you have a simple choice. Either you destroy me and lose $11,736,000—or you give me a little time to find the money." One of the brokers spoke up: "We don't have any choice, do we? We will give you the twenty-four-hours you ask for."

After they had gone, Willi sat looking out of the window and tenderly feeling the stubble of his chin—he had not shaved that morning—wondering if this was going to be the end of him. In his mind he went over all the things he had to sell, and he could think of nothing that might fetch $11,736,000 in twenty-four hours. Besides, by tomorrow the figure would probably have risen to $13,000,000. Where could he find that kind of money? And if the government should now force him to dispose of the Hesslan shares—bought for $60,000,000 and now worth less than half that amount on the market—his losses would be so enormous there would be no chance of holding the Seiermann empire together. In this situation there seemed only one course open to him. He called Helder at U.S. Telephone & Radio and said he would consider selling his sound patents for the amount he needed to get himself out of trouble: $13,000,000. Helder telephoned back within twenty minutes to say that the terms were acceptable.

Willi had survived the worst of the panic. Between October 15th and November 9th, Hesslan shares had dropped from 65⅞ to 48⅜; Seiermann-International shares were down from 105 to 83⅛; U.S. Telephone & Radio were down from 300¾ to 229; Fox Film had dropped from 101 to 71; Fox Theaters from 25⅞ to 15⅛ and Loew's from 64¼ to 49⅝. In other words, Willi was no worse off than anybody else; everybody had been hit more or less equally. His main problem now was that by February the first of the notes on the $60,000,000 loan would fall due, and he would have to find some way of refinancing the entire enterprise. This should not have presented any insuperable difficulty. After all Kabe had used his influence to get the loan for Willi, and with his backing it should be a very straightforward matter to prepare a new issue of shares which would be offered to the investing public—in this way it should be possible to recoup the whole of the $60,000,000 outlay. But now, to his amazement, Willi discovered that the firm which had previously undertaken all his financing wanted nothing to do with him. And as the dates when his notes would be due approached, he found all the banks Kabe had recommended were insisting on payment, refusing an extension of credit, and all the other banks that he went to were refusing to take over the loan. At first he attributed this to the perilous state of the economy, but the economy was supposed to be picking up, there was plenty of money around for others: only for him were all the doors closed. It became apparent to him that there was some design in this pattern of refusals; there could be no other explanation; somebody wanted him not to be able to meet those notes when they fell due, and as a result be forced into bankruptcy. For the first time since the panic of October 28th and 29th, Willi was frightened. This time it was not that everyone was in the same plight; this time there seemed to be a definite attempt to destroy *him*—for reasons that he could only too easily guess. If his companies could be forced into public receivership, then Kabe and U.S. Telephone & Radio could simply step in and take them over. For the first time, he began to see in Kabe's original actions—in insisting on cash payment, in introducing Willi to the banks that would provide him with the money—the seeds of a clever and meticulously worked out conspiracy. He had been tempted to overextend himself; he had been given abundant credit; he had been played along: and now that he was so overextended they could simply destroy him by cutting off his credit and forcing him into bankruptcy. They could play him in like a fish on a line, at their own leisure. With both Kabe and U.S. Telephone & Radio against him, he hadn't a chance of raising $60,000,000. Moreover, they were also obviously the ones who were putting pressure on the government, and even if he could find the money he might find himself ordered to divest himself of the Hesslan shares. He had thought he had power and influence; what he hadn't taken into consideration was that others had even more power and even more influence. Willi realized that he was against the wall. He sought an interview with Henry Kabe. The answer staggered him. Henry Kabe, at his advanced age, no longer concerned himself with the day-by-day running of affairs, but Stafford Deems, his general manager, would be happy to grant Willi an interview. Making a great effort to contain his anger, Willi agreed to call on Mr. Deems.

Deems was a tall, esthetic-looking bachelor of fifty whose graying hair periodically received the benefit of a blue rinse; he wore a carnation in his buttonhole as a permanent fixture and displayed his fine elegant hands a great deal while he talked in a soft and cultured voice. He operated from a kind of salon, furnished with Louis Quinze pieces, devoid of office equipment and innocent of the accouterments of high finance. In this setting even the solitary telephone looked incongruous. His smile was famous. It wrapped itself around you like a warming cloak, and he managed to convey the impression of a man rather pained by the necessity of doing business at all. You felt he would really much rather be playing polo. He listened attentively and with many sympathetic smiles and nods while Willi began to outline his difficulties, then he gently cut him short. "If I may, Mr. Seiermann . . ." An apologetic smile. "I *am* familiar with the situation. Naturally, it is in our interest to help you, and you can rely on us completely. Please don't concern yourself any more, the Kabe organization is quite capable of protecting the interests of someone who has shown himself such a good friend to us in the past."

"Then you will help me," Willi uttered, not able to conceal his joy and amazement.

"But of course. Here is what we propose. One of our subsidiaries will undertake the refinancing of the merger, and meanwhile, so that there shall be adequate time to do this, we shall guarantee your notes as they fall due and thereby obtain an extension from the banks. In return we ask only one small concession from you. That you make over to us the one hundred and fifty shares in Seiermann-International . . ."

"The one hundred and fifty shares . . . to what shares are you referring, Mr. Deems?"

"Ah," said Deems, smiling like someone who knows the solution to a brainteaser. "I refer to *the* one hundred and fifty shares. We know all about them, and I must add that it was not entirely proper for you to have them in the first place."

"Kabe aren't even shareholders in Seiermann-International. Is it their concern?"

"Strictly speaking, that is correct. I speak on behalf of some of our friends, who *are* shareholders."

"Like U.S. Telephone & Radio?"

"You musn't press me, Mr. Seiermann," he said, laughing gently. "We have many friends."

"That I am finding out, Mr. Deems. If I make over these shares to you, you—or your 'friends'—would control Seiermann-International and therefore Hesslan's as well."

"Technically, perhaps."

"You would be taking away my own companies from me, that I built up."

"That's not really an accurate representation of the situation. We should be glad for you to continue as president of the group. We'd just like to have a little more control over you." He gave another of his benign smiles.

"If you can outvote me, you have all the control."

"In theory, perhaps. But why should we wish to do that? We are not picturemakers. We are perfectly happy for you to run that side of it. Your knowledge and experience are invaluable assets. . . ."

"So what you propose is to save me by taking me over. Thank you very much, Mr. Deems, but I don't call that helping me."

For the first time the suggestion of a frown clouded Deems's unruffled features. Willi was seething and trying to hold his temper in check. This smooth-faced bastard with his buttonhole and his fine gestures was a destroyer, as surely as if he were holding a knife to Willi's throat. They've got me in a trap, he thought, and now they are going to cut me up. He pushed back his chair and got up.

"I'm sorry I took up your time, Mr. Deems."

"Now see here, Seiermann . . ." It was Seiermann now, not even Mr. Seiermann. ". . . I think we have made a most reasonable offer. If you refuse it, there is little likelihood of you finding the money to get yourself out of your present difficulties and we—er, our friends—will be in a position to acquire control of the companies in any case. But we prefer to do these things in a civilized way. I'm sure you will agree that is better for everyone concerned . . ."

"What have you got against me, let me ask you? Can

you tell me that? I built up these companies and they have been doing fine. Why d'you want to take them away from me?"

"Let me put it like this. While *picturemaking*"—he gave those words a slightly derisive edge—"while picturemaking was a rather, shall we say, rough and ready business of limited significance in the over-all economy of the nation, it was feasible to run it in rough and ready ways. But that is no longer the case. A great deal of finance is now involved, and we must ensure that the business is *properly* conducted, in accordance with accepted principles of finance. Believe me, we want to interfere with you as little as possible, but we also want to be able to protect our interests should you, or anyone else, go too far in certain respects."

"Like treading on the toes of U.S. Telephone & Radio?"

"Yes, indeed. There are some toes it is most unwise to tread on."

"Will you tell me something, Mr. Deems? Say I refuse your offer? Say I say to you—do your worst: take me over. And supposing you do take me over, and I'm out, who are you going to to get to run this business? You, Mr. Deems?"

"I wouldn't presume to . . ."

"Who is going to run the studios, make the pictures . . ."

"We are entirely satisfied, except in one or two minor respects, with Mr. Sondorf's running of the studio. We see no reason why he should not continue, especially in view of the family connection."

"And say he won't work for you? You know what you're taking over? You're taking over a lot of plant and real estate and theaters and equipment and talent, but what good is that to you if you can't make it work? Seiermann-International is the people who work at Seiermann-International and those are people chosen, guided, developed by me and by Alexander Sondorf. Without us what you're taking over is a pot of paint—so go paint yourself a Leonardo da Vinci!"

"We don't underestimate the importance of the talent factor, not at all. And, as I say, we have no reason to suppose that Mr. Sondorf, whatever you may decide to do, would be averse to continuing on the new basis."

"We see about that, Mr. Deems. We see about that. Good day to you." And Willi got to his feet, gave what he judged to be a withering little bow, and walked out. On his way back to his apartment, he was regrouping his thoughts like a general reforming a badly beaten army. He had thought of a new line of attack. Why hadn't he thought of this before? He could still beat them. When he got back to the apartment he immediately booked a call to Alexander in Hollywood.

CHAPTER SEVEN

It was only from the tower that Alexander could see the ocean. When the house had been built, to the specification of a strange old Spanish millionairess who much admired the work of Gaudi, the Gothic-style towers had been purely decorative. By putting in a spiral staircase, Alexander had converted one of them to give him a sort of superattic, completely away from the rest of the house, from which he had a view of the ocean. Since Paul's death he had spent much of his time here. It was a very plain room—a bunk against one wall, a table with writing things on it, a dictaphone, and a few chairs. He came up here partly because of the peacefulness and also to remove himself from the overpowering richness of the rest of the house. Susan had a passion for collecting things: from her trips to Europe, she brought back Gobelin tapestries, Tudor chests, Venetian balustrades, alabaster clocks, medieval armor, an altarpiece that she had had converted into a dressing table for him—even a Spanish ceiling that had taken her fancy. The wide corridors of the house had a long guard of honor of statuary of very mixed lineage—rather good pieces standing next to the kind of junk that only very rich Americans, and ones who were also in very much of a hurry, could be induced to buy. Susan did her buying in bulk and in haste, and threw out things afterward at her leisure, when their worthlessness had been pointed out to her by someone she considered an "authority." As a result, the inside of the house was perpetually changing. This had a rather disorientating effect at times. Alexander might enter a room he had not used for several weeks and discover that what had formerly been an Italian music room was now furnished in the style of an Olde English tavern. In this ever-changing house—and with Susan's penchant for playing games—he could never be sure in which of the fourteen bedrooms she was sleeping on a particular night, whether it would be in a Queen Anne bed, elaborately draped, or in a convent bunk in a whitewashed room under a crucifix from Madrid. He had no taste now for playing games, and so he kept away from what he thought of as Susan's part of the house, which was most of it. Since Paul's death the panic attacks had been occurring with increasing frequency. He saw very few people. Meeting strangers exhausted him to the point of collapse, and in such states he was most vulnerable to the panic attacks. He still ran the studio, but he did so without going there. The day's rushes were brought to the house and shown for him in his private projection theater; only Stephen Raille and Mrs. Brown were allowed to be present. Alexander's decisions were either dictated to Mrs. Brown, or into the dictaphone, and then taken by one of a relay of messengers, permanently on call, to the studio. Sometimes Alexander did talk to executives on the telephone but most of the time his wishes and decisions were conveyed to them through Stephen Raille.

Alexander had become very thin; such food as he ate he had to force down and often he brought it up again immediately afterward; his thinness emphasized the prominence of his cheekbones and the slightly hollow-cheeked look that was a family characteristic on his father's side, and it made his eyes seem even bigger (and darker against his pallid skin). Dr. Fellowes, who came to see him every day, and had begun to look increasingly worried, insisted that he must stop working for a time and take a holiday to recuperate. But Alexander replied with a thin, sickly smile that a holiday was no cure for hypochondria, on the contrary it would make it worse, and if he stopped working he would die for lack of anything else to do. While he could keep the outside world from intruding, while he could relay his wishes and decisions by dictaphone and telephone, and through Stephen, while he could keep Susan from climbing the spiral staircase to the little room in the tower, he was safe. There was always Mrs. Brown within call to give him an injection, if he should need it, and from the window of the tower he could see the ocean and the eucalyptus trees in the garden, and Susan's friends

392

arriving for dinner. He wanted nothing else. Early in the morning, long before Susan was awake, he could walk in the walled grounds, in the certain knowledge that he would not need to talk to anyone; he could breathe in the fresh morning and watch the sun begin to climb into the sky. And when his pulse had settled down to a reasonable eighty beats a minute, he could walk back to his tower and dictate the first memo of the day. The message that Willi was coming to see him to discuss something of great urgency had disturbed him; he had tried to discourage Willi from coming back to Hollywood, but without success —he would be here in four or five days' time. Stafford Deems, of the Kabe organization, was also on his way to see Alexander. What did they want from him? He wanted nothing to do with any of them. He tried hard not to think of Paul, but even when he succeeded in removing that terrible image from the forefront of his mind it still was there like a sort of faded fresco, and at night the Nembutal did not stop him from dreaming. Often, in his dreams, investigators came to the house and looked through rooms that were strange to Alexander, having just recently been put in, and opened a chest or a sacristy or a trap door that he had never seen before, and discovered the moldering remains of Paul's body. Sometimes, in the dreams, Alexander fled from these investigators, and rushed out of the house, only to find that the garden and streets and the entire neighborhood had been changed, that the streets had different names, and the neighborhood was another neighborhood, and all the familiar houses had gone, and then he could not get back to his own house because it, too, was somewhere else.

Mrs. Brown had just finished taking his blood pressure; it was still low which was why he felt so faint all the time.

"Mr. Raille is here," she said. "Will you see him?"

"Ask him to come up."

Stephen came in frowning painfully. "How are you, Alexander?"

"Not particularly well. Is there anything?"

"Well . . ." Stephen was looking at him thoughtfully, worriedly. "Nothing I *have* to bother you about."

"Come on, Stephen. What is it? Studio matters don't upset me."

"It's not really a studio matter, Alexander, and I'm not sure ..."

"Now you've aroused my curiosity," said Alexander, smiling weakly, "you'll have to tell me. Unsatisfied curiosity, the doctors say, is very bad for me."

"You asked me to find out about Janet Derringer," said Stephen.

"Yes, yes—did you?"

"Well, I've been trying to track her down for days. It was all pretty damn mysterious. At the hotel they had no idea where she was, the apartment is still being paid for, but she hasn't been there for weeks. Alexander, I don't know whether in your present ..."

"Come on, Stephen. Out with it."

"Well, I've managed to locate her—"

"Yes?"

"She's in a place called Kroner's Sanatorium."

"Is she sick?"

"Kroner's Sanatorium, Alexander, is a rather grand lunatic asylum."

"Oh, my God!"

"Now wait a second—she's not mad. I'm sure she's not mad. I've been doing some checking up and I find that Dr. Kroner's sanatorium is a very, *very* expensive place, basically for eccentric old ladies and gentlemen who happen to be very rich and whom somebody wants out of the way. Some of the people there are quite mad, and others not quite so mad, and others not mad at all. The usefulness of the place is that you can get somebody admitted under any of those categories, if you're prepared to pay. In the case of Janet Derringer . . ." Stephen hesitated. He subjected Alexander to an intense scrutiny before going on. ". . . in the case of Janet Derringer, it seems she tried to commit suicide, she was examined by two doctors and she was certified insane—as a result of which she was admitted to Dr. Kroner's establishment. The obvious question occurred to me. How could she afford to be sent there? And why all the secrecy? That's what I've been finding out the last four days. The bills are being paid by Willi Seiermann, and the two doctors who certified her are very, very dubious indeed. It sounds incredible, I know, and one can't really believe that such things actually happen, but

394

it's quite obvious that Willi Seiermann has had her certified and put away . . ."

"Why? What earthly . . . ?"

"I guess if a girl leaves indiscreet suicide notes around, at a time when Mr. Seiermann is anxious to impress upon the world, and Washington, his unblemished respectability . . . that's the only explanation I can think of, Alexander. It fits. Who's going to take the word of a girl, certified insane, against that of Willi Seiermann? She claims to have been his mistress. All right. The product of a deranged mind, delusions of grandeur."

"I don't believe it, Stephen. I can't bring myself to believe it. Even of Willi."

"Alexander, I have spent a lot of time checking and doublechecking. I have absolutely no doubt. The practical question is—what do we do? I've been looking into the question of getting her out, and that's not easy. Once somebody has been certified, to get her uncertified takes a great deal of doing, especially if the people who have her deny you access to her. And Dr. Kroner's establishment will not even confirm that she's there. They say the identity of their patients is a matter between the sanatorium and the relatives."

Alexander had got up from the bunk; the abrupt movement made him feel momentarily dizzy and he had to hold on to a chair to steady himself. His heart was thumping and he had to close his eyes for a couple of moments and try to calm down before speaking. He wondered if his legs would carry him down the stairs, as far as the car. "We're going to get her out," he said to Stephen, at the same time picking up the internal phone and pressing the button that would connect him with the garage.

Oh come on baby palm tree columns all around the room and wallpaper swarming with birds and dolphins and serpents 10 Jack Queen King Ace a top straight oh come on baby a top straight it's the rules slip them off baby slip off the panties oh come on a painted sky with a painted sun and a painted moon come on don't be a spoilsport waterlilies of bronze dripping light like water drops slip 'em off baby hey too much light too much light we want to see something all right but you don't have to floodlight the place the girls are shy the dark-haired girl with the congealed smile white limbs against the yellow trellis dado part of the trellis the moving trellis of intertwined limbs and all those birds and dolphins and serpents and all that yellow and green and gold no no let me watch I can't see like that all right like that all these dolphins and dragons and serpents gilded and silvered and ebonized all that silk there's too much light that's cheating you didn't throw the dice 9 10 Jack Queen King twenty-seven should be enough if you take too many they say you vomit them up okay that gives me an action a full house gives me an action right not like that baby like that darling I want to see you with her I want to see you with her Dear Janet these sort of notes are read by a lot of people so O my God all those lotus leaves lighting up when you switch on the light remember what I said once even what O'Neill said about glue the grace of God is glue hold tight baby hold tight you've got more valor than I have love Paul everything stops oh come on baby give us a show give us a real show everything stops is that me breathing nine ten Jack Queen ten nine eight seven everything stops how can you be sure it's enough if they find you in time they use a stomach pump all those lotus leaves lighting up like that and those white sexless buttocks part of the wallpaper flat like a flattened box with nothing inside gray pallid flesh the color flowing out like blood twenty-seven should be enough in your mouth baby in your mouth is that what it's like to die and Jesus Christ the soft wet mossiness everything stops hold on hold on tight yeah baby hold on and move baby move like that that's great oh great look at those two dancing with her panties round her knees Jesus she's away would you like her instead of me everything stops the darkness is so thick oh God I can't feel anything is this it is this it oh touch me touch me make me feel anything anything just make me feel yuh like that like that I can't feel anything I can't feel anything oh my God I don't want to die make me alive make me alive inside give me life let me be born oh Jesus this is the end this is the end everything stops motions within motions everything stops Ohhhhhh flesh is so white so deathly white but where the blood goes it's pink and warm and hard . . . I can't see like that let me see I want to see but there's no light let's have a little light somebody you can't see their pretty little titties in this Stygian gloom so dark so dark over ripe breasts who would think the human body could take so many shapes white upon white everything accelerates and then stops accelerates white upon white upon white endless repeated patterns like on the wallpaper cries and motions repeated like the patterns on the wallpaper the painted sky is dark and the painted sun has no radiance . . . oh my God . . .

She was lying on the bed, her hand moving between her thighs, when the male nurses came in to remove the uneaten food; she did not know how long they stayed there watching her, but she did not stop, it was only the feeling there that kept her alive, that told her she was still alive, and she could not stop, because if she stopped there would be no feeling and she would be dead.

The walls were padded, but nicely, and if you didn't know, you could take it as being part of the decorative scheme. It was a small room, but comfortable. Janet was looking at the legs of a chair. She had been looking at them for the last three hours. The grain of the wood was alive, swarming, like a slide under a microscope. The legs were not solid. They were a precarious balancing act of matter, the molecules climbing over each other and clinging together. Why did they cling together like that? What lust made them cling together like that? Much later, it might have been hours or days, she went to the window. It had bars on it but they were decorative wrought-iron bars. She looked out. Gray lawns. Tall trees, so tall and thin. There were gray people on the gray lawns. They walked, endlessly, in intersecting circles. Sometimes they lifted their arms and were gray trees without foliage. Such an infinite range of grays. When the sun came out briefly, they looked like overexposed photographs, the excess of light deprived them of their features. Two male nurses came into the room, after unbolting it from outside, and put something on a table that she realized she was meant to eat. The faces of the male nurses had no breadth, they were worn away at the sides, she saw everything thin, all vision had become impossibly narrowed, their eyes overlapped in the vertical plane, now they had no features at all, their features were coagulating wax down the side of a candle. There was no mirror in the room, but that was how she must look too, unformed, an embryo. She realized she was in a lunatic asylum.

The high, spiked walls of Dr. Kroner's sanatorium were concealed from outside and inside by parallel lines of tall trees. The building itself was rococo in style and looked like a cross between a French casino and a German spa hotel; the façade was rich in lions' heads and semidraped female torsos supporting plaster garlands. It was said that the building was an almost exact reproduction of an establishment that Dr. Kroner had formerly run in Switzerland.

The Bugatti had come up the drive at about 50 m.p.h. and Alexander jumped out before it had quite come to a halt; he ran up the stone steps to the main entrance, followed by Stephen Raille, Dr. Fellowes, Frankie, and the other man in the dark, pin-stripe suit. The tough-looking male nurse who sat behind the reception desk looked up inquiringly as they came in a body into the hall; they were past him and halfway along the corridor when they heard the running footsteps behind them and the alarm bell going. There was a bronze plate bearing the inscription "Dr. Krone: Director" on one of the doors, and Alexander opened it without knocking and went in. The others followed. Dr. Kroner was a small man with large eyes which opened very wide, taking up a considerable proportion of his face, as he reacted to this rough invasion of his office.

"Yes? *Yes?*" he said with shocked disapproval, examining them; he had half risen behind his desk. Two male nurses in white uniforms had now appeared and he exchanged coded glances with them. "Yes?" he repeated, frowning in puzzlement.

"You have a girl here, Janet Derringer," said Alexander.

"Yes?" said Dr. Kroner, frowning even more severely, not confirming the statement or denying it.

"You know she ought not to be here."

"Are you a relative?"

"No."

Dr. Kroner had got fully to his feet; the male nurses had moved toward Alexander, like bouncers in a tough dive. "I am very much afraid," said Dr. Kroner in his shocked, incredulous voice, "that I do not see people except by appointment." The two male nurses were standing on either side of Alexander now, their hands lightly brushing his elbows, awaiting instructions. "If you have something to discuss with me," said Dr. Kroner, "I suggest you write in for an appointment."

"I have nothing to discuss with you, Dr. Kroner," said Alexander. "I came here to fetch Miss Derringer."

"That's quite out of the question." He gave a little nod to the two male nurses who now gripped Alexander by the elbows.

"I wouldn't do that," said the man in the dark, pin-stripe suit. Dr. Kroner gave a tiny nod and Alexander's elbows were temporarily released, but he could feel the dangling hands of the male nurses very close to him. "Who are these people?" demanded Dr. Kroner, examining Stephen Raille, Dr. Fellowes, Frankie, and the man who had come along with them. "This intrusion is quite intolerable."

"My name is Sondorf," said Alexander. "This is Dr. Fellowes."

"This girl, Janet Derringer, should not have been committed," said Dr. Fellowes.

"Are you a medical man, sir?"

"Yes."

"A psychiatrist?"

"No."

"Then you'll forgive me if I say that I probably know a little more about these matters."

"On what grounds was she committed?"

"Really, this is incredible! As a medical man you must be aware that I am not at liberty to discuss . . ."

"As I said," Alexander cut in, "we are not here to discuss anything." On the desk there was an official-looking typewritten list which he picked up, causing the doctor to splutter with indignation.

"Oh really, this is outrageous, those things are private, I have never . . ." The two male nurses gripped Alexander toughly, each taking one arm.

"I told you not to do that," said the man in the dark, pin-stripe suit, taking out a gun. Frankie also took out his gun. Immediately the two male nurses released Alexander.

"Now," said Alexander. "We are going to fetch Miss Derringer and we are taking her with us. This is my card so that you know who I am and where I can be found. I am the head of production at Seiermann-International, and if you don't know my face you'll find a picture of me in yesterday's *Los Angeles Times* which will confirm that I am who I say I am. I am telling you this so you won't worry about Miss Derringer's safety, in case you're the sort of man who does worry about such things. When we leave, you can of course call the cops and say that we have kidnaped one of your patients at the point of a gun, but before doing that I suggest you check with Mr. Seiermann. If that's all quite clear, and you have no questions, we'll fetch Miss Derringer now."

To get to the staircase they had to cross a large room, furnished rather like the lounge of a big hotel. People sat around in chairs and settees, either just looking straight ahead or carrying out little ritualistic tasks, some were talking volubly to themselves, one man was playing the piano with evident joy though no actual sounds were evoked by the clumsy movements of his fingers on the dummy keyboard. At various points of the room sat nurses of both sexes in white uniforms.

For a moment, at the foot of the stairs, Alexander felt dizzy, as if he were about to faint, and he had to hold on to the banister to keep from falling.

"What is it, Alexander?" Stephen demanded anxiously.

"It's nothing, just give me a moment." He was experiencing a falling sensation, as if falling at a controlled speed, as if held by elastic that was giving and giving and giving until surely it could give no more, now it must break, now, now. There was a man dressed in the uniform of a Colonel in the Confederate Army, pacing up and down, accompanied by a cynical-looking male nurse. Periodically, he turned to the nurse and commanded: "My horse, bring me my horse. At once." "Sure, sure, general," the nurse assured him roughly. It was comical; the beginnings of a hysterical laugh dribbled out of Alexander's mouth. The mad are comical, he thought. One elderly woman, magnificently dressed as if for a great ball, sat fanning herself vigorously, and from time to time she turned to the pretty female nurse sitting with her and spat out the word, "Slut!" A tall, thin man with a magnificent demeanor and the finest white hair was coming toward Alexander, anger in his eyes. "Why don't they genuflect?" he demanded of the male nurse at his heels. "Don't they know who I am?"

"They did, they did," the nurse told him toughly. "You just didn't notice, Imperial Highness. They know who you are, Imperial Highness. They know you're the Czar. Now come along."

"I demand the respect due to me," the white-haired man

400

said, drawing himself up very high. "You hear? I demand it."

"O.K., buster. Come on now. It's time for your bath. Don't get yourself all excited again, sport."

It was comical, Alexander thought. The white-haired woman at the barred window—her shrieking laughter, when his father was lying dead with the towel over his face. One must not think about such things. But a thought cannot be unthought—it floods the mind with its insidious messages and then smirkingly exonerates itself: only a thought, not real. Anything I *think* can happen *can* happen! On the screen false apple blossom looked more real than the real thing—sweat did not show as sweat and blood did not show as blood. Substances made in the labs photographed more real than the real thing. This madman was perfect casting for a czar, more perfect, probably, than the real man. In movies real Russian princes played waiters, they were perfect casting for that. What was real? He'd told that English director he wanted more light in that scene, he didn't like dark scenes. "But Mr. Sondorf," the man had said, "it's England in February." "I know," Alexander had said, "but I want more light. Warner Brothers make dark pictures, we make pictures with a lot of light in them. All right, it's an exceptional February. I want to see sunlight in that scene. I want to see sunlight streaming through the windows." Was this feeling, now, inside him, real? A premonition? A morbid thought? Death was just a morbid thought, but it happened, though you could never experience it except in anticipation. The actual moment was unexperiencable, because by then the mechanism had stopped recording. Or was that instant, that explosion of a billion brain cells, what they meant by eternity— an instant stretched to eternity? The man was playing the piano, with all the expressions of joy on his face—who could know what sublime music the silence made inside him?

"Alexander, are you all right? Alexander?"

"Yes, I'm all right, Stephen. Let's get her."

He went first up the carpeted stairs. There were various signs and notices on the landing. They took the passage to the right. Alarm bells were ringing throughout the building, some loud and shrill, and close by; others muffled and distant. They could hear heavy footsteps somewhere in the corridors, strident voices, people shouting and arguing; and the commotion was spreading, the patients in the hall lounge had begun to sense that something unusual and threatening was happening, and they were beginning to react like people in a burning building who have just begun to smell smoke. Strange laments came from their lips. The corridor was in the shape of a ring and in places became an open gallery and they could see the patients in the hall below, their mystified faces upturned and full of fear as they watched these figures scurrying above and around them.

"We've gone in a circle," Alexander called to the others. "Back—go back."

They made their way back the way they had come until they found a narrow passage marked E; turning at right angles into it they continued in this direction until they came to a swinging door, beyond which the floor was uncarpeted: fire extinguishers, sand buckets, locked wall cupboards, big red-painted alarm bells, several speaking tubes with call-whistles, overhead a complex tangle of pipes. There was a bad smell in the air, a mixture of body smells and disinfectant and urine and something indefinable—a smell of broken minds.

They came to a heavy door with iron bindings; it was locked and gave not at all when they threw their collective weight against it. The man in the pin-stripe fired four shots into the lock, and then they tried again, and this time the door gave to their joint pressure. The corridor they were now in was wider and had dusty, narrow, barred windows which offered a view across a dim back area of other narrow, barred windows. Open garbage bins, as yet unemptied bucket-type latrines; a couple of beatifically grinning men in overalls mopping the floor with water smelling powerfully of disinfectant. All along one side, plain windowless doors, rather like public lavatories, each with a circular spy hole let into it at eye level.

Hoping to find their way at the junction at the end of this corridor they carried straight on: on their left an open door revealed some two dozen men and women, in segregated lines, wearing old and torn bathrobes. They were watched over by a big, muscular woman in black bombazine, with enormous arms like tree trunks, and the appearance of a German lavatory attendant. She wore a key belt around her waist. Beyond the lines of men and women they could see two doors, one marked Male Treatment Ward and the other Female Treatment Ward. The sound of an alarm bell had brought several startled-looking therapists to the door, and beyond them Alexander saw two large bathtubs, one steaming: an elderly man standing naked and dripping and shivering—one hand shaking uncontrollably. The end of the corridor was blocked by another enormous locked door. Frankie pointed his gun at the woman with the key chain, and indicated with a quick gesture that she was to unlock the door: the keys and her fat bosoms jangling and shaking she ran to the door and unlocked it as instructed, and when Frankie pushed the barrel of the gun into her thick flesh she told them how to get to cell 11, block G, and gave them the key from her belt. Again they found themselves in carpeted corridors, clean-smelling and swept; again they were in the ring gallery, looking down on the patients—these privileged mad ones in their carpeted pit with their private nurses and their indulgent keepers always ready to corroborate their most outlandish convictions. The man playing the soundless piano had begun to sob, affected by the atmosphere of rapidly festering hysteria; the Colonel was pacing up and down, eyes blazing; the dressed-up woman fanning herself let out a scream, continued to fan herself with mounting violence, then screamed again quite matter of factly, functionally. The panic was spreading from one to the other. The nurses were all on their feet now, strait jackets at the ready, alert, communicating with each other with looks and secret gestures.

Alexander felt something going on inside him that was like sand running out of an hourglass too fast, uncontrollably, emptying him before his time. At the same time he felt the sensation of having been to this place—or was it not that he had been here, but that he had always known about it, as part of his inheritance. In some way none of it was unfamiliar. The men and women waiting for their hot and cold baths, these panicky faces turned up to watch him—he knew them all. Room 11 was the third one along. Alexander went in alone. Janet was sitting upright in a chair by the bed, crying softly, and he had the impression that she had been sitting there and crying like that for a very long time.

"Janet," called Alexander very gently; she had not looked round as he came into the room. "Janet." She looked round now and recognized him and began to weep uncontrollably. He put an arm around her and helped her up, and she put her head against his chest and sobbed and sobbed while he murmured in baby talk: "There, there, it's all right now, it's all right, you're going to be looked after, you're going to be looked after."

CHAPTER EIGHT

Willi was waiting by the circular pool. Waiting again, he thought. He had thought he was finished with all that. Alexander hed been talking to Stafford Deems for over two hours now and Willi had tired of sitting around inside the house and had come outside. How many times had he walked around the swimming pools? Twenty times? A hundred times? Why was Alexander keeping him waiting like this? Willi remembered how people used to keep him waiting years ago, before he was anyone, waiting for a letter, for an answer, for a phone call, for a smile, even anger denied him, kept dangling between hope and despair. It was part of the technique, and, later, he had used it himself with devastating effectiveness. "Mr. Seiermann will see you the moment he's free." "Tell him to wait, say I'm in conference, ask him to come back tomorrow." He'd kept the bastards waiting. You never said no; it was always maybe, or perhaps, or as soon as possible, or we'll call you back. Let the anger and the doubt ferment inside them; it was a great weapon—nothing quite so demoralizing as protracted uncertainty. Never reveal yourself as an enemy; always the big smile, the firm handshake, the call-me-any-time, always glad to see you, and then let the bastards wait and stew. And now it was being done to him. He remembered how he used to wait for girls outside Hermann Glantz & Sons—in the rain, for hours—would they show up? Or were they just playing with him? He remembered waiting in that amusement arcade on Rayburn Street. The framed bill on the wall: "Moving Pictures Photographed from Life: Drop nickel in slot—keep turning crank to the right and you will see—HOW THE PUERTO RICAN GIRLS ENTERTAIN

UNCLE SAM'S SOLDIERS." The three coquettishly smiling girls in their feathery hats; one of Uncle Sam's soldiers, in a peak cap, with his arm around one of the girls. Would anyone come in to see how the Puerto Rican girls entertained Uncle Sam's soldiers? Waiting. It was a long time since he'd had to put up with that. When you had the power, you didn't have to wait—that was when you used the rush technique, which was opposite of the stall—you bombarded them with telegrams and phone calls and urgent messages: in the night when they were in bed with their wives or mistresses, at the weekend when they were trying to relax, in the middle of their dinners: you had them paged continuously at hotels, you left urgent messages for them at bars, you radioed them on board ship, you sent chauffeur-driven cars for them before they'd had time to collect their thoughts. You didn't give them time to think. The stall and the rush—those were the two methods, and he was a past master at using them, and now they were being used on him. Part of the technique was never to let people be absolutely sure that they were being stalled or rushed: you didn't give yourself away. Having rushed them, you stalled them; and having stalled them, you rushed them. "My handshake is as good as a contract," you told them. What could they do? Call you a liar? It always worked, and now he could feel it working against himself. Nobody was giving him any answers. With his whole empire in the balance, they were asking him to wait. He cleared his throat and spat into the pool and watched the globule of spittle float on the green water and slowly become absorbed by it.

"Mr. Deems," said Alexander, "as I've been saying for the past two hours, my terms are not open to negotiation. Now if you'll excuse me, I have Mr. Seiermann waiting in the other room."

Stafford Deems gave a pained smile. He looked first at Alexander and then at Stephen Raille. "I'm afraid," he said, "Mr. Kabe will not consider your terms acceptable."

"In that case," said Alexander, "you can tell my grandfather-in-law that he can go to hell. Even sooner than he was planning."

Stafford Deems laughed uncomfortably. "If I may just detain you a moment longer, Mr. Sondorf. . . ."

"Mr. Seiermann is waiting in the other room, Mr. Deems. I believe he also has a proposal to make. In fairness, I can't keep him waiting any longer. He was here before you."

"Mr. Sondorf, as it does seem to be a matter of considerable urgency—very well; we accept your terms."

"I see. In that case, I will consider Mr. Seiermann's offer in the light of your alternative proposals."

"When can you let me know your decision?"

"I will telephone you at your hotel later this evening."

When Deems had gone, Stephen emitted a long-drawn-out sigh of relief and admiration. "Well, looks like you've got it. On your terms. Alexander, I will admit—I am impressed. That is what I call playing poker." Alexander smiled faintly. "You've just obtained virtual control of an empire, and you don't even look mildly pleased."

"I know. Stephen—you know how I've been . . ."

"You're over that. The way you handled Dr. Kroner and Mr. Deems was not like a sick man."

"There are times when I can find some extra energy. Certain things can produce it in me. But it's not something within my control. You saw how I was the past few weeks. That can happen again. And now I'll be running the whole works."

"In my experience," said Stephen wryly, "an increased dosage of power invariably has a very good medicinal effect."

"I can't take it on without you, Stephen. I need you with me; I need to know that you're with me."

"Sure I'm with you, Alexander."

"You know I don't just mean doing the job. I mean all the way."

"You want me to take a blood vow?" said Stephen lightly.

"I'm very serious, Stephen."

"I know you are, Alexander, and I'm not saying this lightly. I am with you, and I think you should accept Kabe's offer."

"All right then. We'll do it, Stephen." And his face broke into a big, happy, boyish smile. "Now. I better get it over with Willi. I'd like you to stay, it's going to be a big emotional scene."

"Sure. I don't mind staying and seeing that louse get his comeuppance," said Stephen grimly.

Together they walked out of the room and went in search of Willi. They found him by the pool. He was looking into the water and for some reason did not see them approach until they were almost on top of him. He looked up abruptly, and there was a silence of perhaps a minute or more while he read the verdict in Alexander's face. He couldn't bring himself to believe it. He gave a big smile—a Willi Seiermann smile—and reached out to take Alexander's arm, to link it with his, in the way that men do on the Continent sometimes when they are going to have an intimate business talk. But, by a fractional movement, Alexander avoided the sought-for contact and Willi's hand hung for a moment awkwardly in the air before it fell again to his side. "You're going along with me, Alexander?" he asked.

"No, Willi, I'm not."

There was a long pause. Alexander had a horrible feeling that Willi might burst into tears and plead—it was not beyond him to use such methods. "Why are you doing this to me, Alexander, may I ask?" he said in a low voice.

"You want to know?"

"Yes, I want to know. I like to know why I'm being stabbed in the back by somebody I always trusted, by somebody I looked on more like a . . . a . . ."

". . . a son, Willi? Cut out the sob stuff, Willi. I'll tell you why I'm doing this. I don't think a man like you should have so much power. You're not fit to have so much power. I'm not exactly lily-livered, but I have to tell you, Willi, that you do things that make me feel dirty to be associated with you. We got Janet Derringer out of that place you had her put in because I happened to find out what you'd done. But God knows what you've done to others—that I didn't happen to hear about."

An expression of almost childlike contrition had come over Willi's face. "About the girl," he said, "believe me I'm sorry. You won't believe me, I know, but I feel a lot for that girl. I was at my wits' end. She was leaving suicide notes that would have finished me. I thought what I did was for the best. I thought she'd be looked after there. Maybe I was wrong to do it—maybe I made a mistake, I admit it. You see, I'm opening with you. Maybe it was wrong what I did. Are you going to crucify me for that? Sometimes a man can make a mistake."

"You're a monster, Willi," said Alexander coldly, "and the fact that people make jokes about how much of a monster you are doesn't make you any less of one."

"That's what you think of me, Alexander?"

"Yes, Willi. You're through. With picturemaking, anyway."

"You've got the right to say that? You? Who gave you the right? Tell me that! Who gave you that right?"

"I took it."

"I tell you something, Alexander," said Willi, his face flushed with hot anger, "I tell you—I love strong, and I hate strong. I don't make any apologies. Not to you. What are you? I made you what you are. I'm a man with big appetites, Alexander, I'm not one of these slender fellows that sips life through a straw. I had to make my way in the world. I didn't have it easy. Millionaires' daughters didn't pave the way for me, and I didn't have anyone to do the dirty work for me. I had to do it with my own hands, and if they got dirty—all right, so they got dirty. That's how it is. You'll find that out. So far you had it easy. I let you make pictures undisturbed, because I respected your taste and your artistry and because I had affection for you. I fought New York for you, I kept them off your back. You know what you're doing to me, Alexander, you're taking my companies away from me that have got my name, that I built up into an empire. You want to run everything, all right, go ahead—that appeals to you. But don't count me out. Not yet. I'm a strong man, and I'm a rich man still. One day this thing that you're doing to me will happen to you."

"Don't get excited, Willi. Take it easy. You don't have to tell me it'll happen to me, I know that." He put his arm on Willi's shoulder and said, almost tenderly, a faint and perilous smile on his face: "You and me, Willi, we're dinosaurs—I know that, sure. And you should know it. In a couple of decades people will marvel that anyone like us could have existed."

BOOK FOUR

PART ONE

CHAPTER ONE

She saw the lemons on the lemon trees become yellow; they had been green before, when she had first come here, and then the greenness had given way slowly over the weeks to the rich, spreading yellowness, until all the patches of greenness had been absorbed by the yellow. She saw a red sun crawling between horizontal layers of clouds: like a train coming out of a tunnel and then disappearing into another. The streaky red of the sky, from the hidden sun. And then the red growing softer and fainter, like dye becoming diluted in the sea. She saw villas with their lovely mellowed, brick-red tiles; she saw the green copper domes of more pretentious houses—the lovely irregularity of the groupings: roof tops, trees, the road going down to the ocean in a series of loops—a stretch of bare deserted beach. In the mornings, she saw fishermen's boats on an ocean like frosted glass, and she saw the ever-varying colors of the day. For the first time in her life, she was conscious of light, realized that it was something that permeated objects and transformed them, and she felt the light as a force, as the green-into-yellow force in the lemon and also in her. On a clear day, you could see so far: the orange trees, opulent with fruit, looked as smug and rich-in-life as pregnant women. Alexander came to see her every day. He had taken complete charge of her; had installed her in this house with a secretary-companion; had arranged for the doctor to see her every day; had arranged for each of his visits to be preceded by the arrival of some gift—flowers, enough to fill the entire house; chocolates; trinkets and items of clothing, which she could try on, and if they did not please her, return to the shop and get something else instead. For weeks, she cried all the time and said very little, and they sat together and he allowed her to cry. She had not wanted to live at first, for a long time she had not wanted to live; but he had said that she must, and there was such a force in him. Almost like an embryo that does not yet have a life of its own, she lived on the energy that he gave her from himself. He was a very important man and he came every day to see her and breathed his life into her, and there was no time of day or night when he was not available to her; there was no conference so important that he would not interrupt it to talk to her and, if necessary, to come and see her. When she had said to him that she could see no reason for staying alive, he had told her that she must live because he loved her. Later, when she was a good deal better, they sometimes slept together, and then she would have liked him to contain her completely, and she would ask him to put her in his kangaroo's pocket, to carry her around with him all the time. The love-making itself was quite different from anything she had experienced up till then: often it went on for a very long time, gently, unviolently, just a long-drawn-out life movement inside her. She wondered a lot about herself in these weeks which stretched into months. She wondered what she looked like: she did not really know. One never knows, she thought. Looking into the mirror, you had a looking-in-the-mirror face; and on the rare occasions when she had been in a movie and had seen herself on the screen, the person she had seen had seemed to have very little relation to her. She wondered if she was pretty when she could not see herself. People told her she was. They told her so many things. But who was she? Alexander had said she was going to be a star, that he was going to make her a star, but she could not see herself in that way. She didn't even want to be a star, but he had such force in him, and he was so sure, and he seemed to know so clearly who and what she was.

There had been one or two quickly muffled groans when Alexander had announced at the conference that Janet Derringer was going to be built up, and that he wanted suggestions of roles that might be suitable for her. Some of the writers had started to make halfhearted protests, but he had silenced them quickly.

"I'll tell you the sort of girl she is," he said, "so you get some idea of the kind of parts I want written for her. She's a different kind of girl—nothing exotic or vampish or Theda Bara-ish about her. That's the first thing to bear in mind. She's a child of the Depression, she's a new kind of girl, very much of the thirties. She's been around—we don't make any bones about that—and she's had some tough breaks, but she's gay and vivacious and optimistic. The way I see her, she dresses simple, nothing frilly or gaudy. Just simple. And she works. She could be anything—a reporter, a nurse, an engineer even, an architect, anything you like. Not a professor of philosophy, but pretty well anything short of that . . . I can see her being under a car with her face all covered in grease, fixing a flat. That's the sort of girl she is, resourceful, self-reliant, able to look after herself, a little brittle on the surface. That's on the surface: underneath she's warm and love-seeking, and though she may be able to fix a flat faster than her man, and maybe she is a smarter reporter or a bigger architect than him, what we have always got to bear in mind is that she's doing all this *for* her man. That's what makes her sympathetic, and takes away the flavor of mannishness. That's the sort of girl I want her to be. I don't want her to be cute or cuddly or precious or some dreamy concoction—I want her to be a real girl, with a sharp line in dialogue and a high melting point when the hero takes her in his arms; *determined* and prepared to go after her man. I think that if we can find the right kind of roles for Janet Derringer we're going to have a very big star, and a very new kind of female star. That's all I have to say. I'd like you all to think about it, and I'd like some story ideas by . . . by next Tuesday, if that's not rushing you."

His happiness had become such a complicated thing—such an elaborate matter of weights and counterweights, it was dependent on so much and on so many people. He thought, sometimes, of those years in New York when happiness had been so much simpler, a matter of having a beautiful girl to take to a première, of holding her in the back of a cab and knowing that he was going to make out, of feeling the night growing brighter. There was one week, he remembered, when he had gone to the same restaurant five nights, each time with a different girl, and he'd made it with three of them. That was intoxication, and that was happiness. They had all been smart, pretty, in-demand girls, and the fact of winning them away from the other men who did the town in the same way was what really mattered, not the sex part. The thrill-moment was when he felt the power in him rising to the point when he knew he could not be refused. Now, to get that same feeling he had to achieve so much. How wonderful to feel all-powerful simply by seeing the compliance in a girl's eyes. So simple, and so beautiful. And now everything was so complicated. Now the nearest he got to being completely happy was that moment of utter exhaustion at the end of a fruitful day: his face stiff with tiredness, his body sweaty and aching from being too long in the same position, his mind numb from taking too many decisions and from expending too much of its energy, but glowing dully with a sense of sureness. He was always one of the last to leave the studio: the change that came over the place when everybody else had left was as dramatic as a change of season—the great hum and turbulence of the daytime subsiding into an echoing silence in which small and irrelevant sounds became meaningful: a long-drawn-out yawn, a sudden laugh, a car starting up, snatches of absurd conversation which the noise of the day obliterated. And then, weighed down by two bulging brief cases, and sometimes with a parcel of books under his arm as well, he would walk through the dark corridors to where Frankie was waiting in the car, and collapse into the back seat. Driving through the town, where they had named a street after him, in this happy, spent state, seeing the lights of the movie houses, gave him a deep sense of satisfaction: it was almost a laborer's satisfaction at having done the day's work, having built a wall or made a table. And, when it had been a really good day, when his mind had made the quick connections in a way that he knew was right, there came that almost mystical feeling of *sureness*.

He was no longer awed by his own power, but accepted it with equanimity and also with a sense of responsibility. He knew that he was the center of many people's lives and he knew how much his smile or frown meant to them. They came to him not only with their career problems but with their personal problems as well; they looked upon him as someone who knew exactly what had to be done in any given situation and he could not risk shaking their faith in him by admitting to being uncertain. He realized that few of the talented people he dealt with had any grasp of reality: he, Alexander Sondorf, was their only reality and their only certainty. If he said they were wonderful, they *were* wonderful, and felt it; and if he refrained from saying this—if he withheld his approval and his praise—they were devastated. Very few of these successful people had had the tempering experience of effort followed by failure producing greater effort and eventual success. It didn't happen that way in movies: with a few exceptions, people made it at the first try or not at all. As a result, the most successful ones lacked the toughening experience of repeated failure and had great difficulty in coping with any form of rejection. It was a curious mutation, this Hollywood breed; as if the law of natural selection had been suspended for their benefit. It was not natural selection that operated here, not the selection of the strongest, the most adaptable, the most fit, but an arbitrary selection of the prettiest, the cutest (not even the most beautiful), the most photogenic, the most exhibitionist, the most love-craving. He knew that he must be their reality. A star might come to him terribly upset, she was losing her looks, she was growing old, she was finished, her husband was leaving her, her box-office popularity was waning; he could say reassuring things to her and as a result she could walk out of his office feeling high and beautiful, and her marriage was on again, and her children loved her, and her public adored her. There was one star whose ability to have orgasms depended on Alexander—while he was a paternally approving figure, it was all right. But should he have occasion to chide her, she became frigid, and this resulted in desperate pleas from her husband: their married happiness depended on Alexander, the future of their children was in his hands. . . . When it was reasonable to do so, Alexander gave the reassurance that was asked of him: and he enabled these fragile creatures, over whom he had unwittingly acquired so much power, to make love and to eat and sleep and to bring up their children and to have self-respect and to feel secure and loved and wanted. He had to do this very carefully: an excess show of feeling could result in uncontrollable attachments: an insufficient show of warmth could result in complete demoralization, even suicide. He had to carefully calculate the amount of warmth and coolness that he showed.

He used this magical power with which they chose to endow him as a means of getting the best out of people. Good work elicited from him a telegram or a green memo —a message written on his half-page-size green notepaper. These telegrams and these memos were treasured; young men—or women—on receiving them went around in a state of euphoria for days afterward: such recognition usually meant the start of a dazzling career. On the other hand, if the green memos or the telegrams diminished significantly then the previous recipients started to worry and to fret. People counted how many of these messages they had received in the course of a year, and if the following year they got fewer of them it made them anxious. The stage after the memos and the telegrams was—and this meant you had really arrived—being invited to breakfast, to lunch or to dine, or—the supreme accolade—to weekend with Sondorf. These invitations, too, were counted and chalked up; anyone who had weekended three times in a row with him was indisputably in; on the other hand an invitation to a really important dinner—at which foreign celebrities were present —might rank higher than a tennis weekend. Breakfasts were usually given to technicians—cameramen, set designers, costume designers, cutters—who had excelled in some respect and earned this privilege. Therefore if an actor was invited to breakfast he would feel pleased, but also piqued at not having been invited to lunch; and if someone who had previously been invited to lunch was now invited to breakfest this was tantamount to a de-grading. And if someone who had previously been invited to a dinner in honor of, say, Bernard Shaw or Winston Churchill was asked when the only other guests were fellow actors, or writers, or directors, and moreover in a lower income bracket, then he would feel definitely slighted. Alexander had to bear all this in mind in arranging his social activities. It wouldn't do to have people committing suicide because, by mistake, they had been invited to breakfast instead of lunch.

Now that he had to deal with the financiers himself, it was necessary for him to make frequent trips to New York. In order that the days spent en route should not be wasted, he had his own railway carriages for these trips, with a drawing room where he could hold conferences, and sleeping accommodations for twelve. He went hardly anywhere these days without an entourage of at least half a dozen: Stephen Raille, Mrs. Brown, a studio secretary, Saul Jessup, and one or more of his production supervisors. On the long train trips there were usually, in addition, a couple of writers and, perhaps, a director. It was said of him that he would look naked with less than half a dozen people around him. Alexander enjoyed working on the train; the fact of being cut off from the day-by-day studio affairs, and relieved of having to make routine decisions, enabled him to concentrate entirely on that aspect of his work which he enjoyed most—the planning and conception of new productions. His filmic imagination was seemingly inexhaustible. Pacing up and down the swaying drawing room, he could ad lib for periods of two or three hours, laying down the line of a story, jumping ahead to sketch in the shape of a particular scene, coming up with some directorial device for which, later, the director invariably received the credit, describing the way a particular set should look, indicating the kind of lighting that he felt would enhance the mood he was after. Sometimes the ideas flowed from him at such speed that the stenographers could hardly keep pace with him. It was rare for him to dry up; closing his eyes he could see the succession of pictures flashing before him, and he only had to describe what he saw, almost frame by frame. He listened attentively to other people's ideas, and never hesitated to accept them in preference to his own if they were better than his own, though sometimes he adapted them, gave them "the Sondorf touch." His critics described his method derisively as "creativity by committee," but anyone who had sat in on one of his conferences knew that a strange, almost inexplicable magic was generated by him—the currents of ideas flowed richly and coalesced into a conception that was not entirely his, or even largely his, but was none the less dependent on his catalytic presence. People who were, normally, merely competent sometimes might find things in themselves being tapped that they had not known were in them. "Yes," he'd say, "go on about that . . . develop that, that's good . . . no, no, that's sidetracking . . . go on about the way he walks after he's killed her, slopping through the puddles . . . getting his

417

trousers muddy. . . . No, let's *not* see her face in the puddle, that's corny, we *know* what he's thinking about . . . this shouldn't be overdone, audiences shouldn't notice it with their eyes, what we want to get is them *feeling*, without knowing exactly why, that now he's done this thing something has snapped in him and he doesn't care about anything that happens to him any more. We should feel it, but we don't need to spell it out. Let the pictures work."

In 1931 box-office attendance had dropped by 40 per cent, and all the major studios were compelled to make sweeping pay cuts. To save on overheads the studios introduced the loan-out system, whereby the contract stars of one company, if they were not currently working, were loaned, at a high price, to a rival concern. Many of the stars, discovering that their loan-out price was very much higher than their actual salary, became resentful of being auctioned off in deals in which they had no say, to play parts that they did not want to play, and some refused these assignments. This resulted in suspensions and lawsuits, and in the realization by many of the top stars that they could do a lot better by being independent, not bound by long-term contracts, and therefore able to exercise their personal judgment in the matter of accepting or refusing roles. But at Seiermann-Hesslan-Sondorf most of the stars, when their contracts came up for renewal, stayed on—if Alexander asked them to stay on. He was able to convince them that they would be better off in the long run with a great studio behind them, to look after their interests, to promote their careers, to present them to the public to the best advantage. If they left, they would be on their own. If they stayed, they would remain part of a great organization, and, moreover, would enjoy the benefits of his personal guidance. He had made many of them into stars, he pointed out; without him, could they be sure of remaining at the top? His magic was so strong at this time that very few were prepared to take the risk—even though the financial incentive was considerable—of cutting themselves off from the source of their nourishment.

That year, a former American Ambassador to France created a sensation by publishing, in a magazine, a list of "the sixty-three men who rule the United States of America."

It did not include the President, Mr. Hoover, but it did include: John D. Rockefeller, Jr., J. P. Morgan, John D. Ryan, copper; Walter C. Teagle, President, Standard Oil of New Jersey; Henry Ford, Frederick E. Weyerhaeuser, lumber; James A. Farrell, U.S. Steel, Charles M. Schwab, Bethlehem Steel; Harry M. Warner, movies; Adolf Zukor, movies; D. P. & M. J. Van Sweringen, railways; Daniel O. Jackling, Utah Copper Co.; seven of the Du Pont family; William Randolph Hearst; Daniel Guggenheim, mining; Henry Kabe; and Alexander Sondorf, movies.

At the suggestion of Dr. Edgar Fellowes, Alexander had started to keep a health diary, the purpose of which was to discover the relationship between external events and his inner feelings, to try and find some pattern in his moods. At first he made entries every day, but later he did not keep this up and often there were months of blank pages.

3rd May, 1934. Long, exasperating talk with union leader, R. Utterly exhausted afterward. They have no objection to how I run the studio—in fact they consider me "a model employer." But they want everything covered by agreements. Told him I can't work that way, that I have to have freedom of action. He came back with the argument that the interests of his members must be protected, that people's livelihoods cannot be dependent on the good or bad whims of employers. Trouble is I can see he's right; when you're dealing with a Willi Seiermann you have to have your rights clearly defined. Depressed—realizing he's right. Still, I have to fight him. They want to put a strait jacket on me with all their agreements and rules and conditions. Going home—sudden feeling of sheer panic. "We are the dinosaurs." Picked up later in evening. (With J.)

15th October, 1935. Premiere of *The First and Last Time*. Felt great—almost as good as after *The Rich, Full Life*. They loved Janet Derringer, I think I'm going to do it with her, I think she's going to be a star. How hard it is now to get that elated feeling—how easily it came once, and I hardly thought about it then as being remarkable. That night with Paul, coming out of the brothel, nothing has ever quite touched that high, high—sure feeling. Work is the only answer, the only real satisfaction.

12th May, 1936. On the boat, very peaceful. Thought came

that I could give it all up and be happy. The real triumphs are inside oneself—is that sentimental? Corny?

13th May. On the boat. (With J.) We have such good times. Swam a lot. Stephen says I've never been young. Is this what it's like being young? How easy and how wonderful—but I'm almost thirty-seven now: too late to be young?

15th May. On the boat. Beginning to get restless—so much for being able to give it all up! Spent morning sending radio messages to studio.

16th May. Told captain to head back. Great sense of physical well-being. It's years since I've felt so good. Weather glorious. Worked on some scripts with Stephen—my God, this is the life! Must do these boat trips more often—I love the sea. Agreed to Stephen's anti-Nazi story. We must mobilize opinion. But we'll lose money on it, people don't want to know. Stephen has found a great story for Janet, very upbeat, amusing, touching. We'll make three anti-Nazi films out of the profits. God, I love this life. It's fabulous being able to get things done. I wouldn't want to be seventeen again—or twenty or twenty-six. How long do I still have—hell! What does it matter.

12th October, 1936. On the set of *It Happens All the Time.* Janet looks fabulous and Gary Cooper plays it beautifully, with such lightness. Sudden moment of dread—for no reason. Feeling of—Europe's about to go up in flames—that's *real*—and here we're making fairy tables. Feeling like that night when I left Paul at the door—the yellow moon . . .

"Did you hear the story about Alexander Sondorf going to heaven?" asked Pete Fenton. "Well," he continued, not waiting for an answer, "Sondorf gets to heaven, see, and he takes a quick look round and he don't altogether like what he sees, so he says to these angels who're showing him round the place: 'There are going to have to be some changes around here . . .'" This produced some deeply felt, edgy chuckles. "Well, after a while," continued Fenton, "he's designed new wings for the archangels and he's revised the whole system on which halos are handed out and he's got St. Peter running around doing all sorts of chores, but still there are some things he don't hold with— just because they've been done that way for eternity he don't see why they still got to be done that way—you know, old-fashioned—so he asks to see God. After a lot of string-pulling, it's fixed up and Sondorf is shown into the presence of God who sits up there on his high throne, frowning. 'Mr. Sondorf,' says God, 'I've heard a lot about you . . .' 'And I've heard a lot about you,' cuts in Sondorf. 'And I don't like some of the things I hear,' continues God, getting madder all the time, 'there are some things that are eternal and unchangeable . . .' 'Sure, sure,' says Sondorf impatiently, 'that's what I want to talk to you about. Now—as man to man . . .' 'As man to man!' thunders the Almighty wrathfully. 'Okay, okay,' says Sondorf, 'as god to god . . .'"

The payoff line gathered up the individual sniggers and chuckles, which had been punctuating the story, into a unanimous roar.

CHAPTER TWO

"In his Aubusson-carpeted private rail car," the *Time* cover-story began, "an old young man of thirty-seven this week paced up and down the swaying carriage, talking most of the time, listening occasionally to tentative suggestions from various members of his personal entourage, and then put an end to all further discussion with his traditional declaration: 'Now this is the way we do it.' Alexander Sondorf, thin embodiment of the American success story, was holding one of his famed conferences-on-the-move while heading East for the première of his latest film, *It Happens All the Time*, starring Gary Cooper and Janet Derringer. In the next carriage a stenographer transcribed memos, instructions, story ideas, casting suggestions, dreaded admonitions and coveted words of praise that he had dictated earlier during a breakfast of black coffee, fruit juice and toast and honey—pots of Karynia honey, 'the honey of the gods,' are specially imported for him from Greece. For Cineczar Sondorf this was just a limbering-up exercise in preparation for a killing 18-hour day as boss of the Seiermann-Hesslan-Sondorf motion picture empire.

"Ostensibly a studio employee, with an annual income last year in salary and bonuses of $1,250,000 plus an undisclosed percentage of S-H-S's total profits, Sondorf is in fact the man who runs the whole show and whose word goes on everything from the color of the lipstick to be used by a female star to the decor of a new S-H-S theater. Only the 97-year-old Henry Kabe, who holds the majority interest in S-H-S, could reverse one of Sondorf's decisions, and Sondorf is married to the aged financier's favorite granddaughter, Susan.

"The one-time Boy Wonder of Hollywood who, at the age of 25, promoted himself from private secretary to studio chief by staging a one-man *putsch* at Hesslan's, has now matured into the movies' most aggressive and controversial trail blazer. He was one of the principal figures in bringing about the wholesale change-over to sound, and then amazed everyone by refusing to go in for photographed stage plays, initiating instead a series of gangster movies (*Enemy of the People, Mr. Bigshot, Gun Rule*), a string of zestful musicals (*Little Girl Lost, Going Places, The Street Paved in Gold*) and a succession of strong dramas of social comment (*The Big Stick, Lynch Law, The Mob, The Grafters, Nobody's Choice,* and *I Am a Jew*—which showed up the persecution of Jewry in Nazi Germany). In addition, he has been responsible for a series of sparkling, 'smart' comedies—with realistic undertones—starring his protégée, Janet Derringer, of which *It Happens All the Time* is the latest example.

"Perhaps starmaker Sondorf's most obviously dramatic achievement was the transmogrification of blonder-than-blonde contract player Derringer into the most poignant light comedienne of our time. When Janet Derringer comes on the screen, she looks like everybody's idea of a blond bombshell; her art lies in playing her roles from the standpoint of being plain. Her momentous achievement is that whereas with some actresses one is induced to forget that they are plain, with her one almost forgets that she is beautiful. She persuades us that inside every beautiful girl there is a plain girl struggling to hide herself. She uses her sex appeal rather in the way that Chaplin uses his physical dexterity, as a last-resort means of retaliation against the bullies of the world—so that when Janet Derringer lays it on, musters her reserves, one is glad for her sake that she has this to fall back on, to see her through. Unlike Jean Harlow, and all the other aggressively erotic sex queens, Janet Derringer is rather apologetic about her power over men. She doesn't, one feels, like to use unfair methods, but forced to it she doesn't protest too much and lets the magic work, rather like a conjuror amazed by his own sleight of hand.

"For the creation of this image, Sondorf is almost entirely responsible. Before he took over her career, Derringer languished for several years as a contract bit-player at Seiermann-International.

"If Sondorf has a great many admirers, he also has his detractors. Says a well-known director who, for obvious reasons, doesn't want his name disclosed: 'Sondorf is the Rin Tin Tin of producers: it isn't that what he actually does is particularly good, what is remarkable is that he can get up on his hind legs and bark with some semblance of al-most-human intelligence.' Says Walter Staupitz, whom Sondorf ousted from Hesslan's in 1924: 'Sondorf is the Judas and the destroyer. Under that exterior of boyish charm lurks a megalomaniac desire for total power. He wants to own everything and run everybody. He is a greater enemy of the art of the movies than Willi Seiermann because Sondorf manages to give the impression of being on the side of culture and art. He is no more in-terested in art than J. P. Morgan was in arithmetic. He has about as much respect for art as Attila, he is what the great American public evidently wants, he is the Diaghilev of the great unwashed.'

"Less virulent, and less biased, critics accuse Sondorf of surrounding himself with sycophants, of being dictatorial and immune to reason. Says one of these: 'He has consid-erable flair, but he is so surrounded by yes-men that all he ever sees and hears are reflections and echoes of himself and of his own ideas. I think that if he heard an idea that had not originated with him, or been inspired by him, he'd think the man was talking Chinese, and fire him on the grounds of not being able to speak English.' In one of his rare interviews, Sondorf had the following to say apropos his dictatorial methods: 'I have a theory about energy. I believe that about 90 per cent of it is wasted on fighting phantoms. Because I have less natural energy than most people, I have to conserve what I've got, and that's why I can't afford the luxury of arguing with people. I tell people what to do because that way I use up less of my energy. I'm not saying this is particularly admirable, I'm saying it's the only way I can operate. To write a truly persuasive line, or to paint a persuasive picture—by which

I mean doing something that persuades people to change their minds, feelings, attitudes about things, about ideas or about the shape and color of a tree—to do this takes ten times more energy than to send a whole army into battle. Because in the latter case you just *tell* them what to do and you don't have to convince them of the rightness of what they're doing. Now I'm somebody who tells people what to do, simply because I haven't enough energy to persuade them, and the way I look on myself is not as an artist or a businessman, or even an administrator—I'm more of a conquistador.'

"To help conquistador Sondorf conserve his valuable energy, he surrounds himself with people who can be relied upon not to argue with him. Studio publicity director, Pete Fenton, is the Court Jester, and he is allowed—and even encouraged—to tell Sondorf the jokes that are going around about him. Sample: 'What were things like at the studio under Seiermann?' 'It was an example of man's inhumanity to man.' 'And under Sondorf?' 'The reverse.'

"Members of the Court include sometime *Life* photographer Jim Kae—whom Sondorf admires for his courage and independence—elderly Mrs. Irene Brown, his confidential secretary, Dr. Edgar Fellowes, one of the movie colony's pioneer psychoanalysts, Frankie Brendano, former grip, whom Sondorf took on as a personal chauffeur and, it is said, bodyguard, and author-playwright Stephen Raille, regarded as Sondorf's right-hand man. Says Raille: 'Alexander Sondorf is the outstanding genius of the mechanized arts. What his critics resent is that, instinctively, he speaks the language of the people. He infuriates all those who feel that art is something for the privileged few, the cognoscenti. He is, of course, a popularizer, a translator, a simplifier. And all those self-appointed guardians of our culture who feel that art is their own private preserve hate him for having introduced art in amounts digestible by the average person to movie-making. To accuse him of having destroyed Staupitz, whom he admires enormously as an artist, is absurd. It was Staupitz's right and privilege to refuse to conform with prevailing conditions in the movie industry, but to suggest that Sondorf was obligated to change the methods and practices of the movie industry in order to accommodate Staupitz is Utopianism gone beserk.'

"Born in the first year of the century, of a Viennese fa-

424

ther and an Austrian-Polish mother, Alexander Sondorf
—his name was Sondorpf in those days but he changed it
because people kept spitting in his eye trying to pronounce it . . ."

A knock on the door made Janet put down the magazine
and slip on a robe. "Yes," she called. "Come in." Stephen
Raille came into the hotel suite, carrying a copy of *Time*.
He came over to her and kissed her lightly on the cheek.

"You've seen *Time*?"

"I'm just reading it," she said.

"Alexander asked me to give you this." He handed her
an envelope, and while she was eagerly tearing it open, he
went across to a table and made himself a drink. The contents of the envelope seemed to upset her, and Stephen
Raille carefully avoided looking at her too closely while she
scanned through two stapled sheets of studio notepaper.

"Anything?" he asked gently, after a while.

"My marching orders," she said, with a slightly wry expression, and began to read from the typewritten sheets:
'From Alexander Sondorf to Miss Derringer . . .' "

"That's real intimate," said Stephen.

" 'I suggest as follows—' " she read out. " 'In press interviews, (1) if you are asked about other actresses, choose to
talk about somebody you like, and be generous in your
comments; (2) if asked about your private life don't refuse
huffily, but use one of the suggested get-outs appended; (3)
play down how much you are earning, without actually
lying or seeming evasive—if necessary point out that actresses only earn these amounts for a few years in their
careers. *At the première:* (1) Don't "pose" excessively for
photographers, but give them enough time to get their pictures; (2) be careful not to cut anyone "unimportant"
—don't worry about leaving Cooper or me standing around
if you want to say hello to someone you know. (People
don't mind about me or Coop being neglected, but they do
mind about Joe Smith who's worked on all your pictures being cold-shouldered.) (3) If you get hemmed in, stay put,
don't brush off *anyone*—let yourself be reluctantly dragged
away by somebody. There'll be people there to do that.
(This holds for the reception and the dinner afterward.)

" 'You have given a great performance, and I expect you'll
get a standing ovation. Be ready for this. Look happy, and
pleased—give Coop a big kiss if you like, give Fred a hug,

but don't make a speech beyond saying thank you.'" Janet put down the typewritten sheets. "And etcetera, etcetera," she added sourly.

"Oh well," said Stephen, "it's good advice."

"He sent no message?" she asked.

"No." He saw the tears come into her eyes.

"Oh come on, baby."

"I'm all right, Stephen. Are you taking me?"

"Alexander asked me if I would. Would you rather . . .?"

"No, no, Stephen, I'm very glad you're taking me . . . I mean, unless it bores *you*."

"Of course not. I'm glad as hell to take you—think of all the envious looks I'm going to get."

"I want to show you something," she said. With little-girlish excitement she ran out of the room and returned some minutes later wearing a full-length white mink. She took up a slinky pose, stroking the fur lovingly.

"It's fabulous."

"It's a present from Alexander—well, from the studio, actually. For being a good girl and making such a lot of lovely money for them." She sighed, and that sad look came over her face again.

"Look, Janet—about Alexander . . ."

"I haven't seen him, alone, for two months."

"He's been awfully busy," said Stephen evasively.

"He *always* was busy, but he used to . . . What have I done wrong? I feel I must have disappointed him in some way."

"No, he's thrilled by your success."

"Is there another girl?"

"I don't think so."

"Then what?"

"I don't know, Janet. Listen. I have a theory about Alexander. Doing what he's doing, he's got to believe that everything is possible. If he should ever find out that some things aren't possible, he'd be finished. If he should ever find out that maybe it can't be done for a man to fly like a bird, he'd—fall."

"But what have I done?" she asked, not understanding.

"I don't think it's anything you've done. It's that—I think —in the end everything disappoints him a little, and then, because he can't live with that disappointment, he has to find

426

something else to give him the sensation of flying, to prove to himself that everything *is* possible."

All the time she was getting ready she cried softly to herself. Then, when she was dressed and waiting for Stephen to return to pick her up, she went to the phone, and asked that the roses in her room should be changed to gladioli, and would they please arrange for the masseuse to come at noon tomorrow, and also book a call to L.A. for twelve-thirty, and have somebody come up to turn down the central heating in the living room and have a log fire made there instead because she preferred it. Putting down the phone, she felt a lot better, and then composing herself settled down, with a serious face, to memorize her instructions for the evening.

She saw very little of Alexander in the ensuing months; when her contract came up for renewal, she took Lewis Sholt's advice and did not sign up again. There were plenty of offers from other companies all the time now, and they were offering her much more money, and much better terms—top billing, director approval, co-star approval, script approval. Lewis Sholt had got a clause in her contract whereby she could insist on script changes, and nominate a writer of her choice to make them, if the part she was asked to play did not in some respect fit in with the established public image of Janet Derringer. She was sometimes offered stories that were clearly unsuitable for her and then Lewis Sholt would return the script, saying that it wasn't really a Janet Derringer part, and that Janet Derringer didn't talk that way and didn't behave that way.

From time to time she saw Alexander, at premières, at parties, at industry functions, and in public he always made a fuss over her, and treated her with great fondness, but she was never alone with him for more than a few minutes and the reason why things had ended between them was not brought up by either of them though sometimes she had the impression he was looking at her with a smiling, dispassionate tenderness that was meant as a sort of apology for the way things had turned out. She thought he was getting to look even thinner and more drawn—as if everything in him was being stretched to its utmost limits—and the gray in his hair was becoming more abundant, making his eyes look so dark and deep, and they looked so removed from whatever was going on. After his divorce from Susan, she saw him with different girls and she had the feeling that though they were with him, for an evening or a night, he was not really with them. With America's entry into the war, she saw no more of him for several years. In 1941 he had left Hollywood, temporarily relinquishing his job, to take charge of making propaganda films—it was said that Roosevelt had personally asked him to do this job, and he could not refuse such a request.

The only time she heard from him was in 1944, when he wrote to her from Italy about Jim Kae's death: "My dear Janet, By now you will have heard about Jim Kae, but I thought I should write to you because I know he was a very old and good friend of yours, as well as mine. You probably know that I always admired him enormously, not only as a photographer—and he was a very fine photographer—but because he seemed to me such a completely self-contained man. He had such resources within himself, and he'd got to that enviable stage of not being dependent on other people for his own happiness—well, not too much anyway. He had a whole lot of qualities that I would have given anything to have—such as not needing people's approval or the acclaim of the world. Though he was getting both, they weren't things he *needed*. People never understood his preoccupation, as a photographer (and a person), with 'sordid' subjects. They said he always had to get a downbeat angle on everything, but that was because, as he once said to me, 'whole' people didn't interest him much—they had so little occasion for valor: what moved him was the struggle of the broken to hold together—in *that* he saw valor, even when they failed. It was always this evidence of valor that he was looking for among the drunks and the deadbeats and the drug addicts and the whores and the wounded and the dying that he photographed so magnificently and with such compassion. I saw him die. It was a very small action, a very minor side show: a dozen men assigned to take a narrow little bridge across a gorge before the Germans could blow it up. It probably wasn't an important bridge for us to have because the gorge wasn't very deep and the bridge was very narrow, and at the most having the bridge might have saved a little time. But they wanted it taken before the Germans could blow it, and maybe they gave us this little bit of action so we'd have something to film to keep us happy and not get in their way too much— I don't know about that. Jim Kae wasn't working with me, but he chose to string along. What happened was quite ridiculous, and in a movie I wouldn't have allowed it, because I always had a down on Errol Flynn heroics in movies. The Germans on the other side hadn't placed their dynamite when we got there: they were trying to pin us down with rifle fire while one of their men crawled along the bridge to plant the dynamite. He was just a kid— we could see that—and absolutely scared stiff. Jim Kae saw it, and he wanted the picture—he wanted this picture of the shit-scared German soldier trying to place the dynamite, and he crawled forward on his belly, ahead of our boys, right on to the bridge, and this German soldier, seeing this man crawling up to him not with a gun but with a camera, evidently was so thrown and got so panicky he just got all confused, and instead of running the fuse back he must have just lit it there and then because quite abruptly and unexpectedly the whole bridge went up with Jim Kae and the German boy. I remember I once ordered a battle scene in one of our early Westerns to be reshot because I felt one of the characters had died unnecessarily and pointlessly—that's how I felt about Jim Kae.

"I've not been too well and I think I'm soon going to be invalided out. One of my plans, when I get back, is to make a picture based on Jim Kae's life, and my hope is that you will be in it. I want Stephen Raille to write it and maybe John Huston to direct—they both knew Jim Kae and, I think, loved him the way I did. It won't be a very big part for you, but you're so big now—and I'm really very happy about that—that it won't hurt you to play a little part, and I would like all his old friends to be associated, in some way, with the picture.

"I hope you are well and that everything goes all right for you. Look after yourself—you are one of the rare and precious ones that we must cherish. Alexander."

PART TWO

CHAPTER THREE

In the early spring and summer of 1947 Hollywood was in a state of indignant apprehension about the forthcoming Un-American Activities Committee's probe into allegations of Communist infiltration into the motion-picture industry. Nineteen of the people called to testify before the Committee had announced that, as a matter of principle, they would refuse to answer questions about their political affiliations—they had been dubbed the Unfriendly Nineteen, and the name stuck. Rumors were widespread that these nineteen, because of their stand, would be banished from working within the industry. J. Parnell Thomas, chairman of the House Un-American Activities Committee, announced that the producers had agreed to the implementation of a political blacklist, but this was vehemently denied by Eric Johnston, the industry spokesman. "Hollywood is weary," announced the Association of Motion Picture Producers, "of being the national whipping-boy for Congressional committees." Prominent stars went on record in opposing the Committee. Frederic March said: "Who do you think they're really after—who's next? Is it your minister who will be told what he can say in his pulpit—is it your children's schoolteacher who will be told what she can say in the classroom? Is it your children themselves? Is it you who will have to look around nervously before you can say what is on your minds?" Frank Sinatra said: "Once they get the movies throttled, how long will it be before the committee goes to work on freedom of the air? If you make a pitch on a nationwide radio network for a square deal for the underdog, will they call you a Commie?" Opposition to the Committee's hearings came from a group that called itself the Committee for the First Amendment, which had the support of many prominent Hollywood figures including Lauren Bacall, Humphrey Bogart, Geraldine Brooks, Phillip Dunne, Ira Gershwin, Sterling Hayden, John Huston, Gene Kelly, Danny Kaye, Marsha Hunt, Shepherd Strudwick, Jane Wyatt, William Wyler, Henry Fonda, Paulette Goddard, Ava Gardner, Janet Derringer, Benny Goodman, Stephen Raille, Van Heflin, John Houseman, Myrna Loy, Burgess Meredith, Gregory Peck, Cornel Wilde, Billy Wilder.

On the other side, members of the Motion Picture Alliance for the Preservation of American Ideals, a militantly anti-Communist, pro-free-enterprise group, vigorously supported the investigation, and circulated producers with *A Screen Guide for Americans,* which contained the following do's and don'ts: "(1) Don't smear the free enterprise system. (2) Don't deify the 'common man.' (3) Don't glorify the collective. (4) Don't glorify failure. (5) Don't smear success. (6) Don't smear industrialists. (7) It is the *moral* —not just political, but *moral*—duty of every decent man in the motion picture industry to throw in the ash can where it belongs every story that smears industrialists as such." Among the "friendly witnesses" who were prepared to co-operate fully with the Committee and approved of the hearings were Willi Seiermann, Howard Rushmore, Gary Cooper, George Murphy, Robert Taylor, Robert Montgomery, Leo McCarey, Walt Disney, and Jack Warner. The question posed by *Life* magazine—"Is it un-American to ask a man if he is a Communist or is it un-American to refuse to answer?"—was being passionately debated throughout the country.

As one of the organizers of the Committee for the First Amendment, Stephen Raille had sought Alexander's support for declarations condemning the hearings, as being contrary to the basic principles of American democracy, and had asked him to join the delegation that was to present a petition for redress of grievances to the Clerk of the House of Representatives. They had many talks about his. So far Alexander had refused to commit himself to any specific action. As the date of the hearings, October 27th, drew closer, Stephen was doing his utmost to convince Alexander of the need for solidarity among those who thought as they did. Alexander was still hedging. "Stephen," he said, "I think

431

maybe your trip to Washington is tactically a mistake, and I am sure it would be tactically a mistake for me, as a studio head, to become publicly identified with any particular group. You don't know the party ties of all your supporters, and it only needs to emerge that some of them *are* Communists for your stand to become suspect as far as the public is concerned. These boys in Washington are pretty smart, and they are going to outsmart you if you are not very careful."

"Is it true that there's a black list?" Stephen wanted to know. "Is it true that the Nineteen are not going to be employed?"

"You know as well as I do," said Alexander, "that the institution of a political black list constitutes conspiracy and is illegal."

"But is there one?"

"I haven't agreed to any black list."

"Has it been mooted?"

"Stephen, you mustn't press me. All I can tell you is that I have not agreed to any black list."

Alexander would say no more than that. Since his return to the studio he had been far more cautious than in the old days: a lot of people were saying that the fire in his belly had turned to middle-aged acidity, that a lot of the drive had gone out of him, that he was far readier now to compromise and to make concessions to New York. To some extent this was a matter of necessity, his supporters pointed out. With the death of Henry Kabe, and Stafford Deems's appointment as President of Seiermann-Hesslan-Sondorf, Alexander could no longer exercise the supreme control he had once enjoyed. Moreover, Willi Seiermann had taken advantage of Alexander's absence during the war to make his way back, and was now—jointly with Alexander—in charge of running the studio. Alexander's supporters pointed out that he was obliged to play things very carefully, but that once he had firmly re-established himself it would be discovered that he was as adventurous and as thrusting as ever. Others said that when it came to playing politics Willi Seiermann and Stafford Deems could outsmart him every time, and that Alexander's creative energies had been drained by the need to involve himself in complex company intrigues that were not really to his taste. There were still others who maintained that his special talents had been peculiarly suited to the circumstances of the late twenties and the thirties, and that his heyday was past, that he was tired out and that his health, never very good, had finally broken. The war, when he had had to take orders instead of giving them, had finally broken him, they said.

Stephen Raille did not believe any of this. He had been with Alexander all through the war and knew how restless and unhappy he had been most of the time, but he also knew that the flow of ideas had not come to a stop, that he had returned to Hollywood bursting with projects, and some of his ideas had a new maturity. He was no longer thinking in terms of controlling the entire output of the studio, but instead wanted to personally supervise the making of a carefully selected number of major pictures with the best talent available. He had realized that with television growing in importance, the routine movie would soon be obsolete and that the public would only pay to see major productions. His most cherished project, which he had so far not managed to get off the ground, was a big film about the life of Jim Kae for which Stephen had written the script. It was provisionally called *The Four Corners of the Earth*, and took in both World Wars. But the reaction of the money men was that an epic about a photographer who never fired a shot in two World Wars, and one or two lesser ones, was not going to bring anyone into cinemas. Now if they would let Jim Kae put away his cameras now and then and pick up a rifle, it might be different, and if he died trying to take that bridge singlehanded, rather than trying to get a picture of a scared German, it might be box office.

The arrival in the hearing room of the Hollywood delegation of the Committee for the First Amendment had been timed to coincide with the appearance before the House Un-American Activities Committee of the industry's spokesman, Eric Johnston. This was on Monday, October 27th. As they took their places in the hearing room, to the accompaniment of photographers' flashes and the whir of newsreel cameras, Chairman J. Parnell Thomas called to the stand, not Johnston, but John Howard Lawson, the most belligerently unfriendly of the Unfriendly Nineteen. In his testimony Lawson turned out to be not merely unfriendly, but aggressively impertinent and bellicose. "It is absolutely beyond the power of this Committee," he declared, "to inquire into my association in any organization. . . . It is unfortunate and tragic that I have to teach this Committee the basic principles of American life." The Hollywood delegation was bitterly dismayed. Their arrival, it was pointed out to them, would be interpreted throughout the country as support for Lawson. Before their departure, William Wyler, one of the organizers, had carefully briefed them, telling them to stay away from "Unfriendly" witnesses: they were going there to attack the House Un-American Activities Committee, not to defend any Communists. Now in their first public act they had already managed to give the contrary impression and had been totally outsmarted by Parnell Thomas. At a press conference, later that day, they were further demoralized by questions about reports in a Washington paper that one of their group was a Communist. The following day Stephen Raille received a subpoena to testify before the Committee, and the rest of the delegation was forced to withdraw in confusion and disillusionment.

Alexander had also come to Washington, but he had been careful to avoid publicity and had stayed away from the hearing room on the first day, anticipating some trick on the part of Parnell Thomas to discredit the Hollywood delegation. On the Wednesday morning, when Stephen Raille was called upon to testify, Alexander took his place in the hearing room. Stephen answered all the initial questions about his place of birth, education, early writing career, war service, with grave courtesy. There was something so quietly distinguished in his manner and bearing that the young Committee counsel almost unwittingly addressed him with the deference due to age and accomplishment.

"In the early days of your career, sir," said counsel, "you were, I believe, one of a group of writers sometimes referred to as the muckrakers?"

"That's right," said Stephen, smiling very faintly. "But I should explain that this was an honorable term. We exposed corruption."

"So-called corruption. In the realm of business?"

"Yes. But also in civic affairs."

"Would you agree that most of these 'honorable' muckrakers held extreme left-wing views?"

"We were against monopolies, trusts, civic corruption, the exploitation of public utilities, gangsterism in public affairs, the rigging of elections, and other abuses of power. I don't know if you would describe that as representing an extreme left-wing point of view."

"Is it not a fact that, in their private beliefs, most of these men subscribed to an ideology of the extreme left?"

"Well, in those days, we didn't investigate people's private beliefs."

"Could you answer the question, please?"

"Some of the articles I wrote were written at the behest of William Randolph Hearst and published in his newspapers. Does that answer your question?" This caused some laughter in the hearing room, and the chairman banged his gavel and called for silence.

Counsel seemed a little put out—he was a very young man, fresh out of Harvard law school, and he covered his momentary confusion by consulting some notes. "Mr. Raille," he said, "could we now deal with your career in Hollywood? Will you tell the Committee of the circumstances in which you came to work in the motion-picture industry?" Stephen told briefly how he had come to Hollywood at the invitation of Alexander Sondorf, after writing an article about him, and how he had decided to stay on, first as a script consultant, and later as a writer for the screen.

"Mr. Raille, the article you wrote about Alexander Sondorf, which resulted in the invitation to Hollywood, was highly critical of him, wasn't it?"

"Yes."

"Will you tell the Committee how you came to change your mind about Sondorf sufficiently to feel able soon afterward to accept his offer of employment?" Stephen appeared to hesitate; he did not look toward Alexander.

"I think the only way I can answer your question, sir, is to point out that a writer cannot always be in complete accord with the people who present his work."

"Are you telling the Committee that all the time you were working for Alexander Sondorf you were opposed to his ideas and beliefs?"

"That's not what I said."

"Then, please, clarify."

"You are asking me, sir, to explain in a few words a relationship that has covered a period of about twenty years. I don't think I can do that in a few words."

"Will you try?"

"I'd rather not, if you don't mind."

"Well, I won't press you on this point at this stage."

"Thank you."

"I hope you won't find my other questions so difficult to answer."

"I will do my best to answer them."

"In 1929, when I believe you were working as script consultant for Alexander Sondorf at Seiermann-International, were you responsible for bringing to the studio, or for recommending the employment of, a man called Rex Norbert?"

"I cannot recall the exact circumstances in which Rex Norbert came to work at the studio."

"Were you responsible, in 1931, when you were functioning as Story Editor at Seiermann-Hesslan-Sondorf . . ."

"If I may correct you . . ."

"Yes."

"I was never Story Editor. I was a screenwriter."

"You were rather more than that, weren't you?"

"I don't think that being a writer is a lesser thing than being an executive."

"I don't want to argue with you about the comparative status of the writer and the executive, Mr. Raille. The point is your position, in relationship to Sondorf, was different from that of an ordinary screenwriter. He relied on you for advice, did he not, on a whole range of studio matters that the ordinary screenwriter would not have been called upon to advise on?"

"I was consulted, officially, on matters not relating to my own work."

"All right. Were you consulted, in 1931, about the engagement of a writer called Greg Tompkins?"

"I may have been."

"Could you try and be more specific?"

"That is very difficult. You are asking me about things that happened a long time ago."

"Did Greg Tompkins subsequently work on a great many pictures made at S-H-S?"

"He worked on quite a few."

"You are acquainted with Greg Tompkins, are you not?"

"May I advise with counsel, please?"

"Certainly."

For a few seconds Stephen consulted in low whispers with his lawyers, then he turned to face the Committee. He said, "I am prepared to answer all questions relating to myself and to my own activities, but I do not feel that I have the right to talk about other people with whom I may or may not have been acquainted and whose lives and livelihood may be affected by being named at this hearing."

"I fail to see, Mr. Raille, how an admission on your part that you are acquainted with Greg Tompkins can in any way have the effect you suggest. I repeat the question. Are you acquainted with Greg Tompkins?"

"In that case I must decline to answer that question on the grounds that it violates my rights under the First and Fifth Amendments and may tend to incriminate me."

"Are you acquainted with Gordon Wolschman?"

"I must decline to answer that question on the grounds just stated."

"Are you acquainted with Harriet Legrand?"

"Decline."

"According to a letterhead dated October 24th, 1945, you were a sponsor of the Spanish Refugee Appeal which was a joint project of the Joint Anti-Fascist Refugee Committee. . . . Is that so?"

"Decline."

"The *Daily Worker* contains a news item, January 3rd, 1946, on page 4, about the death of Theodore Dreiser—he was referred to as 'a member in good standing with the Communist party.' Among those listed as paying tribute to Theodore Dreiser was Stephen Raille. Did you know that Dreiser was a member of the Communist party?"

"I decline to answer on the grounds that it violates my rights under the First and Fifth Amendments and may tend to incriminate me."

"Were you personally acquainted with Theodore Dreiser?"

"Decline to answer on the grounds already stated."

"Did you attend Dreiser's funeral?"

"Decline to answer on the grounds already stated."

At this point, a member of the Committee, Congressman Kaythly, interjected: "Mr. Raille, what impression do you think you are going to leave, not only with members of this Committee, but with the American people, in declining to answer practically every question put to you by counsel?"

"Congressman, you are as well aware as I am," said Stephen, "that it is my right under the Constitution to decline to answer these questions on the grounds stated, and you are also aware that once I have answered *any* questions about a particular individual, or group, however innocuous those initial questions may be, I forfeit my right to subsequently decline to answer other questions about them. I am extremely reluctant to resort to the First and Fifth Amendments in declining to answer questions, and I would not do so if the Committee would undertake to confine itself to questioning me about my own activities and beliefs."

"I'm afraid, sir," said Congressman Kaythly, "that this Committee cannot strike bargains with witnesses in the matter of what it will or will not ask them."

"In that case, Congressman," said Stephen, "I must exercise my rights under the Constitution."

"I would like to put a question to the witness," another member of the Committee, Congressman S. R. Tyler said. "There's been a lot of hedging and hiding behind alleged Constitutional rights on your part. I'm going to ask you a blunt question, sir, because the American people are entitled to know the truth. Are you, or have you ever been, a member of the Communist party?"

"I am not a member of the Communist party," said Stephen, "and I want to say that I am opposed to many of the avowed objectives of the Soviet Government, and anyone familiar with my work will know that this is so. At the same time, I would like to add that there are areas in which the declared intentions, as distinct from the actual actions, of communism have coincided with my own beliefs. After all we have just fought a war in alliance with the Soviets against Nazism."

The young counsel was looking very pink and pleased with himself as he came close to Stephen and declared with thinly suppressed triumph: "I am sure the Committee is grateful for that explanatory statement. However, what you have said is not in accordance with information in the possession of this Committee. This Committee is in possession of information that, in 1938, you held membership card No. 27331 of the Communist party, and that you were assigned to Club 2 of the northwest section of the Communist party in Los Angeles. Did you have a Communist party card assigned to you in 1938?"

This statement produced gasps and murmurs from the people in the hearing room, and the chairman had to bang his gavel and call for silence and declare that if there were any more interruptions the hearing room would be cleared. Stephen seemed to hesitate for a very long time before answering. Then he said flatly: "I decline to answer on the grounds that it violates my rights under the First and Fifth Amendments and may tend to incriminate me."

Before the hearing adjourned for lunch, Alexander was able to get a message to Stephen, through one of his lawyers, suggesting they meet before the hearing was resumed. He suggested the apartment of a mutual friend because it would be better if the press did not learn of this meeting. When they were alone, Alexander said, "Stephen, you've got to open with the Committee."

"You know what that means, Alexander. You know what they're after. They want to show that I used my influence to induce you to make 'subversive' pictures."

"I think you should answer their questions about me. I know you're in the clear, and I know you're trying to protect others. I think the way to play this is to give them so much information about one area that they want to know about—your professional relationship with me—that they will not have the time, or the inclination, to get around to anything else. Don't worry about the possible effect on me. It can't hurt me."

"You're sure of that, Alexander?"

"I'm sure."

When the hearing was resumed after lunch Congressman Swanrigg said: "I have received a message requesting that the witness might be allowed to make an explanatory statement about his testimony this morning. Since the purpose of this hearing is to discover the true extent of Communist infiltration into the motion picture industry, and since it is our desire to explore every avenue in order to arrive at an understanding of the extent of this menace, I think the witness should be given three minutes to make his statement. But I must warn the witness that he will not be allowed to make tendentious propaganda statements, and that he must confine himself to statements of facts. Go ahead, Mr. Raille, and be as brief as possible.'

"Thank you, Congressman," said Stephen. "I am grateful for this opportunity. I would like to say, first, that my un-

439

willingness to answer certain questions this morning was due entirely to my reluctance to involve people unable to defend themselves. Whatever the conclusions of this Committee, or the American people, about my own activities, I do not want innocent people to be implicated simply because I have said that I knew them, or was associated with them in certain projects."

"Mr. Raille," Congressman Swanrigg interrupted, "I have warned you against making propaganda statements."

"So you have, Congressman. So you have," retorted Stephen in his quiet, deliberate manner, rather like a lecturer dealing with a somewhat noisy student. "May I continue?"

"Please confine yourself to factual statements."

"I think what is happening here at these hearings is that you are giving people the choice of being informers—not even *informed* informers, but informers relying largely on hearsay and gossip such as would be admitted in no court of law—or of being in contempt of this Committee and going to jail. I don't think that people should be presented with such an alternative. I don't think that is American justice as I know it . . ."

"You are making a propaganda speech," shouted Congressman Swanrigg. "I have warned you . . . I will not permit these hearings to be used as a platform for subversive propaganda."

"May I continue, sir?" insisted Stephen firmly. "The Congressman is obviously better at shouting than I am, and I shall not attempt to shout you down, sir. You have the floor, sir, if you want it . . ."

"Proceed, Mr. Raille. Facts, please. Facts."

"Thank you, Congressman. You will not intimidate me, sir. If I am not allowed to make my statement then I want the American people to know that I have not been allowed to make it. If the Congressman will refrain from shouting, I shall continue. As far as my own political affiliations are concerned, they are as follows. I was a member of the Communist party from 1938 until 1941, when I withdrew from the party . . ." While murmurings and gasps spread through the hearing room, and the chairman pounded his gavel, Stephen looked directly at Alexander. Alexander returned the look, but his face was expressionless. When the hearing had been brought to order, Stephen continued: "I make

440

no excuses for myself, but I wish to point out that many of us who were Communists in the thirties were motivated by a certain idealism, by a sense of common purpose in the opposition to Fascism and Nazism; that we went through what I can only call a state of political infatuation, and that we were cured of this, later, by the actions of the Soviet Government. Anyone who has read my books will be able to find in them expressions both of the initial idealism and hopefulness, and also of the subsequent disillusionment. I think this process of seeking solutions, of considering different ones, and of discarding them when they are found to be false, is an honorable process, and a necessary process in a democracy. Nothing that I did while I was a member of the Communist party was subversive, and I have no knowledge of anyone else doing anything that might be considered subversive . . ."

Counsel interrupted Stephen at this point: "I think you have been given a great deal of leeway in making your statement. I would now like to put some questions to you."

"Very well."

"In the period between 1938 and 1941, when you have admitted to having been a member of the Communist party, you wrote a great many films?"

"Yes."

"You also, officially or unofficially, enjoyed a position of considerable influence in relation to Alexander Sondorf who was then virtually in complete control of the Seiermann-Hesslan-Sondorf studio, and you were in the position of being able to recommend the employment of writers and actors, many of whom, according to our information, were also members of the Communist party. Some of those films, made by Sondorf, were highly critical of American institutions and the American way of life."

"I think one must distinguish between films that are critical of some aspects of American society and pro-Communist films. I don't think the two can be equated. I never wrote a Communist film, or a Communist book. I do not believe that art can ever be in the service of any ideology."

"At this period, you were attending meetings of Communist cells?"

"Yes."

"Was your work discussed?"

"Yes."

"Were efforts made to influence your work?"

"There were sometimes discussions about the sort of issues that ought to be explored in movies."

"What sort of issues, Mr. Raille?"

"It was felt there should be more stories about the working man, about factories and strikes, about his opposition to capitalism."

"As a result of these discussions, what actions did you take?"

"I took no *actions*. As I've said, I was, and am, opposed to art serving ideology. One of the reasons I eventually severed my connections with the party was because we could not see eye to eye on this."

"But you remained in the party between 1938 and 1941? How come they tolerated someone who was so unhelpful and unco-operative?"

"They probably thought I was a good catch, and were prepared to put up with my recalcitrance."

"I see. Tell me, your relationship with Mr. Sondorf—would you say it was close?"

"Yes."

"Very close?"

"Yes."

"You were in fact what one might term his confidant and principal aide. Yes?"

"We were close friends."

"Intimate friends?"

"If you like."

"Did Sondorf know you were a member of the Communist party and were secretly attending meetings of party cells at which your work for him was the subject of discussion?"

"No, he did not."

"Despite the closeness, the intimacy, of your relationship you kept this from him? If your Communist party activities were really as innocuous as you suggest, no more than literary discussion groups resulting in no specific action, why did you choose to keep this aspect of your life secret from him? It must have involved a considerable amount of subterfuge on your part."

For the first time during the hearing, Stephen seemed put out, the many delicate and pronounced lines of his face seemed to become rearranged in an unnatural way, as if a very clearly drawn map had been suddenly crumpled up. He shot a quick glance at Alexander, then looked down in consternation at his folded hands. "I don't know how to answer that question," he admitted eventually.

"Come now, Mr. Raille," said counsel with mounting triumph in his voice. "You have been commendably frank with us this afternoon. It's not a difficult question. I will re-phrase it. Why, if you were not serving the aims of international communism, and doing useful work for the movement, would you deceive someone as close to you as Sondorf?"

"You are asking me to explain a relationship—feelings, emotions . . ." His voice tailed off.

"That should not be beyond the capability of an experienced author."

"The only honest answer that I can give you is that I don't know. I *have* thought about it, but . . . I don't know."

"Supposing we weren't considering you, but a character in one of your books. As an author, what motivation would you consider might induce someone to behave as you did —other than the obvious motivation that he was a tool of the Communist conspiracy, that this fact overrode all other considerations, even those of personal loyalty to a friend, and that he had to keep his party involvement secret for the very simple reason that if it became known he would be removed from the position of power that he enjoyed, and therefore his great usefulness to the party would come to an end?"

"That would be the motivation in a rather cheap book, if I may say so."

"Can you offer this Committee a better one, a more feasible one?"

"Well . . ." He hesitated for a long time. "It probably had to do with the kind of man Sondorf was."

"Yes? What kind of man?"

"Well, you know, he ran pretty well everything . . ."

"Yes?"

"I don't think this is something you will understand easily, because nowadays it's not the same, and there are agreements covering pretty well all aspects of picturemaking and nowadays it's much more of a joint project, and a man like Sondorf, today, has to be something of a negotiator, a politician, someone who brings people together . . . but in

443

those days he was pretty much of a king, with absolute power . . ."

"I don't quite follow. Are you trying to tell the Committee that you disapproved of him having this amount of power, or what?"

"I didn't exactly disapprove—that's how it was. I accepted that."

"Then what are you trying to say?"

"Let me put it this way. A man has got to a position of great power, and he uses some of that power well— better than anyone else you can think of. The fact that he also uses some of that power badly, and that you don't believe any one man should have this amount of power over people, creates in you certain tensions, conflicts. On the one hand you like the man, admire him, on the other hand, I guess you sort of resent the fact that he has the final say on everything, that you can express yourself only through him and by means of obtaining and keeping his approval. I don't know if that makes any sense to you."

"Not very much, I must admit."

"Well . . ." Stephen closed his eyes for several moments as if overwhelmed by weariness. "Well—these are very personal and painful things that you have somehow maneuvered me into talking about. If you work with a man like Sondorf for a long time, as I did, very closely, very intimately, so that sometimes you can't be sure if a particular thought originated with him or with you—maybe he started it and you finished it—but he has the final say, he has the right of selecting and discarding . . . And add to that the fact that he regards your approval as valuable, that he regards you as a friend, whose approval is necessary to *him* —and yet he has the final say. Well, what happens is that there come moments when you almost lose the sense of having a separate identity, when—after working like this, you must remember, for nine or ten years—you lose something that is very precious to you: the geographical outline of your own personality. You feel absorbed, and that precious frontier-line seems to have become very thin and almost indefinable. I think, maybe, that's when you start to do things in secret."

"I find it difficult to see the relevance of what you are saying. Are you saying that it was the tyranny of Sondorf that forced you to embrace communism?"

444

"No, sir. I don't think it was a tyranny that operated in Hollywood in the twenties and thirties. Or, if it was, it was the tyranny of willful children suddenly given power. What I am saying is that a man like Sondorf . . . I think the very thing he needed from others is the very thing that people cannot give for too long, even if there's a swimming pool and a big salary to go with it."

"I think," said Congressman Swanrigg, "that you have hit upon a most ingenious—and to my mind specious—explanation of your Communist activities. Let us get back to the facts. While you were a member of the Communist cell in Hollywood, did you know a man called Wolschman."

"As I made clear before, Congressman, I refuse to answer that on the grounds stated."

Immediately after the conclusion of Stephen Raille's testimony, the Committee unanimously decided that he was guilty of contempt of Congress in refusing to answer the questions put to him. Alexander flew back to Hollywood. He had a series of important meetings lined up and though he was feeling exhausted, and would have liked to rest for a few days, he knew he could not afford to be away too long from the studio. In his absence, Willi Seiermann would take the decisions. His long years in the wilderness had mellowed Willi, made him diplomatic, and he liked to play the role of the elder statesman—who did not interfere too much in the day-by-day running of the studio, but who, when pressed, would give the company the benefit of his long experience and wisdom. His relationship with Alexander was not close any longer, but he showed no rancor toward him, and never alluded to the circumstances in which Alexander had deposed him. He had been around in the business so long that this, in itself, had earned for Willi a certain respect, and it was fashionable nowadays to attribute to him a great flair for showmanship and an old-timer's understanding of the business. With all major decisions having to be approved by the triumvirate of Willi, Stafford Deems and himself, Alexander could only proceed by getting either Willi's or Deems's support. On the whole it was easier to get Willi's support than Deems's, and this had increasingly forced Alexander into an alliance of expedience with Willi.

"What do you propose about Stephen Raille?" Willi asked

445

him as soon as Alexander was back. Willi no longer attempted to impose his ideas by means of bullying or browbeating; he knew that his strength lay in the ever-present possibility that he might ally himself with Deems against Alexander.

"I don't know, Willi," said Alexander. "What do *you* suggest?" Alexander knew that he must not take an attitude that was demonstrably untenable.

"In my opinion," said Willi, "we have to get rid of him."

"Uhu."

"You don't agree, Alexander?"

"That may not be the best way of playing it, Willi."

"What alternative do you propose?"

"What does Deems think?"

"Deems thinks, and I agree with him, that we can't afford to be picketed. The way things are, Alexander, nobody wants to put money into a film that is going to be picketed. You can't blame them."

"Stephen Raille hasn't been convicted of anything criminal," said Alexander.

"That's true," said Willi, "but he didn't make exactly a good impression before the Committee."

"You want to operate a black list?"

"I don't say we operate a black list. What I say is we got to protect ourselves, our interests. Say the theaters won't play a film with his name on it. If that's even a possibility, we're not going to get the money. Nobody is going to put up a couple of million for a picture that maybe isn't showable. Who wants to take an *extra* risk? My advice to you, Alexander, is—get rid of him."

"That means we have to get rid of all the others who've been named? And all the ones that maybe are going to be named—where do you stop?"

"I know it's hard, Alexander. I don't say it isn't hard. You tell me what is the alternative. I'm willing to listen."

"I don't know," said Alexander. "But maybe if we all make a stand, if we refuse to let ourselves be pushed around by the Committee . . ."

"All right, fine. But are you sure you're going to get Mayer and Warner and Zanuck and Hughes and all the others to agree to that? Say they don't agree. Their films get shown, and ours don't. Can we afford that? How do we justify that to the shareholders?"

"I know it's a problem, Willi. Let me think about it."

After Willi had left, Alexander made a call to Lewis Sholt. "Alexander, doll," said Lewis, "it's lovely to hear your voice. I been meaning to call you."

"I have to have a decision about Janet Derringer," said Alexander.

"That's what I been meaning to call you about," said Lewis. "It's been on my conscience I didn't call you sooner, but I been giving the matter a lot of thought. Alexander, I'll be frank with you . . ."

"Yes, Lewis?"

"Alexander, I get three offers every week for Janet."

"I'm sure you do."

"Frankly, if I thought it was really important for you, I would say to her—look, it's not such a great part, and to play in a Stephen Raille picture is a risk, but I want you to do it out of friendship. Because Alexander Sondorf is an old friend—of yours and mine—so you should do it. But there are two pictures that Zanuck wants her for, Selznick has been on to me all week—he wants her. I got an offer for her from Wyler, who's got a fabulous subject. Let me put it to you like this, Alexander: you really need her? Are you going to get that picture off the ground—we all loved Jim Kae, but does the paying public want to see a war film about a photographer?"

"She doesn't want to do it?" Alexander asked.

"Alexander, frankly, I haven't even asked her. I know she'd do anything for you. But is it fair to ask her? Is it fair to tie her up with a picture that maybe won't get off the ground?"

"The picture will be made," said Alexander.

"All right, Alexander. Supposing it gets made. With Garfield as Jim Kae? It'll be his picture. What is there in it for Janet? It's the man's picture."

"It's a nice part," said Alexander.

"Sure it's a nice part. But *anybody* could play it. You *need* Janet Derringer for that part? Let me put it to you like this. I'm not saying 'No' to you, I'm saying let us off the hook, don't ask for her, as a favor to me—and to her—don't ask for her. Because if *you* ask she'll feel obliged to do it and, frankly, it can't do her àny good."

"O.K., Lewis."

"I hope you don't hold it against me, Alexander."

447

"Naturally not. You've got to think of your client's interests."

"If you see her, Alexander, as a favor to me—don't mention it to her. She'd be mad at me if she thought I'd turned you down."

"Sure, Lewis, sure."

"You going to be at Palm Springs this weekend?"

"Maybe."

"Well, maybe I see you there. And, Alexander, I appreciate what you're doing."

"Sure, Lewis, sure."

"Alexander," said Pete Fenton as they made their way to the executive dining room, "you hear the new story they're telling about you?"

"No, what's that?"

"It's a great story, it'll kill you."

"Yes?"

"Well, there's all these sycophants—who all want to prove they're the most loyal, see? So, finally, there's this guy who wants to prove that whatever anybody else may say he's more loyal and devoted than anyone. 'Mr. Sondorf,' he says, 'I don't want you to think I'm a yes-man or anything, but I just wanted you to know that when I die I want to be cremated, Mr. Sondorf, and I want my ashes sprinkled on your driveway, so your car won't skid.'" Pete Fenton bellowed with laughter.

"That's a very old story, Pete," said Alexander.

"You don't think it's funny?" Pete Fenton seemed hurt.

"I don't think it's funny, Pete. In fact, I think your jokes have been getting less and less funny lately."

"I always thought you thought my jokes were funny," said Pete Fenton, sulkily.

"Well, I don't, Pete. I don't think that joke is funny at all."

"I thought it was a great story," said Pete Fenton, very much put out.

"It was," said Alexander. "When you first told it ten years ago."

"Well, if you don't think that my jokes are funny," said Pete Fenton, very much aggrieved.

"Maybe," said Alexander consolingly, putting his hand

448

on Pete Fenton's shoulders, "it's just that some jokes don't last as well as others."

He could not get out of his mind the sight of that studio messenger who had been thrown from his motorcycle and had broken his neck—Alexander had seen him lying there, just inside the studio gates, so obviously dead, though there was no blood on him or on the ground. You could tell, though, from the way he was lying there, one arm sticking up so unnaturally, his neck out of alignment with his body, his eyes open and staring and his face so white and empty of life. Often Alexander thought of death: it was its arbitrariness that horrified him, and its sudden termination of everything. Why him? Why Paul? Why Jim Kae? He knew that you had to come to terms with the idea of death in order to go on: he knew that it was a trick of the mind, an understanding that death was horrible and arbitrary only from the standpoint of being alive, and since you could never actually experience it in this way, except in anticipation, the dread was not of death but of the living man's conception of it. He tried to think of it in this way, but it did not really work. If only I could finish what I have to do, he thought, if I could be sure of that. He wanted his life to have shape—if it could always have been ended at any given moment, then what meaning had it?

Once, when he was very tired, he allowed Terence Rowley to arrange something for him, the way he used to arrange such things for Willi. He had never gone in for this sort of thing before, believing that his pride would not permit it. But he was tired and he did not wish to talk, only to be lifted out of this mood he was in, and as a young man that was something that had always worked for him. The girls had sharp, common little faces and they flashed like cheap jewelry, and their bodies were neat and taut and very young, and warmer than their faces. They were keen enough, too, willing to enter into the mood of the game and as obedient as figments of his imagination of long ago: belly to belly, their hands on each other's buttocks, displaying each other expertly for his benefit. They were not professional whores; Alexander did not know what arrangement Terence Rowley made with them, whether he paid them, or got them small parts in return, or whether

449

they just did it to socialize, to get to meet important producers. He did not want to think about any of that. They did whatever he asked them to do, unquestioningly, but the deadness in him would not go and only became heavier, more immovable; in desperation he asked more of them, that they should do more: they did all the movements in accordance with his demands, giggling sometimes, and then gasping repeatedly, and then crying out and biting their lips, their bodies entangled—meaninglessly for him—like seaweed. He felt nothing, only the unshifting deadness. And when he got up and left, without having touched either of them, they looked at him in a funny way and made a coarse joke.

In his dream there was a yellow moon, bloodshot, in a hot, black sky. The landscape was flat desert; it was quite desolate except for a filling station, unattended, that sprouted up like some strange variety of desert cactus in the roadless waste. Although there was nobody to be seen in any direction, Alexander could feel the familiar sensation of being pursued by someone. In the crowded emptiness, Alexander began to run. Now, a long way off, across the sand, a distant figure kept pace with him. In whatever direction Alexander turned this distant figure kept parallel with him. Looking up, Alexander saw that the moon had become a slashed eye, dripping blood into the sky, and then he saw that the man who was keeping parallel with him a long way off was himself, but with such an extraordinarily knowing expression on his face, as if he knew things that he could not tell of.

The following week, Alexander returned to Washington. He had agreed to testify before the Committee. He sat listening expressionlessly, while Jack Warner and Louis B. Mayer gave their evidence. Mayer maintained that Communist writers could never succeed in influencing pictures made at M.G.M. because at that studio scripts were read and reread by executives. Jack Warner also denied that there was Communist propaganda in any of the films he had produced, but conceded that probably there were Communists on his payroll who tried to get propaganda into the films they wrote. When he detected a slanted line, he declared, he had that line removed, bided his time and then refused to rehire the offending writers when their contracts ran out. In this way, he said, he had succeeded in cleaning out his studio. He could not agree to an industry-wide ban on Communists because it would not be legal for producers to band together to obstruct the employment of other men. He would continue to get rid of writers he suspected of un-Americanism, but would not join any concerted attempt to black-list them in the industry.

Alexander's turn to testify came in the afternoon. "You have heard Stephen Raille's admission that he was a Communist party member?" counsel asked him.

"Yes."

"And you have heard evidence that several of the writers engaged by you, at his behest, were also Communists?"

"I have heard testimony to that effect," Alexander agreed.

"Would you tell the Committee what your policy is going to be in regard to these writers, and also in regard to those actors named at this hearing as being Communists?"

"Let's take the actors first," said Alexander. "I heard Mr. Menjou's testimony in which he said that an actor could convey Communist propaganda by a look, by an inflection of his voice. Well, I want to reassure the Committee on this score. I would say that the danger of the Government of the United States being overthrown by such means is not considerable." This caused some laughter in the hearing room, and served slightly to diminish the tension. "As for the writers," continued Alexander, "I would not employ any who put propaganda of any sort—whether it was for communism or vegetarianism—in their stories for the reason that I don't consider propaganda is ever good entertainment."

"Would you continue to employ a known Communist, Mr. Sondorf?" counsel demanded.

"Yes, I would, if he was a good writer, and my definition of a good writer is someone who can depict people truthfully, and that rules out anyone whose view of life and people is predetermined by any sort of doctrine."

"Will you continue to employ Stephen Raille?"

"Yes, I will. He is a very good writer."

"You heard him admit he was a Communist."

"I think maybe he thought he was a Communist for a while, but judging from his work I would not have said

451

he was a Communist, not what we mean by a Communist, not what we are opposed to."

"Then you are telling this Committee that you will continue to employ him—and others named at this hearing and found to have been in contempt of Congress?"

"This is a country of laws. And while it is not unlawful to be, or have been, a Communist, I do not consider it is for me, or anyone else, privately, and without sanction, to change these laws."

"Do I understand," interposed Congressman Kaythly, "that the findings of this Committee on the contempt issue do not weigh with you at all?"

"They weigh very heavily with me, Congressman," said Alexander. "And I regret them. And I regret the vote in the House which upheld the decision of this Committee. And I shall support the move to seek a ruling from the Supreme Court on this issue."

"You realize, Mr. Sondorf," said Congressman Kaythly, "that it is people like you, taking your attitude, who give comfort to the enemies of our country, and enable the insidious spread of the Communist conspiracy."

"I'm sorry you think that, Congressman, and I can only suggest, with respect, that if you feel that way you should seek to introduce legislation that will make the enforcement of your point of view a legal obligation. In the absence of such legislation, I shall continue to employ people, irrespective of their private beliefs, unless they have been found guilty, in a court of law, of espionage or subversion."

New York was fiercely cold. There was no snow, but a hard frost covered all exposed surfaces in a bright metallic sheen, and wherever water dripped savage icicles had formed. In the streets, people went around trailing breath-clouds. The wind was sharp and cut the face, inflicting cruel little hurts to the skin. The sun was wrapped in a fine haze, which made it seem to be smoking, like a bonfire whose heat cannot quite reach you. Looking out of the window, Alexander watched the picket lines outside the Seiermann Theater, men and women walking up and down, muffled up to the ears, stamping their feet, carrying placards which said: "This Picture Written by Commie—DO NOT PATRONIZE," and "THIS IS A SEIERMANN-HESSLAN-SON-

452

DORF THEATRE—SONDORF IS A COMMIE-LOVER—PLEASE DO NOT PATRONIZE" and "SONDORF SUPPORTS ENEMIES OF THE U.S.—DO NOT SUPPORT SONDORF." As the sun went down, the tall buildings became gray, fading hulks in the twilight, and then lost their outline, and as the windows lit up one after the other, new shapes grew, erratically, in slabs and rectangles of light. A long time ago Alexander had stood in these streets, had seen the night grow brighter, had felt his pulse quicken in the knowledge that everything was possible. He turned to Stephen Raille at his side, and said: "The Supreme Court will reverse the decision, I'm sure of it."

"They're not going to reverse a vote of Congress," said Stephen softly.

"It can be done," said Alexander.

"It won't happen," said Stephen, "it's not possible." And from the look that suddenly came over Alexander's face, it might have been that he, not Stephen, was going to jail.

On Alexander's return to Hollywood Willi had suggested he take a long leave of absence, go to Europe maybe, give himself a chance to "reorientate his thinking" and, at the same time, give the public a chance to forget his support of Stephen Raille. For the same reason it was proposed that the company should in the future be referred to by its initals only—S-H-S. No point in needlessly flaunting the name Sondorf in the public's face, at a time like this.

One day on a sudden impulse, he decided to visit the house where he and Susan had lived before the war. The gatekeeper was the same one who had been with them all that time ago. "Why, Mr. Sondorf, sir," he said, "it's a real pleasure to see you."

"Is the house occupied, Sam?"

"Oh no, sir. Been empty all this time, sir. Miss Kabe—uh, Mrs. Sondorf—has had it on the market quite a time now, but there don't seem to be the demand these days for this type of property."

"You mind if I go in, Sam, take a look round?"

"Well, of course, Mr. Sondorf, you go right on in. I think you'll find it's been well kept up. I'll get out the station wagon and run you up there . . ."

"No, don't bother—I'll walk."

Sam unlocked the massive gates, with their designs

of palm trees in black iron, and Alexander went in and started up the drive. As the house came into view, it seemed for a moment ablaze with light—an optical illusion created by the sun hitting the windowpanes. He smiled. The forecourt, empty of motorcars, seemed smaller than he had remembered it. Through a window, as he came close enough to see through his own reflection, there was a flash of golden ceilings. Suddenly the fountain in the center of the forecourt began to play, the central jet from the mouth of the captive dolphin, held by the massively muscled male figure in a thigh and arm hold, rose progressively to its full, majestic height, to the height of the house, a rainbow caught in its upward thrust. Sam evidently was anxious to prove how well everything had been kept up. Alexander continued, walked on down the steps at the side of the house and onto the terrace, from which he could see the three swimming pools, and the parallel lines of fountains. The pools were empty. Alexander remembered that Susan used to keep them heated to different temperatures to suit the varying inclinations of guests. The nearest of the pools was fed by an artificial waterfall that also made a fine shower: Sam, evidently still keen to show how well everything was being maintained, had turned on the water and it now began to trickle down among the sculpted rocks and boulders, and then, gathering force, to spray the female figures riding sea lions and winged water horses where they had been arrested by the sculptor, half over the fall. And below them the bathers had taken their showers. What vanity, he thought, what gargantuan vanity! What special people we must have considered ourselves to be. He remembered some of the people who had come here: for whom the invitation was an accolade, and for whom seeing those fountains playing and to bathe in his pools, and to shower under his waterfall, had been the full flush and realization of success. The terrace and the gardens had held such excitement then, such exquisite tensions there had been, arising out of the knowledge that big and important decisions —as they had seemed to all of them then—could be made here, without reference to any superior authority. There had been such certainty in him then, such sureness of purpose, such an awareness of the limitless stretching of himself that was still, in theory, possible. He had thought he had a little time still, but it had run out like a too fast hourglass. What vanity, he thought again. He did not know why he felt this cold grief around his heart, this mourning for some unknown loss. Was it the grief of leaving? He did not know when it was that he had made up his mind, but he knew now that he was leaving Hollywood and America, and for a moment the thought of being a traveler lifted him.

After that day, he was not seen around in any of the places frequented by the big Hollywood producers, and all sorts of strange and fanciful stories about him gained circulation. Like most of the stories that had ever been told about him, they were apocryphal, but they were told with great relish because they seemed to fit in with the legend. The first definite news of his whereabouts was when somebody identified him as one of an unnamed group of people around Janet Derringer in a photograph taken of her at the night club of the winter Casino in Cannes. It had been a purely chance encounter; he had been living for some time in a rented house at St.-Jean-Cap-Ferrat, and he sometimes would drive into Cannes. She'd thrown her arms around him and introduced him to her husband, her third husband, and they'd all had supper together, and when they were all a little drunk and she was dancing with him, she asked him directly: "Why did it end with us?" And he said, smilingly, "I don't know. I don't know why things start or why they end, I guess they just do."

Once it was known he was living on the Riviera the press kept a lookout for him, and from time to time he was photographed in the company of Garbo or Dietrich or Chaplin, and occasionally some reporter on the prowl succeeded in getting him to say that he was planning some fabulous new production, of James Joyce's *Ulysses,* or something, using an entirely revolutionary technique. Maybe he did not actually say any of these things which were sometimes attributed to him, but as he did not complain of being misquoted he was a useful standby for newspapermen stranded on the Riviera without a story, and anyway they loved to write about him because even though he hadn't produced anything lately there was still something rather magical about his name.

THE END